The Unbreakables

ALSO BY LISA BARR

Fugitive Colors

The Unbreakables

A Novel

Lisa Barr

HARPER LUXE

An Imprint of HarperCollinsPublishers

THE UNBREAKABLES. Copyright © 2019 by Lisa Barr. All rights reserved. Printed in the United States of America. No part of this book may be used or reproduced in any manner whatsoever without written permission except in the case of brief quotations embodied in critical articles and reviews. For information, address HarperCollins Publishers, 195 Broadway, New York, NY 10007.

HarperCollins books may be purchased for educational, business, or sales promotional use. For information, please email the Special Markets Department at SPsales@harpercollins.com.

FIRST HARPERLUXE EDITION

ISBN: 978-0-06-291153-7

HarperLuxe™ is a trademark of HarperCollins Publishers.

Library of Congress Cataloging-in-Publication Data is available upon request.

19 20 21 22 23   RS/LSC   10 9 8 7 6 5 4 3 2 1

To David, Noa, Maya, and Maya—
my love and my muses

The Unbreakables

I.

Love never dies a natural death. It dies
because we don't know how to replenish its
source. It dies of blindness and errors and
betrayals. It dies of illness and wounds;
it dies of weariness, of withering,
of tarnishing.

—ANAÏS NIN

Chapter One

Gabe, my husband, still incredibly sexy at forty-two, approaches me from behind in our walk-in closet, wraps his muscular arms tightly around my waist and kisses my neck hungrily. Truth be told, I heard his approaching footsteps thirty seconds earlier stomping across our hardwood floor from the shower, pretended as though I didn't, and let him think he pulled one over on me.

I sink against his bare chest, still slightly damp, feeling those wispy hairs like feathers against my back. *God, he feels good.* His warm hands cup my breasts as he gently turns us both to face the full-length mirror on the back of the door. I look, unintentionally, pretty damn porn wearing a lacy black strapless push-up bra and matching panties, my favorite high-heeled sandals, clutching my new birthday dress—a one-shouldered form-fitting snorkel blue number, which I was about to put on pre–Gabe Interruptus.

His clean-shaven face nestles into my blow-out. It really has been a while—a few months perhaps?—since he's made this particular move, which is slightly surprising. But if I'm totally honest with myself, nothing really surprises me about us anymore and sometimes I wish it did. There are those days when I go for my morning run and wonder what would happen if I just keep going past the three-mile marker and never look back—where would that road take me? It's more of a passing thought than a tangible want. I love my husband. We are each other's history, having chalked up more than twenty-five years together from high school seniors onward. So many years, so many sexual encounters, that Gabe's closet seduction feels a bit rom-com predictable, the left hook you know is coming. And yet . . . I smile into the mirror. We're still good, still us.

"Happy birthday, babe," he whispers into my ear while tracing my body in a more demanding way, which, if I don't put a stop to where this is headed, will definitely make us late to my own birthday dinner in the city. "Do you believe I'm sleeping with a forty-two-year-old?"

"That's *two* twenty-one-year-olds to you, bitch," I retort playfully, as I tenderly pull away but kiss him first, long and lingering, a kiss that says I'm not rejecting you just delaying you. "We have got to get moving. We are already going to be twenty minutes late. You know Samantha and Eric. Dinner is at seven thirty, but they will be there at seven." I tenderly graze my finger over the slim scar next to his left eyebrow. "Continue this later?"

Gabe nods his disappointment, his towel sliding off his waist in the process and I catch it, anticipating the fall as I do just about everything else about my husband.

As predicted, Samantha and Eric are already at Fig & Olive, the swanky new French-Mediterranean restaurant downtown that everyone is talking about. So are Lauren and Matt. Not only are we running a half hour late, but also traffic from the burbs to the city is pure hell, much worse than usual. And it's a Tuesday night. There must be an accident up ahead somewhere. By the time we take the tiny elevator up to the Oak Street restaurant, our best friends are already well into their second round at the large rectangular bar, the ornate centerpiece of the dining room.

"Sophieeee!" my girls scream out, waving their wine goblets in the air, crimson liquid bouncing over the rims. "Over here!" As though I don't see them, as though everyone else doesn't hear them. I laugh to myself. Hillbilly suburbanites—the Clampetts let out of their three-car garages.

"I *love* this place. Everybody is so hip." Samantha points to her extremely low-cut dress. "Too slutty? Eric thinks so. Who cares, right? Happy birthday, gorgeous mama!"

"Perfect amount of slutty. You look great." I squeeze her tightly. Samantha and Lauren have been my closest friends since high school and they both smell amazing. A mix of cabernet and Jo Malone. I, of course, am wearing the same scent. We bought our new perfume together last weekend at Neiman's. We pretty much don't make a move without the others' tacit approval.

Our group of six has been together for years. Eric is a college add-on, but the rest of us have been friends since high school. We vacation together, celebrate every milestone and holiday together. Every important occasion is shared with one another: Samantha & Eric, Lauren & Matt, Sophie & Gabe, and our kids. I am happy this way—like curl-up-in-a-favorite-blanket-on-a-rainy-day happy. No matter what life brings, ups and downs, twists and turns, these are my people.

"So . . . what are we eating?" Lauren asks after we

are seated at our table, her long French-manicured finger skimming the menu.

Lauren's nails, unlike mine, are always perfect, always chipless, even days after a manicure. Mine chip five seconds after I leave the salon because I don't have the patience to wait-n-dry. I don't find beautifying therapeutic, though I do all the maintenance because one must—mani-pedis, blow-outs, waxing, facials, and yoga: the absolute worst. My mind goes into overdrive when I'm told to be still, be present, or hold a pose. I'm an artist—*was* an artist. The only time I ever sat still was when I was in my twenties, studying an object that I planned to sculpt. My artwork back then was considered cutting-edge and exhibited in galleries around the city, and selling. It was everything I had ever dreamed of until severe carpal tunnel syndrome took over and prevented me from doing what I loved most. The doctors (four unanimous opinions) insisted I stop sculpting or I would cause irreversible nerve damage to my hands. I was willing to take the chance, but realized there were things bigger than my passion—actually only one thing. I needed to reserve my hands, my strength, for my then precocious five-year-old, Ava, now nineteen. So, I gave up what I loved most for someone I loved even more.

Now I run the Art Center in town and represent local artists' work. I enjoy my job, but not a day goes by that I don't yearn for what was, who I once was— so much potential cut off before hitting my prime. I buried my own dream, cut my losses, and now I bring others' vision to light. It's the consolation prize that never really consoles.

"Hey, Soph, you with us?"

I smile at Lauren, who has asked me twice what I wanted to eat: my birthday, my choices. I glance at my friends and my husband. "You guys pick. Surprise me."

Eric, who always takes control of every group food event, happily orders us an assortment of appetizers. The marinated olives come first, followed by more wine, six types of crostini, beef something, mushroom croquettes, then more wine. We catch up on our hometown's latest gossip, particularly the Elm Street "temporary" road closure—the town's main drag—a construction project that is taking three months longer than promised to complete, killing everyone's route and making driving around town unbearable.

Matt raises his glass. "Here's to the Great Wall of China, the Hoover Dam, the Colosseum—all built in less time than the goddamn Elm Street construction project."

We all laugh and clink glasses.

"It's like living in the third world," Gabe complains, just as the overly exuberant waiter, who is definitely an actor, brings in the entrées. "It took me nearly thirty extra minutes to get to the hospital yesterday. My patient was having complications and I'm watching that goddamn crane dump cement in slo-mo. I was going out of my mind."

"Can we talk about something other than Elm Street—so boring already. That's all anyone talks about these days." Lauren sighs, then inspects her nails approvingly.

Eric, mouth full, leans forward with a mischievous glint in his eye. "Well, I've got something for us that's definitely *not* boring. I was saving this for later when we were all sufficiently buzzed. I'm sure you all heard about the Ashley Madison lists? Fucking train wreck."

"Ashley Madison?" I slur slightly, after having tossed back glass two. "Never heard of her."

"It's not a her," Samantha explains. "Where have you been? It's a thing, an online company. A despicable website for married cheaters. Their motto is 'Life is short. Have an affair.' Apparently, it was hacked a few weeks ago, and it's turned into a total shit-storm. I read about it on my newsfeed."

"Oh right." I nod. "Someone from the club was talking about it yesterday in the locker room. I wasn't really paying attention." I look over at Gabe, who has begun a meticulous operation on his filet mignon—always the surgeon. I glance over at Eric and Matt and smile, surprised that they have waited this long before making fun of Gabe. Eric sees what I see, points to Gabe, "Steak surgery. Scalpel?" He hands Gabe his knife.

Gabe looks up without cracking a smile. "Asshole."

We all laugh, drink more wine, and Eric holds up his brand-new iPhone with its extralarge face and shines the phone's blaring light directly at us. The restaurant lighting is so dim that the phone casts a blinding gray-blue hue across the sleek ebony table. "Back to more interesting stuff. Apparently, the hackers stole all of Ashley Madison's database—emails, names, home addresses, sexual fantasies and credit card information, and threatened to post all of the details online if the site was not permanently closed. Of course, the Ashley Madison honchos thought they were bluffing, the site stayed open, and the hackers are now making good on their threat. The cheaters are now being cheated out of their anonymity."

"How many people are we talking about?" Lauren asks.

Eric shoots us a wry smile. "Get this, the database estimates are well over thirty-two million cheaters, and the outreach is as far away as Saudi Arabia. And that, my friends, is cheating punishable by death or stoning—not just being kicked out of a house and forced to couch-crash."

"You enjoy this shit," Matt says accusingly, wrapping his arm around the back of Lauren's chair.

"Hell yeah." Eric smirks devilishly, holds up his phone again, this time high overhead as though he is at a Springsteen concert, demanding an encore via phone-cum-lighter.

"What's wrong with you? Put that down," Samantha scolds Eric. "You're embarrassing us."

"Let me tell you what we're about to enjoy . . ." Eric places the phone faceup on the table. "Apparently, the hackers chose today," Eric turns to me, "your birthday, Soph, to release its first round of customer records. This Impact Team—or whatever the bullshit hacker name is—says they are planning to release names of cheaters all month. But today, July twenty-first"—he speaks slowly, purposely building up the suspense—"is the debut of Chicago and its friendly—make that, very friendly—suburbs. Nearly twenty pages of names on this infamous list belong to our very own, very cozy North Grove."

"No shit." Matt takes a generous swig of wine. We all do.

Eric nods. "Yes. Someone from work emailed me the list, and I have held on to this baby for six straight hours without looking at it and you can only imagine the torture. I saved it for us, for tonight. I thought we'd review the list of our town's cheaters together." He turns to me, faux apologetically. "Dark and evil, I know. Happy birthday, Soph."

I laugh because I'm buzzed and because Eric has always been as obnoxious as he is kindhearted. A top-producing investment banker for one of the city's leading firms, we all know that Eric would chuck his job in a heartbeat if he could make a living as a stand-up comedian. He even did a short stint with the Second City after college, taking a gap year before attending the Kellogg School of Management at Northwestern University. And he was talented. He's always been my favorite.

Gabe looks up from his sliced steak masterpiece, shakes his head. "Not on Sophie's birthday. C'mon, dude, no class."

I glance at Gabe, smile, appreciating his care. "This is awful, but the truth is, don't you all kind of want to know if we know anybody? And who better to check the list with than all of us together. I know it's wrong . . . but kinda good-bad-wrong, if you know what I mean."

Samantha, who is sitting next to me, leans her head on my shoulder. "I totally agree. Make that *great*-bad-wrong. Let's have fun with this. I propose a drinking game. It's called Can You Guess the Names of North Grove's Cheaters. If you're wrong, you have to do a shot. If you're right, you get to pick who does a shot."

Gabe turns to me again, his face long and serious. "This is not your thing. This is Eric's demented crap. Let's not do this."

"Overruled," I say, shaking my hair that is so over-sprayed it simply does not move. "I'm now three glasses in—it is *so* my thing."

The waiter appears. Eric orders coffee for all and asks to see the dessert menu. I can tell by his obvious whisper that he also asks the waiter to bring out something sweet for my birthday. I smile. Eric is always on top of things, our group organizer of everything—from PNOs (Parents Night Out) to vacations and group bike rides. Gabe excuses himself to the bath-room, saying something about his stomach. I glance at his empty plate. No wonder. He finished that entire steak.

But Gabe's stomach is ironclad. I'm the one who downs Tums like a grandmother. I gesture to Matt to follow him. "Matty, go make sure he's okay."

Matt gets up, stumbles after Gabe, but then returns

two minutes later. "He said he was fine and just needed a few minutes."

"Screw him." Eric laughs. "I've been waiting hours for this. I'm not waiting another few minutes. I say, let's get started."

"Do it!" Samantha and I squeal. Gabe will catch up when he returns.

"We are all going straight to hell." I giggle. "But you know what, cheaters have it coming. I'm not going to feel guilty—hey, they didn't."

"Cheaters suck!" Samantha clink-clinks my glass.

"That's what she said," Matt adds predictably.

Eric glances at his wife, who is now visibly loopy. Samantha, cheeks flushed, is a lightweight like me. He moves her glass to the other side of his plate. "I can see I'm either going to get majorly laid tonight or I will be holding back your hair while you heave."

"You know it, baby—whip out the damn list. Chop, chop." Samantha reaches over Eric and reclaims her wine and points to his phone.

Eric, laughing, picks it up, types in his passcode, downloads the list, as we all lean in with perverse anticipation. How ridiculous we must look watching that damn spinning loader, which controls all of our lives. "First one up . . . ," he announces as though he's Ringmaster Ned pointing to the Bozo buckets. "Michael Abrams—nice Jewish boy with ten transactions, his own minyan of cheats. Next up, Peter Altman—coming in second with seven transactions."

"What do you mean by transactions?" Lauren interrupts just as Gabe returns. He really doesn't look good. I grab his hand.

"Your stomach?" I whisper.

"Yeah, not so great. Maybe we should hit the road soon."

Hit the road? When does Gabe ever want to leave anywhere early? We are always the last to arrive, last to leave. Even when I've seen him sick as a dog on numerous occasions, he always wants to stay. "Give it a few minutes. See how you feel," I say as he slowly sits down. I turn my attention back to Eric.

"So each time the name is on there, it correlates to the amount of times the cheater paid for a cheat," Eric explains. "Miles Bender with fourteen transactions is—"

"Miles Bender cheating fourteen times!" Samantha shouts out.

"Bingo. Brain surgeon. That's why I married you." Eric smiles at his wife and continues. "Bender—fourteen . . ." The names roll off his tongue in alphabetical order. "Rhonda Black—eight . . . Jeremy Blatcher—nineteen."

"Stop right there!" Lauren interrupts. "Jeremy Blatcher, nineteen times? He's the head of the synagogue's fund-raising committee. And oh my god. Rhonda Black—she's in our yoga class."

"Clearly Blatcher has a lot to atone for this Yom Kippur." Eric chuckles, dips his head to continue naming names. "Neil Blazer—five . . ." Suddenly, he stops abruptly, flips over his phone.

"What is it?" I ask. We're all curious now. "Who is it? Who do we know?"

Eric quickly sticks the phone back inside his jacket. "This was stupid. I was wrong to do this. You guys are right. I'm an asshole."

I glance accusingly at Matt. His face is red. I've always suspected him of hooking up with his flirty secretary. And so has Lauren. I will strangle him with my bare hands.

Samantha eyes Eric suspiciously, then wasting no time, with E.T.-like forceps precision, she snags the phone right out of his jacket.

"Give it back, goddamnit!"

"I know you, Eric. I know you."

Now everyone is getting nervous. I glance over at Gabe, who is not nervous. No, he's white. No, make that albino. I put down my wineglass as my heart stops in midbeat. It's not his stomach, not the steroid steak. I know every move of my husband's, every damn nuance of his since he was seventeen years old. I glance at Samantha, who is now holding her husband's phone to her chest and staring at me, her mouth drops open.

And there it is.

Samantha has never lied to me. Never. She told me right away when a boy I liked freshman year in high school called her first. She always tells me if I have something in my teeth, the right dress to wear, always what is best for me, not what will make her look better. She took care of my daughter, Ava, right after I'd given birth, came over twice a day when I had postpartum depression and couldn't get out of bed. She always puts me first. I glance over at Lauren, who is staring at Samantha, her large doe eyes not blinking. It's always been the three of us together, the no-matter-what friends, the "Jo Malone for three" friends. Always. And now . . . I turn back slowly toward Gabe, who is frozen, fearful.

The burning rage rises rapidly like a tsunami inside me, but the numbing pain is stronger and gets there first. My eyes, the only part of me that can actually move, dart around the table like a 35-mm camera lens taking a panoramic scan. This is my world, equal parts of a whole: Lauren & Matt. Samantha & Eric. Sophie & Gabe.

Sophie & Gabe, TLF.

He'd actually carved that into the large oak tree in front of my house with his Swiss army knife on the night we graduated from high school. It's still there, the jagged scar on the tree—one that I never wanted to heal. For some reason, right now, all I can think about is that tree and an axe in my hand. I have to get to that tree tonight somehow, to chop it down. Right now. I have to—

"Sophie, Soph . . ." Samantha's voice is soft and protective, nurturing like Bambi's mother's just before she gets shot.

My gaze rests squarely on Gabe and I feel sick. This man, this incredibly loving father who smells like Tom Ford mixed with Crest mixed with Degree, who has been my rock my entire life, has betrayed me. I know it without even hearing the words aloud. That sexy move in the closet earlier was not an attempted surprise but a lie, a cover-up, birthday guilt. And now as he stares back at me—his beautifully carved rugged face, that slim scar lining his left brow, those hazel eyes that turn gold when the sun hits them, so many angles that I have once known, touched, kissed, tasted—I no longer recognize him.

Everyone is silent, too afraid to move. I finally find my voice and it is eerily steady, clinical. "Bender . . .

THE UNBREAKABLES · 19

Black . . . Blatcher . . . Blazer . . . Bloom . . ." This stranger's voice that has taken over mine waxes accusatory. "Gabe Bloom comes next. Isn't that right, Eric?" My gaze remains laser-focused on my cheating husband as I speak.

Eric looks to Samantha, not knowing how to handle this. *Do something*, his thick-lashed blue eyes plead desperately, blaming himself for turning a game into the real deal, and counting on her to fix it.

Gabe, barely breathing, reaches for my arm, which has become taut like the rest of me. I'm now in full body armor, and somewhere in the back of my steel-plated brain—the part that isn't drunk, in shock, in pain, enraged, betrayed—I hear a tender, frightened boyishly familiar "Sophie, do you hear me?" echoing, just as the chocolate lava cake drizzled with raspberry syrup bearing a lone pink candle arrives in the hands of the animated waiter. Just as my best girlfriends reach for me and shoo him away, hovering over me like a perfumed igloo, protecting me from the cold, stark inevitable truth. Except there is no protection. Ignorance is bliss and knowledge is definitely its own kind of hell.

I push them all away. I have to see this Ashley Madison list for myself. I grab Eric's phone and he knows better than to stop me. The hackers, I give them full credit, were well organized. The cheat sheet is in Excel format, like a business plan for fucking; a line-by-line attendance sheet. And there he is, front and center. My very own Gabe Bloom, his name listed in one column; North Grove, our home address in another; random letters and numbers that don't make sense in another column, a credit card number that I don't recognize, and finally in the last column is an email address that I've never seen before: GMB18@ gmail.com. Gabriel Michael Bloom. Number 18— legendary high school star quarterback, whose jersey is immortalized in the school's glass case after winning State—the same high school our daughter had attended. The same town that we never left. GMB18. Eighteen is for *chai*—meaning the life that was just swiped out from under me.

Sophie. Sophie.

My name is now surround-sound. It's as though I can no longer hear nor see anyone clearly. Everyone is gesturing wildly, like a sepia-tinted collage of body parts. I hear them all, feel their presence. I can even smell them. My family, my lifeline, my umbilical cord has been severed. The Unbreakables, as Eric once called us, have just shattered into a thousand tiny irreparable pieces.

All I can register in my clogged brain is that Gabriel Michael Bloom—number 18—sole owner of my heart, the father of our only child, Ava, is listed on the hacked Ashley Madison site forty-three times. To be precise: one and a half pages full of Gabe's transactions, along with millions of others, whose spouses are about to wake up to the secret infidelity exposed by mean-spirited hackers seeking an LOL. Ashley Madison—a name that sounds like a preppy clothing line—is an online playground in which you can stay married, stay committed while messing around because it is a quid pro quo affair: You're married, I'm married—why not, nobody gets hurt.

Except everybody gets hurt.

I stare hard at Gabe, the only man I have ever slept with, the one with whom I experienced all my firsts. This being yet another, I think numbly. Dr. Bloom, hot-shot North Grove cardiologist chalked up forty-two paid-for-fucks and one for good luck.

Happy birthday to me.

Chapter Two

The Uber driver makes nonstop small talk. My mouth is moving on automatic, trying desperately not to be rude as I respond with rote replies, but my head, this deadweight on my neck, is spinning out of control. I stare out the car window, watching the passing vehicles on the highway, trying to digest what just happened.

There was the drama, the drink I threw in Gabe's face, the birthday cake smashed like an axe to a tree, and then came the crazy. I stood up from the table and ran to the elevator, which was miraculously open, and got in before anyone could stop me. I bolted out onto the street, hearing snatches of conversations along the way, with Samantha and Lauren racing after me. I was unmoored and fast. There's no motor like rage. I was eight cylinders on stilettos, screaming wildly, "Please, just leave me alone . . . Gabe, get the fuck away from me!" as I sprinted down Oak Street, past all the designer stores without even a single window-glance, in my one-shouldered body-hugging birthday dress like a prostitute fleeing her bat-wielding pimp. I ran until I could no longer, and then hid behind large green garbage receptacles lined up in a scary alley. The rancid smell of rot was overwhelming but I didn't move, barely breathed. In the distance, I caught glimpses of moving recognizable pants legs—Gabe, Eric, and Matt, the three stooges, running in the opposite direction. I hugged my shaking body, feeling my bones, my blood, my guts, all the moving parts within me. They lost me. *I lost me.*

I called an Uber and waited for the driver to come rescue me. And he did within three minutes, just as the app had promised. Stan the Uber Guy with a wispy reddish mustache was my white knight in a dark blue Subaru.

Safely nestled in the backseat, breathing deeply if I'm even breathing at all, I glance at my phone. Fifteen missed calls, alternating between Gabe, Lauren, and Samantha. I check the time. Ten twenty. Without traffic, it should take thirty minutes to get home. Do I even go home? It's my damn home, I remind myself.

I'm not the cheater—*he is*. What if Gabe is there waiting for me? What am I going to do? Forty-three times. *Christ.* I drop my phone back into my purse. I can't breathe.

I open my window and the one on the passenger side as well. Nothing makes sense. I need to think, need to process, but the driver is still talking. I want to tell Stan that I will rate him five stars if only he would just shut up and let me think. But I simply don't have the heart to be mean to a man who is clearly just trying to make a living; a dependable human who said he'd pick me up in three minutes and was not a second late.

"Big night?" he asks, eyeing me curiously in the rearview mirror.

"Big night," I concur, staring at his bushy auburn brow.

"You look very nice. Special occasion?"

I find the words in me somewhere. "Thank you. My birthday."

"Well, happy birthday. You're my second one today. I hope it was everything you wanted it to be."

It was Opposite Day. "Thank you." My tone is crisp.

But he keeps going, not picking up on the social cue. "So how did you celebrate?"

I celebrated the end of my marriage. "I FaceTimed with my daughter who is studying abroad," I say, wondering why I am even telling Stan this and thinking back to my conversation with Ava earlier this morning. She called from Paris, where she studied last semester and extended her stay into the summer to finish an independent project. The call wasn't Ava's usual singing or silliness on my birthday. It felt like a forced call—a because-she-had-to-call-me call. Not her at all. There was definitely something wrong in Ava's face, in her voice.

"There's no way—you're not old enough to have a daughter that old."

I smile despite myself at the back of Stan's head with faint appreciation. Well, I will give him this: he is certainly earning his stars. *But please, Stan. Just. Stop. Talking.* And then, miraculously, as if there is a telepathic chip somewhere in the vehicle, for the next fifteen minutes or so, he does.

As he turns off the highway and heads into North Grove, we pass by my Starbucks, my cleaners, my nail salon, my Whole Foods with its overpriced mung bean salad, my yoga studio filled with pseudo-zen moms, my shoe repair guy, my gas station and bagel place—vignettes of my to-do list, flashes of my daily life—all those things that I love and dread simultaneously.

And then I begin to cry—not silent tears streaming daintily down a cheek, but an all-out bawl. And Stan with all his chattiness, simply doesn't know what to do with me, so he does it all. He pulls over to the side of the road, flicks on his hazards and hands me a tissue and a Wet One, a Q-tip for my runny mascara, a mini-bottle of water, and tops it all off with a Cinnamint. Every amenity Stan has, he gives to me.

"Sounds like it wasn't such a good birthday," he says with true compassion. "I'm really sorry. You seem like the kind of person who deserves better."

"Thank you," I bluster. "I mean it. Kindness goes a long way. I'm just up ahead, over there." I point. "Left at the next light. It's okay. I'm okay. We can go now."

He nods, turns on the ignition, and drives, keeping a concerned eye on me through the rearview mirror. I make a mental note to contact his Uber supervisor—*Uber-visor?*—if there's such a thing, tomorrow.

We slowly pull into my circular driveway and I look up. The outside lights are on, accentuating our new landscaping, and so is the kitchen light, and the one in our bedroom upstairs. I exhale deeply. *Gabe is home.*

"Stan?"

He turns. "Uh yeah."

"What do you do when you don't know what to do?" My nose is running a steady stream and he hands me another tissue.

He shrugs. "I guess, you just do it. Do what you got to do, make it quick, and then get out. That's what I do."

Not so deep but pretty spot on.

I say goodbye and tell Stan he earned every single star and more. I slowly make my way up my driveway as though walking the plank, feeling wobbly in my heels. I stop in my tracks and stare at my big house with its salmon-colored brick, rustic French turquoise shutters, and three-car garage, picturing the once good life inside that no longer possesses bragging rights. Gabe is *definitely* home. I see him watching me from our bedroom window, lifting back the curtain like a leading man in a horror film. Tony Perkins waiting for Janet Leigh.

Then he reveals himself in full. Our eyes meet and lock. Six foot one, 185, tousled black hair—the kind that will never go bald. Long, lean and muscular, perfectly packaged. GMB18@gmail.com: God's gift to forty-three women.

Who are not me. I cringe, turning away from him, wiping my wet face with the rolled-up Kleenex as I press the outside code to open the garage door. I hold my head up high, completely unprepared for whatever comes next. Squaring my shoulders, finding my breath, I enter my home of nearly fifteen years to do what I've got to do and then get out.

And then I stop in my tracks, backpedal out the door and into my garage. *I can't do this. Not yet.* Leaning against my car, I reach for my phone inside my purse. I glance at it before I press the third name listed on my favorites.

"Sophie, thank god," Samantha answers halfway through the first ring, as though she is watching her phone intently, like one of those black restaurant buzzers that light up when your table is finally called.

"Sam." Her name comes out as a bated breath. *I'm dying here.*

"I'm coming right now. I'll call Lauren. Don't move. We'll be there in less than ten."

Chapter Three

Exactly nine minutes later, I hear Pablo, our eight-year-old golden retriever, barking his head off from inside my house. How I wish I could go back in and curl up with him on the couch, as usual. I heave a deep sigh of relief as Samantha pulls up in her Lexus SUV with Lauren. *God knows, if ever I needed them, it's right now.*

I start to walk down my driveway toward them and then I freeze. I note that my sprinkler system must have just turned on. This is my goddamn house; my lilacs being watered. Every inch of it I designed, planned, nurtured. Why am I the one who has to leave?

Because staying in a house of lies is not an option.

Samantha and Lauren face me in the car, watching through the windshield. They both jump out when they see me stalled, staring at my lilac bushes like one of Gabe's zombies in those TV shows I hate. As they quickly approach, I notice that they both have changed and are wearing some version of Lululemon and I'm still in my birthday dress.

Samantha, who's been able to read my mind since the ninth grade, says, "Don't worry, I brought you yoga pants, gym shoes, and a tank. They're in the car."

Lauren wraps her arms around me, points to the passenger side of the car, and says gently, "And you can sit in the front, okay?"

My girls. "Now there's the silver lining . . . Gabe cheats on me and I get shotgun." I laugh instead of cry. But not them—they both begin to cry.

"I'm so sorry, Soph. This totally sucks," Lauren says through her tears while hugging me tightly. She is full-figured, always trying to lose ten pounds, but she's perfect, her curves are gorgeous, and I tell her that all the time. I feel the comforting softness of her body against mine, and it takes every bit of strength I have right now not to fall apart completely. She detaches gradually, then holds me firmly by my shoulders, stares into my eyes. "Stay at my house or Samantha's tonight, and let us take care of you. I know this is devastating, but we've been through everything together, especially the worst of it. We'll get through this too, okay." She gestures to Samantha. "Remember when Sam's mom . . ."

Sophomore year in college. Cancer. Samantha had dropped out of the University of Michigan for the entire semester to be with her mother for those few precious months before she died. Lauren and I came home from college to be with her, rotating every other weekend. It was the most painful time of our lives watching Lynda wither away. I was much closer to Samantha's mother than to my own. So was Lauren.

"How could I ever forget," I whisper, and we both squeeze Samantha. "But this is different. Nobody's dying. Just my marriage, just my life as I know it. That list . . . that fucking list. Who are those women? Do we know them? Do they shop at our Whole Foods? Are they at the club, at yoga? At Starbucks? Laughing behind my back?" I search their anguished faces. "I think I need to disappear for a while, take time to figure it all out. Gabe was my . . ." I wipe my watery eyes.

"You don't need to disappear," Samantha says adamantly, as we get into the car. "We've never gone through anything in our lives apart. Let us help you." She takes my hand and squeezes it. "We're here for you, like always."

Sighing deeply, I gently remove my hand from hers, fasten the seat belt, and glance up at my house as we back out of the driveway. I see a faint shadow in my bedroom window—*Gabe?* I look away because it no longer matters. Samantha is right. We have been through everything together: cancer, suicide (Eric's younger brother), abortion (Lauren, junior year in college), miscarriages (Samantha), postpartum depression (me), fertility issues (me), eating disorder (Caitlin, Samantha's eldest, a senior in high school, struggles with bulimia), bullying (Samantha's ten-year-old son, Brett, had to confront the fifth-grade bully—thank god, that's over), middle school girl drama (Lauren's thirteen-year-old daughter, Riley, still deals with mean girls), and the real estate market crash in 2008 (Matt and Lauren). We all pitched in to get them through that crisis, and eventually they got back on their feet. And now Gabe, the serial cheater.

And yet for some reason, this is the worst thing that has ever happened in my life, and I just want to be alone to wrap my head around this. *I want to and I don't.* I eye my best friends lovingly. I need them. I shouldn't be alone. My suffering is reflected in their eyes, my pain is theirs. We are all so overinvested in one another's lives if there is such a thing, that we don't know who we are without one another. Even our kids think of themselves as brothers and sisters, which I've always loved especially since Ava is an only child. I bite down on my bottom lip to prevent myself from crying again. *What's going to happen to our tight-knit family now?*

"Honestly, I feel like he cheated on me," Samantha says with a side glance as she begins to drive.

"Exactly," Lauren murmurs from the backseat.

I stare out the passenger window and see my reflection in the glass. Gabe didn't just break us, he broke *all* of us. "The thing is, I know Gabe didn't cheat because he hates me or that we had a crappy marriage." My voice is faint, barely there. "Maybe I didn't give him enough attention, maybe we fell in love too young and he didn't have experiences outside of me, us—and he wanted to—"

"Jesus Christ—stop right there!" Samantha shouts, holds up her hand as she drives, staring straight ahead. "Whatever you do, *do not* cave to Gabe wanted this, Gabe needed that, Gabe had to have, you know Gabe. Poor Gabe, the cheater. Maybe that's the whole fucking problem, Soph. Not enough attention? Seriously? You couldn't give him more attention if you tried. He is a self-centered midlife-crisis prick. You know what I think?" She doesn't wait for a response. "I think that you, Sophie, are allowed to go batshit crazy raving mad. Do not minimize your own pain and do not make excuses for him . . ." *As usual*—which she doesn't say, but I hear it anyway.

I turn to Samantha's taut profile. Her lips are pursed and her hands are now perched firmly at ten and two.

"Just so you know, I'm not a total wuss—while I was in the Uber coming home, I actually contemplated stabbing him to death tonight with one of those damn Cutco knives you guys made me buy."

"Not the Trimmer?" Lauren, hand over heart, feigns alarm from the backseat, trying to lighten up the situation.

"Yes, the Trimmer!" I turn back toward her and I can't help it, I do the imitation. "'Slice, dice, and chop with ease . . . This knife will make you feel like a professional chef in your own kitchen.'"

We laugh hard despite ourselves. We all have the identical set—but the Trimmer is considered Cutco slicer royalty. We all endured the same annoying thirty-minute spiel from the same teenage rep—the son of one of Lauren's neighbors. As I look at my besties, my laughter stops in midgiggle and I feel instant panic course through my body. Worse than killing Gabe will be leaving him. Worse than leaving him will be being without him, being alone.

Forty-three times. There's no way back from that.

"**Where are** we going?" I ask, noting that we are not headed to either Samantha's or Lauren's house, rather onto the highway ramp going north.

"The beach," Samantha says.

"The beach? What, are we in high school?"

She laughs. "Sometimes I think we never left high school. But the beach was always our happy place, right?" Samantha shoots a glance at Lauren in the rearview mirror. They clearly have a plan. They must have formulated it on the way to my house. I turn and catch Lauren smirking. I know that smile.

"What is up?"

She reaches into her purse and presents what looks like a flash drive with a cotton-candy colored skin. "Well, I brought treats. You can thank my daughter for this. I found it hidden in Caitlin's underwear drawer the other day with packets of pods stuffed inside socks. As if I wouldn't find it? Put it this way, she lost her phone for the next few weeks, and now we are the proud owners of her Juul."

I giggle despite myself. "This is so high school. Let me see that. I heard about those. Are they even legal?"

"Been on the market for several years—apparently, getting FDA approval in a few months. You know my daughter. There's not a trend she doesn't beat." She hands it to me and I smell it.

"Fruity."

Lauren rolls her eyes. "Mango to be exact."

We pull into the empty Highland Park beach parking lot, and I change into the Lulus that Samantha had brought for me. She opens the trunk, grabs a blanket, three flannel shirts, and a large picnic basket (always prepared).

"You seriously put all this shit together in five minutes?" I look at my best friend and shake my head, the most anal-retentive person on the planet. Prepared even for a marriage collapse.

"Actually, I did it in less than three. Take this." Samantha divides all the goods, and we walk down the familiar winding stone steps toward the beach, which is completely deserted and slightly ominous. Yet none of us cares that it's dark. We've got bigger issues on our minds.

Once we arrive at the bottom, we all kick off our shoes, like the old days. The summer breeze soothes my skin and the sand feels cool and comforting between my toes. The water is glassy and calm, a blackish blue tint as the moonlight shines against it. I loop my arms inside both of theirs gratefully. *This. Them. Us.* All for one, one for all. No matter what. *Always.* What was I even thinking? I don't have to do this nightmare alone.

My eyes pool with tears. I can't believe that just a few hours ago we were all sitting at a trendy downtown restaurant enjoying good wine and celebrating my birthday. My life was still the same: good, comfortable, dependable, oblivious. I was not this cheated-on, pathetic, totally lost, watered-down version of me.

Samantha scrutinizes me closely, reading me as always. "You are not alone, nor are you going to deal with this alone, okay. And there's nothing wrong with you. So get those thoughts out of your head."

"No fucking way will you go through this by yourself," Lauren chimes in.

I stare at the two of them, and weirdly, I wish I could sculpt them right now. The staunch maternal care embedded in their hooded eyes, their clenched determined jaws straining with worry, the unconditional love seeping through their skin, their timeless beauty. Forty-plus could easily exchange with thirty, especially under the starlight that is casting a misty glow around them like an Instagram filter.

"You guys . . ." I manage.

"That was pure hell, hands down the worst night ever," Samantha announces, as we each take a corner of the blanket (Samantha takes two), and lay it gently on the sand. "We love you, Sophie. We're not going to let you fall. You know that, right?"

I nod as I sit on the blanket, and over the soothing echo of the waves, I can practically hear those same words uttered so many times throughout the years. Samantha and Lauren shouting out at the top of their lungs, "*We love you, Sophie!*" when I graduated North-western University with honors, right after the dean had explicitly told everyone in the auditorium to please hold the applause until the end. The same embarrassingly exuberant shout-out when I was twenty-three and had my first art exhibition in the River North art district and was being introduced by the uppity gallery curator. And again, when I gave birth to Ava after eighteen hours in hard labor, no drugs. They were there in the delivery room—not Gabe, who had taken a coffee break—cheering me on. They delivered my daughter and both handed her to me.

Ava. Oh god. How am I going to break this to her? Gabe is her hero.

"What am I going to do about Ava?" I desperately search my friends' faces for answers. "And something is definitely up with her. She called me this morning from Paris to wish me a happy birthday and her voice was trembling, like she'd been crying." I curl my legs to my chest and hug them tightly against me. "Do you believe this fucking mess?"

Samantha, never one to water down the truth, shakes her head and says, "Ava is going to take it hard."

Not surprisingly, Lauren, who is lying stretched out next to me on the blanket, sits up, and softens Samantha's comment with a more compassionate stance.

"Whenever I'm in a bad place, it always seems that one of my kids is in an even worse place. If I have a bad cold, they get a fever. If I break a finger, they break an arm. It's like I'm not allowed to wallow in my shit because I have to take care of their shit. And their shit always trumps my shit." She grabs my hands tightly. "But tonight, Soph, is about you, okay. *You.* You're off mom duty for just a teensy bit. You will deal with Ava, and knowing you, like a pro. It's okay to do that—to take care of you sometimes." Her voice waxes tender. She knows full well that my world revolves around Gabe and Ava. She and Samantha always give me crap about it.

My hands feel limp and clammy inside hers, but safe. We stay like that for a few more moments of contemplative silence. Lauren smiles at me, raises a mischievous brow. "Should we try the Juul?"

I laugh. "Why not."

As Lauren figures out how to use the Juul—a first for us—Samantha pulls out all of her tricks from the picnic basket: a bottle of wine, Cheetos, double-stuffed Oreos, and strawberry licorice.

"Cheetos?" I say. "That's so eighties. No one eats Cheetos or Doritos anymore. Everything is multigrain, quinoa, seaweed, or chia. Cheetos are for those who drink Big Gulps from the 7-Eleven."

"And those have like seventy-two grams of sugar," Lauren adds.

Samantha flashes her a look. "How do you even know that?"

Lauren's eyes pop defensively, always self-conscious about her weight. "I'm not the one who brought Cheetos."

"Well, Eric eats this shit. This is stolen from his secret stash hidden on the top shelf in the garage behind his tools, where I make him hide it from the kids since we've gone organic. There's Hostess CupCakes and Ding Dongs in there too. You would not believe the crap he has . . . but I figured this was an emergency."

Samantha hands me the corkscrew and I open the bottle of wine and raise it high overhead. "Well then, fuck Gabe and fuck organic."

"Fuck Gabe and fuck organic," they shout in unison, and we partake and pass around the Juul, the Cheetos, and the wine.

Lauren shoves an entire fistful into her mouth, the neon orange crumbs decorating her mouth like lip liner. "I have not eaten these in years. Beyond . . ."

I grab a handful and shove it in as well. "Oh my god." I then swig hard and raise the bottle overhead. "Here's to Gabe's forty-three—fuck Ashley Madison."

"Fuck Ashley Madison!" they scream in harmony, my back-up singers.

Samantha, wasting no time, digs into the Oreos, ripping apart the wrapping as if she were Pablo going through the kitchen garbage bin. "I don't mean to be a cold bitch, but let's be clear here. No one—I mean *no one*—has to *find* himself forty-three times, period. And that's just the number of women that we know of."

"Too far, Sam, too far," Lauren says, as she licks off her Cheetos'd fingers.

I put down the bottle, holding it between my legs, and stare at Samantha. *Damn her.* Always a straight shooter—so much so that at times, like right now, her truths are too sharp, bordering on callous. Lauren has always been so much better at smoothing things over, making light of the heavy, softening blows. Not Samantha—she goes for the jugular, especially when she articulates what no one else wants to say aloud: Did Gabe's cheating begin and end with Ashley Madison, or were there more lovers?

I stick the wine bottle in the sand, stand, walk to the edge of the water, and stare out into the abyss. So many women. How could I really not have known? Or smelled it on him? Seen the guilt in his eyes? Heard the tremor in his voice when he'd lie as to why he came home later than usual? Or even, the most basic, why was he showering twice a day? I thought I knew everything about Gabe, anticipated every move of his. How the hell didn't I see this?

I shake my head. Maybe I did . . . There was that flirty fitness trainer with the boobs at the club. That new waitress with purplish streaks in her hair at our local bar who seemed to know Gabe way better than she should. There was the pretty divorced nurse who always seemed to be lurking around every damn time I popped in at the hospital to surprise him with lunch.

Samantha is right. No one has to find himself forty-three times. Perhaps I didn't *want* to know, didn't want to see it.

I hug myself tightly. *But now I do.* Now I want to know it all, every single thing I missed. I turn around decisively, head back to the blanket. "I'm sorry to break up the party, but you guys need to take me home right now."

Samantha's dark eyes open wide. "What? Don't go back there. I have a big mouth. No filter. I'm so sorry."

"It's not you. But you're totally right. I have been a blind fool." I glance down at my feet wet with sand, look up slowly. "We all know Gabe cheated. It's on an Excel sheet, for Christ's sake. But now I need to know how badly he cheated. Was my whole damn marriage a farce?"

I bend down and pick up the almost empty bottle of

wine and cast it into the lake as though it were a shot put. I've never littered once in my entire life, and in middle school I'd even organized a community garbage pickup for extra credit, but right now who I was, what I did, no longer matters.

Samantha and Lauren exchange yet another round of concerned glances. I've chalked up six of those since we got to the beach. But they know better than to mess with me right now. Not like this. Unhinged, in shoot-to-kill mode. They also know that a party-sized bag of Cheetos and a demolished package of Oreos is not going to fix this.

They both leap to their feet, wipe off the sand from their yoga pants. Samantha, on a typical day, would never have left the beach without folding the blanket perfectly, but now she sweeps it up in one fell swoop under her arms. She then points to the emptied Cheetos bag and the finished Oreos. Lauren obeys her silent command, stuffing the trash inside the picnic basket. We all trudge up what seems to be one hundred stairs in collective silence.

Once we pull into my driveway, Samantha quickly locks my door with her childproof switch accompanied by a stern you're-not-going-anywhere-without-telling-me-the-plan look in her eye.

"Well?"

"I'm going to confront him," I tell her. "And then I may just kill him, but first, I'm going to give him an opportunity to tell the truth. All of it . . ."

"I should never have opened my big mouth," she laments. Lauren nods.

They suddenly appear young and scared. It's not their fault. "You guys are my lifeline. Thank you for tonight. The beach, the Juul, and especially the Cheetos. I just need to know what I don't know."

"And then what are you going to do?" Samantha demands.

I shrug. "I have no fucking idea."

Samantha reaches over the wide leather armrest between us, and pulls me in close into an uncomfortable embrace, which feels more like a headlock. "Call if you need me to pick you up. I will keep my phone on my pillow. Anything. I'm here for you."

I can still smell the Jo Malone on her. Lauren tenderly squeezes my shoulder from the backseat.

"Okay," I respond as I grab my rolled-up blue dress at my feet, my voice so tiny and lost as I stare at my house through the car window with dread. *Nothing is okay.*

Chapter Four

I enter my house through the garage, expecting Pablo to jump all over me, but he's not there waiting, as usual, in the laundry room. He must be upstairs with Gabe. I then head into the kitchen, look around. All the lights are off. Except for the outside lights. I peer out the glass patio door. In the past, I would have reveled in the soft radiance shining over my Tuscan garden. Several of my sculptures, which are illuminated, are scattered among the flowers and the trees. But now my prized garden and all the extra touches mean nothing. Everything has changed. Holding my breath, I lean back against the kitchen table for support.

Don't think. Don't feel. Just go upstairs now and deal.

As I slowly head upstairs, I note that my bedroom door is ajar and all the lights are on. I walk in, pause near the bed, when I see Gabe inside the closet reaching for something on his top shelf. How fitting—the night ends where it unfolded, back in the closet with the rest of Gabe's secrets.

Move. Go. Now. My inner Lou Gossett Jr. commands.

I make a beeline into the closet past Gabe, past his going-out clothes, which are in a heap on the floor next to the hamper. No surprises there. He stops what he's doing when he sees me and freezes in place. We face off. He's wearing his old army-green cargo pants and his favorite University of Wisconsin Bucky Badger T-shirt, clearly having gotten comfortable for what is about to be the most uncomfortable night of his life. Pablo (named after Picasso), stands in the middle of us, as though trying to decide who he's going to follow—the Cheater or the Cheated On.

Realizing that I'm holding my high heels and have my birthday blue dress still hanging over my arm, I drop it all at Gabe's feet. We both look down and stare. I then kick the dress childishly, punting it across the closet as Gabe watches. Pablo runs to retrieve it, and drops it back at my feet. He wants to play. I shake my head, then pick up the dress and turn to Gabe. With a strength and a rage that I never knew existed before tonight, I rip the dress in half in front of him. Unplanned and dramatic, but highly satisfying.

"Sophie." His eyes tear up.

"Gabe." Mine are as dry as the Sahara, protecting the Niagara Falls looming behind them. But I can't lie to myself. The dam is about to break, like everything else inside me.

How do I do this? Do I hit him? Slap his face? Gorge him with my stilettos?

He deserves all of it, but the truth is, I'm still in shock. This is so new to both of us. We have fought plenty over the years, but stupid boyfriend-girlfriend fights, then normal marital fights—I did this, you did that, how could you forget, why didn't you, what the hell is wrong with you? fights. But never, not once, an our-marriage-is-over fight. Not even a you're-sleeping-on-the-couch fight. I have nothing from the past to work with—no reference material, no precedent—except for the ghost of Gabe's mother, whom he despises (as do I), who was always mean and bitter. She was a passive-aggressive fighter. She let you know exactly how she felt through her eyes. I know Gabe would rather me throw things or even jab him with my high heel than stare with Gloria Bloom's bullet-laden eyes. I ponder my myriad choices quickly: *Screw him, he gets his mother.*

"Go make us coffee." I glare. I never drink coffee past dinner, and by the surprised look on his face, we're both thinking the same thing. "I will be down in a few minutes."

"Sophie," he says again, repeating my name as if that's his only option. His voice is cracking and if I weren't me right now and we weren't a broken version of us, I would wrap my arms around him and comfort him—the way I had years ago when his dog since childhood died, or when a young patient with a serious heart condition with whom he'd bonded and who he'd operated on four times died, or when we knew we couldn't have any more children after Ava—that it was him, not me. It didn't matter, I told him over and over again, we have Ava, the most beautiful girl in the world. But this, I think, eyeing the now two-piece blue birthday dress at his feet, *this matters*. This, not his low sperm count that he blames on a football injury, has turned our tower of love into rubble.

"Just do it! Make the fucking coffee!" I shout as my eyes begin to water. I can't comfort you now. *You broke us.*

I sit across from him, hands cupped around my favorite mug, which, ironically, reads But First, Coffee, at our new kitchen table from Restoration Hardware. It is country chic, a weathered blond natural wood. I loved it in the catalogue, circled it, had to have it. It seats twelve comfortably with the table leaves. I bought it with our family and our friends' families in mind. Samantha and Lauren each have two kids. I stare at the prized table now and think, who cares? I would settle for Formica, for cardboard even—not to be sitting here right now.

Gabe stares back at me, mute like an Egyptian eunuch, a subservient awaiting his fate. I hate him for putting me in this position. All I can do without falling apart is to focus on the Starbucks Dark Roast at his lips. At another time, I would have asked if he liked the new beans I got from that barista whose nose ring looks like a cowbell, that it's stronger than his usual roast, but now I couldn't care less which type of bean he favors.

I summon my voice. "What I don't understand is *why*? They say a man never leaves a warm bed for a cold one. Wasn't our bed still warm after all these years? If you weren't happy, why the hell didn't you let me know?" My head drops into my hands. "How could you do this to us? Why . . ."

Gabe snaps out of his catatonic state of guilt and reaches for my hand, and I yank it away. *Don't even.* He clears his throat, stares at the hand with the already chipped nails, a hand that he is now forbidden to touch. "I was happy. *Was*, I suppose. Maybe I wasn't.

I think we've been together so long that I just wanted something different, something else. You were the only woman I'd ever slept with. Every experience we've had has been together . . . Something was driving me, Soph, and I couldn't stop it. And this urge became bigger than me, out of control. I wanted something short-term, meaningless." He shakes his head, looks away as if in a private conversation with himself. "I had to have it." His voice lowers to a painful whisper. "I just didn't want to break us or leave you, and the Ashley Madison option seemed, I don't know, stupidly safe. Like I could have other experiences and—"

"Like you could have forty-three other experiences and still come home." I finish the sentence because I know Gabe better than he knows himself. I search his red-rimmed eyes and realize how pompous I am. Clearly, I don't know him at all. Or, rather, I stopped knowing Gabe because I thought I knew everything about him.

"It was enough for me," I whisper, not even aware that the words had escaped my mouth. But was it? Was there something inherently wrong I failed to recognize? Did we stop seeing each other as man and woman and more like good, comfy furniture? Were our spurts of passion really *Just press play* simulations that we could count on to do the trick? I look at Gabe perspiring across the table. The fear, the getting caught, is clearly much worse than he'd ever imagined. I can tell he wishes he could take it all back. But perhaps I'm wrong again. Maybe, just maybe, this is what he wanted subconsciously. *To be free.*

"How long would you have kept this going?" I ask because I have to. "If you weren't caught. Did you have a plan to stop?"

Please lie to me. I need a big fat juicy lie right now, even though I'm demanding truth. *Lie, motherfucker, lie.*

"I don't know, Soph. I think—I think I would have just kept it going."

I slam the But First, Coffee mug down, the liquid spills and is immediately sucked into the table's grainy distressed wood, but I don't care. "Damn you, how could you have done this to me and Ava and live with yourself?" I shout, standing and starting to pace around the oversized table.

"It's unforgivable. I know . . ." Gabe's eyes well up again. "It was so damn easy. Exciting. It was—"

I cup my hands over my ears like a small child screaming blah blah blah when her parent reprimands her, and then my hands drop limply. "Look at me.

Goddamnit, look at me, Gabe. I've kept in shape. I'm a nice person, caring, a good friend, a great mom, a professional, our sex seemed good—"

"Sophie . . . you're perfect. It's not you."

"Stop!" My voice escalates to a shriek and I can't stand the sound of it. "If you give me the 'It's not you it's me' speech, I will lose it!" For a split second, I really do contemplate taking out the newly sharpened Cutco from the knife drawer and stabbing him.

Gabe nods, stopping what he'd been clearly rehearsing in his head and instead goes off teleprompter. "Here's the thing. We got married so young. We had Ava so young. We never had our twenties. We never lived in the city alone in our own apartments and dated. I never went wild in Vegas with my guy friends and did stupid shit. I did everything that I was supposed to do. I lived up to everyone's expectations—my coaches, my parents, my patients, yours. But inside, I felt this deep restlessness that I tried—believe me, I fucking tried—to control but couldn't. I needed passion not comfort, not the familiar. I wanted something that went off the expected course of my life. I needed to be with women who didn't know my every move before I did . . ."

"Not a TLFer," I cut in.

"What?" He raises a brow, not getting it.

"Our tree, Gabe, our goddamn tree. I'm not inhuman. I get that we fell in love too young and there's definitely a danger in that. But there's also something special and pure. Don't you think I ever wondered what it would be like to be with someone else? Or that men haven't hit on me over the years—they have—but then I would look at you and I knew deep down that whoever else I chose, he could never be you. That I would meet other people and still search for you." Tears roll down both of our faces now. Truth is truth, no matter how you twist it.

"See, and the difference is . . ." Gabe says under his breath, "I wanted anyone who wasn't you. Every one of those women are physically opposite of you. Blonde, blue-eyed—I stayed away from anyone who looked remotely like you."

"Thank you for that," I say sarcastically, feeling the heat rise to my face. "I can't tell you how much better that makes me feel."

He wipes the sweat off his forehead. "What I meant is that this didn't happen because I stopped loving you. You're my family. You . . ."

And this, right there, is the slasher of marital moments. "You," I say painfully, meaning me, "feel like a sister—not a lover."

"Yes." Gabe lowers his head, softly acknowledges his truth.

The silence between us fills the room until it smolders and smothers. Truth doesn't set you free—*who the hell said that?* No, truth is suffocating. And then my cell phone rings, bringing me back to the present. Like everyone else, even in my darkest pain, I'm Pavlov's dog when it comes to the phone. My life just exploded, but *ping* and I glance over to see who's calling.

"It's Ava," I announce.

"Please," he begs. "Don't tell her."

"Ava, hi," I answer, ignoring him.

"Mom." Ava is crying and it's hard to hear her over the international call static. "Mommy."

When she reverts to "Mommy," I know my very independent nineteen-year-old is in really bad shape. "What's wrong? What happened? What—when?"

"Is she okay?" Gabe shouts. "Was there a terrorist attack?"

That would have been my top question too.

I hold up my hand, signaling that it's not a terrorist attack. "Jake—what? I can't hear you. The connection is not great. Say it again. Jake did what?"

I glance at Gabe and repeat each one of Ava's words slowly for his guilty benefit. "Jake. Cheated. On. You."

Gabe's eyes are wide. Karma just bit him in the ass. His wife and now his beloved daughter. The two women who supposedly mean everything to him. One he fucked over, the other someone else did. The family crescendo of pain is now at a super max, the soprano of betrayal hitting high C.

I stare at the phone in my hand with disbelief. My daughter and I are so connected. But not this, I think, and not now.

"Mommy," she continues through tears. "I didn't want to ruin your birthday. But I've been crying all day—you don't understand . . . Jake was with Monica."

"Your Monica?" I repeat, sitting back down, understanding the magnitude of this but needing confirmation. Monica has been Ava's closest friend since middle school. Monica is her Samantha.

"Yes, you know they both studied together in London last semester. Same program. Well, they've been traveling with a group of friends. They went to Amsterdam, Portugal, and from there, they're all heading to Spain. I'm supposed to meet up with them in Barcelona as soon as I finish my project. Anyway, I saw Jake and Monica making out on a Snapchat story in the background of another friend's post—I mean, who does that? Everyone saw. Every one. My boyfriend with my best friend. Can you even imagine how I feel? We've been together two years. And with Monica? Monica, Mommy?!"

"Oh honey."

"Monica . . . fucking Monica. I need you. I know it's asking a lot—but please, can you—"

"I'm coming." I finish my daughter's sentence. My home is a House of Sentences I can finish with my eyes closed. Gabe stares at me stone silent as though he's a granite carving on Mount Rushmore. Pre–Ashley Madison, we would have both stopped our lives and gotten on a plane together to comfort our daughter.

"The first plane *I* can take, *I* will be there. Hang in there, okay. You're not alone. *I* am coming." I keep emphasizing the "I"—not "we"—for Gabe's benefit.

"What about your work?" she asks, still crying.

"That's why I have great people working for me. Don't worry about me. It's about you. But I get how you feel, more than you know."

I hang up the phone. Sick to my stomach. Mother Nature is clearly messing with me. I look up. Gabe is standing over me.

"Don't tell her, Sophie, please."

I cross my arms, my eyes grow hard, my voice is sharp. "Did you think of our daughter when you were out gallivanting with Moms on the Make? Did you think about their kids? Their spouses? Ava will hear, Gabe. This is a small town and you are the top cheater on North Grove's public list. Congrats—a couple more you could have gotten first in State once again."

"It will break her," he whispers, head sunk low, defeated. "Break me . . ."

"You broke us first."

"It was only all about Ava," he says under his breath.

I stop moving. "What?"

"Forget it, really." He turns away.

"No. For some reason I think this is the good part."

"All I'm saying is you were always so focused on Ava that you forgot about me." Gabe eyes me closely. "I get that we were only able to have one child, but after Ava was born, I didn't feel important to you. I was an afterthought. And then the postpartum depression. And then . . . after a while, I just needed more."

I stare at him unblinking. *More?* Ava was my everything, but so was Gabe. I gave them both every damn thing I had—leaving nothing for myself. How did he not see that? But was he right? Did I make him feel unimportant? I squeeze my eyes tightly. I can't feel my pulse, my anything.

"Couldn't you have talked to me?" I ask. "Couldn't you have expressed your feelings? We could have worked through this. Did you really need forty-three other women to give you attention?" My insides are burning. "Were you really that deprived?"

"The truth—you want to know the goddamn truth?" Gabe shouts. He never yells. His calm demeanor in the midst of a fight has always made me crazy. "You didn't need me—it didn't matter if I was here or not. You had Samantha and Lauren—I just filled in the blanks. You were married to them. You laughed the hardest with them, not me. You shared your deepest thoughts with them, not me. Yes, I slept with all those women. But you need to ask yourself why didn't *you* fucking notice?"

The heavy silence between us feels funereal—a melancholic din of black and grim. I can't be here any longer with this man. I stand quietly and rinse out the coffee mug in the sink and gently place it into the dishwasher. I return to the table, wipe away the spilled coffee stain as best as I can and toss the sponge into the sink. Gabe watches my rotary movements with a mix of curiosity and not knowing what to do next. I walk past him, through the kitchen alcove and then turn slowly, facing him.

For some reason I focus on that scar near his eyebrow and wonder who will ever know that he fell off his bike while running away from the neighborhood bully? He is dead wrong. I did love him, know him, take care of him, desire him, think of his needs constantly.

We grew up together, Gabe, and no matter what you think, no matter what you did to us, I don't know how to do life without you.

The anger and betrayal dissipate briefly, thawed by an intermission of nostalgia. Our gazes meet in the same way they had when we held Ava for the very first time, when Gabe's eyes traced the planes of my face, knowing the sheer magnitude of what we'd just created. But now our gazes cling to what we've just destroyed. Tears begin to roll and I don't try to stop them, nor does he. Turning around slowly, I head upstairs to pack, knowing the damage is too far gone for any kind of repair.

Chapter Five

As I enter my bedroom once again, a wave of sadness overtakes me, dark and bottomless. I stare at our king-sized bed. The colorful pillows—a pyramid of interrelated shabby chic designs—drove Gabe crazy. *They're ridiculous. How many different types of the same damn pillow do we need?* But it was once a bed that served as a playground for late-night Netflix binges, cuddling, fucking, playing with Pablo, watching old movies with Ava sandwiched between us, reading, heart-to-heart discussions, as well as disagreements and make-up sessions. It wasn't just a bed, but our Oval Office—filled with highly classified information and sheltering the very best and worst of us. His side, my side, and always, finding our way toward each other in the middle. But now . . . I lean against the back wall and brace myself. *There is no now. And there was no then.* Clearly, who we were together in that bed was all in my head.

Taking a deep breath, I walk to my side of the bed, plug my phone into the charger, call Air France, and book a one-way plane ticket to Paris.

"One way," I say aloud just to confirm that it is real. One way, because I feel directionless. I pay nearly four thousand dollars for a same-day reservation, direct flight, first class. I don't even bother using my miles and having to deal with yet another operator for another twenty minutes. I've got to get the hell out of this house, this bedroom as soon as I can. Screw the miles and *screw you, GMB18@gmail.com.*

My eyes rest briefly on the large sculpture in the far corner of the room that I made for Gabe on his twenty-fifth birthday. It is a six-foot-high bronze and metal sculpture of *us*—a man and a woman intertwined like a totem pole; legs, arms, torsos wrapped around each other, mouths pressed together—never letting go. I walk over to it, run my hand slowly along the male's smooth bronzed thigh. My hand drops to my side and I fall to the floor. Tears fill my eyes, and I wipe them away. Enough with the tears. *Get up and go pack*, I order myself. *Pretend you can do this. Pretend you're anyone but you right now.*

Turning away from the sculpture, I slowly enter my closet—the third time tonight. I see the two-piece blue birthday dress, still on the floor, and kick it out of the way. I force myself to turn a blind eye to Gabe's side of the closet, as if it doesn't exist. I don't want to see anything that belongs to him. All those shirts and ties that I bought him over the years. I don't want to think of all the women who touched, unbuttoned, ripped open, fondled, or pressed their perfumed bodies against those annual Father's Day shirts. *Don't think at all*, I warn myself again.

I gather a bunch of random clothes, praying it will all fit inside the carry-on—the only suitcase in our closet. There's no way I'm going downstairs in the basement for a bigger one. As I quickly roll my clothes into tight croissant-like coils, I hear Gabe's footsteps coming up the stairs, a pounding trudge like in one of those Lifetime domestic abuse specials. I stop in midroll, hold my breath, anticipating what comes next. He's going to apologize, beg forgiveness, plead for therapy, say he'll do whatever it takes to get me back. But once again, I call it wrong. In lieu of an apology, there's a total abrupt silence, like someone pulled the plug on Alexa midsong. The footsteps halt, three stairs from the top. Seconds later, they rev up again, only backward, descending, changing their mind.

As I drag my suitcase across the hardwood floor past the family room, I spot Gabe out on the patio deck, draped over a chaise longue. Pablo is curled up at his feet. I stop and stare out the window. He may have slept with all those women, blown up our lives, but I will be damned if he is going to have the last word.

I leave my suitcase, step out onto the patio, which is lit up, and see that he's busy polishing off the new steroid-sized bottle of bourbon I bought from Costco last week. No glass, I note. Swigging straight from the bottle. *Good,* I think, standing over him with crossed arms. *Sufficiently buzzed with truth serum.*

"Sophie." He bolts upright with surprise. He places the bottle onto the small round glass table next to him. "I thought you were leaving."

"I was, until I realized I forgot something."

"What's that?"

I scan the length of Gabe's lanky body. Hate him or love him, the man doesn't age. He is still lean and fit, still boyishly handsome with the kind of unfair face like Bradley Cooper's that just gets better, more re-fined, with each passing year.

"The truth, Gabe. All of it." I sit across from him on the twin chaise, peer into his bloodshot eyes. "When Ava called I was focused on her and we didn't finish our conversation. But now . . ." I can barely get the words out. "No more lies."

He averts his gaze, stares down at the bluestone at his feet, then looks up in slow motion, his mouth dropping. "What more do you want from me? You already know everything."

"See, that's the thing. I have this nagging feeling that I don't." I grab the bourbon and drink straight from the bottle too. The alcohol burns right through me as though it were lighter fluid—exactly what I need right now. "I need to know if there *is* more. More than just Ashley Madison." I place the bottle down, meet his wide-eyed gaze squarely. "When exactly did we end and the betrayal begin? I have to know before I go." My voice begins a shrill climb to a sharp peak, and I don't try to tone it down. He remains unnervingly silent, and it's infuriating. "Damn it, Gabe, tell me now."

He buries his face in his hands, then looks up with those remorseful eyes. "I'm so sorry for hurting you. How many times can I say it so you believe me?"

I shake my head. "'Sorry' doesn't begin to cut it."

He lets out an exasperated sigh. He's a guy. An apology should have been enough. "I don't know what more you want from me."

"The hell you don't," I snap. I have zero energy for pulling teeth. "Let's start with this . . . when did you have time to fuck forty-three other women?" My voice is getting louder and I can't control it. "Tell me now, goddamnit."

Gabe shakes his head, guzzles more bourbon, then slams the bottle back down on the table. "Okay, fine. You really want to know? Things began to change between us with the Tuesday at 7:54," he says, shame-facedly. "That's when."

I furrow my brow. "Tuesday at 7:54? Is that some kind of cheater's code? What does that even mean?"

His jaw constricts. "It means when we couldn't con-ceive after Ava . . . all the treatments, all those months of monitored ovulation, all that goddamned timed-to-the-minute sex—if you could call it that. I remember specifically watching a Bulls play-off game and you came downstairs and said, 'It's Tuesday, 7:54—exactly one day before ovulation and the exact time when my eggs are strongest. So it's right now, Gabe—let's give it a go.' And I remember thinking all I want to do is watch my fucking game and not ejaculate on call. That I was so sick of how scheduled it all was, what we'd become . . . so tired of how exacting you were, like my dick was some kind of science experiment." He points a finger. "That's what killed us."

I stare at him and that menacing finger. My stom-ach twists, and if my eyes could shoot bullets, he would be dead on arrival. Sound and motion begin to split all around me. With this admission, everything comes to a screeching halt and then a sudden lurch forward. And that's when I stand, pick up what's left of the bourbon and dump it over his head. "Let me remind you that *I* wasn't the problem. It was you, your goddamn low sperm count. So screw you for making me out like I wanted to ruin the Bulls play-offs so I could . . ." I can't even finish. My head is reverberating with *7:54, 7:54.*

But I'm not done. I can actually feel my blood pressure elevating beneath my skin, the steam oozing out of me, and I'm about to blow. I tower over Gabe like a shrew from medieval times—even my voice has taken on a strange cackle. "*You* have low sperm count and *I* deserve to be betrayed forty-three times because you missed a stupid Bulls game that they lost anyway? *I* was the science experiment—not you—you selfish prick!"

Gabe bows his head in silence. And I know his brand of silence. It is the kind which says that's not all, that there *is* more to this story, more depth to Tuesday at 7:54. I know this man better than he knows himself. Although who am I kidding? I clearly missed the Ashley Madison gang bang going on right under my nose. But I do have options right now. I could retreat and slam the patio door behind me. I could throw more things and berate him, but if I want real answers, it's now or never. This is *the* conversation—there won't be another chance. His defenses are down. *Choose now.*

Exhaling deeply, I feel the tears forming once again in the corners of my eyes, and I will them away. "So just to be accurate, you stopped seeing me as a love object while we were trying to conceive." I blow more air out of my cheeks. *Keep it together.* "If I do the calculations beginning with Tuesday at 7:54 p.m., then it's clear the Ashley Madison harem were not the only cheats, were they? They came later . . . much later."

His eyes are glued open, a thirteen-year-old boy caught with his dad's *Playboy.* I'm no longer me. I'm Gloria Allred, investigating a highly controversial case, deposing the defendant, who is *so* guilty—and now it's just a matter of finding out *how* guilty.

A faint sweat breaks out across Gabe's forehead, but he admits nothing, knowing that it's in everyone's best interest to take the Fifth. Feeling my cheeks growing feverish, I begin to enumerate the facts on my fingers. "Let's see . . . that pretty nurse, Holly, right? She was always lurking whenever I popped in for lunch. I'm guessing she was on your journey."

He nods without moving his head; just his eyes confirm my worst fears. *The first dagger goes in.* "Then I'm betting on that trainer at the club—Tammy with the boobs? Her too?"

Nod two. *Twist in, thrust hard.*

I can barely breathe now, but push myself to keep going. I snap my fingers. "Oh, oh—and of course, that bartender over at Billy's. You know the one I'm talking about with the purple hair, or was it magenta? She was in a band, played drums. You kept asking her about her concerts—as if you actually give a shit about alternative goth rock. On your bucket list as well, am I right?"

Gabe's cheeks are now stained the color of cabernet. He starts to say something, some form of apology, that he has a problem—maybe the words "sex addiction" come out of his mouth, but I don't hear it. I just feel it. *Stab, repeat, stab, repeat.*

I'm floating out of my body and not in a good way. The man I've loved for so long, gave my whole self to, raised a child with, not only Ashley Madisoned me, but also cheated on me practically our entire marriage. How long would it have continued? How long would I have been blindsided had those hackers decided to get their LOLs elsewhere?

I gather whatever remaining scraps of breath I can find to pull out the final accusation—the lone allegation that matters most: "Did you ever cheat with someone I know?" I silently pray for one morsel of manna, one toss of a dog bone. *Say no. Spare me that, at the very least.*

Gabe is silent. And not just monastic silent, but stock-still, like a soldier who finds himself standing in the middle of a minefield. That's when I hit him for the first time ever, a swift slap across the face. "Who? One of our neighbors? Who?" I yell, feeling like I could go all-out postal. "One of our friends? Who?"

His hand soothes his stinging cheek, then he squeezes his eyes shut, too tightly, too briefly, and lets out a deep exhale. *The final tell.* The one truth too awful to even release. I circle him now, a lion trainer with an airborne whip. "You sack of shit—who?"

His terrified eyes are dilated saucers and I know exactly what he sees: the blushing girl who stood at her decorated locker when he asked her to prom. *That girl.* The young bride walking toward him, aglow with all that possibility. The first-time mom cradling their newborn baby girl—after giving everything she had, her whole body, to that pregnancy. The woman in the messy kitchen who made him his favorite pasta for the first time, homemade spaghetti with those special meatballs—his grandmother's recipe—and his mouth forms the one word that I hear but fail to process: *Lauren.*

"What?" I say, squinting.

"Lauren," he whispers.

"*My* Lauren," I confirm, leaning in. "Lauren, Lauren?"

His eyes—*Ava's eyes*—are brimming with tears. Any prospect of saving us, any chance of recovery is gone, destroyed, decimated. *Lauren, Lauren.* So many lies, so much betrayal, no beginning, no end.

"Just once . . ." he says, his voice so far away that it sounds like an echo.

"I'm done." I grab my purse off the chaise and clutch it to my chest. "There's nothing left of me to break. We're over, Gabe. But I guess we were over at 7:54 on a Tuesday so many years ago . . . So much deception, so much of my life that you stole from me."

"Sophie, please."

I hear nothing, see nothing, feel nothing. I'm a shell with a voice. "Here's what's going to happen. I'm leaving now for Paris. I'm going to nurse Ava through the Jake breakup, then I'm going to tell her the truth about us. And then . . ." I don't finish my sentence because I have no idea what *then* is.

"This will destroy her," he pleads. "Please, give *me* a chance to fix this, to tell Ava myself in my way, to explain." He looks grief-stricken as if *he* has been violated, and I no longer care. "I'm so ashamed. But I'm still her father."

I'm suddenly shivering, my purse begins to shake against me. "You've lost all rights. You've lost your way."

I run into the house, sick to my stomach, and lock myself in the downstairs bathroom near the kitchen. I bend over the toilet and wait. *Lauren, my Lauren . . .* worse than all forty-three women plus bonus sluts combined. I picture her thick, red wavy hair, that voluptuous body and creamy skin in Gabe's roving hands. I see them laughing. I can actually hear it. I replay the loop over and over in my head like it's on redial, and I want to die. Does Samantha know? *No way.*

Somehow, I manage to reach inside my purse for my cell phone. "Sam," I barely breathe out her name. "Come get me now."

"Soph . . . oh no. I'm coming. I will call Laur—"

"Do. Not. Call. Her!" I yell at the top of my lungs, dizzy, as I lean against the bathroom wall for support, my head detonating so many vivid images at once, spinning mercilessly out of control, until it expands, big-bangs, and ultimately, explodes.

Chapter Six

I hear the screech of the tires against the driveway as Samantha pulls up. I splash water on my face, quickly dry off, and head out. As I pass the kitchen windows, I see Gabe still lying out there on the chaise in the backyard. I sprint down the driveway, throw my luggage into the backseat of her car, slam the door. "Just go!"

"That bad?" she asks softly, looking at me as she pulls out of the driveway.

I can't even respond. There are no words to define this kind of bad. I have nothing left to give. "I want to go to the airport now."

"What? The airport? No. You're coming back to my house with me." Samantha freezes. "Where are you even going?"

"To Paris to be with Ava," I say. "Jake cheated on her too. She needs me. My flight is at 5:30 this afternoon, but I'm going to try and catch an earlier one. Honestly, I don't care how I get to Paris. I just need to get out of this town now."

"Jesus Christ. You're not going anywhere like this. You need me, goddamnit!"

"Please, Sam, just take me to the airport." I can barely keep it together.

"It's barely 3 a.m. Nothing is even open. Sophie, c'mon, you're not thinking." She slows down. "Please, just talk to me first."

I burst out crying, sobbing in a way that I haven't since Ava was born. "Stop the car somewhere," I manage through the tears.

Samantha gets off the main road and pulls onto a side street and parks.

"Lauren, Sam. Do you . . ." But I can't even finish the sentence.

She leans forward, her lips purse tightly, her dark eyes grow wide and round like a kewpie doll. I know that look. *Her tell.* Suddenly, all the crying stops as if a director wearing a leather bomber jacket and baseball hat shouts "Cut!" I stare in disbelief. It can't be. Anyone else—*not her.* Not Self-Righteous Samantha. *Christ, she knows.* "You know exactly what I'm going to ask," I growl, shocked by the sheer magnitude of the betrayal encompassing me on all sides. "You fucking know . . ."

Samantha opens her mouth, about to defend herself, and then stops. There's no point. "Yes," she confesses. Her whole body seems to contract like the bellows of an accordion. "Yes."

Yes?! Twenty-eight years of friendship and that's it? The admission releases a fusillade of bullets, each tearing my heart out. "How long?" is all I can muster.

She exhales hard through her nose, and I recognize that particular Ujjayi breath from yoga class. "A long time, Soph."

"When, damn it?" I hiss.

"Five years ago."

I speed-flip through my mental datebook. "That Nashville trip? When I had food poisoning?"

She nods, her forehead breaks out into a sweat. "Believe me, it killed me not to tell you, but it wasn't my place."

I shake my head furiously, like Pablo when he's wet, not letting her anywhere near off the hook. "It was *so* your place." I point my finger between her eyes. "When have we ever lied to each other about anything? Seriously—when?"

Samantha points back. "It wasn't my lie and you

know that. It would have broken up the group, torn apart two marriages when it meant nothing—a drunken night of sheer stupidity. Believe me I ripped Lauren to shreds over it."

I place my hand over my mouth, unable to comprehend the magnitude of this. "Broken up the group? See, you're wrong. It means *everything*. I would have told you about Eric and Lauren in a heartbeat if that happened. I wouldn't have thought twice, only about protecting you, making sure you were nobody's fool. Broken up the group—are you kidding me?" I spit back at her. "Just get me to the goddamn airport."

"Soph."

A name I no longer recognize nor respond to. I'm deaf, broken, muted, emotionally stripped.

We drive in a painful silence for the next twenty-five minutes to the airport. Samantha doesn't even turn on the music. As we pull up to the drop-off lane, I turn to her. "Gabe broke me, Lauren destroyed me . . . but you, Sam—you just buried me."

Tears stream down her face, and she is not a crier. She's a thrower. Guilty by association. Guilty by omission. I look away. *Guilty is guilty.*

"What can I do?" she whispers, grabbing me by the arm as I try to open up the kid-locked door. I push her away.

"Release the fucking lock," I say coldly.

I get out, slam the car door with Samantha still inside, still crying. Completely numb, I grab my bag from the backseat and don't look back. I push through the glass double doors toward the check-in counter, barely breathing, just sensing my forward movement. Perspiration glides down the back of my shirt and in between my breasts. I didn't just lose a husband, my marriage—I lost my entire support system in a blink of an eye.

But as usual, Samantha was right. The reservation desk for Air France isn't open yet. I sit on a random chair and wait, feeling the sheer terror mounting inside me. I have given the very best of me to those I love— and they took it all, leaving me nothing to hold on to. I've never felt more alone, betrayed, and lost. *What now? How do I do life now?*

II.

Life beats down and crushes the soul
and art reminds you that you have one.
—STELLA ADLER

Chapter Seven

I t's the middle of the night in Paris, and from the hotel room bed I see Ava standing outside leaning over the balcony, a slim grainy silhouette against the charcoal sky. Deep in thought, she looks like she just stepped out of a film noir, only without the cigarette. I sit back against the headboard, rub my mascara-encrusted eyes, and study my daughter through the open French doors.

She never changed into pajamas, probably never fell asleep. She is still wearing the same baggy boyfriend jeans and faded white tank from the day before. Her hair is piled high in a messy bun. Except for her eyes, the cleft in her chin, and lankiness—all Gabe—she has my features, just an improved version. Like me, Ava is an artist, a painter who looks like a model with her willowy height, dark riotous hair, long-lashed hazel eyes, sharp cheekbones, and slightly squared jaw with that tiny cleft—the spot where the angels kissed her when she was born, I used to tell her when she was a little girl.

Only Ava is no longer a child. She's a budding young woman, betrayed and in pain, and I feel every inch of it. Standing like that, propped up against the night, she appears so vulnerable. I grab the blanket off the bed, wrap it around me, and walk toward her.

"Honey, you need to sleep. Come to bed." I glance over the balcony and see the shades of night accentuated by flickering lights in the distance. I hear the loud honking and orchestra of motors—scooters, ambulances, police cars. Europeans are big on honking. Even in the wee hours, everyone still seems to be in everybody's way.

She stares, nods absently. Her eyes are tired, her gaze is strained. "I think it hurts even more that Monica betrayed me. Does that make sense?"

"Yes," I reply, having gone over this with her at least a dozen times already since I'd arrived yesterday. The same scenario. Monica and Jake caught making out on someone else's Snapchat story. Monica begging for forgiveness. Jake saying that they had been drinking. It was a mistake that happened only once, said Monica. Only Jake admitted that it happened twice.

"Believe me, I get it."

Tears stream down Ava's face. "You just don't understand."

I don't even try to convince her that I do. Instead I grab her hands and hold tightly. Lithe, slender fingers—*my hands.* Heartbreak devastates. It's a selfish, all-mine-not-yours emotion.

It takes everything I have inside me not to envelop Ava into my arms—she hates that. Ava is not a hugger and can be a bit standoffish. I've always found it fascinating how she can paint her emotions so freely, just not emote them with words or public displays of affection. Unless she is with Gabe, her hero—then she is all hippy love. I'm the heavy in our house, the discipliner, the one who takes care of things. Gabe rides in on a white horse and steals the girl but I tend the stables. And yet, when Ava's in pain or in a tough spot, it's Mommy to the rescue. Mommy, who for the first time ever needs to be rescued herself.

Christ, how do I do this?

Once Ava finds out that her hero is no better than Jake, that he, too, has fallen headfirst from his pedestal, it will break her. I have to somehow keep it from her and protect her for as long as possible. But I cannot help but feel like I'm a fraud, Mary Poppins dropping in with her magic carpet bag, which is empty inside.

How can I mother her pain when I'm in deeper pain? Who's going to give me a spoonful of sugar?

"Why are you looking at me so weirdly?" she asks.

"Just thinking." Thinking that I have no answers.

"Well, there's something else I have to tell you . . ." Ava's forehead scrunches, her eyebrows slope inward. Gabe makes that same face when he comes home from a hard case at the hospital and I'm asking if he wants sushi or Thai for dinner.

She leads us from the balcony back into the room, sits on the edge of the bed. "Don't judge me," she says, bunching the bedspread between her fists. Her eyes are fearful. This can't be good.

"Why don't you give me a chance first?" I say. Truthfully, I'm mentally drained and I've only been with her for less than ten hours.

She begins to cry. I know this is an awful thing to say but Ava is not a pretty crier. She looks exactly how she did when she was born. Like an old man in a stained white T-shirt watching a losing Cubs game.

"I think I may be pregnant."

"Pregnant?" I sit bolt upright. *Oh god. Talk about keeping the punchline under wraps.*

She bites down on her lip, shakes her head. Now I know *that* look. Yes, she did take my new black sweater from my closet. Yes, she was smoking pot in her bedroom. Yes, she did let her friend cheat off her on the algebra final—and they both got a detention. Deep exhale. I know what's coming next.

"It's not Jake's," she says, predictably.

"Not Jake's," I repeat to buy myself processing time.

"Stop repeating what I say."

"Stop repeating what you say?" I move in closer and feel like I want to spank her although I've never spanked her before. "How am I supposed to react, Ava Rose?" The middle name thrown in says it all; it is my homegrown verbal spanking. "You had me come all this way because Jake cheated on you. And now this … pregnant? You saw Jake in April, when he visited during spring break. If it's not his, then whose is it?"

She ignores the question, rolls her eyes, shakes her head. "I should have called Dad."

Fuck you, I think but obviously don't say. "Maybe you *should* have called Dad. Or maybe you should have just told me this from the beginning. This is clearly much more important than a Snapchat story."

Who are these people in my life? Tiny family, big lies. My husband the cheater and my daughter, who still has one more year left of college, who may be pregnant with what is clearly not her boyfriend's sperm. What type of people have lived under my roof? These dark impulses are killing me.

"I don't know who I am anymore," she says dramatically, cupping her face in her hands, as if she's in a scene from *The Bold and the Beautiful.*

Right now, my sympathy factor has a gun to its head. "Back up. First, why do you think you're pregnant?"

"For starters, I missed my pill. My entire cycle is off, and I was supposed to get my period three days ago, and I'm always on time—always—and nothing. Not a damn thing." The tears, which took a brief intermission, now return in full force.

Oh Christ.

"Did you take a pregnancy test?"

She shakes her head no.

"Why not?"

She wipes her eyes with her hand. "Because I have a portfolio to present tomorrow, and I had to stay focused."

I stare at Ava, not sure what to do first. Scream at her for sheer stupidity? She didn't take a pregnancy test because of an extra credit presentation? Is she kidding? But my daughter, who skipped fourth grade, still has to ace everything. This is crazy. I stand, swipe my hands against my pajama bottoms. "We're going to a gynecologist tomorrow, doing this properly."

"My presentation is at noon."

"Seriously, Ava? Fine. Let me see what I can do. I'm

going to call my gynecologist's office back home and see if they can recommend someone here."

"I'm so sorry, Mom." Her eyes are downcast, her bare feet shuffle against the almond-colored carpet.

I hold up my hand. "Wait a minute. Who is the guy?"

She glances up slowly, red faced, then blows out a deep breath, looking too much like her guilty father. "You're going to hate this . . . Please don't freak out."

At this point, Ava, freaking out doesn't even make the cut.

"Who?" I push.

She speaks in rapid double time to get it out and over. "My forms and figures professor. It's all my fault. I told Monica—that bitch—about the professor and she must've told Jake. And then came the Snapchat makeout. And now this . . ." She stops talking when she sees my mouth drop open. I use the nightstand next to me as a crutch to prop me up.

Her professor? My heart sinks and won't stop falling. This shit doesn't just happen in real life without a script and a demented reality show writer to go with it. So the missing piece of the story makes sense: *Ava cheated on Jake first.*

She sees my face, the harsh judgment that I cannot conceal in my eyes, nor do I bother. "It happened, okay, Mom. I'm not proud of it."

"Is he . . ." *Please say no.*

"Yes, he's married. I'm so screwed."

I give my daughter hard-core side eye, I can't help it. It's *his wife* who is *so* screwed, Ava. *You are your father's daughter. You are the Other Woman, no better than an Ashley Madison mom.* My anger is close to the boiling point, and I can barely contain it.

"Did you know he was married before it all began?" My voice is gravelly, on the verge. I have to know how badly I raised my own child.

"Yes."

And there you go.

"And that didn't stop you?"

She shrugged. "I didn't think about it. He's so brilliant and talented."

"And married . . . with kids?"

"Yes on both. But it was his choice."

Let's see your response when I tell you about your father's forty-three choices.

"Does this professor know you may be pregnant?"

"No. I haven't told anybody but you."

I sit back down on the bed. Now I'm squeezing the bedsheet into tiny orbs in my hands, feeling my own nails jab into my skin. "How old is he?"

"Forty." She pauses. "Forty-four."

From bad to worse. I squint tightly, trying to figure

out what to say here. *Does my daughter even have a conscience?* No words come.

"I know you're so upset, Mom. I get it. I just don't know what to do. I really care about him and I don't want him to be mad at me."

"Mad at you?" I repeat, wanting to beat this man to a pulp.

"Can we just fix this together, and leave him out of it?"

Fix this, like I always do. That's who I am—the Sweeper. No, I tell myself accusingly: *YOU are the Enabler.* You are *that* mother, the one whom all the parenting books snigger about—the one who brought the biology book to school after your daughter had left it on the kitchen table. *Yes, that one.* I find my mind wandering from the Maybe-Pregnant Teen in front of me to the Cheater Back Home. What kind of protection did Gabe use? Did he wear condoms? Did he care about STDs? Care about giving me chlamydia or herpes? What if Ava *is* pregnant? What if she wants this baby? My thoughts are spiraling. The contorted images of Gabe's and Ava's follies are flashing and fighting for space inside my bursting head.

I stand with arms folded, my back facing her, and then I begin to pace around the room, wondering how to say *I'm so fucked* in French. *Okay, think.* First things first. She needs to see a doctor. No matter what I'm feeling, Ava needs my support not judgment. What time is it in Chicago? I count backward seven hours. The gynecologist's office is already closed. I will have to call their emergency number. Honestly if I could, I would bolt out the hotel room door, run from a life that no longer makes any sense. Either I screwed up so royally, or everything that I once thought was so perfect is simply a fantasy that I bought into.

Ava surprisingly reaches for me. I feel the hot anger inside me subside just a little as I bring her close to my chest. Did I give Gabe and Ava too much rope that they choked themselves on it, not caring for repercussions and who got hurt in the process?

I have been mulishly loyal to both of them, the family doormat, purveyor of satisfying their needs. If they are happy, then I'm a good wife and mother. If they are hungry, then I feed them. If they forget a book for school or lose their wallet/glasses/phone/car keys, then I drop everything and begin a search and rescue. I have given both all the support they need, and still I produced cheaters. They made those choices, but I made their beds. Am I the problem? Did I create two monsters—*am I Dr. Frankenstein?*

Chapter Eight

"Really, Mom, Café de Flore? Why there? So touristy." Ava is clearly annoyed as we walk along Boulevard Saint-Germain toward the renowned café in the Sixth Arrondissement, a mere fifteen-minute walk from the hotel for brunch before her presentation.

"Because I've always wanted to go there, that's why," I say tersely.

Ava knows better than to argue anything at this point, and I allow myself a few moments to indulge in window shopping along the way while she walks and texts. In the distance, I see the famous ivory awning with its giant olive-green Café de Flore lettering and the legendary scripted sign above the coffeehouse that lights up at night, and I feel a surge of excitement. Celebrated for its famed literary and artistic clientele, the

Flore has been a backdrop in so many French movies that it was déjà vu—like I have been there before.

When we arrive, the café is predictably crowded and I'm hoping we can get a table on the terrace. Speaking in flawless French, Ava tells the maître d' that we would like an outside table if possible. There are a few tables opening up so the wait shouldn't be too bad. We decide to take a quick peek inside the restaurant, which is magnificent. I'm amazed by the classic art deco interior of cherry red seating, mahogany tables, and gilt-framed mirrors that apparently have not changed since World War II.

I turn to Ava. "This is where Hemingway hung out with Gertrude Stein, where Sartre and Simone de Beauvoir spent their evenings, where Picasso sat," I exclaim, ignoring her exaggerated eye roll. "If I'm going to eat croissants and drink coffee—it's going to be right here."

She shrugs and, with a glint in her eye, says, "And then from here, I'm betting while I'm at school, you will be going to Shakespeare and Company and then off to the Louvre to see the *Mona Lisa*?"

Sarcasm. If only it were that simple. I assess my daughter, who is wearing a stylish white miniskirt and a flowy off-the-shoulder blouse, and silently pray she isn't pregnant. "And while you're busy mocking your mother . . . ," I add, trying to keep things lighter between us but inside I feel sick, "just to mention that Dr. Vivienne Goldberg's office happens to be near the Eiffel Tower—another tourist trap to add to your list."

"*Your* list. Vivienne Goldberg. Only *you* would find me the Jewish gynecologist." Ava laughs—as if finding a Jewish doctor is an actual effort. I smile thinking that my grandmother, a Holocaust survivor and an activist for women's rights, would be pleased that of the three names recommended by my gynecologist, who answered my emergency call last night, I chose a woman who is not only Jewish but also according to my Google search a renowned gay rights activist and patron of the arts. I figured that my progressive daughter would appreciate that part. And I got the appointment with Dr. Goldberg only because there was a last-minute cancellation.

We are seated at a small round bistro table near the sidewalk and order cappuccinos and croissants. Smiling to myself, I notice that all the waiters are wearing identical black vests and bowties, with long aprons practically reaching their ankles. White towels are draped over their left forearms. It's as though I've slipped into another era. I glance at my daughter, whose cheeks have suddenly become rosy, and she looks lovely. That is, until I follow the direction of her bright gaze and see exactly what that blush is all about. A Javier Bardem-but-better clone waves at her from the sidewalk and seems to be walking toward us, but first stops briefly on his way to say hello to someone.

"Tell me that isn't him." *Christ, he's a full-fledged man.* He looks like someone who would play racquetball with Gabe—not like age-appropriate Jake, who plays Baggo-for-beers. I lean back hard, bracing myself. My brief fantasy that I'm sitting in Simone de Beauvoir's chair just blew up. *My daughter may be pregnant with that man's child.*

"It is him." Ava challenges me with her eyes— *Gabe's eyes.* This girl has always pushed the envelope. But this time, too damn far.

"Are you kidding me?" I manage to scrape out. "Why is he here?"

She smiles at him while talking to me. "I texted him that I was with you. And he said he was actually on his way to school but would stop by and say hello."

How very French of him. My cheeks begin to burn. No shame. She's a teenager. He's married with kids and her professor. And he wants to stop by for a meet and greet? *I'm not equipped for this.* I glare at Ava. "Really? This is happening right now?"

"Please, Mom, just be nice. You'll see why . . ."

Oh, I can see why. The cheating professor wears a

loose black button-down shirt unbuttoned a few too many, dark jeans, loafers, and his hair is Euro-shaggy. He's ridiculously sexy. But not for a teenager. *My teenager.* I can only imagine Lauren's and Samantha's side comments right now, beginning with *I would definitely Eat Pray Love that guy,* and then going straight to the gutter from there. And then I remember . . . *there is no more Lauren and Samantha.* My heart drops with a thud as the professor stands in front of us, a handsome blur, as an even deeper sadness clouds over me.

He and Ava cheek-cheek kiss, and the worst part is Ava's reaction to him—the sheer electricity between them. My stomach twists as he turns toward me. I wonder what his wife, who probably picked out that shirt, would think of this little rendezvous. She would want to kill my daughter. *I want to kill my daughter.* Whoever thought that I would be in this position, when I could easily have gone to high school with this guy.

I sip my cappuccino without blinking, staring over the top of the white ceramic rim, while Ava introduces us. I hear my name, but in a fog. I wish Gabe were here right now—*is that crazy?* He would have taken over, known what to do.

The professor slowly removes his Ray-Bans and smiles gallantly. "*Bonjour, je m'appelle* Olivier," he says for the second time, only a little louder.

Of course, you are. I snap out of my trance. "I'm Sophie Bloom," I respond to his velvety French in a crisp authoritative English, though my college French conversation is still pretty good. He eyes the empty chair next to me, waits for the invitation that doesn't come.

"May I?" he asks in English and points to the chair. *And if I say no?* But I nod instead.

His and Ava's eyes remain locked across the table as he sits down, and suddenly I feel like I'm in the middle of a seduction—a Nabokov/*Lolita* moment, a *Last Tango in Paris* engagement—and I can't breathe. *This is my daughter you're playing around with, mister.*

Olivier cocks his head slightly, weighs his words. "Forgive me, but you look so much like Ava. It's very . . . disconcerting." He appears almost pleased with himself for using such a big English word.

This is insane. He's discussing my looks? "Olivier," I begin, clearing my throat, more than ready to cut the crap. "This for me"—I gesture to both of them—"is not at all acceptable."

"Mom, please," Ava interjects angrily. I glare back. *What is she possibly thinking? That we are going to bond and discuss the artistic differences between Picasso and Braque, Monet and Matisse?*

"Yes, I understand," he acknowledges, signaling

the waiter over simultaneously and quickly ordering a double espresso. "I know how this must look."

"Look?" I repeat incredulously. I sit on my hands to prevent them from ramming the butter knife into his throat. "Ava still has another year left of college. You're married with kids. And she may be pregnant," I blurt out.

"Mom!"

Olivier turns to Ava, his mouth dropping. "Is this true?"

"Jesus, Mom!"

Jesus yourself. "Ava, answer him."

"*Oui,*" she says. "I missed my period. We're going to the gynecologist this afternoon."

"I'm coming," he says, not blinking.

"You're not coming," I snap. "This needs to be over, Olivier. I'm sorry, but it does. You're married," I emphasize again, as if no one understood me the first time around.

"Oh my god." Ava turns, giving me the evil eye.

"Sophie, please, it's not like that," Olivier says softly.

"Do I look stupid?" I ignore Ava and continue the prosecution. "You have tenure, I presume, at the École des Beaux-Arts? Does this allow you to do whatever you please? I also assume—but who knows, this is Paris—that they must have a no-sleeping-with-students policy?" My bitchiness is in full swing. "It is *exactly* like that."

"Mom, why are you being like this?"

The truth is, Ava never sees me like this, so undone, so clawing. But I am undone, clawed by life, and ready to pounce on this Playboy Professor. *I hate him. I hate Gabe. I hate all men like him.* Thinking they can cheat, that they can get away with it, that they can meet the mother of their teen mistress and casually order a double espresso, that they can sleep with your best friend, that they can do anything they damn please and still come home and have sex with you in your closet on your birthday. That it's all somehow okay. I glare back at my daughter—so young, beautiful, talented—so goddamned enamored. *I can't stand it.*

Olivier makes some sort of French dismissive hand-flicking gesture accompanied by a tsk sound, which I interpret as *policy schmolicy.* "Madame, I truly understand how you must feel. Believe me."

Did he just Madame me? "Honestly, I am out of my league here. Olivier, you seem completely comfortable with this . . . what exactly are your intentions?" I demand, crossing my arms tightly.

"My intentions are perfectly clear." He pauses, as if trying to find the right words. "Ava is—"

"Too young," I interject. "Too damn young. And what if she *is* pregnant—what then?"

Ava is clearly not happy being discussed in third person by the only two adults at the table, and that, instead of the lovely discussion she stupidly envisioned, *this* is happening. Her lips tighten as she holds her head high. "For the record, it's my body, my decision, Mom," she says predictably. I refrain from rolling my eyes.

Olivier reaches over and tenderly touches her hand. *The supportive cheater.* I pick up my fork, gripping it tightly, picturing myself bludgeoning him right here at the table and all the waiters having to use their forearm towels to clean up the mess. *How can he do that in front of me?* And isn't he remotely worried that someone may see him touching her like that? The school is just blocks away. I turn to my stubborn daughter. If I say no, she says yes. If I say high, she goes low. Maybe I need to switch tactics here and tell them both I plan to be called Grandma Sophie if there's a baby on board, and let's all go baby furniture shopping together. Then, perhaps, she and the sexy professor will come to their senses. On the other hand, it *is* Ava's body. While severely headstrong, she has always been extremely mature, the result perhaps of being an only child. I exhale deeply—experiencing no toxin relief.

Everybody within a four-mile radius could see that my daughter is smitten by this man. *Does he see how she looks at him?*

Olivier meets my protective glare with warmth as if to counteract my anger. Close up, his eyes are a soft brown, and if I didn't hate his guts right now I would admit that there is kindness inside them. You can't hide that. But Gabe's eyes are kind too. He is known throughout the hospital for his exceptional bedside manner. I laugh to myself, totally appreciating the irony.

"I take full responsibility here," Olivier stresses. "I can only imagine everything you are feeling. Whatever Ava decides, please understand, I will fully support her."

"And your wife—will she be supportive of your *full* support?" I ask bluntly as Ava's eyes pop into a *quelle horreur* expression. *Seriously, Ava? Yes, I am so going there. I'm done being nice, being accepting, not seeing what's in front of my face.*

"No," he admits. "This will be a shock. It will . . ." His voice fades out just as a car honks over it.

"Is this your first time sleeping with a student?" I continue my interrogation and I think Ava is about to throw something at me. I ignore her.

"No." He sips his espresso. "But it is the first time that I'm in love."

Christ. Yet another cheesy line from *The Bold and*

the Beautiful—just the schmaltzy Euro version. I glance at my awestruck daughter, who after that one-liner is no longer looking at me venomously. She is all in, drunk on the syrupy Kool-Aid this guy is pouring out.

"We need a plan," I say adamantly. "I'm taking Ava to the gynecologist this afternoon—*alone*—and then we will meet again and discuss options together."

Ava's cell phone rings before Olivier responds. She looks up at me, startled. "It's Dad."

Bam. Could this be any more Theater of the Absurd?

"Hi, Dad," she says nervously. "Yes, Mom's here. Yeah, the hotel is really nice. Way nicer than my apartment. We are just having . . . umm, brunch. No . . . really, you don't need to come here. I'm doing okay now. Do you want to talk to Mom?" She extends her phone to me.

Come here? I will kill him. I shake my head no. Ava looks at me with surprise. I gesture with my eyes toward Don Juan next to me, not intending to give Gabe the time of day.

"I will call you back later, okay, Daddy . . . Love you too." Ava hangs up the phone and stares at me. "What's going on with Dad? You always take his call."

"Nothing," I lie, thinking *everything*. It's probably a good thing Gabe is not here. I glare at Professor Olivier Messier (yes, his name rhymes), who suddenly doesn't look so cool now that Ava's father weighed in. *Yes, this shit just got real. And if Gabe were sitting here, you wouldn't know what hit you, buddy.* Gabe would definitely not be seduced by your wily charms and impeccable manners, your lingering double-cheeked kisses. You thought you could just drop by and say hello . . . Well, *absolument pas*—as in Hell to the No. I'm not buying any of it.

Ava glances at her phone, exhales deeply. "I have to go now."

Olivier wipes the sweat off his brow, puts back on his sunglasses to hide the visible alarm in his eyes, but I catch it anyway just before the Ray-Bans land. The pregnancy news and the father calling to check in clearly threw him off his game. "I will walk you there. I was on my way to pick up something in my office anyway," he says, signaling for the bill.

Ava stands, gathers her things. "Mom, can you just call Dad back and deal with him, please?" She eyes me with tight lips, flared nostrils, clearly still pissed off, as if I owe her.

And there it is. Ava's independence and defiance disappears when she's uncomfortable with something and defers to me to clean it up. And usually, in this exact scenario, the *deal-with-Dad* situation, I'd feel like a hero, ride in and save the day. I shake my head.

Not this time. I've coddled her, coddled him, coddled all of them, and where did that get me? An unfaithful husband, a promiscuous daughter, and best friends who betrayed me.

The new bruised, broken me stands up and throws down a bunch of dollar bills. "No way. This is on you, hon. Deal with your dad after school. See you at the gynecologist at three p.m." I turn to Professor Olivier Messier and, surprising myself, I say, "You're coming with me."

Chapter Nine

Ava refuses to leave the café. She's clearly furious with me. Olivier takes her off to the side, and to his credit, and by his body language—lots of arm flails—I can tell he convinces her that it's okay for him to talk to me alone. Finally satisfied, she reluctantly turns to go, waves hesitantly in my direction, and I'm left standing with my daughter's lover, who smells unnervingly good, at the intersection of the most celebrated establishments in twentieth-century Parisian history: Les Deux Magots, Café de Flore, and the Brasserie Lipp.

I step away from Olivier, making sure our shoulders do not brush as we walk down Boulevard Saint-Germain. "Let's get this straight," I say, after a few minutes of uncomfortable silence. "I appreciate that you are taking the time to talk to me, but you're not coming to the gynecologist."

"Ava wants me to be there. I promised her."

I flick my wrist dismissively. "She's nineteen. She doesn't know what she wants and you know that." The threatening tone in my voice is at a solid number seven.

Olivier appears nervous, as if I'm a woman on the verge who has just taken him hostage, and he's half right about that. He peers at me sideways. "Sophie, I know this is—"

"No," I cut him off. "You have no idea what this is like. This has to end."

"I don't run away from things," he says heroically.

Just your marriage, you coward, which I don't say. And he looks like a runner, the type who bolts the second an affair becomes a complication. And this is not just a *thing*—if Ava *is* pregnant, it could blow up his career, his marriage, his all too *libre* lifestyle. And this guy, mark my words, will sprint like an Olympian.

"Can we at least talk this through? I presume that's why you wanted to meet me alone?" he implores, clearly seeing the anguish all this is causing me. "Do you want to go somewhere private? Inside? Outside?"

I pause, having no plan at all. I want to go home. But there is no home.

He lifts up his sunglasses halfway, and this close, I

catch a glimpse of his sparkling nut-brown pupils with lashes that are unfairly long for a guy. *A man*, I remind myself. *My daughter is sleeping with my peer.*

"How about the Rodin Museum?" he suggests. "It's nearby. There's a lovely garden. We can sit and talk this through privately."

Rodin. This guy doesn't miss a beat. I surrender slightly. "Yes, that works."

"Okay then, this way." Relieved, he leads me down a side street. "Ava spoke about you quite often. She showed me photos of your sculptures that she kept on her phone. Your exhibit, 'Mermaids and Madmen,' was breathtaking. Truly magnificent." Turning sideways, he smiles broadly—a dazzling smile that I imagine has gotten him laid on more than a few occasions. "A sculptor cannot come to Paris without seeing Rodin."

I blush. I can't help it. I haven't been called a sculptor in years. *Don't let him charm you*, I warn myself. He's a snake, and an extremely attractive one at that. And the last thing I want to discuss with Olivier is my has-been talent of the past. "Thank you," I say politely. "But that was a hundred years ago, another life ago."

"Art never leaves you . . . even when you leave it," says the Jean-Paul Sartre impersonator. "Believe me I know."

I don't believe him. I don't believe anyone these days.

"My first love was sculpting but I wasn't very good," Olivier explains as if I care, as we stride in the direction of the museum. "I had the inclination but not the talent. Yet I could paint. I was considered more than acceptable. But sculpting . . ." He gazes into the distance. "There is no comparison, is there? The feel of clay, wood, plaster, stone, the chisel against marble."

I close my eyes briefly. No comparison. He is right. The muscle memory is still there, never leaves. I think about all the twisting sensations, the turning, the bending into shape, the hammering, the carving, the varying textures inside my hands. *God, I miss it.*

"Why did you stop?" he asks, seeing my reaction.

I glance down at my hands, once considered gifts. "I didn't have a choice. Medical reasons."

He waits for a more elaborate explanation but I offer none. "I see . . . and now you represent other artists?" He either is interested in getting to know me better or is extremely adept at trying to avoid the pink elephant between us—my daughter.

"Yes. I run a small museum and gallery in my town. We promote local artists and organize the annual art fair in our community. It's lovely actually." I think about my cadre of artists, how they depend on me, and that I need to call my assistant later today and explain why I'm in Paris and not in the office. Our big art festival is coming up, and knowing Rachel, her anxiety level is probably through the roof. "It's just that . . ." *Let it go. Don't go there. Especially with him.*

"You miss it." He finishes my sentence anyway.

I nod honestly. "Every single day."

We continue walking, pick up speed, immersed in our own thoughts. We turn left along Rue du Bac, a lovely street lined with art galleries and pastry shops. Ava loves macarons. She must have come here often. Of course, I don't mention that to Olivier but I wonder if he's thinking that too. *Does he even know that about her?*

Once we turn onto the ritzy Rue de Varenne with its majestic homes, my attention is drawn immediately to a convoy of black town cars at the end of the street. I point. "Mafia? Funeral? Government?"

Olivier laughs hard and the sound is rich, the kind of infectious laugh that takes center stage at a cocktail party. "Yes, on all three. Actually, that's the prime minister's house, called Hôtel Matignon." He gestures across the street. "See that walled garden on the other side of the street up ahead? That's the museum, a refurbished mansion called the Hôtel Biron—it is where Rodin worked and collected."

I look across the street with dismay. A long line of visitors is wrapped around the wall. It's the height of tourist season. "Damn," I say, visibly disappointed. "There's no way we can get in. We don't have enough time."

"You could say there are some small benefits to being with me." Olivier chuckles and taps his chest. "Given my position at the Beaux-Arts, I have free access. No lines. I often go to the sculpture garden to think or to paint. Come with me—this way." He lightly touches my arm, and his hand on my skin sends a slight tremor through me, an unexpected electrical jolt. I stop in my tracks. So does he.

He appears uncomfortable. "Look, Sophie, I know this has all been a shock for you." He eyes me squarely. "I'm truly sorry. I didn't mean to wreck your family or disrespect you. It just happened."

Nothing just happens. You pursued her. I bite down on my bottom lip and don't respond. *Wrecked our family.* That's the understatement of the century. I wonder if there is a double-jeopardy clause: Can an already wrecked family be rewrecked? I stare back at him, sunglasses-to-sunglasses.

"I'm sorry," he whispers again. His voice is sincere, not assholey at all.

Aside from the obvious, I can see why Ava is drawn to him. But I can no longer hold back. "How could you have been so totally careless that she may actually be pregnant? You're an adult. You know better, damn it."

My voice when it scolds becomes shrill and I've always hated the sound of it. People start to look. Olivier is embarrassed, but I don't care.

He exhales deeply, croaks out his words. "I am very careful. Ava, as we both know, forgot to take her pill. I'm not blaming her, but whatever this may be—and it may all be okay—it was truly an accident. But I'm on board with whatever needs to be done."

Done, as in *get rid of it.* What if . . . Ava doesn't want that? I can't even go there right now until we have an answer. I feel a ripple of unease move up my spine. "See, I don't believe that you're on board. I don't believe you when you say you don't run . . ." My voice trails off, and the lines become blurred—*is it him I'm speaking to, or is it Gabe?*

People are circumventing us on the sidewalk. Olivier clearly wants to move to a more secluded spot, making it obvious with his eyes that this open discussion may be very American but it is certainly not the French way. My feet are grounded.

"Why her?" I press on angrily. "My guess is that you know damn well your effect on women, particularly impressionable young female students. Why was Ava this semester's target?" I know I sound mean and accusatory, and I'm basically calling him a lecher, a cheater, and a pedophile.

"*Aucune idée.*" He raises his shoulders, holds up his arms at the elbows with palms facing out, raises his eyebrows, and sticks out his lower lip—clearly some kind of full-bodied French gesture meaning *No idea.* His voice loses its calm demeanor, his forehead furrows, and he appears to change his mind.

"Actually, I do know." He corrects himself. "Have you not seen Ava paint? Her incredible ability? There are many pretty girls who rotate in and out of my classes but she stood out. Yes, she's lovely, and there was the obvious physical attraction. But then it became something more . . ." His shoulders lower, the jutting lip retracts, and his gaze is now direct and uncompromising. "Teaching can be exhausting, but every once in a while, a student comes along who reminds me why I love what I do. Have you never felt inspired by someone and it surprised you, moved you to the point of immobility or perhaps even caused you to make a reckless decision? Tell me, Sophie . . . never?" His eyes search mine.

I look away, refusing to comply with his I-showed-you-mine-now-you-show-me-yours game. I should never have come here with him. I should have just gone my own way while Ava was at school. "I'm not here to discuss my reckless decisions, Olivier. And I certainly don't need you to tell me that my daughter is exceptional." My tone is brusque bordering on rude, but I'm too emotionally wiped out for niceties. "Ava's teachers recognized her artistic ability early on. She got accepted into every top art school that she applied to, but she wanted the full college experience, and her dad and I pushed her in that direction. I knew that no one could take away Ava's natural ability, but I didn't want her talent to steal her youth. I wanted her to have it all—to experience a full life outside of art—but certainly not this." I point to him. "*Definitely* not this."

"*Oui.*" Olivier's cheeks turn red. "I understand."

There is an awkward silence between us. I pivot slightly in the direction of the museum. "Let's go see the master's work, shall we?" I say. My eyes bore into his uneasily, not knowing what else to do.

He nods, clearly relieved to get off the hot seat for a while. "Rodin also slept with his students, by the way," he says with a lopsided grin, hoping to lighten the situation. "Another imperfect man."

I laugh despite myself. My emotional palette seems to be changing by the nanosecond. "Yes, another imperfect man. I feel surrounded by them."

Given our time constraints, we decide to bypass the main museum with its vast collection of bronzes, marbles, and plasters, and instead, head straight to the sculpture garden. We pass through fragrant rose-bushes along the front and sides of the Hôtel Biron, toward the expansive gardens behind the building.

Greeting us at the garden entrance is the "gatekeeper"—perhaps the most famous of all Rodin sculptures, known as *Le Penseur*—The Thinker. I freeze at the foot of the imposing bronze sculpture. I have studied and analyzed this statue for years, but only on paper. To see it in real time is nothing short of spectacular.

Barely catching my breath, I stare at the hunched muscular torso—Dante in deep thought. Olivier watches my struck-by-lightning reaction with amused interest in the way that an opera aficionado eyes the mesmerized face of a newbie hearing Verdi's *La Traviata* for the very first time. The last time I felt this affected by a sculpture is when I stood in front of Michelangelo's David.

It was four summers ago when Gabe and all of our friends had rented a villa in Tuscany for five days, and then spent two days touring Florence to celebrate Eric's fortieth birthday. After visiting myriad churches and boutiques, I dragged everyone to see the David.

Eyeing the daunting seventeen-foot marble nude up close left me immobile and speechless. I stood at David's feet and did not budge for more than a half hour. My friends all made fun of me and my new "boyfriend" at dinner later that night—especially Eric and Matt. Needless to say, the "David dick jokes" flew back and forth all evening. I laughed with them, but I also remember much later that same night going out onto our hotel balcony while Gabe slept, crying as I stared at my broken hands. I would never sculpt again. I would never achieve a David of my own, and that was unbearable.

"What are you thinking?" Olivier asks, leading me toward a nearby garden bench. We sit a little too closely together as we look out onto the maze of ornamental shrubs and the numerous sculptures erected between them, so I inch away from him. "You are very deep in thought."

"More like *lost* in thought," I tell him with a heavy sigh. He appears willing to listen. "Not that it matters to you, but Ava's father cheated on me. I found this out right before I came here to see Ava to deal with . . ." *Does Jake cheating with Monica even matter at this point?* "Anyway, all of this—the infidelity, the likely pregnancy, and yes, meeting you—has been beyond overwhelming. And now seeing all that Rodin created reminds me that I haven't sculpted in years." *Why am I even telling him this?* He is the enemy, not a friend. He's a cheater too. My eyes well up. *But I have no friends.* And I'm not myself. Averting my gaze, I cup my eyes with my hand. I don't want him to see me cry or, worse, to pity me. Olivier is definitely not the shoulder I want to lean on.

Observing me closely, he starts to rest his palm on my back to console me, and then changes his mind when he sees me flinch at the approaching hand. I wipe my eyes and move farther away. *Please don't touch me. I don't know why I opened up to you.*

He places his hand back on his lap and releases a full-scale tension-filled breath. "I get how this all appears to you, so . . ." He makes a tap to the side of his head gesture. "So cliché. The married professor and the beautiful student. *La muse.* This was an affair—it was wrong, I know—but a lovely affair that has perhaps become complicated," he admits.

"What about your wife?" I ask, thinking about Gabe, thinking of me. "Where does she fit into the equation?"

"Look, I've known Sabine since we were kids . . ." His voice becomes distant. "We have an understanding. She lives her life, and I live mine. Our boys are our priority."

I groan, and don't try to shield it. *An understanding.* Code for an open marriage. How convenient. And there it is—the French version of Sophie and Gabe. Puppy love once again that has no chance of survival in the grown-up world. As Olivier goes on about Sabine, a prominent architect, and his two young sons, about their so-called arrangement, I listen but not really. Instead, I see only the breezy sway of the beautiful trees around us and I think about the carved *Sophie & Gabe, TLF* tree. I can still see the tender look on Gabe's face like it was yesterday when he carved it, and I loved it, loved him, loved us. How naïve I was. There was no 'understanding'—there would never be one. It's not me. I will never understand how he did this to us.

"I can see that this has all been a great burden on you."

"And what about you?" I challenge. "What if Ava *is* pregnant? Does this 'arrangement' of yours have a clause for that?"

Olivier's face falls hard. "No."

He reaches over and places his hand on mine—*for him, for me?*—and for one frozen second, I stare at it. His slender hands are smooth on top with proud protruding veins, serrated fingernails lined with permanent paint, palms callused—artist's hands. And then I remember who he is, who I am, and I quickly yank my hand away, locking it protectively between my thighs.

He tilts his head slightly, looks at me, then stands. "Come, Sophie. You must see more of the gardens and of course the room dedicated to Rodin's muse and partner, Camille Claudel. It will be okay. It will get better. It always does."

And Olivier was right. It did get a little better. My mood shifted as we spent the next hour immersed in the spectacular gardens. We perused the rose garden first and then the large rocky garden—the "Garden of Orpheus"—and finally we ended up in the "Garden of Springs." Each turn presented its own unique gift. Rodin had created his very own Garden of Eden and, as Olivier led me around, I couldn't help but let my guard down, push aside my troubles, and revel in the exquisite beauty surrounding me.

"Before we go, you must see *Le Baiser*," he says, pointing inside the museum.

"Yes," I say excitedly—I can't help it. *Le Baiser*—*The Kiss*—is considered by many to be Rodin's most erotic sculpture, and I've been dying to see it up close my whole life. It represents Paolo and Francesca, two star-crossed Italian lovers who had been condemned to wander eternally through Hell for their crime of passion, but not before they shared the most sensual of all unrequited lip-locks—suggesting that they were interrupted and met their deaths without their lips ever having touched. It is a forbidden embrace immortalized by Rodin.

We walk through the museum for another half hour or so, and decide to head toward the hôtel terrace for a quick coffee before we leave. Once we are seated under the shade of lovely linden trees, Olivier insists once again that he accompany me to the gynecologist appointment, and that he had promised Ava he'd be there, to please allow him to do that—*for her*, he emphasized.

"Fine." I finally give in. "But then, whatever happens, your relationship with Ava must end immediately— are we clear?"

He nods, and although I have warmed up to him, I have no illusions who this man is, and don't trust him at all.

"I don't believe you."

Sipping his third espresso of the day, he leans forward. "Sophie, please, you're making this so difficult. I care a great deal for Ava. But I will end it, okay, I promise. For you."

"For *her*, damn it, for her." My voice rises threateningly.

Olivier looks around the café. "Fine, yes, for her."

We sit in silence for a few more minutes. I down my cappuccino as if it's a flaming lemon drop. "This is not who I am, you know." *Why do I feel an urge to explain my behavior?* I owe him nothing. "You have to understand my life has blown up completely."

"I really do understand," he says as the waitress hands us the bill. I reach for it but he grabs it first.

"Thank you for . . ." I begin and then stop myself. *What am I thanking him for?* Taking me to the Rodin Museum so I can beg him to stop seeing my daughter? For listening to me open up about *my* cheating husband? That's like asking for sympathy from the devil. I am really losing it.

"I'm glad we came here, talked, and spent time together," he says, his voice lingering as he moves in closer to me. *A little too close.* His musky scent mixed with espresso fills my nostrils.

Is he fucking serious? I lean back, reestablishing the appropriate boundary, while internally scolding myself. *You're not some young, carefree woman enjoying an afternoon tryst under shady trees. You're you*—Hester Prynne's mother. There's no dropping your guard. No opening up to him. No thanking him. No 'let's discuss art and find a common bond.' And definitely no need to apologize about anything. Olivier is Gabe in French drag. *Pull yourself together.*

"Let's go," I say abruptly and stand. Smoothing out my shirt, I turn in the direction of the exit with Olivier following a few sheepish steps behind me. I don't even want to know what he's thinking. Unlike the rest of my impulsive family, at the very least, I know the difference between wrong and *really* wrong.

Chapter Ten

The taxi pulls up in front of the building on 29 Avenue Rapp in the Seventh, along the left bank of the Seine with the Eiffel Tower in full view. I stare out the open window in awe. I have never seen a doctor's office that looks anything like this. It's a sculpture not a building.

"Are you sure this is the place?" I ask the driver, who responds with some sort of thrusted bottom lip and chin lift gesture that must mean yes.

"It's the Lavirotte Building," Olivier explains, letting out a low whistle as he pays the driver. "The doctor must be quite successful to have an office here. It is a well-known historic apartment building, one of the best examples of art nouveau architecture in Paris."

We get out of the cab and stand together in front of

the outrageous multicolored structure, faced with ceramic tiles, lavish sculptural decor depicting animals and vegetables, curvy windows, embellished balconies, and curling wrought-iron railings. Most shocking are the erotic stone sculptures of Adam and Eve surrounded by beasts and phallic symbols flanking the arched entrance, which looks like a supersized vagina.

"Welcome to French gynecology," I say under my breath. Olivier laughs.

"I haven't been inside this building in a few years," he tells me. "It's had quite the history. It caused a major scandal when it was erected at the turn of the century and then won the Paris competition for new façades in 1901." He smiles mischievously.

Yet another scandal, I think wryly, gauging Olivier, and scolding myself again for even thinking about him with anything other than disgust. Olivier leads me toward the creepy-looking wooden entrance ornamented with wrought-iron lizards. He turns slightly before opening the door. "Sophie, are you—"

"No," I cut him off. "Not okay. Just really nervous."

"Me too," he says, slowly running his hands through his dark wavy hair like a lawn mower through tall grass. Yet another sexy gesture to add to his repertoire.

Tears fill my eyes as I stare at him. *And I miss my husband.*

———

Olivier and I arrive on the third floor of the building. The entire floor seems to belong to Dr. Vivienne Goldberg. We enter the waiting room and I quickly look around and let out a small sigh of relief that Ava is not here yet. At least I have a few minutes to get situated. And it's not a waiting room at all—it's more like a reception hall. The ceilings are vaulted and the flooring is black and white marble partially covered with an oriental rug—not your typical cadet-gray just vacuumed carpet. Not to mention the large chandelier. *Yes*—an actual ballroom-sized chandelier dripping with crystals. Unbelievable. I laugh to myself, imagining the fourteen-karat gold stirrups on the examination table.

If only Samantha and Lauren were here to see this. *Stop thinking about them—they betrayed you, remember?* But I can't help it. They would be enamored by this place. We always brag that our gynecologists have the hands-down best waiting room around because every single magazine is up-to-date. No exaggeration. If you visit Drs. Miranda Kelly or Emily Stein in May—all the magazines on the coffee table and on the wall display are May/June issues. And we're not talking typical parenting/pregnancy/vaginal health magazines—Kelly and Stein have all the top fashion mags, as well as *O*,

People, Us Weekly, Vanity Fair—and even *W*. What doctor's office has a subscription to *W*? Most people go to K and S (as they are known in the burbs) because they are the best, but I go for the magazines. It is the only doctor's office in which I'm actually thrilled when they tell me there's a wait.

As I scan Dr. Goldberg's elaborate waiting-area-cum-salon, I notice there's not even a single magazine on site, rather a filled floor-to-ceiling built-in bookcase. Who reads a book at the gynecologist's office? I glance around and take inventory. One elderly woman is accompanied by a young aide and three pregnant women are reading their phones. No one even looks up. Olivier sits down on the Louis XIV–style canapé—where does Goldberg do her furniture shopping, Versailles? The office is so over-the-top, I'm beginning to feel underdressed. Squaring my shoulders, I walk up to the receptionist, who is sitting behind a large antique vintage writing desk. No glass partitions in this place.

"*Bonjour*, I'm Sophie Bloom. For Ava Bloom," I say slowly. "My daughter will be here any minute with her passport and international insurance information."

The woman, who looks like she just jumped out of Robert Palmer's "Addicted to Love" video with her sleek blonde chignon and pursed crimson lips, says without smiling, "The American, *oui?* You called this morning."

"*Oui, c'est moi,* the American." I continue to respond in French-lish, a kind of half and half.

The woman nods with no affect. "Very good. Please, madame. Have a seat and we will call you shortly."

I take a seat across from Olivier. "Books not magazines," I point out. "Not even a *Paris Match.*"

"Sophie, why are you acting so strange?" he asks as though he's known me for years and could possibly know what my strange looks like.

But he's right. I'm anxious about everything. Ava. Him. A potential pregnancy. Most of all, I can't believe Gabe is not here with us. We've never missed a single big moment together in our daughter's life. Our motto has always been *Ava first, Ava last . . .* and now that it's Ava in the middle of a crisis, to be here without him feels like I'm missing an arm or a leg.

The door flings open, and of course, it's Ava on cue. She walks in, cheeks flushed, hair loose and wild around her face, as though she's been running. "Sorry I'm late. Don't ask."

She acknowledges me but barely, clearly still upset at how I handled myself at Café de Flore, then breaks out into a wide smile when she sees Olivier. *Yes, he came,* I yearn to scream at my idiot daughter.

But she sits next to me.

"So, how did it go?" I ask, as if she just got off the school bus and is ready for her snack. Her presentation is the last damn thing on my mind. In fact, it doesn't even make the top ten or bottom twenty.

"Intense but over," she says, her eyes resting on Olivier. "How was your time together?"

Over, which I don't say. "Fine."

Olivier leans forward, grinning. "Nice actually. We went to the Rodin."

She turns to me. "You must have loved that."

Loved it? What is this? Let's play pretend? None of this is "nice actually." None of this is normal. Not you, Ava. Not him, not this gilded gynecologist's office, which looks like it could be rented out for bar mitzvahs and weddings. I don't speak, because I'm afraid of what wretched thing may come out. I smile with tight lips and throw in a nod—that's the best I can do.

"Ava Bloom," the receptionist calls out loudly, pronouncing our last name as though it were "Plume." The three of us stand and walk toward her. The receptionist shakes her head. "*Non.* Just Mlle. Bloom and her . . ." She looks at Olivier and clearly cannot decide who the players are here. She settles on me. "Mother."

Ava glances at Olivier longingly. *Puh-lease.* I inwardly roll my eyes, more than grateful that he is stuck out in the waiting room. Ava hands the receptionist her documents to copy, then I follow her through the door leading to the examination rooms. Ava turns and whispers, "What's going on with you and Daddy, by the way? Something's wrong and I know it."

Not this too. I can't deal with that right now. "We had a fight, honey," I semi-lie, then fake-clear my throat, buying myself a few extra seconds to pull an alibi together. "Before I came to Paris. Not a big deal. We will work it out. Obviously, I have had bigger things on my mind. Don't worry about us."

She scrutinizes my face, searching for clues, and then relaxes. My lame explanation is enough to hold her over for now. "Okay . . . so did you really have a nice time with Olivier, or was that just a cover?"

I avert my gaze, because the truth is, I'm not sure what I feel about what we had at the Rodin. I can see what she sees in him. He's handsome, sophisticated, makes you feel like you are the only one . . . that is, until the next one comes along. I've seen his type in just about every chick flick. He's Daniel Cleaver in *Bridget Jones's Diary*—an irresistible asshole, the guy we fall for head over heels, but never the one who stops long enough to pick us up.

"Olivier is intelligent." I give him that. "He showed me around the Rodin Museum. But . . ."

I never get to finish my sentence as to why he's not trustworthy because a nurse says something to Ava in French and directs us into Room 3 with her. Like the no-nonsense receptionist, she immediately gets down to business and asks Ava the standard questions about her medical history, then weighs her and takes all of her vitals. When she's finished, she instructs Ava to undress, put on a gown, and that the doctor will be in shortly. All the usual stuff.

Ava sits up on the examination table, her long, tanned legs dangling over the side. She swings them like she did when she was a little girl on the playground. *This is killing me. She is too young for all of this.*

"Mom, I'm really nervous," she says finally, when the nurse walks out.

Me too, baby. I stand, give her a hug, and she accepts it.

The door opens slowly, and Dr. Goldberg enters the room. She is tall and regal-looking with medium-length coiffed honey-streaked hair and bright blue wide-set eyes. A handsome boxy woman, she wears a cream-colored Chanel suit with black piping, accompanied by layers of chunky gold chains around her neck and wrist—no shapeless white doctor jacket with an embroidered pocket bearing *Dr. V. Goldberg* for her. She matches the décor of her office.

Dr. Goldberg addresses me first. "Madame Bloom, please extend my regards to Emily Stein. We met at a convention in New York several years back. Truly lovely and talented."

In contrast to her commanding appearance, Vivienne Goldberg's voice is surprisingly kittenish, suggesting sensuality beneath all that Chanel. I can only imagine that she must be a hit with the ladies.

"Thank you, I certainly will. Dr. Stein is a wonderful doctor," I say, and she has the best magazine rack in town, which I don't say.

Dr. Goldberg examines Ava's chart. "So, Ava, I understand you are nineteen and from Chicago, studying at our excellent École des Beaux-Arts." She tilts her head slightly. "And you think you are pregnant, yes?"

"*Oui*," Ava responds, playing with the ends of her hair, a nervous habit she's had since middle school. "I forgot my pill, missed my period. I'm nauseous, and I'm having this weird sharp stabbing pain in my pelvic region."

I turn to her, surprised. "What pain? You didn't mention that."

Ava shoots me a wide-eyed, annoyed, just-stop-it's-my-body look. I exhale deeply. One second she wants me, the next she wants me to jump off the nearest cliff. I don't know how to be anymore.

The doctor's gaze shifts briefly from Ava to me. We share a knowing glance that is universal in any language. This is not optimal, her eyes express. I return the volley. *Not optimal at all.*

"Did you take a pregnancy test?" Dr. Goldberg asks.

Ava blushes slightly. "No, because I had a final presentation at school, and I was too scared to take it. Stupid, I know, but . . ."

"I understand." The doctor examines Ava, and when she presses down on the pelvic region, Ava lets out a shrill wince. "Well, given the pain—let's skip the pregnancy test and go straight to the ultrasound, which will tell us the whole story," Dr. Goldberg says decisively. "Pauline will bring you to the ultrasound room, set you up, and I will meet you there in just a few minutes."

"Can my—"

"Yes," the doctor says, snapping shut her file. "I heard there is someone out there waiting for you. He can join us."

In my wildest dreams, I never imagined this particular scenario playing out for at least another ten years. Olivier (extremely quiet, picking at his fingernails) seated on a chair in the corner of the room, Ava lying anxiously on the examination table, and me, standing next to her, waiting for the doctor to arrive, as Pauline the technician sets up the ultrasound machine.

Dr. Goldberg finally enters and acknowledges everyone in the room. She sees Olivier and stops in her tracks. *Oh God, now what?*

"Olivier?" she says with open surprise.

Olivier's eyes pop. "Yes . . . do we know each other?"

"Not very well," she tells him. "We actually met a few years ago at a hospital benefit. Your wife, Sabine, and I sat on the board together."

With my rudimentary French, I pick up exactly what's going on here: *Your wife Sabine* being the only words that actually matter. I look at Ava, who turns white. She understands perfectly. It doesn't take a brain surgeon to comprehend that Olivier has just been busted.

Dr. Goldberg clears her throat, visibly uncomfortable with what appears to be a "situation." There is dead silence in the room, and instinctively, I jump in—

"You know Olivier?" I turn to the doctor, my voice higher pitched than usual. "What a coincidence. We are so fortunate that he came here with us. He is Ava's mentor and advisor at the École des Beaux-Arts." I glance over at Olivier, who seems to be wondering where I'm going with this. As do I, but I just keep talking. "You see, I asked him to come with us just in case we had difficulty communicating."

Everyone in the room knows I'm lying—including Pauline the technician. Why would Ava's school advisor be sitting in an ultrasound room? *More important, why did I jump in to save him from exposure?*

Because I can't just let him fall. If Olivier falls, Ava falls. If Olivier falls, then Sabine falls. If Sabine falls, then so do all the cheated-on women. But most important, my daughter comes first. I don't want anyone to gossip about her. My interjection—ridiculous as it may have been—is all Mama Bear instinct.

The doctor, like everyone else, sees through the bullshit but resumes her professional stance. "Well then, let's see what we have here, shall we." But not before she eyes Olivier with a piercing blue you-don't-fool-me glare. "And if we have any issues, then how fortunate we are to have our very own translator in the room."

Good French sarcasm, I think. Bedside manners must not be a thing here.

Pauline spreads the ultrasound gel over Ava's tummy. My heart flutters. *Please, God*, I pray, *may my baby NOT be having a baby.* Tears rise once again, my throat tightens, and I will myself not to lose it. Pauline steps aside and Dr. Goldberg takes over the probe and begins to place it on various spots along Ava's stomach, eyeing the machine closely, highlighting various areas in neon, and calling out numbers that Pauline records.

Dr. Goldberg leans forward, studying the screen closely. Olivier is shaking his head to himself, wanting to comfort Ava but refrains from touching her because of the *your wife, Sabine* comment. But there is no doubt in my mind: something is wrong.

"What is it?" I ask finally, breaking the unbearable silence.

Dr. Goldberg places her hand over Ava's. "Well the good news, and I assume it is"—slight side eye at Olivier—"Ava is *not* pregnant, but she does have a large ovarian cyst, which looks like it may be erupting very soon, as well as a few polyps that should be removed—hence, the sharp pain."

Not pregnant is all I hear. *Not pregnant. Thank you, God.*

Instant tears stream down Ava's face. She reaches out for me and I hold her hand tightly. Ava, a teenager who has her whole life ahead of her, will miraculously not have to make a crippling choice that would surely haunt her sensitive soul and change the course of her life. She has been spared. The cyst and the polyps we can manage.

I glance around the room, see the high-five in Olivier's eyes: *We are all free.*

The doctor wants to meet me and Ava in her office; she purposely excludes Olivier. I excuse myself to the bathroom as Ava gets dressed, and I hear Olivier walking behind me. Actually, I can smell him, that musky cologne. I turn in his direction.

"You're leaving," I say.

"*Oui.* I don't think I was invited to the doctor's office. Please, walk me to the elevator," he says under his breath. "I must go home." He stops there, choosing not to elaborate. It's obvious to both of us that Ava's nonpregnancy just bought him his life back. It's also evident that being recognized by Dr. Goldberg shook him up. "You are right about what you said at the Rodin. I need to reassess everything," he says, moving in closer. Once again, I take a reflexive step backward, keeping my distance. He smiles slightly. "I don't bite, Sophie, I promise. Look, thank you for what you did in there. You were not even remotely believable, but thank you for trying to protect me. You could have easily tossed me to the wolves and I deserve it. You could have—"

I lean against the wall. I'm so mentally exhausted by everyone. "I was simply protecting my daughter,"

I say, sighing deeply. In the distance, a door opens and a pregnant woman waddles toward us from Dr. Goldberg's office. "I hope by 'reassess' you mean that you are ending things with Ava," I whisper firmly. "You need to do it, because from where I stand, I don't think she will."

"Yes, but it's not so easy to just—"

"Let me be clear"—I notice the woman stopping to drink some water—"I saw the fear in your eyes when the doctor recognized you. You are now free from the responsibility you never wanted. Do you hear me, Olivier? *C'est fini*—it's over. You are free to go ruin other people's lives." I bite my lip. That was really nasty and I instantly regret saying that. "I'm sorry, but please just let Ava resume her life without you."

He nods with full understanding, but is he really listening?

"All I ask is that when you *do* break it off," I press on, "just remind her how wonderful she is and that what you two shared together was special but that it was wrong. Tell her that you must take care of your family, and as a father and a husband it was a big mistake that you cheated on Sabine." I know I'm projecting Gabe all over him—but really, it is one and the same. "I want her not to be afraid to love and trust again." I stare deeply into his eyes with those dense lashes that rival a makeup model's. "Please, Olivier, no bullshit, okay. Just let this go. You don't need her and she certainly doesn't need you."

He takes a bold step closer. That scent, that raw male sexuality, invades my personal space like it had at the Rodin Museum, but this time I don't step back. I cross my arms, stand my ground. I mean business. His infallible charm is no match against Mom Kryptonite. He doesn't dare move another inch.

His thick brows narrow inward like parentheses, as though organizing his thoughts and sentences within, translating the French into English. "This afternoon, seeing Rodin through your eyes was really meaningful. I wondered how your husband could possibly give *you* up for another woman? Then I looked over at Ava, so young and beautiful, so afraid on the examination table, and I hated myself. And then I thought of Sabine at home with our children . . ." His mouth becomes taut, determined. "I promise, Sophie, I will end it properly. I'm even contemplating giving up on the arrangement altogether." His words are strong and promising, but his body language, like molten wax, tells another story. He is a man fighting himself, a player who suddenly sees the light but who will surely be blindsided once again. "Maybe I'm not capable of fidelity. But all I know right now is that I will try . . . thanks to you."

"Goodbye, Olivier." I exhale deeply. The pregnant woman, who looks as if she could deliver any second, is now just a few feet away from us. I turn to go and he lightly grabs my arm. I stare at him over my shoulder with surprise.

He leans in to kiss me French-style, the right cheek first, his mouth landing dangerously close to my lips. But before he can get to my left cheek, I pull away quickly, wanting to slap him but conscious of the approaching woman. The elevator arrives. Olivier stands to the side, ushers in the woman first, then turns to me. "*Au revoir*, Sophie," he says as he enters the elevator. I don't respond. I give Olivier's newfound resolve one month. *Tops.*

Chapter Eleven

I tuck Ava into the hotel room bed the way Gabe and I used to each night when she was a little girl. We didn't rotate back then, do the it's-your-night/my-night thing like most other parents. Neither of us wanted to miss a single minute of her—our one and only. We would each read a book, take turns saying good night to all her stuffed animals, and sing songs. Off-key, wrong words, it didn't matter—it was our treasured time to-gether, the three of us, bookends positioned on either side of Ava, our hands entwined over her head.

But not today. Today it's just me. Ava had a minor laparoscopic procedure last night at the hospital after experiencing sharp pains and heavy bleeding from what turned out to be an ovarian cyst eruption two days after the gynecologist appointment. Dr. Goldberg was the consummate professional. She met us at the hospital and took care of everything. She was surprisingly warm and nurturing, still in Chanel, even at ten in the evening. She told her team to speak to us only in English and made sure that we were comfortable. She knew better than to inquire about our "translator" Olivier. I texted Olivier, letting him know what happened because Ava had insisted. He texted back how sorry he was, that he wished Ava well, no further explanation. Harsh, but better that way.

"Call Daddy please, Mom," Ava said, before drifting off to sleep.

"I will. I promise." *Damn.* I can't hold back anymore, I will have to deal with Gabe directly. He's called at least twenty times and sent just as many "call me now" texts.

I wait until my heavily medicated daughter is full-on asleep. I gently stroke her head, pull away the stray strands of hair from her face. Ava is so beautiful when she sleeps. Her skin is luminescent as a sliver of light seeping through the window glances over her face. I then stare at my phone on the nightstand, searching for answers, as though it were the Magic 8 Ball that I used to consult when I was kid. I picture Gabe sitting on the couch with his feet kicked up on the ottoman in front of the supersized flat-screen TV, Pablo at his feet, waiting to hear from me. We still haven't talked directly to each other, but we've played pretend for Ava's sake. I decide it's best to FaceTime him, not deal with the international call static, and just get it over with. But first I grab a bottle of wine from the minibar and head out to the balcony. There's no way in hell I'm doing this sober.

I sit at the bistro table for two, plop down my phone, and chug the pint-sized chardonnay. The air is balmy and fragrant, and I take in the city's twinkling lights. The romance of Paris at night is not lost on me, I'm just lost in it. Ironically, at another time, I would have sat here on Gabe's lap, feeling his strong arms wrapped around me, our legs intertwined, as we'd point out all the magical sites in the distance— the Eiffel Tower, the glittery Seine, the imposing Arc de Triomphe. I would have leaned into him, thinking how happy I was, and he would be leaning backward, thinking, *Tuesday at 7:54.*

I finish off the bottle, which is not an effort—four swigs until I hit backwash—and notice how the flickering lights that just moments ago appeared enchanting now seem to mock me, the Eiffel Tower looks fake, and if Gabe were here and happened to drown in the Seine . . . oh well.

But he's still Ava's dad. And no matter what he did

to me, I owe her that. *Just do it.* I pick up the damn phone, hit FaceTime . . .

Gabe accepts even before the first ring finishes out its course. "Really, Sophie? I've only called you twenty fucking times to check in on her. How is she?" I was wrong. He's not on the couch. He's sitting at the kitchen table, looks sleep deprived and anxious, and is justifiably pissed off at me.

I pretend not to notice. "Sleeping soundly. Everything went well," I say clinically, as though I'm the doctor looking at my chart. "Ava just needs a few days of rest and then she can resume her normal activities."

"I wish I were there." He looks at me through heavily hooded lids.

I say nothing.

"How are you doing?" He tilts his head, leans into the phone. "You look tired."

I don't respond to that. No woman ever responds to that, even if it is true. Everyone knows tired is code for old. I just stare blankly back at his face, at those deep-set amber eyes; a face I've loved, and, I can't help it, still do. But it's now spoiled for me, ruined, no longer mine. "I'm . . ." I look away, feeling tears spring uninvited into my eyes. Jesus, not again. *Don't cry. Don't give him that.*

Together practically our entire lives, Gabe sees

what I'm trying to hide anyway. "Sophie, please don't cry." He shakes his head, purses his lips. *Guilty Gabe.* "I've done a lot of thinking these past few days, soul-searching. I am so sorry for all of it."

But that ship has long sailed, right along with trust, communication, and integrity. I meet his remorseful expression straight on. "This is about Ava," I tell him firmly. "*Only* Ava—okay."

"Well, I'm not doing this to piss you off, but I've decided I'm coming there. I worked out coverage at the hospital, bought a ticket, and I'm arriving the coming weekend. I have to see her. You know that, right . . . I have to." His voice fades out.

Ava first . . . Ava last—our family motto.

My wet eyes turn into dry sockets. "Please don't come."

"I'm her father. I'm coming."

And Ava would want him here. "Fine, but I will be gone before you get here."

"Where the hell are you going?" Gabe's face, pressing into the mini-screen, is now close up and distorted, abstract like a Picasso. He then pulls back and walks around the kitchen—*my kitchen*—and I can see the dirty dishes piled high in the sink behind him.

"I don't know," I say honestly. "But somewhere else."

"We need to talk. You can't just run away."

I stop breathing. *He did just say that.* Like one of those Stupid Things Guys Say memes. I throw my head back and howl with laughter, because it's actually funny, especially if you weren't me. "Says the man who *ran* after every woman wearing a tennis skirt, as if fucking were a marathon."

"Sophie, please." His eyes beg.

"I've got to go." *Because I love you and I hate you, and I can only pick one.*

"No, stay, please." His eyes glaze and I'm not remotely moved. The *you can't just run away* comment is still instant-replaying in my head.

"Bye, Gabe." Looking at him is unbearable.

I hang up, then turn my phone power off. *Gabe's coming, and I've got to get out of Dodge.* I head back into the room, shed my clothes into a pile on the floor, grab my Northwestern T-shirt and sweats from the lavender-scented drawer, climb into bed next to Ava, and curl my arms around her slim shoulders. If only I could protect her from the inevitable that is waiting to crush her. I pull her in close, and in her drugged state of sleep she melds into me like she did when she was little and had a bad dream. She was so tiny then, I used to jokingly call it teaspooning.

The hours pass and sleep is not an option, so I shoot for stillness. I've lost everything that I've ever counted on, believed in, trusted and loved—everyone *but Ava*—and the guy who nuked my life is now coming here to invade my safe space. No fair, I think. *Life's not fair*, I used to tell Ava. And now I know I was telling her the truth all along.

I toss and turn. The pillow is hot and mushy. I can't lie here any longer. I get up, wrap the duvet around me, and head back out to the balcony. I sit at the table and watch the sparkling flicker of the city lights around me. Only this time, I count each light, beginning with one and hoping to reach five million—anything to muzzle my racing mind, anything to cut off the images of Gabe with his harem of infidels, Gabe touching Lauren. Even the dirty dishes in my kitchen sink make a cameo appearance in my head. And when the counting stops, I follow the hypnotic pattern of the illuminated street grid from right to left, left to right, until the sun rises and night bleeds into morning.

Chapter Twelve

After a few days of taking it easy, Ava's color finally returns to normal and her mood improves immensely. I can see she is antsy to get back to her own life. We have been busy doing low-key activities together, wandering along Boulevard Saint-Germain, Champs Élysées, and Rue du Bac—eating, strolling, shopping, café hopping—keeping things light and easy. Gabe is coming in two days, and I'm determined to be gone before he arrives. As I button up my white capri jeans, I see my daughter Snapchatting someone from the bathroom. *It's time. She's ready.*

"Ava, we need to talk." I stand in the bathroom doorway as she puts on her morning makeup.

"We've done nothing but talk." She laughs. Her old laugh, the happy kind. "I love you, Mom—but no offense, I really need to be around other humans besides you."

"No offense taken, I guess."

She turns to me, waving the mascara wand. "I mean I really appreciate everything you've done but I've got to get on with my life . . . and now Dad's coming."

"About that . . ." I begin, seizing the opportunity.

Ava pauses and has that mischievous look of Gabe's that says there's more there than meets the eye. "Actually, there is something I want to talk to you about first."

Christ, not Olivier again. I will kill him. "Ready when you are." I gesture toward the bed—the same one we've been sharing since I arrived in Paris.

She finishes up in the bathroom and we both sit on the bed. Our plan today is to get breakfast and then head over to the Jeu de Paume museum. I have a feeling that after this conversation, the museum followed by a walk through the Tuileries Garden is not going to happen. I almost want to tell her *not* to put on the mascara, knowing it's going to be all over her face in just a few minutes. I feel sick to my stomach, but I've rehearsed this little speech for the past twenty-four hours in my head.

"You first," I say, chickening out.

She pushes her long hair behind her ears, then

nervously plays with the ends. "Well, things with Olivier are officially over." She lets that settle in. "I'm
sure you are happy about that. It was my choice, just
so you know. I did a lot of thinking. He really was not
there for me at all once I found out I wasn't pregnant. It
was like he just ran away, done with us, you know." She
stops talking for a minute, appears deep in thought.
"We were even planning on spending a few days together in Provence—he's teaching a seminar there next
week, but I decided after everything, not to go, and to
end things. Look, he has a family and I get it—but the
being there part—it was never going to happen. I was
crazy about him, but he's not reliable. Not like Dad,
who is always there for you and me no matter what.
That's the kind of guy I want."

Oh god, this is going to break her.

She stares at me, expecting me to comment but I
remain mute. *Say something now.* "Good decision,"
I say with a slight tremor in my voice, knowing I'm
about to destroy the institution of marriage for her permanently. Maybe I shouldn't say anything. Maybe she
isn't ready. Gabe's coming. Let him do it. But I need to
explain why I'm leaving. This has to happen now.

"But that's not exactly what I wanted to talk to you
about," Ava continues. Her gaze lowers to the floor and

she picks up her sandal lying there with her toes, like one of those claw arcade games.

"There's more?" *The sky already fell, what's left?*

Ava releases the sandal and stretches out her long legs in front of her. She's in teensy jean shorts and a skimpy tank top—all of nineteen. "Well, I know I shouldn't forgive him, but Jake and I have been talking again."

"Since when?" I ask. *Where was I?*

"Since the day before yesterday, after I broke it off with Olivier. I told Jake everything."

My mouth falls open. "You told him about the pregnancy scare?"

"Not that part." Her nose crinkles. *As if.* "I'm keeping that between you and me."

Ava's eyes are wide and expectant as she awaits my judgment, the maternal gavel to come down followed by the requisite soapbox lecture on being honest followed by a sublecture called "Don't Jump into Things So Quickly; Give Yourself Transition Time." But I say nothing, none of that. That was the old me—the *before* Me. I've got way bigger fish to fry, and I would take ten Jakes over one Olivier for her right now. And selfishly, she's going to need Jake once I break my news.

"Okay," I say simply.

She raises a suspicious brow, as if to say *That's it?*

"Well, now that my lease is up, and I'm not going away with Olivier, I decided to meet him in Spain right after you and Dad leave, to see if we can fix things," she says slowly, gauging my reaction. Then her eyes grow instantly hard and unforgiving. "But Monica—*fuck her*—so done, so over."

When Gabe and I leave together . . . that's what she's thinking. My stomach drops. This is really going to be hard for her. *And Monica . . .* she can somehow forgive Jake but not Monica. I so get it. Lauren's cheating on me is almost worse than Gabe's. I can't explain it, but the betrayal of Girl Code surpasses anything and everything. My eyes swim with tears. *Gabe and Lauren.* My god, I just can't stop crying.

"What's wrong?" Ava grabs my hands, confused. "You think I shouldn't see Jake, is that it? Jake said Monica left the group and went back to North Grove. They're not talking anymore either." She searches my face for clues and seems to find one. "You've got more on your mind than just me and my screwed-up life. It's Daddy, isn't it?" *She knows.* She always had an uncanny ability to see through me. I make a split decision not to lie.

"Yes, it is about your father." I hold in my breath and then let it out with a whoosh. "It began the night that you called me about Jake and Monica and asked me to come to Paris."

"Your birthday."

"Yes, my birthday." I pause, thinking I'm going to need to find another birthday because my real one was blown to shit forever. *Now. Say it now.* "I found out that same night that Dad has been cheating on me."

"On your birthday?" she repeats, her forehead scrunching with disbelief. "No. It can't be. You guys are so in love. You've had your fights but the way you guys still look at each other, and your PDA—especially in front of my friends—they all make fun of me about it. I've always thought I would never find that. What happened?" Ava is trying hard to keep it together, processing her father, her hero's betrayal. It's not real. It hasn't sunk in. Those were just words. Words that float. I get it. It's still not real to me.

The actual truth is too awful for anyone's child to handle. I decide to minimize it. "The details aren't important, but it happened." And here I go defending Gabe for Ava's sake. "But no matter what he did and how wrong it was and how much it hurts me, he loves you. He dropped everything to come here and be with you. He—"

"Wait!" she yells, cutting me off in middrivel, and

stands. "Did you just say Daddy cheated on you? How is that even possible?"

"Ava, I'm trying to tell you—"

Her eyes begin to spin wildly like pinwheels, her voice builds to a crescendo. "No, you are trying to minimize and protect. That's what you do. Damn it, Mom—tell me the truth. Stop defending him and stop protecting me. For Christ's sake, I thought I was pregnant with my married professor's baby. I'm not twelve. What the hell happened? And with who?"

But I don't take the bait. I know my daughter. Tough on the outside, soft and vulnerable within. No amount of heartache will allow me to destroy her. "Please, Ava, for once, stop pushing. It just makes it even more painful."

"Who did Daddy cheat with that could possibly hold a candle to you?"

There. Right there. That's the moment I lose it. All gloves come off. I shed my maternal skin and expose the woman scorned. "It was more than one woman."

"No, no—not Daddy. It can't be, it can't be." The reality seeps in, the pedestal Gabe is perched on crashes, and she begins to cry. "How could he do this to you? To me? To our family?" Ava is crying, not just about me and Gabe, but about all of her losses and betrayals— Olivier, Jake, Monica—her entire support system exploding inside her with one thrown grenade.

I stand and open my arms, as she falls limply inside. I hold her or she holds me until she calms down. Whatever it is, whoever is mothering whom, we are intertwined, twinning in pain, clinging to each other—the only two people in this world whom we can depend on, who understand exactly what we're going through.

We stand there like that for a really long time. I finally pull back when her tears subside, her body loosens, and I feel myself strengthening. "We have both come to a crossroads, Ava. And there are choices now, for you and for me."

Her eyes are bloodred and I'm sure mine are the same. "What are you going to do?"

What *am* I going to do? "There's no going back, no fixing this. Your dad and I once had a great love. But somewhere along the way it fell apart. He betrayed me and I'm not going to minimize that. But a broken marriage takes two to destroy, even if one person did the crime. I'm so beyond sad, believe me. It kills me to even tell you any of this. And I can't even comprehend that this is my life now. I'm trying to figure it out and I don't have any answers yet." I avert my gaze because I don't want to break down in front of my daughter.

"I'm a terrible person," Ava says softly. "This is what Olivier's kids would have felt like, and the thing is, I didn't even care when I was with him. I didn't even think about them or his wife. So selfish, so shitty of me. Look at you. I'm so sorry for everything you've been through, with Dad, with me." She wraps her arms around my shoulders, stares into my eyes. "You were going through your deepest pain and as usual, you put me first."

Ava then drops her arms to her side, becomes still as a statue. A moment of calm passes between the crash of waves, but in a few seconds or so I know, because I know my daughter, she's going to lose it all over again.

I summon up my soothing voice, the one I've always used to calm her anxiety. "I don't know who I am without your father and I've got to go find out. While you travel with Jake, I think I'm going to head to the South of France for a bit. Somewhere quiet, beautiful, surrounded by nature and lavender, wineries and perfumeries. I need to clear my head, to think about everything that happened and figure out what I want to do. I have so much noise going on in my mind right now that I'm hoping to find some inner peace. But I will be back, I promise." I search her anguished face, wishing I could retract everything aired in this room but I can't. "Can you handle that? Can you know that I'm not leaving you, just going to go find me for a while?"

"Do you want me to come with you? I will cancel with Jake. You need me."

My baby, this incredible young woman, sees me and that's enough. I cradle her delicate chin inside my hands. "I love you but no. I want you to go be nineteen, be with Jake and figure that out—if you two can really forgive each other, and if being together is something you still want, or even discovering you want to move on. Go, okay. Take that time for you. I need this time for me. I love that you want to be with me, but I have to be with me alone. Do you understand?"

She nods reluctantly. "What about your work? The festival? Rachel is probably having a total freak-out."

Oh my god, Rachel. I have to call her at the office today. She's left ten messages that I've ignored. Who could think of work with everything going on? I'm usually so on top of everything. "Timing is terrible." I sigh deeply. "But I really do need to figure everything out. Work will be fine." Ava is right. Rachel is probably out of her mind with the arts festival just around the corner. But I simply can't think about that right now. "I'm more concerned about you, honey."

Ava gnaws on her chapped bottom lip, trying to be brave. *Give her more, she needs more.* "You and Dad have always been so close," I tell her, taking her hands into mine. "He's coming to be with you and to tell you the truth in his own way. I know this is going to put a strain on your relationship, but that's not what

I want, okay? I'm not asking you to choose sides. Our marital problems are separate from being your parents. You have always been the most important part of our lives, no matter what. Just work it out with him, honey. That's what I want for you. You never have to choose."

"But we will never be the same, never be the three of us again." Her voice is tiny, retro. The little girl who can't fall asleep, standing next to my side of the bed, clutching her special blanket and stuffed elephant, wanting me to make it all better.

I press my forehead lightly against hers. "We won't be the same. But our love for you is always the same. You are going to be okay, and I'm going to be okay— you know that, right?" I don't know that. But I want her to know that.

"How long are you going?" she asks, eyeing me with worry.

Don't lie to her or to yourself. "I'm not sure," I say. "But I'm leaving before your dad arrives this weekend. I need to do that for me."

Her brows knit, calculating the timing. "I don't mean to be selfish, but will you be back to drive me up to school like usual, to help me decorate the new apartment, and get things organized?" Ava's eyes are hopeful, clinging to ritual, to anything she can count on right now.

School drop-off has always been our thing. Bed Bath & Beyond, Target, the Container Store. And of course, our annual spa day spent downtown at the Peninsula Hotel before we part ways. Ava finds comfort in rituals, lists, habits, sameness—as do I. In her eyes, it shouldn't take me more than a few weeks while she is traveling with Jake to find myself. As long as I'm on her time line, she's thinking this could work. I'm not so optimistic. A few weeks is nowhere near enough time to mourn my marriage. But hell or high water, I will take Ava back to the university for her senior year, which begins on September 1. I squeeze her tightly. "Of course, I will be there."

Ava first, Ava last . . . Ava in the middle.

III.

Your gifts lie in the place where your
values, passions and strengths meet.
Discovering that place is the first step
toward sculpting your masterpiece—
Your life.

—MICHELANGELO

Chapter Thirteen

Fuck them, now me.

Four words, my newly customized version of *Om*, repeat feverishly inside my head like a mantra, as I drive from Nice, where I spent the past three days while Gabe is in Paris, to Saint-Paul-de-Vence, one of the oldest medieval towns in the French Riviera. I've flipped a switch from pain and sadness to rage and wrath, which is spreading inside me like wildfire. Speeding down the road, I merge in and out of the roundabouts—ironically in the same reckless way that I once imagined I would make my Thelma and Louise getaway during my morning runs in North Grove. *But this shit is real. This shit is not going away.*

My heart feels as though it's pummeling through my

chest. *How did my life fall apart so fast, so completely?* I once had everything and now it's gone—my marriage, my home, my best friends, even my daughter's innocence. It's as if I have been blown to smithereens and somehow survived the trauma with no arms, no legs— just remainders: a head and a heart to comprehend and feel it all. I want to die and I want to live. I want to cry and I want to scream. I want to laugh at the absurdity and I want to go stark raving mad. As I careen in and out of lanes, a violent sensation overtakes me, wrapping its meaty hands around my throat and won't let go. I pick up speed, now going a solid twenty-five over the limit. *Fuck them, now me.*

I hightail with the wind in my hair, knotting and twisting into dreds until I'm forced to slow down due to construction. Ultimately, I mosey up to the finish line: *You have arrived at your destination.* Siri with a Brit accent, my only friend and companion along the way, congratulates me after I round the serpentine Route des Serres, passing by charming rustic homes, and slowly approach the hotel entrance. Hotel? The elegant wrought-iron gate provides a window into the courtyard. It looks more like a château for the rich and famous. Full admission: I picked the priciest place I could find. Did I mention my car? It's a vintage white Alfa Romeo convertible that I chose from the exotic car rental place in Nice. My new goal: *Live large and let Gabe pay for it.*

This is not how I've ever operated. I don't deprive myself, but I never spend money recklessly. I didn't grow up with it, so those ingrained frugal habits never really died. But today is a new day, a new me, and all financial prudence is dust in the wind. *Lauren? How could they do that to me?*

I stop the car to pull myself together before entering the exquisite hotel grounds. I chose La Cachette because the reviews called it a "secret gem," bathed in quietude, elegance, and the lush fragrances of Provence. Surrounded by elaborate gardens and aged olive trees, citrus fruits, and thousands of wild Provençal plants, it is a far cry from the SUV-infested landscaped suburban jungle of North Grove—and solitude is just what I need right now.

Inhaling deeply, I give my name at the intercom and the gate opens. I drive slowly around the pebbled driveway, passing a ten-foot-high modern stone and metal sculpture, and stop at the entrance and wait for the valet's meet and greet.

Without Gabe. Everything I do from now on has a Without Gabe tag. It's all so strange. I have never checked into any hotel without him or my besties. Until now, I never knew how codependent I was on all of them. I have always considered myself independent, a go-getter, but now I know the truth—I'm emotionally crippled and terrified of going it all alone.

Breathe, I tell myself, just breathe. And then the valet arrives, a vision in black. The elegantly suited young Frenchman gallantly opens the car door with a disarming Chiclets smile, and a full head of gelled hair. As he leans in, I briefly close my eyes beneath my sunglasses. He smells so good. I take my time uncrossing my cramped legs as I get out just to whiff him fully as though he were a human aerosol, a revival spray. I read his name tag: *Jean-Paul.* Of course, it is.

I then check into the hotel for the week with the option to extend my stay and walk down the fancy corridor, which is lined with ancestral portraits and oversized antique clocks that all tell the wrong time, toward my room. I take the winding staircase up to the second floor and open the door. The room is stunning, immaculate, smells like fresh flowers, and is decorated in spalike hues of cream, peach, and pale blues. I spin around and spot the best part—the large balcony with a small sitting area and two stuffed chairs—another table for two. I swallow hard. *Without Gabe.*

I drop my purse on the bed and kick off my sandals. My dinner reservation at the hotel restaurant is at eight thirty. It's just after six and the sun, slung low, is still shining bright. I stick my knotty hair into a scrunchie, wash my dusty face, then fling open the balcony doors and step out into paradise. Everything around me is as aromatic as the handsome valet—an onslaught of intoxicating lavender, lilac, basil, and musk. I raise my arms in a sun salutation. So, this is what on-my-own looks like. This is what a sensual five-star hotel room *without Gabe* feels like. Alone—but for the first time in hours, I'm not enraged. I'm calmer, defused by the postcard-worthy beauty casting a giant welcome mat over my problems.

The sun, still warm, radiates a rich topaz glow over the hills and valleys on all sides of me, and I see myself as I am: a wounded woman who has come to heal. In the near distance, I look below and spot a luxurious pool bordered by elegant private cabanas and a Jacuzzi surrounded by exotic flowers. To my left, there is a small sculpture garden and an adjoining spice and fragrance garden. Near the pool, off to the side, I see a young couple having cocktails at the elegant white-clothed terrace restaurant. I stare at them. I was once them—hands laced, foreheads practically touching, sexy half-smiles, wine-stained breath. Now I'm not. Now I'm this. Whatever this is.

I sink into one of the plump chairs, kick my feet up

on the rattan console and stare out into the abyss. Now what? What's the damn plan? *What do I want?* God knows I haven't asked myself that question in years.

The hard truth is that everything hurts—my heart, my body, my head. Is the only remedy for pain time? Am I supposed to follow the heartbreak diet and curl up in a ball and cry it out? Where's the damn when-life-goes-to-shit handbook called *What to Expect When You're NOT Expecting It*? It doesn't exist. It simply doesn't exist.

I lean forward, elbows on the small table, head in hands. What would happen if I did something totally radical like make the decision *not* to suffer at all? To *not* mourn my losses. Is that denial? Do I have to go through the five stages and follow some kind of grief timetable? Can't I make up my own rules? I look around. There's no grief police to tell me otherwise.

What if I choose *not* to be angry, sad, vengeful, and destructive? What if I choose *not* to wait out a year of mandatory processing and acceptance? What if I don't go comatose, drown myself in Ambien in order to sleep and wake up on Prozac for breakfast to get me through my day? What if I skip the essential mourning, self-mutilating part, cut my losses, and start my new life right now? Yes, it's denial—so what.

I hug myself tightly as the tepid evening breeze

passes over me. I yearn to shout: *Embrace denial!* It feels right, less painful, and certainly less destructive than the Danica Patrick impersonation of an hour ago. *Embrace denial.* I have picked my poison and that's the one. I sit bolt upright, holding my head up high, and it feels as though I'm about to meet a new person, as if I'm about to date myself and she's kinda hot. I laugh for the first time in what feels like a lifetime. Who cares that I seem delusional—who's going to stop me?

I stand decisively. First things first in Denial 101 . . . What does one wear to dinner when dining alone? Another admission to self: I have never dined in a restaurant alone. Never, not once in forty-two years. I've picked up morning coffee a billion times, salads, sushi, etc.—lunch alone. Even movies on rare occasions. But that doesn't count. I have never walked into a fancy restaurant for dinner and asked for a table for one.

No blacks or browns or neutrals, I decide. Nothing dark or drab. Go bright, go bold. Flowers perhaps? I shake my head. Too prissy. Yellow—that's it. I step back into the room and open my suitcase and pull out the form-fitting taxicab yellow maxidress that I threw in at the very last moment. I hold it up, stare at it, press it against me, and glance in the mirror. I allow myself thirty seconds to remember when I'd last worn this dress. I bought it in Florence on the David trip with the whole crew. Samantha and Lauren also bought the same dress in different colors—I chose yellow, Samantha, orange, and Lauren, emerald green. I smile to myself, remembering how Eric called us the Lifesavers when we all wore our new dresses to dinner at that Michelin-starred restaurant near the Duomo. I wore it just that one time, thinking it was too electric, too neon look-at-me for judgy suburbia.

I shed my clothes and stand naked in the mirror, something I've always hated and avoided but something that Gabe used to get turned on by—making me face the mirror and look at myself while he touched my body from behind. *No Gabe this time to feel me up.* So . . . I do it myself. I caress my own breasts as he once did, slowly in clockwise circles, breasts then nipples, while looking in the mirror. Strange but surprisingly sensual. Full, still firmish. Not so bad at all.

The rest of my body is not what it used to be, but still holding its own. My stomach is strong from obsessive core work—Pilates, yoga, and Samantha's boot camp that she drags me to on Saturdays, which I hate but never miss. Legs, long and muscular, slight cellulite but not too noticeable unless you get up close. Still me, with a few good years left.

I take a shower, pull my hair into a low ponytail and then twist it into a sleek knot at the nape of my neck, mimicking the French chignon style that the receptionist wore at the gynecologist's office. Large hoop earrings, bangle bracelets, mascara, blush, liner, a little brow filler, nude lip gloss, and funky sandals with a three-inch wedge complete the table-for-one look.

I return to the mirror for a quick once-over. Nice. Not a lonely look, rather an empowered I'll-get-there look; a look that pretends what I don't yet feel. I glance over at the nightstand clock. An hour until dinner. Hmm, why not? I grab a bottle of rosé out of the minibar, take my laptop, and return to the balcony, my newly designated office for Denial Inc. You need a plan, I tell myself, reverting to my anal-retentive habits. *You need a to-do list.*

I kick off my wedges and create a new file I call "Me_The Sequel." The obvious buzzwords come to mind: mind, body, spirit, healing, presence. I shake my head. No. I need much more than a self-care plan; I need a life overhaul, a Reinvention Manifesto. A *without Gabe* covenant. And I need a title. Something bold, that commits and binds me to this contract.

I begin to brainstorm and type: *Twelve Steps to Finding Sophie Bloom.* Trite, sounds like a *Cosmo* manual. *Twelve Ways to Heal Sophie Bloom.* No—too Alcoholics Anonymous. Something powerful and gutsy, like *The Ten Commandments.* This contract must be unbreakable.

The Unbreakables, I think sadly, recalling the name Eric had dubbed our group—Sophie & Gabe, Samantha & Eric, Lauren & Matt. But we came apart anyway, like those red plastic monkeys holding on to their linked arms for dear life until one falls off. *I fell off.* No, Gabe pushed me off. This new me is not going to depend on anyone—no more clinging monkeys.

What do I really want?

I glance out at the rolling hills in the distance and stare at the sculpture garden beneath me, filled with small, intricately carved stone fountains. *I want to sculpt again,* I whisper. I want to chisel marble, twist clay, create something. And I want to fuck passionately, just like that young couple down at the restaurant will surely do right after dinner. I want to smile and mean it. Most important, I want to *feel* my life, to live it, to connect, and not just exist where one day fuses into the next. I want to do things because *I* want to, not because I have to. Okay, and this is totally childish, but I want to *out-Gabe* Gabe. I want him to regret what he did, to see me grow and blossom, to really know all that he gave up when he chose Ashley Madison and friends over me.

My fingers begin to type furiously, taking on a life of their own.

THE UNBREAKABLES
by Sophie Bloom

1. **WEAR WHATEVER I WANT.** No age barriers, no fashion rules. First Move: Get bangs.
2. **EAT ONLY WHAT TASTES GOOD.** Fuck fat-free. No calorie counting. No scales. No pleasing anyone else but me first. Eat in combos—sweet & salty, appetizers & desserts. It will balance me.
3. **SMILE—FEEL IT, NOT FAKE IT.** No North Grove air kisses and playing pretend. I'm in France. Find the *joie de vivre*. No "settling" on any decision— and most of all, no matter what I do, no regrets.
4. **NO MORE RUSHING. SLOW DOWN, TAKE CONTROL OF MY LIFE, MY WAY, ON MY TERMS.** Stop the rigidity of a schedule, must-do workouts, and all the accompanying stresses. Those days are so over.
5. **SLEEP AND REJUVENATE.** Nonnegotiable. Seven-hour minimum. Even if I have to lie in bed and watch the clock. Read again. No TV and other life-wasting binges. Get off Facebook, Instagram, Twitter. Stop squandering precious time

and energy in an alternative universe where *everyone lies* anyway. And most important: don't be a slave to the phone.

6. **EXERCISE**—but *only* what I enjoy. No machines. No treadmills. No StairMaster. Nothing that stays in place and gets me nowhere or hurts. No more boot camp, punishing trainers, or spin tyrants.

7. **MASTURBATE.** Nonnegotiable. Get to know my body again and what turns me on.

8. **MUSIC AND DANCE**—play it loud, play it often, and feel it. '70s—my fave. Joni, Carly, James Taylor, Carole King, Cat Stevens, Donna Summer, and Aretha, and of course, the musts: Sheryl Crow, Stevie Nicks, and Tom Petty—music and lyrics that fill my soul. Dance again—even alone—*especially alone.*

9. **NATURE IS NURTURE.** Long walks and hikes whenever I can. Surround myself with natural beauty. It will heal my spirit, empower me.

10. **PASSION**—whatever that means and in whatever form. Remain open to new experiences. No rules—except for one: guilt-free *but* no hurting anyone in the process. Unless that someone happens to be Gabe. NO MERCY.

11. **ART—SCULPT AGAIN.** Fourteen years in exile using the medical excuse is too damn long.

No more fear. My hands are fine. My hands are ready. Now *go.*

12. **EMBRACE MYSTERY**—Not everything has to be a plan. Prepare to be surprised by life.

I lean back against the chair, pleased with what came out of me without thinking too deeply. I smile hard—a *real smile—a Rule No. 3 smile.* And for the first time in what feels like a really long time, I actually feel my lips grazing my teeth. *I want this.* I close my eyes to take it all in, and then from inside of the room I hear my phone ringing. *Damn. Just let it go,* I tell myself. Don't answer it. *But what if it's Ava?*

I jump off the chair without thinking twice to pick it up. My heart sinks. It's not Ava but Samantha for a Face-Time. I just blew Rule No. 5—failed myself three seconds out of the gate. I stare at my best friend's number and her picture in the little round circle at the top. It's the one I took at her fortieth birthday luncheon at Neiman's Zodiac Room. Samantha's long, dark hair looks like a sheath of silk, her thick eyelashes with extensions look like mini-brooms, and she is wearing the new Tom Ford red lip-stick we all bought together. She is all mom-glammed but giving me the finger—*still Samantha.* This photo makes me laugh every time she calls—except this time. One ring left before it goes to Missed Call. *Do I answer?*

I swipe right. "Sam," I say. And there she is, in 2-D. Once my best friend, my sister, and now part of the team of liars.

"Christ, Soph, I've been trying to get a hold of you. I know you don't want to talk to me but I'm glad you finally answered. This is the longest we haven't talked. Wow—you look amazing. You never wear your hair back like that." Her eyes are glassy. "I'm so sorry about everything. I'm sick about it. I haven't slept since you left."

I just stare at her, detached, as though I'm Jane Goodall observing chimpanzees in the wild. Samantha is in her Lulus with a small towel wrapped around her neck. It's Monday post-hot-yoga with Jenna, our fave. I don't even have to ask, I know. I would have been there with her, wearing a similar outfit, matching white towel.

Embrace denial. My first act: *I deny you forgiveness. I deny us this conversation. Seeing you, hearing your voice, just hurts more.*

I then do something I have never done to my best friend. I hang up without a goodbye. I return to the balcony, about to throw the phone as far as I can, and then my arm drops limply to my side. *Ava.* All the pain in the world—crushed, bulleted, betrayed and stabbed— but I'm still her mom. I can't just disappear, disconnect.

I stare at the phone. If I can't destroy this hateful

device then at the bare minimum I'm going to delete and block every single number on my contact list but two: Ava and my office. Tomorrow I'm going to resign from the art gallery and give my fabulous assistant my job—a job she is more than ready to take on. Then I will delete that number as well, which leaves just Ava. Hers will be the only number left on my phone, the only one that matters. I press my hands against my broken heart for what feels like an eternity, and then I let go.

Embrace denial.

Zombielike, I walk back inside the room, glance at the digital clock on the nightstand: 8:28. Time to claim my table for one. I reach for my Tory Burch clutch, put back on my wedges. I can't feel my body move but I'm still breathing, still standing. I've got my list now—the only thing I possess that makes any sense. I toss the phone onto the bed. No more slips. No one else deserves a piece of me—except for my daughter. Sophie Bloom has officially gone rogue and is not coming back any time soon.

Fuck them, now me.

Chapter Fourteen

So I didn't get bangs. I went to the nearby shopping mall less than a mile away from the hotel, where the hair stylist persuaded me to skip the bangs and instead go for a trendy layered bob. She lobbed off six inches (I was terrified) and insisted I get highlights, and it's perfect. Gazing into the Nike store window, I don't recognize my reflection between the sneakers and the Just Do It sign, but I love it. It's younger, flirty; a forty-two-year-old train wreck determined to get back on the track look.

I then buy skinny jeans, a form-fitting white T-shirt, and chunky-heeled red sandals. I wear the whole getup right out of the store. After that, I purchase a French pocket dictionary, a Riviera guidebook, and a blank leather journal. I'm a walking-talking cliché and I'm okay with it. Grabbing a cappuccino, my second one before noon (no longer care), I head toward my car. I plan to spend the afternoon at the Fondation Maeght, a small museum of modern art on a hill overlooking Saint-Paul-de-Vence, about ten minutes away.

Driving toward the museum with the wind in my new hair, I feel strangely free, lighter, having no set plan, no one to answer to, no responsibilities, except to see where the day takes me. I park in the lot and walk toward the lovely, lush garden entrance. I take my time before entering the museum itself. No rushing (Rule No. 4). Meandering through the sculpture garden, I encounter an amazing ceramic by Fernand Léger, a fountain sculpture by Pol Bury, a sculpture by Alexander Calder, and a wind sculpture by Takis. Eyeing the incredible art while inhaling the warm fresh air, I feel rejuvenated.

Entering the museum, I take a brochure and roam my way toward the main gallery, stopping when I come upon a magnificent painting called *La Vie*—by Marc Chagall, my favorite painter. The whimsical composition covering an entire wall chronicles human love and life. It depicts the artist's real-life events juxtaposed with his vivid dreams—from his humble Hasidic upbringing in Russia to the end of his days in Paris. Colorful images of his rabbi grandfather, his marriage to his first wife, the birth of his daughter, his lover, are all mixed in with acrobats, dancers, and musicians—representing the vibrant saga of a man whose life was filled with beauty and torment.

I stare at the painting, imagining my own life and how Chagall might have painted it: my parents' messy divorce when I was five, my cold, aloof mother, my estranged father and his new family, meeting and marrying Gabe, my short-lived sculpting career, giving birth to Ava, the postpartum depression, the pregnancy struggles, our close-knit group of friends, Gabe's lovers, Ava's pregnancy scare, and now me alone—with no acrobats or musicians to prop me up. Like Chagall, I, too, am at an intersection in France, amid beauty and torment. I feel the painter's brushstrokes roiling inside me. His world, like my new one, is volatile in both mood and color. I stand in front of the masterpiece, feeling both alone and less alone.

Other visitors gather around the painting. I notice a young couple to the right of me, arms looped casually, heads cocked, jointly assessing the Chagall. I cannot help but stare at them. The guy looks vaguely familiar. How can that be? His hair is gelled and his sinewy arms are filled with colorful swirling tattoos like in one of those trendy adult coloring books. The woman standing next to him is slim and lovely, angelic, with dark blonde hair flowing down her back in waves, wearing a loose peasant dress and booties. I try not to stare, and then it hits me.

It's Jean-Paul, the hotel valet. It can't be, but it is. I suddenly have that displaced feeling like when you were a kid and spotted your teacher at the grocery store—it just didn't make sense. Teachers don't shop, hotel valets don't go to art exhibits. Jean-Paul out of his elegant suit and tie wearing tight faded jeans and covered in tats is deceptive. It's as though this doppelgänger is the so-phisticated Jean-Paul's badass identical twin.

He feels my intense gaze on him, turns in my direc-tion, trying to place me as well. And then his crystal blue eyes light up. "*Bonjour, madame.*" He smiles at me.

I retract slightly. *Madame* feels like I'm the Old Maid discovered in a deck of cards. But I return the warm smile, run my hands self-consciously through my new hair. "Yes, *bonjour.* Jean-Paul, right?"

"*Oui*—yes." His eyes twinkle or maybe it's my imagination. But he is definitely looking at me differ-ently than he had at the hotel. There, it was all about graciousness and protocol, but here he seems to be eyeing me as a man would a woman from across the bar. *Man?* He's not a day over twenty-five.

"You changed your hair since yesterday," he says.

"Yes." I blush slightly. He noticed. "Something dif-ferent."

"It's nice," he says. I'm embarrassed but secretly pleased. He points to the Chagall. "You like?"

"Brilliant." I nod. "The colors . . ."

"I love this painting. It inspires me. You know what Picasso said?" He tilts his head in the direction of the painting. "'When Matisse dies, Chagall will be the only painter left who understands what color is.'"

"Yes . . . I totally agree."

He then whispers to the woman, probably telling her that I'm a guest at the hotel.

"Are you here alone?" he asks, now holding her hand as he moves in closer.

"Yes, I am."

"This is Lea, and this is . . ." His face reddens.

"Sophie." I notice a sketch pad sticking out of the girl's leather bag. "Are you an artist?"

She laughs. "Yes. We both are." Up close, she has tiny exquisite features, doe eyes against pale skin, bridge-of-nose freckles, a small but determined mouth. She raises an inquisitive brow. "And so are you, am I right? Your hands. I can tell."

My hands. I glance down. Do they still give me away? Hands that betrayed me. I *was* an artist. I still am, I suppose. There's a permanence. "Yes." I try on my renewed persona for size. "I . . . I sculpt. Not in a long time. But yes."

There, not so bad.

They both move in closer. I'm suddenly more interesting, a little hipper, a little less Madame. "We are about to go for coffee," Jean-Paul says, pointing to the staircase. "There's a lovely café near the entrance." He looks at Lea, who nods. "Please join us."

"I don't want to impose," I say, dying to have coffee with them. *Do it. They're asking you.* "You know what—I'd love to."

I'm going to move past the coffee part, the animated conversation, the laughter. I'm going to cruise beyond the American-Franco comparisons of nuance, innuendo, and gestural meanings, the discussion of alternative music and great and not so great art. Here's what *does* matter . . . She paints, he's a photographer— both are twenty-seven. They have lived together for four years. She works at an art gallery in the village of Saint-Paul; he works at the hotel. Both are originally from small towns outside of Paris, both studied at the École des Beaux-Arts. And yes, both know exactly who Olivier Messier is. I'm going to fast-forward, and let's just say that the coffee turned into wine. And the wine turned into . . . well, it's all a blur right now.

The way Jean-Paul's left hand is on his girlfriend's, and his right hand casually slides along my thigh under the round table. Only it isn't just his hand, there are two of them, on both of my thighs. *His and hers.* I gasp slightly. Two sexy millennials seducing me at the Fondation Maeght café with three families eating ice cream and cake at nearby tables. My mind races with images of what may happen and the fact that I want it to happen, whatever "it" may be. The truth is, I felt the chemistry the second I saw the way Jean-Paul looked at me near the Chagall with fuck-me eyes. It was a look I had not seen in so long—but now I've experienced it twice in just over a week. Jean-Paul and Olivier. *And Lea.* Three times.

Rules No. 10 and 12: *Be open to sexual situations and prepare to be surprised.* Do they do this often? Do they know I'm old enough to be their mother (a teen mom). Is it my new hairstyle? It doesn't matter. This is really happening. My mind is static and my body is on fire.

Jean-Paul pays the bill, refusing to take my credit card. Lea lightly squeezes my wrists and asks if I would like to see her paintings in their apartment. I say yes, and they trade knowing looks, shared smiles.

It's on.

We leave the café and drive to their apartment, which is a few miles away. They both admire my sporty convertible. I follow them and try to imagine the conversation that they are having in their car. I feel excited, scared, stirred, knowing I am way out of my league here. If only I could call Samantha and Lauren to share and strategize this. *Stop! Don't go there.* Don't think about them or home. Instead, concentrate on the way those lovely artists' hands sent tremors through your body. *Stay present.* Exhaling deeply, the doubts begin to fester anyway: They are just eight years older than Ava, which makes you not much better than Olivier if you pursue this. They are a couple. This is taboo. He works at the hotel you're staying at. You can't do this. You're a mother. Think Stranger Danger—what *might* happen. You're not gay. This is not okay. Make a U-turn and go back to the hotel now.

I glance into the rearview mirror. No one is driving on the road but us. It's a sign. Who says it's not okay? I don't see anyone. You wanted something to transport you from your present state of hell, right? Isn't that why you're here in Saint-Paul—to reclaim life's beauty, to heal, to be surprised? Life doesn't stop because you're a mother. There is no downside. You've been with one man—a man who betrayed you. You are not hurting anyone (Rule No. 10). They clearly have an open relationship. They want to share you together. They are not cheating on each other. This—whatever this is—*is* their thing. Embrace their free spirit. You're wearing good underwear.

Done.

Lea and Jean-Paul's small apartment reminds me of Ava's dorm room freshman year. It's cluttered but funky and colorful with a large mosaic tapestry and string lights tacked to the wall above the bed. The other walls are filled floor-to-ceiling with her paint-ings. Abstracts—some good, some mediocre—but who cares. I'm not here to judge the art.

"Lea, do you mind if I use your bathroom?" I ask, trying to hide my nerves and wanting to douse my face with water and do a quick full-body touch-up before . . .

"Of course." She points to the obvious door and smiles as she grabs wineglasses and a joint. Pot too? *Who am I right now?* I have not smoked weed since college. The Juul on the beach with Samantha and Lauren doesn't count. That was an e-cigarette. Lea's joint is tightly rolled by hand, old school. I've officially entered a time warp, a reboot of sorts.

Once inside the bathroom, I peer closely into the small mirror doubling as a medicine cabinet over her sink. I can't help it. I see myself in the reflection and think of Gabe. He must have felt just like this. The anticipation, the excitement, the adrenaline rush, the newness. *This* is what he clearly craved and exactly what I could no longer give him.

I stand in front of the mirror, immobile. I forgot about my new haircut and for a second I don't recognize myself. I brace my hands on the sink, my stomach turning from the number of internal butterflies swarming. *This is so happening.*

I quickly wash my face, then borrow Lea's deodorant and her Fragonard body lotion, which smells of jasmine. *Do not overanalyze this*, I warn myself. *You're hanging with the go-with-the-flow crowd now.* I hear music being turned on—something French and seductively jazzy. I use her mouthwash too, and then take a quick peek down there. I showered before I left for the museum. So, all good. *You got this.* I open the door and it's just Jean-Paul alone in the room. Lea is mysteriously elsewhere.

"If you call me 'madame,' I will have to kill you." I laugh, trying to camouflage my obvious nervousness and lack of kinky experience, shortage of lovers (the understatement of the century).

Jean-Paul, with a sly confident grin, slowly removes his T-shirt and poses like a Calvin Klein model in his low-rise jeans with the white underwear band peeking out. His torso is a perfect V and he is a painting, not a man. Every part of his chest is a road map of colorful brocadelike tattoos. I'm fascinated and turned on. He stands where he is, waits for me to approach him. I take a long, deep breath, then move toward him. I don't want to fuck him right now, it's even more hardcore: *I want to sculpt him.* I want to feel his Greek-god body covered with graffiti against my hands, like clay waiting for me to transform it. Suddenly, I'm not overthinking and I'm no longer powerless and vastly inexperienced. I may not have the lovers to chalk up, but I do have the touch. I have created so many bodies with my own hands. I can do this.

The music, the waft of weed, the woozy lighting—Sophie Bloom has gone fishing, and this other being, this Sasha Fierce begins to emerge. Jean-Paul with all his swag is no match for me right now. I approach him with confidence and without hesitation. I kiss him hard on the lips, full and demanding. He leans back slightly, blatantly surprised by my aggressiveness. He mumbles something I don't understand and then grabs my ass and roughly pulls me toward him. I feel his hardness press against me, jeans to jeans—and I smile. *I did that.*

"Take my clothes off now," I order. *Who am I right now?* I've never ordered sex before. I've never even asked. Gabe just knew what to do, what I liked. But now I want to do more than what I know. I want to do everything I don't know.

"You're hungry," he says under his breath in English.

"You have no idea," I respond seductively in French.

I feel his taut chest with my hands. His beautiful body—the bulging biceps, the perfect contour of his pecs, the curve of his shoulders, the rock-hard abs, the pronounced crease of his pelvic muscles. My hands are all over him and then my mouth. His body is so young and dangerously sexy, I yearn to devour him. From somewhere above me, I hear him moan. I unbutton his jeans and release him. He pushes me backward onto the bed and I let him. My shirt is off now and so are my jeans, the new red sandals are flung across the room. *Where is Lea?* crosses my mind and then disappears, knowing I'm in a triangle, that the young artist with an affinity for abstract body parts will soon make her entrance. This is their game, I've just collected $200 and passed Go. They have their own rhythm, and she clearly knows her cue. Right now, Jean-Paul is mine. But soon, I can feel it in the air, we will share him.

His breath tastes like cigarettes, espresso, and cabernet, and his tongue is rammed down my throat. Normally, I'm not big on ramming tongues—but now I can't get enough. That tongue moves expertly from my mouth to my breasts to my stomach and continues heading south. He's saying dirty things to me in French—who knows, who cares—I just don't want this to stop. Closing my eyes, I experience every tingling sensation at once. This spectacular young man is exploring me in places where only Gabe has traveled before. His touch is markedly different, demanding, experienced, rousing, and wildly erotic. And then, as I predicted, the real game begins . . . I feel a second tongue on me. Light, flickering, softer. She's here now, the waiflike temptress, the one who calls the shots.

Jean-Paul roughly pins me down. Our eyes lock and I don't dare look away. I feel her below, spreading my legs and that expert sharp tongue darting in and out. I feel out of control, propelled to a higher place than I've ever been, until it is unbearable. The orgasm comes hard, too quickly, unexpectedly. I ball up the sheets in my hands. I don't want this to end.

As I lay panting and satiated, the artistic duo gives me time to process, and by the anticipatory looks on their faces, a return favor is clearly expected—*him and her*. My turn. Catching my breath, I sit up and examine them fully. Like a beautiful Rodin nude, her skin is as smooth as ivory and a glaring contrast to his, which is vibrant and decorative like Christmas wrapping paper. They are entwined, eagerly awaiting me to join the party. I reach over and stroke him first, then touch her softly, hesitantly.

"You've never been with a woman, have you?" she whispers.

"No," I say honestly. She releases him, angles toward me and kisses me tenderly, clearly relishing being the first. Her tongue tastes like peppermint and wine, her cherubic lips are supple and inviting. She stops momentarily, reaches over me toward the nightstand, grabs the waiting joint, lights it up, and hands it to me.

"Now let me show you what I like," she says with the confidence I only wish I possessed at any age. These millennials—say what you will about them, but they know what they want and are not afraid to take it. She removes the joint from my hand, tokes hard, and then hands it to Jean-Paul. Gently, she guides me over her body—the perky breasts, the taut nipples, her bare mound—as Jean-Paul sits back against the headboard, smoking and watching us with lazy half-mast eyes.

I begin to explore her, taking my time, learning her body, and it's lovely—feminine, soft, and sensual. Like the principal dancer in a ballet that they choreographed, I leap from her to him, back to her. And they, too, begin to rev up the sensual dance—he touches her, then touches me. She's on my breasts, I latch onto hers. She and I then take care of him together. It is all so communal, tangled, and knotted, an erotic game of Twister. Gabe never enters my mind. Not even once.

They orgasm within seconds of each other, and I do too, yet again. They hold each other tightly as I lay next to them, her free arm draped over me—all of us satiated and blissfully depleted. Soon after, they separate, lie on their backs, and we listen to another album. Miles Davis. We laugh about nothing in particular, share a bottle of wine and an extralong crispy baguette in bed. It's all so natural.

Suddenly I do think about Gabe. About standing at the Maginot Line of temptation—the divide between Faithful and Unfaithful. About losing all control. This is what my husband must have felt as he inhaled a strange woman's scent; a not-mine scent. Just like this: slightly breathless, heart beating rapidly, a smoldering, taboo, full-body sensation. No wonder once Gabe started down that forbidden path he could not stop himself. He tasted the apple and wanted the whole damn tree. Once you choose *more*, you want more of more.

Lying here with them, I realize that, like Gabe, I too want more of *more*. Rule No. 10: Guilt-free passion—whatever that means and in whatever form. But unlike Gabe, in my beginner's playbook of exploring uncharted territory—no one gets hurt.

Chapter Fifteen

I wake up feeling strangely elated this morning. Yesterday I spent the entire day at the hotel, rejuvenat-
ing from my night spent with Lea and Jean-Paul. I
slept late, lounged at the pool, worked out, had a mas-
sage, then dinner at the hotel restaurant. Indulgent, but
I don't feel guilty.

It's as though the sexual encounter was an awaken-
ing, igniting an internal lava lamp, a seductive bubbly
levitation. It was a different kind of high than anything
I have ever experienced; a kaleidoscope of sizzling
colors, sounds, scents, sensations that seems to absorb
itself, break apart, and come together in different
forms in my mind. It's as though I have suddenly redis-
covered my appetite for life—not realizing that I was
even hungry. All day yesterday, I chose not to speak

to a single person except for the waitstaff. Selfishly, I wanted to remain in my own head and replay the sexy soundtrack—him/her/me—and then reshuffle the sensual images repeatedly without interruption.

As the hotel staff passed by me at the pool, I couldn't help but wonder if any of them were personal friends of Jean-Paul's, if he bragged about sleeping with the hotel guests, or if they exchanged tales about horny vacationers over drinks. But none of it really matters, I told myself. *Don't make it matter.*

I stretch out in bed, glance over at the nightstand clock, and sit bolt upright. *Christ, it's nearly 11 a.m.* When have I ever slept past 8 a.m.? My usual wake-up time back home is 6 a.m. I liked to get things done around the house before my family woke up and before I had to leave for work. *Shit. My office. I've got to call Rachel today.*

I get out of bed, fling open the curtains and the double doors leading out to the balcony, instantly feeling the warm rays of the sun on my face. In the distance, I see an older woman with what looks like her daughter strolling arm in arm through the spice garden. I watch them for a while, taking pictures of each other and laughing. Suddenly, my elated feeling begins to dissipate, and an old wound fills the void.

I only wish my own mother were someone I could call, cry to through all this, but she's cold and reserved—the last person in the world who could console me. Sadly, she is still the part of me that remains unresolved, the piece that always hurts. She never remarried and barely dated after my father left her for another woman when I was five. I sigh deeply, wrap my arms tightly around myself. *The irony of that.* We never received any child support or alimony from my father, and it was tough making ends meet. My mother claimed she wanted nothing to do with his "dirty money" anyway. We could have used that dirty money plenty of times over the years, I used to think, but I never dared to express that aloud.

Now retired, my mother was a high school English teacher, more absorbed by her books and grading papers than she was by being a mom. I always felt that she cared more about Holden Caulfield than me. She did what she had to do—doctors' appointments, clothing, school supplies, food in the fridge, attended my art exhibits at school, but no extras. She was incredibly organized, but never loving or affectionate or emotional. Any animation she could muster was given to her freshman and junior English classes, where everyone said she was the "best" teacher ever (that always killed me). Although it was just the two of us, there was this impenetrable wall between us, a permanent separation, no matter how hard I tried to break through.

After dinner, she would plan her lessons, grade her papers at the kitchen table, and in order to be near her, I would sculpt at the table quietly. Clay at first and then anything else I could find. Rocks, hangers, coins, pieces of metal. Television was not allowed in our small house (apparently, it ruined the mind), but with art and classical music, I had free rein. Just no paints—the smell irritated her. My mother would make us a big bowl of microwave popcorn, place it at the center of the table, she on one side and me on the other. She'd turn on the classical music station. We didn't talk, we created. That was my childhood. Me, my mother, and the "three Bs"—Bach, Beethoven, and Brahms.

My father, with whom I maintained a distant relationship, having reconnected with him in my late teens, never took a real interest in me or my artistic pursuits. I was determined that I would never be like either of my parents, and when I met Gabe—captain of the football team, smart, funny, with a big, boisterous personality, he became more to me than just a boyfriend: he put noise into my life. His mother was crazy with a mean streak, but his father and two younger sisters were lively and warmhearted. I couldn't get enough of the

Blooms and their highly energetic dysfunction. The yelling—especially at the kitchen table—the loud TV going on in the background at all times. Game shows. Everybody played, everybody talked over one another, shouting out answers and swearing, and I loved it. There was no silence in the Bloom household, ever.

By the time I started college, they had become the only real family I ever had. And, of course, I was an honorary member of Samantha's and Lauren's families too. There was not a single day that I took those relationships for granted. That's how I survived: I had to leave my house to find a home.

The sunlight against my face no longer feels soothing. I step back inside the room, glance at the mirror across from me, seeing the heavy sadness veil my eyes. It's all gone now—my big extended family—that precious noise and cherished camaraderie. I'm orphaned once again, back to the unbearable quiet of that lonely kitchen table of my childhood. Don't go there, I tell my reflection gently. *You woke up feeling good. Don't let the new light extinguish so quickly.*

Perusing the small closet with my limited choices, I settle on a strappy floral sundress—a happy dress— grab my new wide-brim straw hat, aviators, and beach bag. I decide to spend the afternoon exploring

Saint-Jean-Cap-Ferrat, the jewel of the Riviera. According to my guide, back in its heyday in the fifties, Cap-Ferrat was the epitome of glamour, *the* vacation destination for the glitterati. With its magnificent coastline, art galleries, boutiques, and mountainside villas, Cap-Ferrat is known as the "see and be seen" haven for wild parties, soirees, yachting, and fashion shoots. *Sounds perfect.* I encourage myself to push through the pain I'm feeling. The excursion will be light and adventurous, an uplifting diversion from my dark thoughts.

But first things first. I sit on the edge of the bed, glance at my phone. Dozens of emails, texts, from my office, questions about exhibiting artists—everyone needing something—had poured in overnight, adding to the slew of messages that I've ignored since I arrived in France. Rachel's last email message reads like an SOS:

Sophie, call me any time of day or night. I NEED TO TALK TO YOU!

I glance at my phone: 5:15 a.m., Chicago time. I feel a sharp pang tug at my stomach, then I text her:

SOPHIE: Rach, I know it's very early there. You up?
RACHEL: YESS!!

Of course she is. The girl doesn't sleep. Rachel, who has been my assistant for the past five years, who knows what I need before I even say it, answers on the first ring. "Sophie, thank god it's you! I left you like a zillion messages. Are you okay? I got the one message that you were leaving for Paris, and then a second message that you will be spending a few weeks there with Ava. But it's been absolute chaos here without you. The Berland exhibit, you cannot even begin to imagine . . ."

Oh, but I can. Renata Berland is the most difficult artist we've ever worked with, but one of the best. "I know, Rach. I'm so sorry I didn't get in touch with you earlier. I've had to deal with a personal crisis. And I apologize for calling at this crazy hour."

"Don't worry, I'm up. You know I never sleep. Is Ava okay?" she asks, concerned. Rachel and Ava have always liked each other.

"Yes . . . she's okay now," I say, deciding not to elaborate. "But Gabe and I are separating."

The phone goes dead silent. "Gabe? What? No. You two are the perfect couple." I can hear the shock in her voice. Rachel, like everyone else apparently, had a crush on Gabe. His charm followed him wherever he went.

"Far from perfect," I tell her, trying to keep it together. Somehow saying this aloud to Rachel makes it all so real, so permanent. "Here's the thing . . . I'm, well, I need to take some time off." I take a deep breath. *God, this is hard.* "Actually, a lot of time."

"How much time?" she whispers, and I can hear her panic rising. The arts festival begins on August 28— in three weeks. We both know this is crunch time, do or die.

"I know things are tough," I say carefully. "I know Renata is Renata, and I'm so sorry."

"And I'm sorry you are going through hell," she says, and I know she means it. "But this is our biggest show ever, Soph. Nearly one hundred and fifty exhibitors and yes, Renata is off the chain. Please just tell me what you want me to do." She pauses to take a loud, nervous sip of whatever it is she's drinking. I bet it's a Diet Coke even at this early hour. She drinks at least five of those during the work day. It's no wonder she doesn't sleep.

Rachel is on the ledge. I've been there dozens of times with the exhibitors, I get it. "Listen to me closely," I tell her. "You are beyond capable, amazing at what you do, and I know you can handle it all. Give the shit work to the interns, okay. The deal is, I'm not coming back is what I really want to tell you."

Rachel laughs loudly, unnaturally, like a haunted-house actor. "Yeah, right. Is this a joke? The festival is your life, your baby—everyone knows that."

Was my life, was my baby. I release a heavy sigh. "Do you want my job—because it's yours. My life is upside-down right now and I need time to figure it all out. And . . . I need to sculpt again." There, I said it aloud. It's official. Another cat let out of the bag.

"Wait—what? Not coming back?" I can see her shaking that wisp of a blonde ponytail held together by a gaggle of bobby pins, her tortoiseshell glasses fogging up with worry. "You can't just leave, Sophie. I can't do this without you—nobody can."

"Yes, you can," I say gently, hearing the sheer terror in her voice, wishing I could hug her right now. "You have been the backbone of the entire center. I'm sorry to do this to you. Timing is terrible, I know. But I need to take care of me. So, it's all yours, my office, our clients . . ."

"Soph." Rachel, bookish and brilliant, begins to cry. "What if I can't—"

I interrupt her. "I chose you for a reason. Don't doubt yourself. Bye, Rach—you got this." And then I hang up. Just like that. Barely breathing, I fire off a quick email explaining my situation to the board of directors, and then I delete my email account. I erase the part of me that spent the past decade mothering a network of artists, mothering an assistant, mothering a new fine arts center for the community, mothering suburbia's much anticipated summer arts festival, turning North Grove into Burning Man for one week every summer. An annual festival so hip that even city dwellers make the trek to the burbs without complaining. I delete it all. I glance at my phone just to make sure. Gone, wiped out, *finito*. The only contact I have left on my phone and all my networks is my daughter.

I feel an overwhelming surge of relief for a split second, and then just as quickly, the floodgates burst open. *Holy shit, I just deleted my entire life.* I think of Gabe, and my stomach lurches. *No, my life deleted me first.* I was forced into deletion. I start to feel queasy and shaky, and I make a run for the bathroom. I loved my life, my assistant, my artists, my festivals—even Renata and all of her pain-in-the-ass demands.

Perspiration trickles across my forehead and under my arms. I splash water all over me, stare into the mirror at a face I no longer recognize.

What have I done?

Chapter Sixteen

The drive to Cap-Ferrat is just over forty-five minutes and even lovelier than I imagined. The scenic route helps lift my mood, and slowly, with a lot of deep breathing, I allow myself to fall under its spell.

The winding narrow road leading to the center of town is slightly scary in my convertible, and I wish I had one of those vintage Hollywood scarves to wrap around my hair, à la Audrey Hepburn. It's that kind of look, that kind of day. As I navigate the snake turns, I catch glimpses of sprawling villas behind manicured gardens, and beyond, the azure sea blends into the turquoise sky. The sea air is invigorating and once again I feel ageless, lighter, and surprisingly high on life, determined to enjoy the day.

Up ahead in the distance, I see a sign pointing to

the Villa Ephrussi de Rothschild, a palatial seaside museum filled with eighteenth-century art. I decide to check it out—*why not?* I read about the museum and its long-gone proprietor, Béatrice, the socialite daughter of Baron Alphonse de Rothschild, a banker and renowned art collector. At nineteen, she married a hapless Russian banker fifteen years her senior in 1883—a gambler and a cheat, who gave her what sounded like a severe case of syphilis, which prevented her from ever having any children. Finally divorcing the scoundrel after twenty-one years of a miserable marriage, Béatrice turned her attention to her greatest passion: collecting art and creating her dream home filled with masterpieces and furniture. A year before her death in 1934, she bequeathed the mansion to the Académie des Beaux-Arts for the purpose of creating a museum.

I park my car and walk briskly toward the museum, then stop and stare. It's breathtaking. Surrounded by nine gardens and sea views on all sides, the gorgeous rose-colored villa is evocative of an Italian palazzo. I browse my guide for a quick tutorial. The museum boasts a major collection of Sèvres and Vincennes porcelain, Flemish and Beauvais tapestries, and eighteenth-century furniture and paintings. But apparently, the lush exotic gardens steal the show—Japanese, Spanish, Provençal, Florentine, and rose—each with magnificent ornate fountains that are switched on every twenty minutes with a musical accompaniment.

It's so beautiful outside that I decide to check out the gardens first. I sit on a remote stone bench outside the villa to take in all the panoramic beauty and read about each garden. There's no rush. The day is mine. A few minutes later, I hear loud chatter in the distance. I look up and see a group of college students equipped with sketch pads congregating near the rose garden. I smile to myself. I was once them. I remember visiting the Art Institute of Chicago with my class, armed with my sketchbook. I had painted back then, but sculpting was my true love. I remember feeling so important, so cultural, so part of the world I was soon entering. As I reminisce, I watch as the students gather around their instructor and I lean forward in disbelief.

What? No—it can't be.

I take off my sunglasses for a second look. My jaw goes slack. There, standing in front of the students wearing jeans and a royal blue button-down shirt and those same Ray-Bans, looking like George Clooney playing the part of an art teacher, is none other than Olivier Messier. I close my book with a slam. I can barely breathe. *Why the hell is he here?* And then I remember Ava telling me that Olivier was teaching a seminar at the Université de Provence, and she was supposed to join him before they broke up. *Christ, I've got to leave this place before he sees me.*

I wait until Olivier turns around, pull the brim of my hat low on my face, and try to slither out of the garden without being noticed. But that man, I swear, has eyes in the back of his head. Somehow, he turns around at the very same moment I sneak behind his students. I keep walking as I hear him tell the students "just a minute," that he will be right back. His quick steps are approaching and I move faster. *Do I run? Do I hide?*

"Sophie! Sophie!"

Damn, I'm trapped. Just keep going, pretend you don't hear him. *Go where?* Anywhere—before he smothers you with that swarthy charm. Before he tries to kiss you on two cheeks. You're not you right now. You're this other person—the one to whom strange things are inexplicably happening. I feel his long stride sidle up next to me. There's no way out.

"Running away?" He laughs. His voice is husky as he eyes me from head to toe. "What are you doing here? And you look fantastic, by the way."

I ignore the fantastic part. "Olivier, what a surprise." I'm so transparent, so bad at being fake. "I'm spending the day in Cap-Ferrat."

"Alone?"

"No," I lie.

He moves in closer. One eye on me, the other on his students, who have now turned to watch us. "I'm teaching my summer course in Aix. Where are you staying?"

I pause. There's no way I'm giving him that information.

"You're traveling alone, aren't you?" he persists, looking around. "I know Ava left for Spain."

Is she still in contact with this asshole? "I'm meeting someone," I say. *Stay away from my daughter, and stay away from me.*

His eyes glisten. "We should get together."

I purse my lips tightly. There's no chance in hell of that happening. "I don't think that's a good idea," I say, forcing a smile. "But nice to see you. I'm going to go check out the museum and you should probably go back to your students." I gesture to them over my shoulder.

But he ignores the students, leans forward, his warm breath grazes my neck. "I'm here for just two more days with my class. Nights are free. Why don't we get a drink?"

I stop in my tracks. This man is infuriating. "And how *is* Sabine?" I sneer, tossing in a bitchy reminder. "And the kids?" I throw in for good measure. "No drinks. No dinner. No lunch," I say adamantly before he can respond.

Undeterred, he takes a bold step closer. *That musky scent of his is overpowering.* His mouth sets in a hard line. "It's just a drink and conversation—not a lifetime commitment. Really, Sophie, I don't bite."

If Ava knew this conversation was even taking place, she'd feel so betrayed. "Yes, actually, you do."

He lets out a huge belly laugh, the opposite of my intention. "Think about it."

"I don't need to think. It's a hard no. But enjoy your time here." I take a step sideways, but before I can walk past him, he grasps my arm gently with an unmistakable glint in his eye.

"I will call you."

Is he delusional? Did Gabe use those same scripted lines? I feel my face burning up. *Just go.* Leave, and pretend this run-in never happened, but I can't. I turn to face him squarely. "You can't possibly believe that I am interested in you. And if you do, it makes you some kind of monster. Ava is part of every decision I make. But even if Ava were not in this picture, this"—I wag my finger between us—"still wouldn't happen. You see, I'm not very French and apparently not very American these days either, but Sabine exists for me— arrangement or no arrangement."

He squeezes his eyes shut as though physically wounded by my words. A little dramatic, but for a man who lives by a code of pleasure, it's rejection, which I bet rarely happens to him, if ever.

"I am not a total bastard." His pained look turns puppy dog. "I do have a moral compass. Not often, but it's there." He glances over at his students, who are staring at us as though we are a telenovela. "I also follow what's in my heart. As wrong as it is, and I'm sure you're going to hate me for saying this, but I was attracted to you from the very first time I saw you. It was as if Ava had walked into my life as a fully formed woman. Sexy, bold, experienced . . ." His eyes gleam like new pennies, and it takes all of my restraint not to slap him. "It's no coincidence that we are meeting again. I felt we connected at the Rodin and—"

My hands ball into tight fists at my sides. "There was no connection, do you hear me—*zero*. I asked to meet you alone *only* to make sure you ended it properly with my daughter. It was a get-out-of-her-life conversation. That's all—no more, no less."

Olivier shakes his head. "You're overreacting. All I was suggesting is a harmless get-together. One drink," he persists.

"Jesus Christ—no fucking drinks!" I shout loud enough not only for his students to hear, but all of Cap-Ferrat. "Not now, not ever."

On that note, I bolt out of the garden, past the

musical fountain, the museum, the tourists waiting in line, and head straight to the parking lot. Trembling and out of breath, I lean against my car for support, but the hot metal scorches me through the back of my dress. *And fuck you, Gabe.* I scream inside my head, like a wolf howling at the moon. *For making this my life.*

Chapter Seventeen

Exhausted and still traumatized by the Olivier incident, I pull into my hotel around 7 p.m., deciding to order room service and just detox from the day. As I round the driveway to drop off my car, Jean-Paul walks out of the hotel in his tailored suit and tie and slicked-back hair, his colorful tattoos carefully concealed. When he sees it's me behind the wheel, he smiles broadly and I perk up like a wilted flower doused with sugar and water.

"*Bonsoir, madame,*" he says with a naughty grin as he opens the car door.

"If you call me 'madame,' I will have to kill you," I whisper seductively, feeling the instant electricity between us.

"You look beautiful," he says under his breath as he assists me out. The doorman nearby is watching us. "Where were you?"

"Cap-Ferrat for a bit . . . and then I drove to Monaco and walked around."

"So touristy."

"Well, I'm a tourist." My mouth curves into a half-smile as I hand him my car keys. I inhale his spicy aftershave, which smells like a cross between cardamom and cloves. Immediately, the rated-X memory of the other night floods my brain, easily drowning out the Cap-Ferrat fiasco. "You have a better suggestion?" I add demurely. In a split second, I've morphed from me to Jenna Jameson.

His eyes narrow in, his bottom lip distends slightly, eyeing me in the same predatory way he had in his bed when he pinned me down. "Maybe, yes." With a sly smile, he gets into my car and drives off to the private parking lot.

What was that?

I look back, but he's already gone. As I head up to my room, my whole body tingly, I try to decipher "Maybe, yes" and its myriad meanings. The way he looked at me, stripped me with his eyes, was enough material to get me through the night. I remove my clothes, order room service, turn on the TV, and try to decide between two faves that I've seen dozens of times—*Bridget Jones's Diary* or *Under the Tuscan Sun.*

Ten minutes later, I hear knocking at the door. Room service was much quicker than I'd anticipated. "Just a second." I quickly grab one of the plush hotel robes, put it on and answer.

My breath catches in my throat. *Maybe, yes* has turned into a Definite Yes.

My heart races when I see him. "Are you doing room service now?"

Jean-Paul glances behind him. "I have a half-hour break. Can I come in?"

I open the door wider and he walks inside.

"Nice suit," I say.

"It's nicer off." He locks the door behind him. "I will be fired if they find me. So . . ."

"So . . ."

"The other night was good, yes?" Wasting no time for my response, Jean-Paul runs his hands down the length of the opening in my robe, along the curvy lines of my cleavage. I moan softly and then remember my rules: passion without hurting anyone. *Lea.*

I stop his hand from opening my robe any farther and hold it there. "But Lea—"

"What about her?" he says with a shrug. "She's at home painting. Happy."

"Will she be happy knowing that you're here with me without her?" I shake my head, raise my brows in an I-don't-think-so.

"We are open. She has her experiences as well." He looks surprised, as if it's strange that I'm even bringing her up right now.

"But you shared me together. Is that allowed in your rules?"

"Of course. And we don't have rules." Jean-Paul's eyes are wide and unblinking. He lies and I let him. *I want him to lie.* Everyone has rules. Even sexually fluid millennials.

"I'm too old for you." My unconvincing last-ditch effort to give him an out.

He smiles and I see a tiny dimple that I hadn't noticed before. How did I miss that? "You seem very young actually," he says.

I don't know if that is an insult, pointing to my inexperience, or if it's a compliment. He sees the confused look in my eye and rewinds. "My English is not very good. What I meant to say is you are a woman and yes older, but you have much to learn."

And there you go. My face turns flush.

"Wait, I said that wrong too." He places his hands lightly on my shoulders. He's not tall like Gabe. Perhaps just four or five inches taller than me. "It's the language barrier. What I meant is you have much you *want* to learn—am I right?"

"Yes." I nod. "More than you know."

"I know." He runs a long finger through a stray hair sticking to my cheek, pulls it back gently.

"And how do you know that?"

"Lea told me. She sees things that other people don't, the details. A beautiful woman alone in Saint-Paul-de-Vence wearing a wedding ring. She said you either murdered your husband or he hurt you very badly." He takes my hand and leads me toward the bed. It's the only place to actually sit in the room, unless you count the uncomfy decorative chair in the corner.

I laugh nervously. "Lea's right. I murdered my husband."

No one needs to know the details about Gabe. I don't want anyone to feel sorry for me. I couldn't bear it. I glance at my wedding ring. But it is the details that count. My ring . . . I still haven't taken it off. It belonged to Gabe's grandmother and I loved her nearly as much as I loved Gabe. She lived with Gabe's parents until she died, when we were in our late twenties. She was kind and smart, and like Lea, she too saw things that other people didn't see. Gabe's grandmother was her own version of an artist—the things she could crochet—and she was the one who encouraged me to make sculpting my career, to do what I loved. I still miss her and her precious pearls of wisdom. Suddenly without warning, I begin to cry and I can't stop.

"I'm so sorry," I say, wiping the tears, embarrassed. "This is clearly not sexy and definitely not what you came here for. And you have like eight minutes left."

"No . . . still sexy. I like sensitive women," he says, which makes me laugh. "And I have nine minutes. I'm truly sorry about whatever happened to you that has made you so sad. But I don't live in the past or with regrets. I'm here with you now. And Lea would want me to be here too. She wants me to be happy. Be free. That's why we work. I'm not going to lie to her. I will tell her. She tells me. Do you understand me? This is okay."

No rules. No regrets. Never looking back in the past. If only I could be that free.

He runs his hands through my choppy hair, his fingertips trace down along my neck, and I moan aloud—I can't help it. He leans in and kisses my neck lightly, and then my lips hard. "I've thought about you all day. I touched myself this morning, thinking about you and us together."

"And Lea," I say, still feeling guilty.

"Yes, and Lea. But right now, just you. I want *you*."

He takes off his jacket, loosens his tie, undoes his pants and places them neatly over the chair. Just then there's a knock at the door.

"Room service," a woman's voice calls out.

Jean-Paul puts his finger to his lips. "Yes, *merci*," I answer. "Please just leave it at the door and I will take it in a few minutes. *Merci beaucoup.*"

We wait until the footsteps disappear down the corridor. Four minutes left.

"Take me in your mouth now," he orders.

I don't think—I do. I get down on my knees, about to wrap my mouth around him when my phone rings. *Christ.* There is only one caller left on my phone and she is in Barcelona with Jake. I have to take it. From the corner of my eye, I can even see her picture popping up on the phone screen.

Jean-Paul sees my face. "Someone important?"

"Very."

He pulls away, reaches for his pants. "Take it then."

I can't tell if he is angry or annoyed or both. But I lunge for the phone anyway. *Ava first, Ava last.* I'm sorry, I mouth. "Hold on, honey. Let me get into a spot with better reception."

"What time do you get off?" I cup the phone and whisper.

"Ten," he says.

"Come back?"

"Maybe, yes."

"Ava—how are you?" We talked the day after Gabe arrived in Paris, which apparently didn't go so well, and then yesterday morning when she was leaving Paris for Barcelona to meet Jake. Things had improved with Gabe by the time he left for Chicago, and she seemed excited to see Jake again.

"Dad was in a car accident and you need to go home. I think I do too."

"What are you talking about? What kind of accident?" I forget that I hate Gabe, that he betrayed me. Gabe was in an accident. I can barely catch my breath. "Is he . . . okay?"

Ava starts to cry. "I don't know. He's really hurt. And I'm still really mad at him, but please just go take care of him, Mom. Be there for him, like always."

My heart is beating fast. I sit on the bed, shaking. "Ava—please, tell me slowly, exactly what happened."

Her voice is trembling. "Samantha called and told me to tell you. Why wouldn't she have called you directly?"

Because. "Doesn't matter—what did she say?"

"She said that Dad is at Northwestern Hospital with a severe concussion, two broken ribs, and a broken arm. Please go home and fix this. He needs you and I need you to be there for him." Ava in a panic sounds like she's twelve.

"Can I talk to Jake for a minute?"

"Mrs. Bloom?"

"Jake—call me Sophie—listen to me. Ava is all over the place. I want you to take care of her. I'm going to find out exactly what's going on with her dad and I will call you directly. Is she okay . . . are you guys okay?"

"We're good, Mrs. Bloom—Sophie. Not good right now obviously—but you know, good."

"Good," I say, thinking I've got to call Gabe. And if he's not there, I've got to bite the bullet and call Samantha. "Okay, tell Ava I will call back as soon as I have more information. No reason to fly home yet. Just keep her calm. Can you do that, Jake?"

Gabe, Gabe. What happened to you? So much bad stuff has hit our family and now this. *I hate you, but I can't lose you.* I call him. Four rings. *Pick up, damn it.*

"Sophie?"

Thank God. "Gabe, what happened? I just got a call from Ava. She's hysterical. Are you okay?"

"Not my best. I was hit on my way to work by someone who ran a light. I was uh . . . Sophie, where are you? I tried calling you several times but couldn't get through."

You've been deleted. "How bad are you, really?"

He hesitates. His voice is weak. "A few broken ribs, my arm, my head—the headache is excruciating. I won't be able to operate for weeks, maybe more."

"Who's there with you?"

"My mother just stopped by and that just about did me in. And our friends have all been here . . ." He starts coughing, clearly hard for him to breathe.

Lauren? I wonder, barely hearing him choking on his words. They're not "our" friends anymore. "Good," I say absently, stealing Jake's lone, dependable word.

"Soph, I need you. Come home. I know I fucked things up but . . ."

Cabo. The time when Gabe swam out too far and the waves were so choppy. I told him not to go swimming, that there were warnings, but it's Gabe—a challenge is a challenge. Too far means not far enough. He defied the signs and swam anyway and, predictably, got pulled down by the undertow. I watched from the beach, screaming for him. It took two lifeguards to save him and when they did, he lay in my lap on the sand, waterlogged and tears filling his eyes. "I'm sorry I did that to you, Soph. I know I fucked up but I'll never scare you like that again."

"How long will you be in the hospital?" I ask, thinking *should I go to him?*

"I don't know. When are you coming home?"

I have no home. I'm landless. My home is this hotel room.

"Please, I need you," he begs softly.

I think of Jean-Paul and his psychedelic tats, those hard abs, and heavy breath—*I want you*—there's a difference. But Gabe is hurt. Ava's dad is hurt. Think of her, not you.

"I don't know, Gabe. I'm not sure."

"Soph . . ."

"Tell me more again," I say, trying to buy myself time to figure out my next move. "How exactly did the accident happen? Were you alone?"

There is quiet. A pregnant pause. Maybe it's a bad connection. Maybe the concussion?

"Gabe? You there? Gabe?"

"No."

"No—you're not there?"

"I wasn't alone."

"Who was with you?" I hold my breath. I don't allow myself to feel anything. I don't want to know. But I have to know. "Who, Gabe . . . answer me now."

I can hear his difficulty breathing. "A nurse from the hospital. She's hurt bad, much worse than me. She's in surgery now for her—"

"Wait, wait—back up." I literally put up my hand like a school crossing guard stopping the kids from running across the street. I know Gabe. And I know exactly who the injured nurse is. "Holly the nurse? *That* nurse. Are you fucking kidding me?"

Silence. And it's definitely not the concussion. It's guilt this time.

"Get well and goodbye, Gabe."

I lean against the wall and slowly slide down. I stare at his grandma's ring and then remove it. I hold it up to the light and peer through the tiny loop. He almost had me again, drew me in. I was back in Cabo, on the beach, his beautiful head of glistening curls nestled in my lap. I was stroking his drenched forehead. I was praying. For a moment, our past trumped our present. For a moment, I still loved him, still cared. And then along came Holly. And I hate him all over again.

It's 10:05, *Bridget Jones* is almost over. Bridget's running through the snowy streets wearing just a tank top, an unbuttoned sweater, panties, and untied sneakers to get Darcy back. *Go, Bridge, go.* He's not leaving you—I scream inside my head—he's inside that store, buying you another red diary. And then, just before the final kiss, my favorite part, there's a three-tap knock at my door and I realize that *Maybe, yes* is no longer a maybe.

I open the door. Jean-Paul walks in and doesn't wait for my objections, my rules, my regrets, my phone to ring. He doesn't care. He's been parking cars for the past three hours and working the front desk dealing with demanding hotel guests and their room issues. He doesn't need me. *He wants me.* And right now, I don't care if Gabe is concussing. I don't care if Holly the flirty nurse comes out of surgery. I don't care if Lea is at home happily painting body parts or if she's majorly pissed off. I don't care if Olivier Messier is plotting how to seduce me or spending the night with one of his students. I don't care if Ava wants me to go take care of her cheating wounded father. I let my robe fall to the ground. I'm naked and more than ready. My forty-two years old presses up against his taut twenty-seven years young—and you know what—I just don't care.

Chapter Eighteen

The text comes the second I open my eyes the next morning. I hear the *ding*, search around for my reading glasses, and bring the phone up close to my face.

O: Sophie. I am sorry about yesterday.

I sit up, find the glasses on the floor next to the bed, not knowing what to think or how "O" even got my number, and then I remember. I texted him after Ava's procedure in Paris. I'm about to erase his text, block him for good, and then *ding*, another message comes in.

O: Please don't ignore. There's someone you should meet while you are here. She's a sculptor. It is my gift to you, my sincere apology for my behavior.

His gift. Admittedly, a pretty good apology as far as apologies by assholes go. But again, it's Olivier, there's got to be a catch, something in it for him. *Delete, block.* I warn myself. *Do it now.* I tap at the phone, hesitating. The sculptor part is definitely intriguing. *Who is she and why does he want me to meet her?*

I reread the message again, trying to find a clue between the letters. Okay, I'm going to regret this but . . .

SOPHIE: Who?

I stare at the dancing dots as he writes back.

O: First, how long will you be here?

I shake my head. *Now I'm the asshole.* I'm not falling for this. It's a trick question. This time I don't answer. And like the man-child that Olivier is, his patience level does not exceed twenty seconds, and the dots begin to shuffle once again.

O: I'm leaving for Paris tomorrow, if that makes this easier. I won't be around.

I respond.

SOPHIE: It does. Will be in Provence for a while. Who is the sculptor?

The dancing dots appear and then:

O: Nathalie Senard. You've heard of her?

I nearly drop the phone on my sheets. *Heard of her?* Who in the art world has not heard of Nathalie Senard and her handsome husband, the painter Luc Senard? It's like asking a teenager if they've heard of Beyoncé and Jay-Z.

Nathalie, who is only in her midforties, has paved the way for contemporary women sculptors. She is famous for her larger-than-life Amazonian sculptures of women made out of every medium—metal, glass, clay, but particularly marble—always in powerful poses. Nathalie Senard's women—"Les Bitches," as the French press lovingly refers to her sculptures—are synonymous with Joan of Arc in stilettos. Her pieces have even been featured in several popular movies, both American and French. I can barely breathe. *How does Olivier know her, and why does he want me to meet her?*

In my excitement, I forget that I despise him. I pick up the phone and call him.

He laughs. "I had a feeling . . ."

"I'm sure you did. What is your connection to Nathalie Senard?" I don't mention that she is an idol of mine, because it sounds pathetically fangirl. Nor will I tell him that one reviewer actually compared my "Mermaids and Madmen" exhibit to her work. It was the greatest compliment I ever received.

"Nathalie and I go way back, since art school," Olivier explains, and then, as if reading my mind, he adds, "and no—we were not together. Just friends. Believe it or not, Sophie, despite popular opinion, I actually *do* have a few of those. Her husband is a wonderful painter in his own right, but Nathalie is in a league of her own." He sips something loudly into the phone. Probably the first of his daily espresso lineup. "But what I'm about to tell you is between us . . . can I trust you to keep it that way?"

I nod to myself. "Yes, of course."

He takes a long, drawn-out breath. "She's dying. Ovarian cancer. Stage four. They've done everything they can for her. The best doctors, all the possible treatments. It was discovered late and Nathalie has just months left to live."

"What?" I gasp, shocked by the news. "That's devastating. And yet, I've read nothing about it."

"No one has. It's not public knowledge. The Senards have paid a lot of money to keep her illness out of the press for as long as they can. They have lots of friends in high places. But between us, she has stopped all treatment because she wants to finish her final installation . . . which is truly magnificent." He clears his throat and doesn't try to hide the sadness in his voice. "The treatment has been brutal on her body, her hands. It incapacitates her. But she is determined to fight this until the end. For Nathalie, the art, of course, always comes first—even before her health. Anyway, I've put together an exhibition for her—an unveiling of this last sculpture. It will be held in Paris, at the Musée d'Orsay in mid-October." I can hear the click of a lighter as Olivier sparks up a cigarette, and then his protracted exhale. "I'm scared she might not make it until then, and though she doesn't say it, so is she."

I feel sick to my stomach with this knowledge. What a true loss of one of the greatest talents. She must mean a lot to Olivier.

"The problem is Nathalie is very stubborn, determined to finish her work all on her own, refusing to accept assistance," Olivier continues. "But the woman can barely hold a chisel. She needs help. I don't know how she would receive this—it's a long shot. But I think *you* could help her."

"Me?" I'm taken aback. "I haven't sculpted in years. Not just years, Olivier, but *fourteen* years."

"I know . . . but I've seen the images of your work, from Ava. Your technique, especially with marble and women . . . there's something there that reminds me of Nathalie's work—especially the shine. I can't explain it."

The shine, my signature. Everyone used to talk about the gleam of my sculptures. But that Sophie Bloom is gone and buried, a suburban relic.

My mind wanders from Olivier to "Mermaids and Madmen." That exhibit was volatile, passionate, and it took everything out of me to create. I had tapped into the sheer elation of being pregnant and about to give birth to Ava—I was so young then, so in love with Gabe—and overwhelmed by that precious moment of Ava's birth. Seven giant marble mermaids materialized out of those joyous emotions—frolicking, swimming, diving, fins flapping—such freedom depicted in those sculptures. And then . . . it was followed by the ugly— the nemeses—seven monsters rising up out of the ashes of a postpartum depression so aggressive that I never thought I would come out from under it. I had turned gleaming blocks of black marble crisscrossed with veins of gold into vicious, violent creatures of the night. It was a shocking display of extremes that put my name on everyone's radar in the art world, especially because I was so young—just shy of twenty-six when I finished it.

But I owe it all to Samantha and Lauren. Just weeks after Ava was born, I couldn't get of bed, could barely lift my head off the pillow. I hardly remember Ava or Gabe during that dark period, just whirring silhouettes that would move in and out of our bedroom. Samantha and Lauren didn't leave my side during those lost, melancholic months, encouraging me—*begging me*—to sculpt during the worst of it, shoving instruments into my limp hands—anything to bring me back to life, back to me. And eventually, their joint maternal force overpowered the darkness.

I remember the day, the exact moment when everything changed, when I finally got out of that bed. It was a breezy, sunny morning, nearly thirteen weeks after I'd given birth, and I lay awake watching the golden rays from the window traverse my covers, demanding that I rise, urging me to come back to me. Obeying finally, I threw off my sticky pajamas and walked naked into my tiny studio, which was adjacent to our bedroom. I knew after the first chisel, that everything I had been feeling would hemorrhage out of me, through my hands. "Mermaids and Madmen" emerged two years later from the ashes of my greatest joy and my deepest pain.

But that was so many years ago. I'm not that same sculptor anymore. I get up out of the bed and pace the room naked. I then grab a robe and cover up, as though Olivier could see me through the phone. "Why me, Olivier? I'm sure there are brilliant young artists you know who are French, who sculpt daily. I'm—"

"You," he interrupts, "have the one quality that may just appeal to Nathalie—your anonymity. You are a stranger here who knows no one in our community, and could quietly help her with no one finding out about it. You don't strike me as a braggart and god knows, you're overprotective. And, you are ready to work again, *oui?* I saw it in your eyes at the Rodin—"

"Don't even start with that," I warn him. *Yes, Olivier, I'm dying to sculpt again, to wrap my hands around tools, to feel the coolness of marble against my fingertips.*

"Nathalie has a studio in Paris and one in Èze. She's there now. Where are you staying?"

Èze is about forty minutes away, I calculate. "I prefer not to say, but not far."

"You're as difficult as she is," he says, not hiding his irritation. "Okay have it your way. But is this something you would want to do—*can do*—before I ask her? And will you stay here until it's done?"

I want to do it with all my heart, but *can I do it* is a different story. This opportunity won't come knocking again. *Don't be afraid of it.* "Yes, Olivier, I want this," I say adamantly. I press my lips tightly. "I'll stay as long as it takes."

"Excellent. Then I will talk to her, and hopefully, convince her. I must warn you that Nathalie is very difficult and demanding." He pauses for another long drag on his cigarette. "She was difficult even when she was well and now, understandably, it's much worse . . ."

Suddenly, I feel a sharp pang in my chest, like a stab. *What if I disappoint her? She doesn't have much time left.* I sit back on the bed as the panic sets in. It's Nathalie Senard we're talking about. "Maybe the timing is wrong, Olivier. I'm not a sculptor anymore," I stammer. "I need practice. Maybe you are better off finding someone else."

"The timing is *only* now, and yes, you are." Olivier cuts me off. "Talent at your level doesn't disappear. It's just hibernating. I believe you are exactly what Nathalie needs to cross the finish line. I thought about it last night. I feel it. When I feel things here"—I picture him pointing to his gut—"I'm never wrong. Especially about art—never."

"There's always a first time," I counter softly. I hate this man but at this very moment, I kind of love him.

"Look, I will show her images of your work and ask her to consider this proposal." His voice is cautious. "I know Nathalie—her damn pride, her strong sense of dignity. You would not get any credit. You would be a ghost. Can you handle that?"

"One hundred percent yes."

"Sophie . . ." My name lingers a little too long on his breath.

Here's the catch. Right now. I feel it. "Yes?" I clench my teeth in anticipation of the fine print. *Please don't make me hate you all over again.*

"I can't promise anything, but I will try my best."

I heave a deep sigh of relief right into the phone. "Thank you, Olivier. I mean it."

We hang up, surprisingly, without any strings attached. I climb back into bed, pull the covers up to my chin. I stare up at the ceiling. *Nathalie Senard . . .* If this works out and she agrees to me coming on board, I will be Olivier's parting gift to his precious friend before she dies. And ironically, his gift to her is also a gift to me. Sadly, I may be finding my new beginning with someone else's ending.

Chapter Nineteen

I spend the rest of the day roaming the village of Saint-Paul. I walk in and out of boutiques and galleries for a good two hours, then have a late lunch at a tiny bistro with a magnificent view overlooking all of the village. I enjoy a delectable dish of *escalope de mérou au citron*, sea bass in lime, then indulge in a two-scoop Nutella gelato for the finale, topping if off with my third cappuccino of the day.

I keep checking my phone. Olivier said he will call as soon as he speaks to her. *Stop checking.* To keep my mind occupied, I decide to google Nathalie instead. An interview from the *Paris Match* three years ago pops up, headlined "The Power Art Couple." I peruse the long interview and pretend to understand the French. After a while I give up on the content, but stare at the incredible photographs of the Senards taken at Le Jardin Exotique d'Èze—the exotic garden—apparently her husband's favorite spot and where a few of her famous sculptures of women are installed amid the flowers, succulents, and cacti. I zoom in on each photo and check out all the details closely. The gorgeous couple stands intertwined, arm in arm, leaning against the mountaintop garden's protective stone wall overlooking the coastline below, next to a giant marble sculpture of a woman with her arms raised high as though she is about to fly. The wind rustles through Nathalie's long blonde hair, Luc's arm wraps tightly around her waist. Partners, lovers, artists. I stare at the photo for so long that their features begin to merge from two people to one. So much love and beauty this couple has brought into the world, and obviously to each other. Tears prick at the corner of my eyes, then the guilt sets in, and the excitement turns to gloom. *And now she's dying. His heart must be breaking. She's dying . . . and her illness may just be my big break.*

I'm not surprised when I return to the hotel later that evening that Lea has left me a message. Jean-Paul had his turn and now she wants hers. Everyone, it seems, wants a piece of me. I stare into the small, narrow closet mirror. I look so put together—

the hair, the dress, the makeup—but the truth is, it's all a lie. The damn truth is I really just want to click my ruby red slippers and reclaim my old life. I sigh loudly. But there is no Kansas anymore. I slip off my dress and watch it fall into a black puddle around my feet. I kick it away, glancing at the nightstand clock. Nearly seven p.m. Maybe I can catch Ava.

"Mom?" Ava answers on the first ring. *That voice. God, I miss her.*

"Hi, honey, how are you?"

"I'm good now. I spoke to Dad this morning and he said he's feeling better and will be out of the hospital tomorrow. He told me to stay in Barcelona. So Jake and I decided to stay but we cut our trip short. I'm heading back to Chicago at the end of next week." She pauses. "When are you coming home?"

I feel a hard twitch in my stomach. Do I tell her about Olivier? No. It doesn't matter—even if it does. "I don't know yet . . ." I say evasively. "But as soon as I figure it out, you will be the first to know. Tell me, are you and Jake having fun?"

"Yes, we're good. Right, Jake?" I can practically see the way she is looking at him. Her lively dancing eyes. And Jake smiling back at her with that dumbass frat-boy grin of his. Though he's not dumb. He just parties as hard as he studies. *They're good.* I smile to myself. Somehow, they are finding their way back, post-Monica, post-Olivier. Could I ever be that forgiving? Could I ever find my way back to Gabe?

I think back to the one time when we broke up for three weeks during college, and it was all my fault. Gabe was studying at the University of Wisconsin–Madison, where Ava also goes to school, and I was at Northwestern. Two and a half hours separated us and yet we somehow made it work, alternating weekend visits. That particular weekend it was my turn to travel his way. It was late Thursday night and I was working hard in the art studio because I knew I would lose the weekend and had to finish a piece. A few of my sorority sisters barged into the studio and insisted I go with them to the Sigma Chi fraternity party. I just wanted to sculpt and not be bothered. They literally pulled me out of the studio with plaster all over me. Nancy, who was also my roommate, was carrying my going-out clothes with her—a miniskirt, a cropped top, and boots—which meant I had no excuses. So, I went with them reluctantly, and unfortunately for me, I stayed, as in all night. There was a local band playing cover songs on the fraternity's front lawn. It got crazy, and I downed several shots of tequila and a few plastic cups full of rancid neon yellow Everclear mixed with pineapple juice. I found myself lying in a bed in a dark musty room at some point during the night. Everything was so brown, so muddy, even the ceiling. I remember the wood-paneled walls spinning around me and that the room smelled like urine mixed with Clorox mixed with body odor. I was a sophomore and the guy lying next to me was the frat house president. I had seen him around campus but never officially met him until that night. I knew I should have left with my friends, but I was drunk and wanted to stay. I missed my ride to Madison the next morning to see Gabe. I didn't sleep with Sig Chi's president but it got close—what was his name— *Mark, Craig?* After at least a dozen calls discussing "the situation" with Samantha and Lauren, I decided not to lie. Terrified, I told Gabe the truth and we broke up. He wouldn't talk to me—though I begged, apologized, left him one hundred messages. Two and a half weeks later, he finally called me back and said simply, "Now, we're even. Do you want to get back together?" And I did. Tit for tat. We never talked about it. *Why didn't we ever talk about it?* Gabe had evened the score and that was all that mattered.

Are Ava and Jake even? He was with Monica, but she had an affair with her professor. Am I supposed to somehow even the score with Gabe? My mind wanders to the nurse in the ICU recovering from that car accident. Did he sleep with her the night before? Did he take her to our home, to our bed? Did she sleep on my side? It just doesn't end. There is no evening it up.

Ava shares a few details about their trip—the Miró museum, the Sagrada Família. Her animated descriptions move through my brain but my thoughts are elsewhere. I can feel the exuberance in her voice, and it's enough.

"Mom, are you there?"

I snap back to the present. "Here."

"How are you—really?"

"I'm . . . I'm really pretty good, managing."

"Managing?" Ava pauses, clearly not convinced. "Have you met any friends? Who do you go out with for dinner? I just can't picture you eating alone."

If she only knew about Jean-Paul and Lea. My face instantly flushes. *What kind of mother does that?*

"I cut my hair," I tell her. That should change the subject quickly.

"What?! You've had that same style since forever. Short? I'm FaceTiming you right now. Don't move."

I quickly put on a robe and take the phone with me out to the balcony, and she calls back. I see her beautiful face light up the phone screen, and at the sight of her I feel my eyes swimming with tears. *I really miss her.*

"I love it!" she shrieks. I can see that she and Jake are sitting in an outdoor café. "Look at my mom. So hip. And . . . you got highlights."

I laugh, happy that she approves.

Ava is drinking wine. She takes a sip and holds up her glass as proof that yes, she's only nineteen and underage in the States, but in Europe, wine is ageless. No fake ID required. Her carefree gaze waxes serious. She does this squinty thing with her eyes that Gabe does. She puts the glass down.

"By the way, why aren't you talking to Samantha?" Her face is now up close to the phone, as if she's trying to gauge my real reaction. "What's up with that?"

There is no way that I am going to tell her about what happened with Lauren and Samantha. "How about we discuss that another time," I say.

Ava's eyebrows narrow in. She is reluctant to let it go. "Hmmm. Okay . . . well, I'm still really upset about things with you and Dad." Her eyes flicker with sadness. "You know that, right?"

"I know. Me too, baby." My heart breaks, aware of how much all this is hurting her. I can actually feel it cracking.

"But I really hope you are okay. Jake—say hi to my mom," she says brightly, her moods changing with the wind, as always. She then presses her mouth to the phone and a giant kiss appears in the miniature screen. So resilient. How does she do it? A boyfriend breakup, losing her best girlfriend, an affair with her married professor, a pregnancy scare, our marriage breaking up, and *poof*—back to being Ava. Unlike me, falling apart at forty-two and unable to catch myself.

Jake sticks his head into the phone screen to say hello. His hair is longer than I remember and his face is scruffy. He smiles that silly smirk but it looks right on him. He looks happy.

Ava grabs the phone back. "No matter what, I will see you in three weeks for college drop-off. Can you believe it's our last one? Love you, Mom."

I stare at the phone, long after we say goodbye, calculating the timing. *Three weeks.* It's just not enough time. Ava automatically assumes I will be on a plane to North Grove and taking her back to school as usual. Why wouldn't she? I'm her mother. That's what I do. I'm a given. And what if . . . it *does* work out with Nathalie Senard? I place my hand on my chest, feeling the quickening of my breath. *I don't want to go back, not like this, still in pieces.* And they will all be there— Gabe, Lauren, Samantha, Eric, and Matt—their lives the same, continuing on without me. Did Gabe and

Lauren discuss that I know what happened between them? Was it only one time? *Goddamnit—how could they do that to me?*

I bring my knees up to my chest into a fetal position on the cushy balcony chair. I just want to rewind, start again from the very beginning. Gabe and I should have talked about the Sigma Chi incident back in college—as if evening up the score were enough. There are so many things we should have talked about over the years, but didn't. Instead we clung to our history, to all of our firsts—we held on to a version of us that no longer existed.

Three weeks . . . what then?

Chapter Twenty

I call Lea back because I don't want to be alone any longer with my thoughts, which are becoming increasingly bleak and anxious. She answers the phone right away.

"I was wondering when you'd return." Her voice is soft, seductive. "How are you?"

I avoid answering that. "How are you?" I ask instead, leaning over the balcony. No one is around except random cleaning staff roaming the grounds.

"Great. There's an interesting exhibit opening in Nice tonight—a friend from one of the galleries in town organized it. Around nine. You want to come?"

"Jean-Paul too?"

She pauses just enough to take a long drag on her cigarette. I hear her breathy exhale. "Just me."

I didn't see Jean-Paul when I arrived at the hotel earlier, but I wonder if he is here. *Or with someone else?* I feel a twinge of jealousy and let it pass. "Yes, I'd love to." Anything not to be with me right now, alone inside my head.

"Pick me up," she says. It's an order not a question.

When I pick up Lea at her apartment, I notice how clean and organized it is and that it smells lemony. The other night, the place was a disarray of clothes and art supplies, and reeked of marijuana. And she looks different too. Not all hippy artist, rather sophisticated and clubby in tight black shorts, a black tank, gladiator sandals, and bright red lipstick. Her hair is pulled back into a high sleek ponytail, reminiscent of Madonna circa the Blond Ambition tour, which of course I saw with Samantha and Lauren. Her colorful geometric earrings dangle like a Calder mobile. She looks sexy and elegant at the same time.

"Wow, you look fabulous." I glance down at my skinny capri jeans, sandals, and flowy halter top. A very suburban-mom-getting-salad-or-sushi outfit. *Why did I wear this?* "I feel underdressed."

"You're perfect."

She kisses me hard on the mouth, as if she now has the license to do that. I pull back reflexively. Though we shared a bed the other night, I cannot help but think of Ava. How I wish I could be edgy, carefree, and twentysomething again, and slide my tongue into Lea's inviting mouth, but I'm not and I can't. Perhaps I shouldn't have come. What was I expecting? To sit cross-legged on the floor with a bottle of Tito's and braid each other's hair?

"Something wrong?" She regains ground, takes a step toward me. I recognize her perfume. That same Fragonard scent I had smoothed on the other night while I was in the bathroom.

I hesitate because I'm not sure how to articulate how I feel. I clear my throat, point toward the chairs around the kitchen table. I sit down and she sits next to me, her bare leg pressing against my jeans. I pull away just enough to allow a slim ray of air between us and not be rude.

"You're lovely," I say because it's true and I can't ignore the other night's acrobatics. "But I'm not gay, not bisexual, not pansexual. The truth is . . ." *What is the truth? Does it even matter?*

She grins, reaches for the pack of cigarettes lying at the center of the table. "I know. Our lifestyle is a bit radical."

"It's not that I didn't enjoy the other night—I did. It's just that suddenly you remind me of my nineteen-year-old daughter, whom I miss terribly. And my life is a bit of a hot mess. And all of this just feels . . ." *Icky*, which I don't say.

She lights a cigarette, offers me one, and I take it even though I don't smoke. This is a smoking conversation. "Funny, you didn't complain the other night," she says. "What changed?"

Me. I changed. I keep changing by the nanosecond. I don't know Lea well enough to even tell her that. I think about all my ambitious rules, which I had created that first night—the Unbreakables list. They're unrealistic. Not even doable. I mean do I really want to hear Carly Simon right now belt out "Anticipation"? Do I really want to be the best version of myself, climb the highest mountain, ride a horse into the sunset? Do I really want to dine alone and pretend I'm bold and daring? Do I really want to be sexually free and easy and be surprised by life? Those rules for the new, improved Me are like Facebook—an alternate reality to the life I *want* to lead but that doesn't really exist. Perhaps, I have to slow it all down and digest. Maybe that's the problem. I'm skipping steps, leapfrogging the pain, and I can't. I have to go through the grieving process to get to the other side like everybody else. I'm not an emotional Olympian. I can't outrun grief and hurdle betrayal and then walk off with the *I Did It* medals if I don't do the time.

"You look like you could use a drink. Maybe two." Lea gets up and heads toward her pantry and pulls out a bottle of red. I follow her to help with the glasses.

We sit back down at the kitchen table. She pours, I talk. "I probably should explain . . . I've been through a huge personal trauma. My husband cheated on me and it has destroyed me. I came here to figure it all out. And on Day One I met you and Jean-Paul. So you could say that the night we spent together was more than radical for me—it was mind-blowing. My emotions keep shifting, and I just can't keep up."

Lea nods, absorbing it all, and then it hits me. Perhaps I'm having postpartum depression Part II. Separating from Gabe has been so similar to what I felt after having given birth to Ava. The only way to describe it is a perpetual fall, a rock-bottom sense of hopelessness.

Lea smokes and listens patiently. I keep talking, rambling. "I really don't want my marriage to end. I liked my life. Was there passion? Now and then. Comfort, yes." I sip my wine and she says nothing, so I keep going. "The night that I found out my husband was cheating was on my birthday. And the crazy part is that earlier that same night he wanted to fool around, but I pushed him away. I stood in my closet mirror like a porn star in heels and panties and pushed his hands off me because we were going to be late for our dinner.

In the old days, when everything was still new, time never trumped fucking, right? I think that's what Gabe wanted—what he was clearly starving for—no boundaries, no one saying, 'Get off my boobs, we will be late for our dinner party.' We became an Old Married Couple and no matter what you do, you simply can't Benjamin Button that."

I take another cigarette, light it up. Lea probably has no idea what I'm even saying. "The thing is, I didn't see him anymore. Gabe was no longer a man to me. He became a habit, like brushing my teeth. I have to take responsibility for that. He betrayed me in the worst way possible, but infidelity is a two-way street."

When I'm done with my Hamletesque soliloquy, Lea folds her arms, tilts her head with knitted brows as though she is Dr. Freud psychoanalyzing me. Infidelity is just another day at the office for her and Jean-Paul. It's their way of life, but not mine. Tears sting my eyes. "I didn't see it coming," I whisper. "That's the part that really gets me. I thought I was so in control, when really I was totally blind to what was going on around me."

"Or perhaps you wanted to be."

"There's that." I raise my glass.

"And now?" She leans in closer, our legs touch again. "What do you see?"

"Just flashes of truth, pop-up memories, and it hurts like hell." I search her lovely, caring face. Her skin is like porcelain and lineless. I would kill for that dewy uninjected skin; so would about forty other women I know. Had I been following my Unbreakables list, going to bed with Lea again would surely be the best diversion from all of this. I sigh deeply. No matter how much I want to, I can't separate sex from my emotional state. "Look, I really did enjoy the other night, don't get me wrong. And I couldn't stop thinking about it, but I just can't . . . I guess I'm old-fashioned at heart."

Lea arches a brow, accompanied by a wry smile. "Jean-Paul told me everything. Not so old-fashioned."

I blush. It's true. I did things with him in my hotel room last night that I had never done before. But it was just after that phone call with Gabe. It was angry sex. Revenge sex. Against-the-wall only-in-the-movies sex. On-the-balcony sex. Three back-to-back orgasms in one night—my record sex. But Jean-Paul is not mine. He was borrowed. "Jean-Paul is yours. And thank you for sharing him. But that too is not going to happen again." I decide this as I'm saying it.

"I don't own him." She snaps at me in a way that I'm not sure if it's angry or French. "He makes his own decisions." She takes another long drag off her cigarette. I watch it burn halfway up.

"Jean-Paul doesn't have to be anybody else's, you know," I say carefully. "He can be just yours."

Lea rolls her eyes. "Boring."

"You know that's not true. He is far from boring. And you—"

Her eyes become fiery. I just struck a nerve. "Look, Sophie, I respect your decisions. But please don't try and make mine." She points the cigarette between my eyes, a bright orange bull's-eye. "Commitment brings pain and monogamy is bullshit, a waste. Life is short and brutally unpredictable. I accept what is, not what should be."

She definitely has a point. Commitment is a lie, but for that precious time when it is real and good and romantic, nothing beats it. Even with everything that happened, I wouldn't trade my marriage with Gabe, especially the early years, for anything.

We are quiet for a while. Lea sips her wine. I eye her curiously. There is clearly something else lurking there beneath the surface. It's strange how much she reminds me of Ava: that fiercely independent streak, the way she carries herself, headstrong, proud, and defiant.

Her face changes color slightly, a rosy bridge across her milky complexion. "I lost my mother at a young age. It was devastating. It changed me. I was forced to grow up too quickly. I learned what really matters, what doesn't. All this pain you have—it's just not worth it. Trust me. Let it go before it strangles you."

I reach over and place my hand on top of hers. "I'm deeply sorry for your loss, and I really appreciate that you are listening to all of this. On a different level, I lost my father. He abandoned me and my mother when I was five. He started a whole new family and I wasn't part of his world. I didn't matter to him. But even worse, I lost my mother then too. She was there physically but not present at all. I could never get close to her, no matter how hard I tried. She never recovered from him leaving her for another woman. I don't want to be like that, Lea—*like her.* Bitter and alone. And that terrifies me the most—what if I'm never able to let go of this pain?"

She studies me for an uncomfortable minute or two, then stands. "Can I show you something?"

"Of course."

She takes my hand and leads me across the room. She unlocks a door that opens to a small room the size of my walk-in closet at home. She enters, but I stop at the threshold and peer inside, blown away by what I see. Hundreds of enlarged black-and-white photographs of women's faces cover the walls from floor to ceiling— even the ceiling. Not models, but real women: young, old, fat, thin, wise-looking, interesting, beautiful, and ugly-beautiful. Each face is soulful and expressive, each radiates a unique quality. Whatever this is, it's magnificent. I slowly enter the room and all my senses are roused simultaneously. The faces are so alive. It's as if I can actually hear the depth of their laughter, the shrill of their cries, even tears of joy—so much emotion is popping out of each photograph. "Who are they?" I murmur as I make a panoramic sweep of the room.

Lea's eyes light up. "This was Jean-Paul's gift to me a few years ago. These women are strangers and yet they are now part of me. He is so talented. I tell him that all the time. I come in here whenever I feel lost, when I need to center myself. I have those days just like you, when it all hurts, when I doubt everything, and I miss my mother. But in here, my sanctuary, I have so many women surrounding me, to mother me, sister me, friend me—so that I'm never really alone." She whirls around. "He did this for me out of love. This—not who we sleep with—is our version of commitment. It's about what we give to each other, *not* what we take away."

I gaze with appreciation at this French no-nonsense Tinker Bell. Turning slightly, I reach out and graze the walls lightly with my fingertips. One particular photo stands out. It is of an old Italian-looking grandmother with glistening jet-black hair. There are so many life-lines carved into her face that the topography of her wrinkled skin looks like a road map. "This is spectacular and should be displayed in a gallery, not holed up and hidden away."

Lea shakes her head, juts her bottom lip defiantly. "This is *my* gallery. And yes—it's an exhibit like no other. But some art is not for others, you know. Some art is meant just for you."

I get it. "Can we skip that exhibit in Nice and just hang here for a while?"

She nods, smiles, then goes back into the other room, and returns several minutes later, standing in the doorway with paintbrushes in her hand. "We will stay but on one condition. Since we've established that we are not going to bed together, you are going to paint with me."

Bossy. I laugh, but shake my head no. "I'm not a painter."

"All I've heard tonight is everything you're not."

She gestures for me to join her back in the main room. She hands me a paintbrush. "You told me the other night that you haven't sculpted for years. So I researched you and saw old photos of your work. You're very talented. Do you want to know what I really think?"

By the look in her eyes, probably not.

"I think you are afraid *not* of your husband's betrayal but of yourself. Reclaiming your own power.

You are terrified to bring your talent to the surface again. You say your husband abandoned you"—she points her brush at me—"but I think *you* abandoned you long before that." Her gaze is faraway, but her potent words linger. "My mother used to tell me when I doubted myself that no one wants to be with a shell. Be the pearl, Sophie, and you will find you again."

We change out of our clothes into sweats and oversized T-shirts that probably belong to Jean-Paul, and it all feels a bit like a teenage sleepover. Lea blasts out a young French singer who is covering Janis Joplin's "Piece of My Heart."

"First you paint me and then I will paint you," she says firmly. "We each get an hour."

I shrug and don't even try to argue. "Fine, whatever."

Lea's hair is loose now, freed from the tight ponytail and draping around her face like heavy theater curtains. I paint her as I feel her. Not as a person or a figure, but as bold, fiery colors. My version of her is all purple, orange, and red. I don't think, I just paint broad mercurial brushstrokes, swirls and slashes and dashes of strong, provocative color. As novice of a painter as I am, I'm really enjoying this.

And then it's her turn. I sit on the bed, legs curled to

my chest, and pose for her. "Close your eyes," she calls out. "Don't be so uptight. Let it all go."

After her painting hour is up, I expect that we would examine each other's work. But once again, I am wrong. Once again, Lea surprises me. She doesn't even glance at my canvas. Instead, she takes me by the hand and leads me back into the Women's Room. I follow Lea blindly, having no idea what her plan is, but knowing better than to question her modus operandi. She was definitely a general or a prison warden in her last life.

"Stay here. I'll be back." She lightly kisses my cheek, then quickly shuts the door behind her and locks it before I can respond.

I stare at the locked door and I'm immediately claustrophobic. Why did she lock me in here? What was I thinking? Maybe Lea is crazy. Maybe I'm crazier to have trusted her. Maybe she really is pissed off that I had three orgasms with Jean-Paul and I'm not evening up the score with her. I start to panic and bang on the door. "Damn it, Lea—let me out! Open the door now!"

"Relax," she says calmly from the other side. "I'm not going anywhere. This is for you. Trust me, okay."

Trust her? I don't know her. I mean I know her, but not really. I lean against the door and eye all the women staring back at me. Before they welcomed me and now they are judging me. The bright-eyed blonde with a large mole near her lip, the pursed-lipped middle-aged woman with a perm and crooked teeth, the sexy redhead with light green eyes and long lashes with a perfect rosebud mouth. The serious-looking Asian woman with spiked hair and Harry Potter glasses. The beaming black woman with a huge afro and sparkling eyes. And the old Italian mama's unwavering gaze has seemingly hardened. So many women—so many expressions that they all begin to merge in a haunting way. *Get a hold of yourself.* And then the tears begin to fall once again. I've cried more in the past few weeks than I have in my entire life.

I cry for me and for all of them. None of us gets by on a free ride. I cry for a marriage that I thought would last forever, but fell apart right under my nose. I cry for Ava and our soon to be broken family. I cry for my mother, the one I had and the imaginary one I always wanted. Finally, I cry for Samantha and Lauren— mourning the loss of my two best friends. Despite everything, I really miss them. My gaze lands hard on the photograph of the redhead—she reminds me so much of Lauren. Instantly, I stop crying and then I freeze.

Was it more than just a one-night stand? Was Lauren in love with Gabe all along? And him with her? My head begins to spin. There was that Nashville trip when that one-night stand apparently happened. But there was more . . . that weird moment during our trip to Italy when our group was together at dinner and I caught them looking at each other across the table in a way that wasn't brotherly and sisterly—the way I am with Eric and Matt, the way Samantha is with Gabe and Matt. I thought I had imagined it, because when I looked again, it passed as though it never happened. But it did. I felt it inside my body and said nothing. Why? Was I too afraid to hear the truth? And that biking trip in Michigan, two years before Nashville, when Lauren hurt her ankle and she leaned up against Gabe, while he held the ice pack against her leg and then lightly massaged her foot. Where was Matt? Why didn't I question that?

Pressing my face right up to the redhead's photo, I stare into her green eyes accusingly, demanding answers. And there were more looks, right? Before that . . . way, way before that. Senior prom, the second-to-last slow dance, the teen band was singing "With or Without You." I followed Gabe's straying gaze to the other side of the room, to where Lauren was standing. Lauren, with her long cascading russet hair, leaning against the gym's back wall, laughing with Tommy Winslow, her date that night. Laughing with Tommy but actually staring back at Gabe—that same long, lingering look. Her full breasts were bobbing from that low-cut blue dress that we got together at Marshall Field's—mine was a similar version but in red.

I can barely breathe. *Was it Lauren all along?* Did they stop themselves from each other because of me? And because of Matt, Gabe's best friend and her husband? Was Gabe my One, and Lauren his? Did Samantha know this? Did Matt see things, feel them too? The women surrounding me now become my jury. Their silent voices culminate into a Greek chorus collective verdict: *It was Lauren all along.* The Ashley Madison moms, Holly the nurse, the hot bartender, the personal trainer, and me, and most likely more—we were all merely substitutes. Gabe was too loyal in his disloyalty, too dedicated to us and to our group of friends to ever reveal the truth about Lauren to me, or perhaps even to himself.

I cry harder. Our marriage failure was not about comfort or lack of passion, but really about him carrying a torch for Lauren and hiding it. I cry until the tears thin out into drips, leaving in their wake a void so deep that Lea with all her might and infinite wisdom cannot save me. The truth is not brutal—it's decapitating. It severs any hope, any thoughts of reconciliation or forgiveness. Perhaps I was never Gabe's first—I was his second, the consolation prize. No wonder he couldn't be faithful. I wasn't the one he was cheating on.

Minutes pass, hours perhaps. Time is irrelevant. The door finally unlocks and opens, and there she stands, hands on slim bossy hips, eyeing me impishly, holding something flashy at her side. It's not a brush this time but a long, shiny knife.

My mouth drops. "What now? Are you going to kill me? Is that how this all works—cry and die?"

She laughs. "Not exactly but close." She hands me the knife, which looks like it was a prop from *The Shining*, and I reluctantly take it.

I don't ask questions. I follow orders. I'm numb now. I'm Lea's science experiment. I'm anyone but me. Together we exit the Women's Room and head back over to the paintings, which she has propped up onto twin easels.

"Now stab them, Sophie." She gestures toward the knife.

"What? That's crazy. No." I step backward, drop the knife to the floor, hold up my hands. She picks it up and points it directly at me in the exact way that I had taught Ava repeatedly when she was younger to *never* point a knife or scissors. "Stab the damn paintings. You want to release the pain? This is what I do. I go to my women and then to my artwork. You can't do one without the other. Now, stab!"

I've never stabbed anything in my life. I'm not

violent. I don't throw things. I don't kill spiders—I'm the type who puts a glass over them and takes them outside. Although I did rip apart that blue birthday dress pretty damn good. And right now, thinking of Lauren and Gabe and all the years of betrayal—I could Jack Nicholson the fuck out of anything. Taking a deep breath, I walk in front of the first canvas—the one I painted. Lea grabs a glass of wine from the kitchen table, sits on the bed cross-legged, and watches me as though I'm a spectator sport.

I turn to her, hesitating. "But I'd be stabbing you."

"Yes, and I welcome it! Now go!"

I raise the knife high overhead and I stab right through the center of the canvas.

"Again!" she shouts from behind me, my rage coach. "The other one too. Let out all that pain, all that anger."

I stab my painting first, and then I turn to the one she did of me. It's simple in form, painted with fluid black lines and bright splashes of color, like a Matisse—and it looks like me. I don't hesitate. I stab it right through its belly, then repeat. Again and again, each thrust becoming increasingly violent. Each stab is for all of them, all those women in the closet, who, like me, have felt sheer joy and the darkest betrayal. I stab for Lea. For Ava. Even for Sabine. I stab as though what's left of my life depends on it. I stab at everything that I had refused to see—even when it was all right there in high def. Truth is ugly, commitment is a lie, love is shit, and marriage is betrayal. I murder and pillage both canvases, until there is nothing left but two large squares, emptied frames, through which I can see the hardwood floor. Shards of still drying colors are scattered everywhere. Breathless and depleted, I turn slowly to Lea. Our eyes lock. She nods. She feels me. She knows.

Coming toward me, she gently peels the knife from my trembling hand, then tosses it into the sink, and leads me back to the table where the evening began. I'm still shaking as she pours more wine, then lights up yet another cigarette, and hands it to me. It doesn't matter that I'm not a smoker, a lesbian, or a slasher—I have earned my rite of passage.

"Life is messy," she says through the opaque haze of smoke. "Love is messier. But pain is the messiest of all. Now you can begin to move on. Now you are ready."

IV.

At the end of the day, we can endure
much more than we think we can.

—FRIDA KAHLO

Chapter Twenty-One

Nathalie Senard agrees to meet me at her home in a private villa just outside of Èze, a picturesque medieval village situated between Nice and Monaco, nicknamed the Eagle's Nest because of its spectacular view 427 meters above the Mediterranean Sea. The drive itself in the early afternoon was stunning with surprisingly little traffic. After being admitted through the Senards' electric gate, I park along the pebbly circular driveway, where a giant marble sculpture of a wild-haired Amazonian woman guards the entrance of the bougainvillea-wrapped villa. I can hardly wait to see what's inside.

As I slowly make my way to the front door, I can't help but think how ironic it is that Nathalie is celebrated for her fierce depiction of women. Just wait until she meets me. Zero control of my life right now. I'm excited for the meeting but nervous. When Olivier called from Paris yesterday, he emphasized repeatedly that Nathalie is not to be touched, not to be challenged. Her illness has made her extremely irritable, he added just before we hung up, so be aware.

An Asian woman in a crisp white uniform answers the door and welcomes me inside. She leads me directly through the art-filled foyer, past the kitchen, and out onto the backyard terrace, where Nathalie is waiting. I only wish I could have stopped to peruse all the incredible artwork covering the walls of her home along the way.

Nathalie sits on a large cushioned chair next to a stone wall facing the sea and does not turn when I go out to the terrace. I take a quick look around. The backyard has a luxurious pool, a large Jacuzzi, and a colorful Moroccan-style garden with an ornate fountain at its center.

"Nathalie," the caregiver announces loudly. "Sophie Bloom is here."

"Good afternoon," I say, still standing behind her chair after the caregiver leaves us alone together.

Instead of responding, Nathalie waves me over to join her as she continues to stare silently out into the abyss. I stand next to her quietly and follow her concentrated gaze downward. The view is gorgeous. Clusters of terracotta-roofed houses are perched on rock outcrops above the cliffs leading down to the sea. The sun-kissed beach at the very bottom is accented by a rainbow of beach umbrellas. White yachts sail across the sea. The sky is bright and cloudless, the water crystal blue. I steal a glimpse of Nathalie's aristocratic profile, so pale and long-necked that she reminds me of a cameo. I wait patiently until she acknowledges me.

"Lovely, isn't it," she says with a half-smile as she slowly turns toward me. Her eyes meet mine and I'm struck by the startling shade of turquoise. They pop from her pale, ravaged face as though someone had colored them in. She wears a vintage fire-engine red Hermès scarf wrapped like a turban around her bald head, a throwback most likely to much better days.

But those piercing eyes hypnotize, draw you in, and hold you hostage. I have seen eyes like those only once before. When Samantha's mom, Lynda, was dying, she insisted on taking Samantha, Lauren, and me for high tea at the Four Seasons, accompanied by a nurse from hospice and an oxygen tank. It had been our annual ritual together since freshman year in high school—the four of us—just before the holidays. We all knew that it would be Lynda's last high tea. Once so stylish and commanding, Lynda before she got sick was a high-powered corporate attorney who never lost a single case, except her own to cancer. She had those identical daunting eyes—determined and unstoppable—to the very end.

"Olivier said nice things about you." Nathalie gestures to the chair across from her, nods to her caregiver, who is standing in the kitchen window watching us. Within seconds, the woman appears carrying two tall glasses of fresh lemonade and an assortment of pastel-colored macarons. I reach for a pink one and laugh. "My daughter's favorite. Thank you."

"Yes, Ava . . ." Nathalie says her name with a look and a pause that tells me she knows everything. My cheeks begin to burn slightly. For the first time ever, I'm deeply ashamed of my daughter's actions.

"You know," I say.

"Of course." She doesn't elaborate and it's better that way. "Tell me, Sophie, why are you here?"

My eyes widen. I lean back against the chair. Clearly, Nathalie knows exactly why I'm here. I know her type. She doesn't really want to know why I'm here, rather why I *deserve* to stay. But a dying woman is entitled to the truth. "I was once a sculptor and had early success in my twenties," I tell her. "I stopped sculpting because I developed severe carpal tunnel syndrome, which was debilitating. After that, life took some turns." I pause to gather my thoughts. "I'm here in Provence because I'm recovering from a broken marriage and I'm trying to put my life back together. Olivier told me about you and your situation. He's seen my work and thought I could help you with the installation at the Musée d'Orsay."

"But I don't want help," she says defiantly.

So why *am* I here? I don't hold back. "And yet you agreed to see me, why?"

Nathalie looks slightly shocked, as though nobody in her right mind would dare challenge her. And my guess is people don't. "Because Olivier insisted. He is a selfish man, you know. And for him to help someone other than himself required a viewing." She assesses me critically. "I can see why . . . but you're older than his usuals. First the daughter, now the mother. Interesting, even for him."

She may be dying, but I don't have to sit and take this. For a brief second, I want to tell her to go to hell, but something even stronger keeps me in my chair. She's volleying, waiting for my return, seeing what I'm made of. Olivier had said to be aware, but what he really meant was *beware*. "Just so you know, I am not interested in Olivier in that way at all." I can feel my eyes blaze, and I fight to keep my voice even. *I need this job.* "I'm interested in you and in how I can help you. Here's what I do know. You've had a phenomenal career. You stood alone, broke ground for so many women sculptors. You are working on a final installation but . . ." It's obvious what the *but* entails. I don't finish that sentence. Nathalie raises a barely-there eyebrow and something tells me she's waiting for me to continue. This is a woman who clearly disdains pity. Our eyes remain locked. I sip the lemonade slowly. "Everyone knows you, Nathalie. I'm totally alone here. No one has ever heard of me. I don't move in your circles. In fact, I don't move in any circles. But if my hands prove their mettle, I can still sculpt. Olivier told me that this installation is in marble, which is my expertise." I exhale deeply. "So here's what I propose . . . You be the eyes, let me be your hands. Let's finish this together. I know it means a lot to you." I lick my dry lips. I don't know whom this voice/these words belong to, but they come and there's more. "You're dying. I'm alive but dying inside, desperately trying to recover. I believe that alone makes us compatible, right? But should we agree to this relationship, let's respect each other. There's no need to test me or to cut me down. I've been tested and I promise you, I can't fall any farther than I already have."

I stand. I've said my piece. She watches me with piqued interest and an amused smile, but remains unnervingly silent. So be it. "I'm staying in Saint-Paul-de-Vence. I'd like to hear from you in the next few days," I continue. "If you want to work with me, it would be my great honor. And it would, of course, remain our secret. The installation would be in your name alone. But if not . . . I truly do understand and wish you well."

Her swimming-pool blue eyes shimmer as the sun beams down, contemplating me. This woman needs me even more than I need her. She just has to decide if her ego will allow it. I may be desperate but I'm nobody's doormat. "There is one other thing," I say, turning slightly. "If we do work together, you need to know that my daughter is the most important person in my life. She is the sole reason I'm still standing, still breathing. So, whatever you know about her and her silly teenage mistakes—which I'm sure you've made plenty of your own, as I have—please respect that I'm a mother first and last. You can say anything to me and we will work it out. But as far as Ava is concerned—she's off-limits, my line in the sand."

I've never used this reprimanding tone of voice with anyone and certainly not with a dying woman who is a national treasure. But my gut tells me that if I show any weakness of character, if I allow her to berate my own daughter, Nathalie will boot me out with whatever strength she has left. Weakness is the deal breaker here.

I gather my purse and turn to go. Nathalie's caregiver watches me from the kitchen window.

"Please, Sophie . . . sit back down," Nathalie calls out from behind me. It is not a request or an order. It is an agreement.

I stop in my tracks without turning around. I see her reflection behind me in the glass patio door. Her hands are crossed, she's leaning forward. I have passed her test. Glancing down at my unused hands, I flex them. Electricity charges through my fingers. *This is happening. I'm about to sculpt again.*

Chapter Twenty-Two

It's nearly 5 a.m. and I can't sleep. I flip the pillow to the cool side and puff it up once again, and when that doesn't work, I decide to watch CNN for a while. Too antsy to concentrate, I fling off my covers, grab my robe, and head out to the balcony. I sit and stare out into the sepia-tinted nothingness until my restless gaze meets sunrise, a jubilant display of orange and gold illuminating the shady distant hills. My mind, finally, begins to calm. I bring my knees to my chest and hug tightly. I'm going to sculpt today after so many years, to carve actual marble, to feel the tools inside my hands that I've avoided for far too long.

The hardest part is that I cannot share my good news with anyone because I promised Nathalie no one would know that I would be her ghost sculptor—just Olivier, of course, and her husband. So that leaves me with just Olivier, which basically leaves me with nobody. I try unsuccessfully to meditate to pass the time, then I go back inside the room, and check my phone. An "I miss you" text comes in from Ava, and there's another one from Gabe.

GABE: Hi. Tried calling you. Can we talk? Are you okay? Pablo misses you.

Pablo misses me. I stare at the text, at Gabe's cheap attempt at being cute by using our dog as a mouthpiece, and I feel nothing and everything at once. *Am I okay?* Yes and no, depending on the moment. But today, right now, yes.

First, I respond to Ava with a "Miss you more" text, and then I delete Gabe's text altogether. Cold, but what does he expect from me—emoji kisses? Those days are over.

I put away the phone, read for a while, shower, order an early breakfast, and an hour and a half later, I walk inside Nathalie Senard's enormous studio, which is adjacent to her home. My gaze shifts immediately upward, toward the vaulted wood-beamed ceiling that must be twenty feet high. I then turn in Nathalie's direction. She is waiting for me on the far side of the studio, sitting on a sturdy chair wearing a denim work shirt, jeans, and a blue Hermès scarf. I'm sure she has one in every color. There's a radiance to her face that wasn't there yesterday. Her caregiver, whose name is Claudia, is there too.

As I walk toward her, I scan the studio, an imposing, barnlike structure. The walls are stark white, lined with vibrant pottery, mounds of clay, plaster, casting materials, odds and ends, and every tool imaginable. At its center, and unmissable, is a giant marble statue nearly touching the ceiling, enveloped inside a womblike scaffolding. *It's her.* The installation. From my angle, through the metal guardrails, I see the unfinished backside of a woman; the long sturdy legs, the carved indentations of her hamstrings, the athletic muscles straining through her calves, the sensual smooth curve of her buttocks, the long, stalwart back, the protruding shoulder blades. She is formed, yet far from finished.

"It's 5.17 meters high," Nathalie says when I approach her. No good morning. No how are you. Just that.

"Isn't that the exact height of . . ." I interject. Seventeen feet high, I translate inside my head.

"Yes. Michelangelo's David. And that's the point." She smiles broadly. "This is my answer to the David." Nathalie begins to cough hard, and it sounds painful.

Claudia immediately hands her water. My heart goes out to Nathalie. I stay where I am, respectfully waiting until she steadies and signals me over. *Her answer to the David?* Every artist knows that no one has ever been able to measure up to Michelangelo, including Michelangelo himself—his own fiercest critic. His last works were full of self-doubt and struggling uncertainty— nowhere near the perfection of his early work.

"Come," she whispers finally when her breath evens.

I walk toward her with trepidation, excited and overwhelmed by the statue's size and the magnitude of the work ahead of me. I turn to glimpse the front of the statue, hearing Nathalie's voice emanating from behind me.

"Meet Eve."

Eve. I stare upward and take in the powerful body. I touch my hand to my chest. I can barely breathe. Eve is usually depicted as a long-haired naked beauty, a rib derivative best known for succumbing to a serpent's temptation—but not this version. Nathalie's Eve is far from weak. She clasps the serpent by its throat in one hand and holds a spear in the other. This Eve is no second-class biblical character but a warrior, a marbleized fuck-you to the doubters of a woman's true power. My gaze slowly travels upward, absorbing every illustrious detail of this masterpiece—the powerful thighs, the indentation of her mound, the flat yet muscled torso, the proud breasts, erect nipples— all still needing work but already well-defined. Yet it's Eve's face that is most commanding. Chiseled, shined, finished. And strangely familiar. Not just familiar . . . I cover my mouth, take a clumsy step backward, and grab onto the nearest chair to prevent myself from falling. I turn to Nathalie with an accusatory glare. She doesn't look at me. She knows exactly what I see.

My inner rage, a hot bubbling magma, rises to the surface. *That's not Eve. That's Ava.* The long neck, the refined nose with the slightly flared nostrils, the almond-shaped eyes, the perfectly arched brows, the prominent cheekbones softened by a full, sensual mouth. But it's the chin that is unmistakable, the give-away. Lightly squared, with a tiny indentation. The woman representing all women, clutching the serpent, is the nude image of my nineteen-year-old daughter. Nathalie holds up her hand before I can speak. "Yes," she says with all the strength she can muster. "It is who you think."

Heat boils inside me. I've been played. Olivier ne-glected to mention this part. *The catch.* My voice echoes loudly throughout the studio. "That bastard used my daughter, and you did as well. I'm an artist. I get it. I understand nudes—I've sculpted them. But she is just a teenager, damn it . . ." The affair, the pregnancy scare, and now posing nude for a very public exhibition. My heart begins to palpitate. "I'm leaving." I turn to go.

"No, Sophie. Wait!" Nathalie calls out.

"Please, stop!" Claudia shouts at me. I stop.

Nathalie clears her throat. "Just hear me out." She gestures toward the chair next to her, but I stand in place, crossed arms. "Okay, fine," she concedes, clearly understanding that she may control everyone else around her—but not the mother of her muse. "I visited Olivier's class months ago when I was in between treatments. I was receiving an honor at the École des Beaux-Arts. I saw your daughter there. You must understand that I have been working on Eve on and off for nearly ten years. I've thrown away three different versions of her. Nothing felt right. I had been working with another model for the past year to carve the form, and yet something was still missing. I'm a perfectionist, I know. But being sick, I was running out of time, and *voilà*—there she was—sitting in a classroom, taking notes. *That face.* Those strong cheekbones, the long line of her neck, the fierceness in her eyes, the willpower set in her chin. Eyes, both young and old at the same time, and I knew—"

"You knew what?" I demand, cutting her off. "That

Olivier was sleeping with his student? Did you know back then that she was with him when you 'found your Eve'?"

Her face drains of color. "I had no idea that they were together. Not until later." Nathalie looks away from me as though hiding something else. She glances back, her blue eyes fasten onto mine. "After that class, I asked Olivier whether he would mind if I asked his student if she would consider modeling for me." Her voice lowers. Her forehead begins to perspire profusely. "I am suddenly very tired."

She closes her eyes briefly. Claudia walks over to her, but Nathalie holds up a shaky hand to stop her. "Not yet, Claudia." She turns back to me. "I met with Ava and told her about my final installation. That I'm sick and she was under no obligation. But she said yes immediately and that she didn't need time to think about it. It was *her* choice to pose for me, but I was determined to make it work for her. I took photos, drew sketches, made a mold of her face, even carved a small two-foot-high clay sculpture of her—all the prep work was done in my Paris studio so that I did not interrupt her studies. She came to Èze for a few weekends throughout the semester to pose for me. I promise you that Olivier had nothing to do with it." She nods to Claudia, who brings over a pill and more water.

My daughter. So much I don't know about her. I've always felt our bond was strong, that we talked about everything. *Why didn't she tell me?* But Ava has always been so independent. I stare at Nathalie and think about Ava, then about me at nineteen. If the great Nathalie Senard had asked me to pose nude for her final installation, told me that she was dying, I too would have said yes in a heartbeat. I wouldn't have had to think twice about it. It's art, not porn. I wouldn't ask my mother. *So get over yourself.* But still.

"It was all Ava's decision, Sophie. No one pushed her into it," Nathalie emphasizes again. "I have known Olivier since art school. I won't lie. I knew that if he hadn't already, he would fall for her. Ava is his type. But I didn't care about that—I had found my muse. That's what mattered to me. It was your daughter's face I had to sculpt." She points to Eve. "A snake and a spear can be done with my eyes closed. Bodies are important, of course, but a face—a face is everything. It tells the whole story."

I stand there, immobile, trying to absorb all of this. Nathalie starts to look slightly feverish, but she refuses to be coddled by Claudia, who notices it too. "So when Olivier mentioned that you sculpt, that you worked in marble and showed me photos of your work, I knew even before meeting you that you would be the one to help me complete Eve. Most important, from the photos I had seen, it was clear to me that you understood what it really means to polish a sculpture." She smiles to herself. "Or as the Italians call it, the 'prolonged caressing.'"

I press my lips together. I know all about "prolonged caressing." The finish on marble is everything. I've always felt that way. While other students in my sculpting classes took advantage of contemporary finishing materials, I preferred going old school, using rasps, emery cloths, and even straw to polish my pieces. It was more labor-intensive, but it made all the difference from a sculpture being simply glossy to sheer luminescence.

"Your work didn't just simply shine, Sophie—it glowed—even from a photograph on a phone," Nathalie continues. "That's why you're here. I thought to myself how could I be so fortunate to have met my muse and then have her talented mother finish my life's work? That doesn't happen. I'm not lucky. My life has been beautiful and full, filled with hard work, great success, great love, and great loss—but never lucky. And never without a fight. Now facing death, I'm suddenly lucky." She smiles again, a sad, forced smile. Remnants of her beauty radiate through her flushed face. "We were destined to meet. My vision, your hands. Your daughter, my Eve." She reaches for my hand. "There is something else . . . You must know that I have never let anyone except for my husband and my models into this studio. I'm very private, possessive of my space and my work. I've never had an assistant before . . . I've refused. Until now. So please, don't leave, Sophie."

It's the way she says my name that is fully loaded. I'm all she has. Time no longer exists. We both know it. I hesitate. Olivier had told me not to touch her, but I do anyway. I reach out and take her frail extended hand into mine, feeling the thin, clammy translucent skin. I stare at the early-onset age spots and bruises covering a woman who is not much older than I am. *My daughter, her Eve.* I gaze up at the spectacular unfinished sculpture, at the masterwork in progress that will be celebrated long after Nathalie Senard is gone. Long after I am gone. Long after Ava is gone. *Her vision, my hands.*

She gently pulls away, eyes Claudia and nods, giving in with a long, rasping sigh. Her caregiver immediately begins to pack her up. Where is she going? Home? Bed already? It's not even 11 a.m.

"We will begin again tomorrow," Nathalie says weakly. "Stay here as long as you like. Take your time. Get to know Eve. I must rest now."

Claudia lifts Nathalie onto a wheelchair that was

discreetly hidden in the corner of the studio. Nathalie doesn't say goodbye. Her eyes are already closed. She is a woman with fierce pride. This deteriorated version of herself is a humiliation that I imagine she cannot bear. She is staying alive, clinging, *only* to see her final work actualized. We both know that an artist whose hands have been tied is already dead. I glance at my own unused hands. Perhaps I, too, have been dead without knowing it all these years. I stare up at Eve, at my Ava, and I see the familiar lines of her body, that face—no doubt casted with the finest flawless white marble—strong, proud, nobody's victim, and eerily alive.

Once Nathalie leaves, I circle Eve. She is barefoot, with feet that are still unfinished blocks of marble begging to be shaped. Nathalie must have done the torso first, the snake and the spear, then the face, given the timetable. I climb the scaffold stairs slowly, observing Eve inch by inch. Most sculptors working with such a giant piece of marble would use a hydraulic lift. My guess is Nathalie is like me, old school too, perhaps meeting Michelangelo on his terms by using traditional tools and methods.

I think back to my art history class freshman year in college, recalling how Michelangelo's friend and biographer Giorgio Vasari, also an artist, described how the master carved his figures by actually laying his model inside a coffinlike box. He'd then fill the box with water until the figure was submerged. Slowly, he'd let the water run out of the box and the parts of the figure that emerged first are what Michelangelo would cut out first on his stone block. Authenticity for Michelangelo was not everything—it was the *only* thing. Every detail counted. My hunch is Nathalie's perfectionism is the same.

Unlike Rodin and other sculpting giants who utilized assistants, Michelangelo, famously, also did all of his artwork alone, paranoid that his secret techniques would be stolen. Like Nathalie, no one was allowed to watch him. It must be so difficult for her to even have me here, invading her precious sanctuary. The hefty price tag of her illness is not just artistic impotency, but also much worse than that—dependency. *On me.* I wipe the tears forming in the corners of my eyes, look around at her magnificent studio, all the genius that been created within these secluded walls. Soon, it will be gone.

But not yet. She's still here, still fighting.

Inhaling deeply, I assess Eve from the back again, from the sides, taking notes inside my head. I envision it all. I see exactly what needs to be done, and I can even hear her voice. It's Ava's, calling out to me, to complete her, to refine her, to free her from the confining marble that still entraps her.

I return to the ground, surveying the sprawling studio filled with myriad tools—chisels, mallets, hammers, rasps, angle grinders, rifflers, pumice, sandpaper, cloths. I can't believe it is all mine for the taking. I spin around the studio as if I have a skirt on that swirls. I imbibe every inch of Nathalie Senard's secret world like a kid in a candy store. This is what she wants—my passion, not my pity.

Eve is Ava, Eve is me. If this marble vision of Nathalie's, symbolic of all that is woman, can stand alone and fight the good fight, well then, so can I. I lightly trace my hand over the smooth marble base. It's cold and satiny. God knows, I remember this velvet-to-the-touch sensation. Eve is now mine to shape, mold, and mother. I don't have to learn this Eve or study her. I know her, I feel her. I gave birth to her. *I can do this.*

Chapter Twenty-Three

When I arrive at the studio early the next morning, Nathalie is already there, and surprisingly alone. Her scarf today is school-bus yellow and she wears large gold hoop earrings. She looks like a gypsy, upbeat, and ready to work. Within seconds, I can tell she is high, even before I smell the marijuana.

"Where is Claudia?" I ask, looking around.

"At the house. She will come soon. I wanted to be alone with you."

I smile at her. "Is there anything I can do to make you more comfortable?"

She giggles, and it's warm and a little loopy. "The point is I want you to make me *uncomfortable*," she says. "You were here for a good two hours after I left yesterday. You had time to think. What would you change about Eve?"

Our eyes meet—I've thought of nothing else all night. Eve is stunning, a contender, but nowhere near the level of the David. There is still much work to be done. I can't tell her that—*but can I?*

Make me uncomfortable. I think back to what one of my professors told me when I'd asked him, *How do you know when you are done with a sculpture?* When you think you are done—ask questions, he said. If your answers match your intention, only then the piece is complete.

"So . . . ," I begin, "David is beauty personified, yet Eve appears angry. Is that what you intended to convey—her anger? Or do you want wisdom? Or beauty? What is Eve's true power for you? Looking at her now, I'm not convinced."

Nathalie smiles with closed lips, her eyes shine bright. "The old ask-questions-find-the-intention technique—I know it well. I've taught it." She laughs airily as though reminiscing. "But yes, let's play that game and see where we go. I want Eve to be battle-ready. David is beautiful, but don't forget that he has that slingshot over his shoulder, the rock in the other hand. His physical power is not overwhelming—not to mention that his, shall we say, genitals, are less than extraordinary. They are underdeveloped like a boy's—not man-sized. The way I see it, our David had something to prove. And so does Eve, but differently. David takes on Goliath and is triumphant. I want Eve to take on the world and challenge it, defy it. Do you understand me? I want her created with great beauty, but her mind and body even stronger. Fearless . . . that's what I want for her. I want her to be what I once was." Nathalie's smile vanishes completely. "Not as I am."

Time stands still for both of us. I'm staring imminent death in the face and we both know it. I walk over to her, kneel in front of her chair. "I don't know you well. But I know you are unbelievably strong. It's okay to be afraid. It's human."

She shakes her head and one gold hoop falls from her ear to the floor. I pick it up and gently put it back in. She touches my hand. "It's not death that I'm afraid of—it is dying before I'm done. I'm afraid to leave Eve with her feet unfinished, her back imperfect, her face still searching. I have nightmares about it. I need to ground her before I go. Do you understand me?" Her voice trembles with what little force she has left.

"More than you know." I pull up a chair and sit next to her, urging her to let it out, just like Lea had done for me the other night.

"I never had a child, Sophie. I wanted to, and we tried, but lost multiple pregnancies. I could get pregnant, but couldn't keep it. I finally stopped trying because I couldn't take the loss any longer. My work, my sculptures, are my children. Eve is the young woman I would have wanted to raise. I want you to give her everything that I won't be able to." Nathalie's sparkling eyes are eclipsed with tears.

"I understand you," I whisper, thinking of all our unsuccessful attempts to get pregnant after Ava was born. So many tries, so many failures.

"So you know."

"Yes."

She wipes away her tears with her sweater sleeve. "My husband is a wonderful man, a gifted painter in his own right. He was there when I was on top of the world and is here for me at the bottom, at the very end. I am not so wonderful," she laments. "I am selfish, demanding, rude . . . I take what I want, give when I want to. I have hurt him when he has been so good to me."

I think about Gabe. All that hurt and I was good to him. "Mistakes," I say carefully.

"Yes, but some of us make bigger ones than others."

We both turn to look at Eve. "She, on the other hand, will be flawless. Eve *will* be the counterpart to David when we're done," she emphasizes with fire in her eyes.

"That's my dream—it's always been my dream since I was a young art student and saw the David for the very first time. I believe Michelangelo's intention was to present the singular moment just before David decides to fight Goliath. It's *the* decisive moment that impacts all humanity—the crossroad between choice and action—that's what I want for Eve as well. To confront that inexplicable moment of reckoning with strength—can you do that, Sophie? Can you capture that? Can you make sure of that even if . . ." *Even if I die before Eve's finished,* which she doesn't say, but lingers heavily in the air between us.

I hold her lucid gaze. "I will make sure of it. No matter what."

"Then let's get started." Her eyes transform almost instantly from relief to animation. She springs into action without even moving from the chair. Squeezing the sides of her chair, ready to go, Nathalie is no longer a dying artist, but still the creator, still in command. I can only imagine her in her prime. She must have been a powerhouse.

"Feet first," I say, knowing that grounding Eve is of utmost importance to her.

"Yes, exactly."

"Then I need yours."

Nathalie doesn't question me as I reach down, slip off her ballet flat, and expose her right foot. I walk briskly across the studio, grab a block of clay, bring it over, and place her foot on top of it.

"Point your toes, then flex," I say. She knows the drill. I need to see all the joints, the muscles and especially the twitch of the tarsal on top of her foot—the most widely used muscle of the entire body. I place my hand on her foot, close my eyes, and trace it, feeling the topography and texture, transmitting the image into my head.

Only when I'm ready do I release the foot, stand, and walk toward the statue. I eye the chains binding Eve, holding her firmly in place so that I can work. I circle her slowly, cautiously. I envision the foot, the strain of the tendons, the muscles and ligaments running along the surface and alongside it. The Achilles is crucial, connecting everything, then come the bones of the feet, even the shape of the toenails is all being sketched in my mind before I dare make a single move.

Taking a deep breath, I first draw my incisions on the marble and begin the roughing out, then taking the point chisel and the mallet, I give it a hard blow—not too hard, but just enough to let the stone swim. The exactness, the knowing, comes from years of practice.

Never mind that I've been in hibernation. I then grab a finer-toothed chisel to model the form, removing the stone and debris quickly and efficiently. I inhale the familiar powdery scent of the dust particles and I'm intoxicated. Using the rasp with its sharklike tiny teeth, I grind it into the stone with my entire body. Sculpting is not about technique; it's about losing your ego, refining, and flowing with the demands of the stone—it's lovemaking in its highest artistic form.

I don't even see Nathalie anymore as I work, even though I'm aware she is watching every move I make. She begins to blur and blend with the rest of the studio. I have entered the Zone. For so many years I have been dead, passionless, left out in the cold. But not now. I'm once again inside the room, flowing and alive. I smell the sweet-scented marijuana filling the air around me. The pain must be getting worse, but Nathalie doesn't say a word, doesn't complain, asks for nothing, just watches me and smokes. I'm already higher than I've been in years. It's an indescribable ride: first the heart thumping, the jitters, the stomach drop, then floating trancelike, as though I am flying wingless. My body begins to dance the sculptor shuffle, twirling around Eve much like Pygmalion, the mythical Cypriot sculptor who carved the perfect woman out of ivory and then ultimately, unequivocally, fell in love.

Hours pass, but time is irrelevant. I don't even notice until Claudia comes in, announcing a mandated break. Nathalie and I both ignore her. According to Claudia's watch, which she holds up for both of us to see, Nathalie has had more than enough for the day. She must eat, must rest. This has been too much action for her patient, Claudia says, blaming me with her eyes.

"What's the worst thing that could happen—I die?" Nathalie laughs. "Leave me alone."

"Madame Senard, your husband made it very clear—"

"And let me be even clearer: no!"

I ignore them both, letting them duke it out, knowing Nathalie will win. I'm deeply immersed but see them from the corner of my eye as though I'm on a fast train and they are passing images. Sadly, I will never recapture all the years I've lost as an artist. But now I'm no longer feeling shattered. It's as though I've suddenly been put back together: the woman, the mother, the chiseler, the cobbler, the archaeologist, digging through stone until uncovering my hidden treasure. I stand back slightly, as Eve's right foot finally emerges from the block of marble like a baby from its womb. I turn to Nathalie for approval. It's her foot, not mine, I remind myself.

The room is silent.

"Slimmer toes. The third one especially. It's not precise. Fix it," she says, closing one eye. I walk over to the foot, stand back. She's right.

Claudia retreats to her corner of the studio, knowing better than to challenge Nathalie, who refuses to stop the momentum as I spend the next few hours fixing that toe, and then the others. Tomorrow I will refine it, polish it, and then on to the other foot. When I'm done, I look up at Nathalie and she nods her approval. Her lips are pressed together, her eyes are illuminated. She glances at Eve's new toes, clasps her hands together—it's exactly what she envisioned. I know—we both do—Eve, her muse, my daughter, is finally being grounded.

Chapter Twenty-Four

As I pack up to leave for the day, Nathalie asks if I would care to join her in the garden, have a glass of wine, perhaps? Her husband is not expected home from Paris until later that night and she would love the company. Can she drink wine with all her meds, all that weed, being that sick? I don't ask, I say yes.

I help Nathalie into the wheelchair and together we head over to the house. Staring at the back of her scarfed head, my heart breaks thinking about everything she's going through, all that she's lost. I recall the unwavering look in her eyes earlier—that she'd rather die before allowing Eve's toes to be less than perfect and not meet her vision. She is a perfectionist, and while time races, she stubbornly refuses to skip any steps. Eve is keeping

Nathalie alive, the way Ava in my darkest moments is what keeps me going.

I grip the handles of the wheelchair tightly, pushing it over the pebbled walkway. I wish I could somehow take away Nathalie's pain, her daily disintegration, but I can't. It's out of my control. Once again, I can't fix it. All I can do is this.

Claudia opens the door, taking control of the chair, and I trail behind them. The wine will definitely be a great segue into the evening. I'm having a late dinner with Jean-Paul and Lea in the village of Saint-Paul. I follow Nathalie and Claudia through the house. This time, I walk slowly, taking in the incredible art collection hanging along the hallway. The paintings—both figurative and abstract—are magnificent.

"These are stunning," I say, observing the myriad landscapes and seascapes, several nudes, followed by a provocative series of young lovers.

"Mr. Senard's work," Claudia says.

Of course, it is. How they must inspire each other. I look down at my hands self-consciously. "Nathalie, do you mind if I wash up a bit?" My hands are grubby, my fingernails are dirty, and I feel the powdery dust from the marble covering me.

"Absolutely," she says. "Use my bedroom up ahead

to your left. You will find everything you need in there. Claudia—show her the way, please."

Claudia leaves Nathalie where she is, and quickly ushers me into the master bedroom, points to the bathroom in the far corner and waits and watches from the doorway until I walk inside. That woman is more than an aide to Nathalie—she's a bodyguard and a watchdog.

Entering the bathroom, I stand perfectly still against the door until I hear Claudia leave and walk back down the hallway. I wait a few seconds longer, take a deep breath, and then I tiptoe back out into the bedroom.

That painting.

I lean against the nearest wall and stare at the large framed canvas suspended over the king-sized bed I passed on my way to the bathroom. I place my hand to my chest. My heart begins to palpitate as I absorb the painting. It's so realistic that it feels as though the scene is happening right in front of me. A naked woman lies on a bed, rosy nipples erect, her legs splayed, as a nude man stands over her. She is exquisite, her body is graceful yet carnal, like a ballet dancer and a pole dancer in one. Her eyes are closed and her thick, golden halo of hair fans her face as she pleasures herself. I can actually feel the rapture in the strain of her eyes. But it is the man, gazing upon the woman with raw sexuality, who magnetizes. His lustful expression, the hungry way his lanky, defined body leans over her, desires her, is the most erotic image that I have ever seen. Two people who are intimate but who never actually touch, like Rodin's sculpture *The Kiss*. All of my senses are aroused at once.

It's them—Nathalie and Luc Senard.

I recognize her face, those prominent cheekbones, that swanlike neck. It is the image of her *before*; when her incomparable beauty had not yet been ravaged by cancer. Nathalie in all her glory, naked, sensual, and commanding. And the man in the painting is clearly Luc, and so is the artist. The bold, expressive brush-strokes are identical to the paintings in the hallway.

I can't help it. I'm reminded of the sculpture I created for Gabe in our bedroom, the two of us at the height of our passion, just like this. *What does Holly the nurse think when she sees that sculpture in our bedroom?* And Gabe—what does he think of it now?

When Nathalie's gone, how will Luc feel about that painting, and it's just him lying in that bed? Alone, without her, next to an unslept-on pillow that may still have her lingering scent.

I walk toward the bed, and gaze at a small framed photo of Luc as a young artist on the nightstand. The photographer had captured him in his studio, canvases and art supplies surrounding him. Luc was dreamy, in that Alain Delon French-movie-star way. Piercing green eyes, close-cropped dark hair, full almost-womanly lips, three-day neat stubble over a sculpted jaw. He wore a crisp white T-shirt, worn jeans, and, of course, the requisite loosely wrapped gray scarf around his neck. A face that demands to be photographed, painted, sculpted. *What's he like now?*

I stare again at their bed, and again at that spectacular oil above it. Such love and such loss. My heart no longer races, it seems to have stopped beating. *This is where that painting once came alive for them, and this is where it's going to die.*

I hear approaching footsteps coming from down the hall. I shouldn't be here, a stranger in their bedroom, snooping around, prying into the most intimate side of this prominent couple—a side that belongs only to them. I quickly step back into the bathroom, turn on the sink water at full blast to buy myself a little time to pull it together. I stick my parched mouth under the faucet, drink, then wash away the dusty remnants of Eve still stuck to me.

"Is everything okay?" Claudia knocks lightly on the door.

"Yes." *No. Maybe. I don't know.*

I pull my hair up into a clip and quickly leave the

bedroom, closing the door behind me and walking with Claudia back down the corridor, without looking at the paintings this time. Up ahead, through the window, I see Nathalie outside on the patio, in her large chair surrounded by pillows, waiting for me. Two glasses of red wine have already been poured.

Taking a deep breath, I walk toward her, somewhat afraid—not of her, but for me. Olivier, Jean-Paul, Lea, Nathalie, and soon Luc. This is my new life; a new cast of characters linking up like those plastic red monkeys. *Where do I belong? Who do I hold on to, and will I fall off once again?*

Chapter Twenty-Five

Jean-Paul and Lea sit across from me in the bistro, his arm draping her bare shoulder. They fit. Best friends, lovers, cocreators, and strangely, my only friends here.

We decided on Le Tilleul. It's a perfect night and we sit outside dining and drinking around the famous tree at its center. Everything they ordered so far has been beautifully displayed—the salad niçoise, the foie gras, the linguini with clams—but my head is still in *that* painting, not the meal.

"Tell us where you've been hiding," Lea says, clasping her hands together. "We haven't heard from you in three days."

"I haven't even seen you at the hotel," Jean-Paul

chimes in. "You're gone before I get there and still not back before I leave."

They look at me, expecting an answer, as though they are my parents. "I've been, well, actually . . ." I throw up my hands. "I've been helping out an artist, but I can't really talk about it."

"Yes, you can," Jean-Paul says, pouring us all more wine.

I shake my head. "No, I can't. Really. I signed a nondisclosure agreement."

They look at each other. Jean-Paul reaches over and places his hand on mine while squeezing Lea in closer. I look around. No one seems to care. "Sounds exciting. Tell us."

"I wish I could. One day, I promise."

He glances at Lea, who shrugs. "Well then, we will revisit that later," he says, digging into the salad. "We wanted to tell you something." He winks at Lea. "The hotel has asked me to fill in at a sister hotel in Capri for a month—and how could I refuse? The good news is that Lea got permission to take time off from the gallery and can join me. So, we are both going." He drops his fork, smiles broadly, his face lights up as he wraps his arm tightly around Lea, and she leans into him. I feel warm inside just watching them, but sad for me. I will miss them. I try to hide what I'm feeling.

"That's fantastic," I say effusively, hoping I sound genuine. "I'm so happy for you both."

"We are going to miss you, Sophie . . . it all happened so quickly," Lea adds. "We have to leave tomorrow evening. No time—it's crazy. But we want you to stay in our place while we're gone." She leans forward. "No is not an option. You've probably spent thousands of dollars at the hotel. It's enough. Stay, water our plants, and take in our mail. Yes?"

I sit back in my chair, hearing muffled music pulse from the building next door. How grateful I am that I met these two—so open, inspiring, and generous. Lea is right. The hotel has been ridiculously expensive. Staying at their apartment sounds perfect, actually. A month buys me time, and now I don't have to look around right away for a sublet. "I would love that. I have been thinking that I need to start searching for a place. But please let me pay you whatever you would have charged someone else. I insist or no deal."

Jean-Paul shakes his head. "Absolutely not."

"We will revisit that," I joke. "But I'm paying for dinner and I won't take no for an answer."

"Absolutely yes." Lea laughs. "Tell us about the art, at least a little . . ."

I look around. No one I know. "Well, I'm sculpting again, and I am so happy to be back in the studio."

"And your hands? Are you in pain?" Lea asks.

I smile at her. With all her tough talk, she's very caring. "Not at all, that's the crazy part." I'm dying to tell them everything about the Senards, but I can't. "I really wish I could talk about it with you both. Please understand." I reach over and squeeze Lea's hand while my eyes meet Jean-Paul's. Is it wrong that I want to be with them again? That I don't want to go home alone tonight? I say nothing, but they feel my vibe anyway. These two familiar strangers who play by their own rules sense my silent longing, know the cues. The sculpting alone would have been enough to make me feel this way, so charged. But that painting taps into something deeper that I cannot describe but that feels famished.

"You look different. You look . . . ," Jean-Paul says slowly, lightly rubbing the inside of my wrist.

The word he is looking for is "hungry." I look hungry.

"Come back to our place with us tonight." Lea knows. She doesn't look at Jean-Paul for permission. "You want to."

"Yes." My eyes bore into hers, then his. "I want to."

I lie naked on their bed, just like *she* did in the painting. On my back, one arm extended overhead, the other hand touching myself. Jean-Paul, also nude, stands over me. Lea sits naked on a chair near us. They let me call the shots, not knowing that I am reenacting the painting. They are so young and accepting, so passionate and patient. They don't ask questions. Jean-Paul is clearly aroused. I'm flush with wine, loose with longing, and I'm ready for the two of them in a way that I was not before. I'm no longer the student. This time I'm in control, the artistic director.

I sit up against the headboard, see Lea in front of me, watching us, and I begin to explain myself though she asks nothing of me. "I saw this erotic painting today that made a huge impact on me. And I—"

"Tell us exactly what you want . . . what you need," she implores, understanding me completely.

"I don't know what I want." I search her face. "It's weird, right?"

She looks at Jean-Paul, who nods. "Not weird at all. You've been lost. What you really desire from your time here is to find yourself. You're still searching, Sophie, and it's okay. Discovery is not a destination, it's a process." She folds her arms, tilts her head. "Do you want me to paint you like that, just as you are now?"

It's uncanny how this young woman seems to understand me so much more than I ever will. "Yes," I whisper. "Paint exactly how you see me." I look up at Jean-Paul who appears ready for action, and not to stand still and pose with an erection. "This was not your plan."

He gives me an open-handed surrender. Lea is in charge and he accepts it. "Let things roll. That's my only plan."

Exactly, I think. I am so grateful to both of them. So much so that I get up off the bed, walk over to Lea, lift her chin upward and kiss her. Her lips are soft against mine. My tongue dances with hers, and then I walk over to Jean-Paul and kiss him too. His mouth is rougher, his breath warmer, his tongue hotter. I feel his excitement rise, becoming firmer, and I slowly pull away. I lie on the bed and tell him to stand over me again, but not to touch me yet. I instruct Lea to paint us, just like that, the moment *before*.

The next morning, I drive with trepidation, slowing to a crawl as I approach Nathalie's driveway, and then punch in the gate code. I can hear the crunch of the pebbles beneath my tires as I advance toward the studio. I spot the sleek silver BMW sports car parked in the driveway and I know Luc is there with her inside the studio. I park and then carefully open the heavy studio door. I notice my hand is unsteady against the doorknob.

Luc's back is facing me. He is standing across the studio with Nathalie, who looks exhausted, unwell. But when she sees me enter, her whole face lights up. He turns around, squinting slightly as though trying to place me as I slowly walk toward them.

"I'm Sophie," I say, extending my hand, which he takes.

"I heard all about you from Nathalie. I'm Luc." He smiles broadly, speaking in English for my benefit. "It's a pleasure to meet you. Nice work on the foot, by the way."

"Thank you." I smile back, trying not to stare, to appear normal—whatever that is. Casually dressed in jeans and a black V-neck T-shirt, Luc is even handsomer than the younger version in that old photograph. And the more recent photo with Nathalie taken in the exotic garden does not even begin to do him justice. In real time, he's more sophisticated, more chiseled. His eyes are an even brighter shade of emerald. *Say something.* Tell him how inspired you were by his paintings that you saw in their home. *No, don't say anything.* You're the ghost sculptor, remember. Simply here to help his wife, to lie low. It's not about you or him, but all about Nathalie. I glance over at her. She really looks sick today. Her face is pallid, and there appear to be deeper, darker circles beneath her concave eyes.

"Luc." Nathalie interrupts my thoughts. "You need to go now. You're stealing our time." *Time that she no longer has*, we are all thinking.

He turns away from me, eyes his wife affectionately, as though happy to see her still alive, still bossy. He leans down, places his hand over her gaunt shoulder. "Not too much today. You need rest. Claudia told me—"

"Don't listen to Claudia," Nathalie snaps, then offers him a hint of a grin. "We need to work. I will rest when I'm dead. See you at lunch."

Luc shakes his head, as in why even bother telling his wife what to do. He turns to me, still trying to place me. "It's Ava. You look so much like her. That must be it," he says.

And then it dawns on me. My daughter has met Luc. *Did he see her posing naked?* My breath catches in my throat.

We hold each other's gaze a second too long for two people just meeting. Maybe it's only in my head. My mind briefly flashes back to last night, keeping up with the millennials, as we acted out Luc's painting. If he only knew what his gifted brushstrokes inspired . . . a night so wildly unexpected. I was insatiable, somebody I didn't recognize at all. Unleashed, raw, and voracious.

I try to shake off the memory. If Nathalie knew that I had re-created her husband's artwork in Lea's bedroom, that I assumed *her* role . . . A crimson flush spreads across my cheeks. I feel the heat beneath my skin. *Can they see it?* We are all artists here. It's all in the details, the nuance, the unsaid. We perceive those things invisible to the naked eye.

I quickly avert my gaze, reach for the pitcher of water on the small, nearby table overloaded with the fruit, crackers, and various cheeses that Claudia lays out each day. From the corner of my eye, I see Nathalie and Luc talking quietly. I down a glass of water, then head to the other side of the studio to prepare my tools—Nathalie's tools. I feel their eyes on my back, watching me. *Ignore it, focus.* Turning slightly, I see Nathalie kiss Luc good-bye. He waves to me on his way out.

"I will begin working on the left foot," I announce quietly, awaiting Nathalie's approval.

"Yes, but today let's see if we can get those toes right on the first try." Her voice is surprisingly terse—perhaps I'm only imagining that? Her barely-there brows draw tightly together. This isn't about me, I remind myself. Nathalie is running out of time.

Chapter Twenty-Six

I can't sleep again, and it's becoming a problem. I definitely need something to take the edge off. I glance up at the loud ceiling fan hovering over Lea and Jean-Paul's bed, a bed that is now mine, and am counting rotations when the phone rings on number eighty-two. I see Ava's smiling face light up the screen. I grab the phone off the nightstand.

"Ava! How are you? You're home." I am excited to speak to her. I check the clock. It's late afternoon there.

"I'm sitting here with Dad."

"How was the rest of your trip?" I ignore the Gabe part, picturing them both at the kitchen table.

"Jake and I had the best time together," she says. I place my hand on my chest, grateful. Ava sounds good. "But it feels really strange to be home after nearly eight months abroad . . . and yes, Mom, I can tell you don't want to talk about Dad."

That obvious? "Tell me more about Jake." I cross over to the only neutral subject available.

"Love the diversion," she sniggers. "Jake is amazing. We're good again. He's back in Seattle with his family. But I'm still not talking to Monica." Long pause. "When are you coming home?"

I sigh deeply. *What home?* I don't want to go home, go there. I'm not ready. And how can I leave Nathalie right now? I just started. But Ava's last year in college . . . "I don't know exactly yet."

"You don't know yet? Mom, school is in, like, a few weeks. Aren't we going together as usual? Why are you being so weird?"

And why didn't you tell me that you posed nude for Nathalie Senard—that you are Eve? "I'm not being weird."

"You are and we both know it."

"Okay . . . maybe a little. Big news." Another diversion. "I'm sculpting again."

"You're what? Oh my god—where?"

"At a studio, nearby. I'm just beginning, but I absolutely love it and realize how much I missed it."

"I'm so happy for you." And Ava means it. "But school starts in *eighteen days*," she emphasizes again.

"Are you coming home or not?" She sounds hurt. In the old days, we would have been planning the back-to-college weekend together weeks ago.

I wonder briefly what would happen if I announced that I'm not coming home. "I'm thinking I will come home on August twenty-seventh and I will stay through the weekend. We can shop then and get it all together." I decide this as we speak.

"Four days? That's all? Coming from France—that's crazy."

"Yes, I know."

"Will you be staying here at the house at least?" Ava is pushy, always has been.

"I don't know. I don't think it's a good idea." I don't ever want to go back there. It will be too hard. But god knows, I miss my dog, my lilacs. "How's Pablo?"

"The best. Right here next to me . . . Just come home, okay. Please. For me."

We are both silent. Ava knows I will do anything for her. "We'll see."

"Do you want to talk to Dad?" she asks. Her voice is wistful and young.

"No. I'm sorry, Ava, but I don't." I have to draw a line somewhere.

"Can't we just fix this somehow?" she pleads. She is now standing outside on the deck. I can hear the neighbor's dog barking in the background and Pablo barking back. "Even for me?"

No, this I can't do, even for you. Instead, I say, "I love you. I will see you very soon."

I place the phone down on its face in slow motion, knowing sleep is no longer an option, and having no patience to count fan rotations. The worst part is that I don't want to go back home. I don't want to see Gabe, deal with my broken marriage. Not now. I want to stay here and work on Eve, immerse myself. What is happening to me? Being a mother has always been first and last. Ava needs me. I used to drop everything for her, no questions asked, no matter how it impacted me. But now . . . Luc's face flashes inside my head. *What the hell is wrong with me?* I cut off the image quickly, looking up to the ceiling for safety. Eighty-three, eighty-four . . .

Chapter Twenty-Seven

"I need to leave for four days to take Ava to college," I tell Nathalie the next day. "Thursday, August twenty-seventh and be back the following Tuesday."

Her face drops. She doesn't hide her reaction. For Nathalie every minute, every hour counts. She doesn't have Thursday through Tuesday to spare. I know exactly what she's thinking. I'm thinking the same.

"Ava can't take herself?"

Nathalie has no clue. "Yes, she could, of course. But it's our ritual. She's my daughter. We do this together. And she's dealing with a lot right now. Honestly, I don't want to go, but I have to."

"I see." She sniffs deeply.

No, she doesn't see. She has never been a mother. She doesn't understand that umbilical pull, only to her artwork. "I don't want to lose the time either, Nathalie. So here are my thoughts . . ." I planned out this speech in the middle of the night because I never fell back asleep. "I will work late nights until I leave. We will work together as usual during the day. You can rest and then have Claudia bring you back to the studio in the evening for a little bit just to make sure you are happy with the progress. How does that sound?"

Her eyes light up. It's better than nothing. "I appreciate that. But driving back and forth from Èze to Saint-Paul so late? No. Maybe you should stay in our guest room for the few weeks before you go?"

I think of Luc, the painting, their private time. *No way.* "I don't want to disrupt your family time. What if we brought a bed into the studio? That way if it's really late and I don't want to drive back to Saint-Paul, I can sleep here and work without having to worry."

Nathalie turns to Claudia. "Arrange a bed in here for Sophie. A small refrigerator and amenities as well."

Claudia nods with pursed lips. It's clear she cares deeply for Nathalie but is not at all thrilled that her famous patient is spending her final days holed up in a dust-filled studio. But this is what makes Nathalie happy, this is what keeps her alive. This is the job. "I will get on it immediately," she says.

Claudia leaves, heading back to the house, and Nathalie removes a fat joint from her purse. "And how is Ava doing?"

I light it for her. "She is good. With her dad."

"And you?" She tilts her head, scrutinizing me closely. The pungent scent fills the air. I presume I'm high every day due to secondhand smoke.

What is she getting at? I shuffle my feet against the dusty floor.

"How do you feel going back there, seeing your husband again?" She raises a curious brow. This is the first time she's asked me about Gabe.

"Not thrilled. But I'm going for Ava." She offers me her joint and I take it, inhale deeply, and quickly hand it back. It's just after nine and I haven't even eaten breakfast yet. "Truthfully, I don't want to leave now in the middle of all this. I feel like we have real momentum going here, and I love it."

She sighs deeply and releases a fat plume of smoke in the process. "Life tends to get in the way of our art, doesn't it? If only we could freeze those we love while we finish those we create. Believe me, my work has hurt me so many times over the years. It has destroyed friendships and relationships. And—" She stops herself. She has that same angsty look that she had that very first day in the studio, like she wants to tell me something but is hesitant.

"And what?" I push gently.

"It has hurt my marriage. Only he doesn't know it." Her voice is barely audible.

"I'm not sure I understand."

She hesitates. "Before I was sick, or at least before I became very sick, I was with someone else . . ." She eyes me closely, gauging my shocked reaction.

"Someone you still care for?" I manage, every mixed emotion hitting at once. I think of *that* painting. That love. Yet another lie.

"Yes . . ." She coughs, and then steadies herself, eyes me squarely. "It's Olivier."

Olivier. I cover my mouth, mortified. That despicable man has no boundaries, no morals. And he lied to me again, used me somehow . . . and she lied too. I glare back at her, sick to my stomach, unable to hide my disgust.

"When?" is all I can muster.

"When?" she repeats, her gaze becoming misty. "It's complicated. So many years I have known him, since art school, we were barely twenty, and never once did we take it further. Oh, make no mistake, he tried countless times. But I wouldn't allow it. He was a player even then. I respected myself too much to fall prey to Olivier's charms. I enjoyed our friendship too much, our light flirtation—but that's where it ended. And then I met Luc, who was a few years older in school, and then Olivier did not stand a chance." She reaches for her water and a pill. I watch her in stunned, gut-wrenching silence. "I used to think that I was the only woman alive who Olivier had *not* slept with. I'm still surprised that he didn't try to hit on you."

I maintain a poker face. I'm not going there, no matter what. She keeps smoking, talking, as though I'm an attentive audience and not the mother of Olivier's latest conquest, who *did* go there. "Never loyal to Sabine. Not a single day—although, she didn't demand it. She has lived her own life. Not like Luc—loyal to me from beginning to end." Nathalie's words are measured. "When I heard my cancer had spread, actually the very same day I got the bad news that it was stage four and all downhill, I was in Paris at the time. Luc was working here in Èze. I went straight to Olivier's apartment. Not to his home—to his private apartment."

I picture Ava there at that same apartment, the revolving door of women, my extraordinary daughter just another peg in an assembly line. I can barely breathe, but I say nothing, just listen.

A tender expression comes across Nathalie's face. "I told Olivier everything. I cried to him and he held me. And then it happened. Just like that. Perhaps I knew deep down it would. Perhaps I wanted it, needed it.

And it was like nothing I'd ever experienced before . . . or at least for a very long time." Her blue eyes are bold and unblinking, locked in her memory. "I love my husband, Sophie, but we met when we were so young, before our careers even began. It was once so beautiful between us, and then it became like anything else in life, old. A gorgeous piece of art that you once loved so much at first, that you had to have, treasured, and then as time passes, it becomes just another picture on the wall. You no longer stop to admire it. And with Olivier, the passion was so new, so reckless." She dabs her now watery eyes with a tissue. "And perhaps because I had just received my death sentence, suddenly I didn't want comfort—I wanted life, to live what little I had left. I became so lost in Olivier, we got lost in each other, and then I got really sick so quickly. I had to let him go, which I did, but not in my head, not in my heart. I lied to Olivier. I hurt him very badly, told him that it was a mistake, a meaningless fling and I broke it off harshly . . . because I had to."

"And Luc," I prod, unable to mask my anger.

"I got lucky. He never found out."

If Ava weren't involved, I would perhaps feel sorry for Nathalie, living out her last days like this. Tormented. Sad even for Olivier, who had fallen in love with the one woman he couldn't have. But I'm livid that Ava was the rebound, a consolation prize. Too damn young. It's all so wrong, so totally unforgivable.

"And then came Ava." It pops out defiantly, my resentment steaming on a platter.

Nathalie releases a deep, knowing sigh. She sees my anger, hears it. "Yes, and then came Ava."

"You wanted to keep her close," I say accusingly. "It wasn't just that she was the perfect face of Eve."

Nathalie looks at me with guilty glazed-over eyes. "She *was* the perfect Eve. They weren't together at first. But I knew Olivier, and I knew it would be just a matter of time. So yes, maybe you are right—I wanted to keep her close, him close. I was dying. I had rejected him. My hair—that beautiful hair—was gone. The drugs, the treatment, stole everything from me—my looks, my fire, my sex drive, my ability to sculpt. I was so sick that I accepted it all. Even watching him and Ava in motion, seeing him happy once again, was a fitting punishment for betraying Luc. And I owed Luc loyalty in my final days." Tears begin to fall and it's unbearable to watch. I grab more tissues from a nearby shelf and wipe her eyes for her. "But I didn't want to die carrying this secret alone." Her voice is opaque but I can see through it. She still loves Olivier. "The truth is, this is breaking me, Sophie. I felt you might understand all this."

So many secrets. My daughter, who was really a pawn in a game of lovers' Ping-Pong, is now immortalized as a statue, and loyal Luc was betrayed in the same cruel way that Gabe had betrayed me, only he doesn't know it. *No, Nathalie, I don't understand any of it.* But when she reaches for me to comfort her, I can't help it: I take her frail hand inside mine anyway, and hold it tightly. *For her and for me.*

Chapter Twenty-Eight

It is 10:30 p.m. and I'm standing on the scaffold sanding down Eve's backside to remove shallow scratches. I forgot how much I love working at night when no one is around. For the past eleven days, I've done what feels like my best work with Nathalie and Claudia out of the way. The studio, with its high-arched ceiling, was constructed nearly a decade ago to fit Nathalie's mammoth artwork. From the skylight, the stars twinkle down on me, and through the large windows surrounding me, the colors of night stream through— inky shades of blue, gray, purple, illuminating Eve's marble physique to an alabaster glow.

My music blares from a boom box and I don't hear the door creak open. Nor do I hear the footsteps walking toward me as I work and harmonize with Sheryl

Crow. When the song is over and my concert is done, I hear clapping from behind me. I stop working, embarrassed, afraid to turn around. Oh god, it's *him*, I feel it.

"I thought you might like a glass of wine," Luc calls up from the base of the statue.

I stand where I am, pull up my goggles, turning slightly. "You didn't hear me sing."

"Oh, I did. I think all of Èze heard you sing." He laughs, and the sound is hearty, warm. I notice that he brought only one glass of wine.

"I'm mortified." I laugh nervously, wondering if he can see how red I am as I slowly descend the ladder.

"Don't be. I'm thoroughly entertained." When I reach the ground, I take Luc in. The casual elegance of his navy blue crewneck sweater with a white T-shirt peeking through, jeans, and loafers. Straight out of *GQ*. He hands me the wineglass, then crosses his arms. "I got home from Paris last night. Nathalie told me that you've been working around the clock. So I thought I would come by and see how you are doing." He pulls up a nearby chair, gesturing me to sit down as he grabs another one for himself.

As he sits next to me, I'm conscious of the sweat at my temples and that my hair is plastered from the sculpting workout. "It's going really well."

"Funny, isn't it? Here you are in Èze, helping my

wife. And your daughter was the model for Eve. What are the odds?" He laughs again. I can see his eyes shimmer even under the grainy lighting of the studio.

"What *are* the odds?" I repeat, because there are no odds. This doesn't even feel real. I point to wine on a nearby shelf. "I do have more—can I get you some?"

He shakes his head. "No, I really just wanted to take a moment to thank you, and make sure you were comfortable out here." He smiles, but it feels forced. He clears his throat. "Nathalie, as you know, is in very bad shape." He points to Eve, his voice barely above a whisper. "This is really the only thing keeping her alive and happy, her mind off the inevitable."

"I'm so sorry, Luc," I say softly. "I feel grateful every day that I get to work with her."

"And she feels the same about you." He takes a deep breath, trying to control his emotion. "I owe you a lot."

"You owe me nothing. This is truly an honor and privilege. I don't know if Nathalie told you but I haven't sculpted in a long time."

"Why did you stop?" he asks. "You're clearly very talented."

I feel my cheeks heat up, not sure that I want to go there. "It's a long story. I was young when my career took off, and then . . ."

He leans back in the chair, head tilted, assessing me intensely. It's unnerving. "And then?"

I inhale, release slowly. "And then, in the middle of everything, I developed carpal tunnel syndrome, which led to nerve damage, and I couldn't sculpt anymore, or it would get much worse. It was, as you can imagine, devastating. When my hands eventually healed, I was afraid to begin again. I guess I was terrified that I had lost my touch." *Why am I telling him this?* He doesn't want to hear my whole sob story. "I'm sorry. I'm going off on a tangent, and it's late."

There's an awkward silence between us. He checks his watch, stands. "Yes, it is late, and you've been working nonstop." He points to Eve. "Fantastic what you've done, really. I can see why Nathalie is so pleased." As he turns to go, he stops momentarily, gazes up at the beaming skylight. "Still gorgeous every time I look at it. Never gets old. She used to work in the middle of the night, you know, all night sometimes—especially right before an exhibition . . ." He cuts himself off. "Now I'm the one going off. *Bonne nuit*—good night, Sophie." He waves, walking toward the door.

"Luc . . . wait," I call out just before he leaves.

He turns, looking back at me. I don't even know what I'm going to say. *Say something quickly.* "Do you want to talk just a little longer?" I ask hesitantly. "I'm not so tired."

He shuffles his feet against the floor, like a little boy. "Yes . . . I think, perhaps, I do." He returns to the sitting area, to his chair. I point again to the few bottles of wine that I have on the nearby shelf. "Then please, at least let me pour you a proper glass of wine," I say. "Pinot noir. I know you will enjoy it—it's one of yours that Claudia brought for me."

"Actually, that does sound good."

I open the wine, pour him a glass, aware of his eyes on me as I hand it to him. He sips the wine, looking a bit more relaxed. "Tell me, how did you even end up in Èze, sculpting for my wife? That's a long way from Chicago."

"I think this story requires a refill." I laugh, pouring myself more wine. Never mind that he'd brought me chardonnay, and I'm mixing the red into the remnants of the white. Admittedly, I've become a daily drinker. Wine is the new Evian. "It's been a difficult summer for me," I tell him. "I came to Paris to visit my daughter at the end of her semester abroad. I'm . . . newly separated from my husband. It's actually a long, awful story— believe me you don't want to hear about it. Anyway, the short version is that I came out to Provence for a little soul-searching."

"Was the search a success?" he asks delicately.

"You could say that I'm a work in progress." We both laugh lightly.

"Sounds like there are a lot of missing details to that story." His eyes flash. The way he is looking at me is suddenly different, less intense. There's a casual ease to his gaze. I'm sure I'm imagining it.

"My husband cheated on me," I divulge, and then cover my mouth. *What am I saying?* It's the wine talking. It's the fact that I've barely eaten today. But I keep going. "To be honest, it's not a soul-search, more like a rescue mission." *Just stop*, I warn myself. He doesn't need to know any of these details—especially *those* details.

He stares at me, unblinking, and it's uncomfortable. I look away. I'm really such a mess. "Nathalie cheated on me too," he whispers, setting down the wineglass. *Oh god.*

I don't blink this time. No matter what, I will not betray her trust. Let him talk. Better him than me.

His eyes suddenly turn somber, darker. His forehead furrows. "I actually haven't discussed this with anyone. I'm very private, not the type to just open up. But it's all very strange, isn't it, all of these connections. You, me, your daughter, my wife, and . . ."

Olivier is what he wants to say.

"Yes." My heart is thumping.

"I was lying in bed last night, thinking that everyone is connected to . . ." Luc searches my face, shaking his head. "That guy," he says.

That guy. He definitely knows.

"I can't even begin to imagine how you feel about him regarding Ava . . . but it was also Olivier who had an affair with my wife."

I know, Luc, I know. I'm too afraid to move or speak.

"They think I don't know." He leans forward, cups his chin in his hand. "But there were so many signs, sloppiness—which isn't like Nathalie. She's a woman who is always in total control. But these days . . ." He looks away, visibly pained.

These days are shit, I think. His wife of nearly twenty years is about to die, and all she wants to do is spend her last days alive in this studio with me and Eve—*not him*. Her heart is with Olivier—*not him*. She's with Luc out of guilt and history. And he knows. My heartbeat quickens. The pain he must feel.

He clenches his jaw and I wish I could run my hand along it, soften it somehow, and tell him I know exactly what he's going through—the betrayal, the abandonment, the loss. "My wife . . . sometimes I think I know her *too* well. In many aspects it's a good thing, but really if you think about it, it's a curse."

I don't need to think about it, *I know.*

His hands fidget. He's no longer relaxed, no longer *GQ* cool. "We've been together so long and we don't have children, so the focus on each other is perhaps even stronger. I know what she's about to do before she does it. And Olivier—I've known him since art school. He's a pig." The golden flecks inside Luc's eyes blaze like torches.

"Yes, but a complicated one," I say honestly. "I wanted to hate him for having an affair with my daughter, and I do, believe me." I don't mention the almost-pregnancy. "And then he set this up for me with Nathalie. So yes, I hate him for what happened with Ava, and yet I'm grateful to be here."

Luc doesn't say anything for a long while. He stares out the window over my shoulder. I turn to look. There's a shadow of a leaning tree, its branches lightly slapping at the window. "I cannot help but wonder if Nathalie didn't get sick, would it have continued? Is she still with me *only* because she's sick?" Again, he searches my eyes for answers. *Stay neutral. Stay Switzerland.* "She's dying and I promised myself that I would never let on that I know. I think she's at peace thinking that she got away with it, without hurting me. And somehow that hurts even more. But really, what's the difference now, right?"

I yearn to save him from the torment I also feel. What *is* the difference now? Nathalie is dying and my own marriage is already dead. I yearn to reach out, to comfort him—but I don't. The part of me that is still me knows better. Find words, I tell myself, soothe this beautiful man somehow. "The way Nathalie talks about you, looks at you still, it *is* love. Don't lose sight of that. Maybe it's not perfect. Maybe it's a long-term love that turned into friendship. But it is still love built on history. You grew up together. No one can take that away. Trust me, I know."

"I appreciate that, I really do. But does history require lies?" he asks, sounding so vulnerable. I can feel his rawness as though I'm inside him. *He loves her.*

"I can't answer that, Luc. I just can't."

His shoe grazes mine accidentally, and I feel a shooting sensation throughout my body. I quickly pull away. Strangely, we are bonded by Siamese betrayal. "I have never cheated," he says. "I'm probably the only Frenchman alive who can say that." He laughs in a sad sort of way, then places the half-full wineglass on the small table and stands. *It's enough.* We both know we crossed too many boundaries. Our conversation is much more intimate than it has a right to be. "Thank you again for being here for her."

I remind myself that this is a good man—*not a Gabe*

Man. A man with a cheating, dying wife who loves another and he knows it, but is too honorable to reveal the truth to her, even at the expense of himself.

After Luc leaves the studio, I don't even have the strength to remove my soiled, dusty clothes. I collapse on the bed next to Eve. I lie on top of the covers, staring at the glittery stars above and then at Eve towering over me, a milky goddess. I replay every word of the conversation with Luc in my head, twisting, turning, reinterpreting—playing mind games until my eyes finally shut, until Luc becomes nothing more than a dream, and tomorrow becomes a reality I don't want to face.

Tomorrow I head home.

V.

If I create from the heart, nearly
everything works: if from the head,
almost nothing.

—MARC CHAGALL

Chapter Twenty-Nine

In the old days, Gabe would have picked me up from the airport, and if he couldn't because of work demands, it would have been Samantha or Lauren. There was never a thought that I would one day get off a plane—after traveling for hours and managing mishaps from Nice to Heathrow, missing my Chicago connection, having to fly to JFK instead—spend a sleepless night in a crappy airport hotel, and then onto a Chicago flight early this morning, and be alone. That I would pick up my suitcase, meeting no one in Baggage, and return to a home that is no longer mine, alone.

I check my watch as I quickly make my way outside to meet the Uber: *9:30 a.m. here, 4:30 p.m. in Saint-Paul.* I feel displaced, a stranger in a strange land. I told Ava, who isn't a morning person, not to come get me, and I warned her not to send her father. She promised. And yet, I find myself looking around for Gabe anyway.

When the Uber arrives, I'm half hoping it's Stan the Uber Guy, but it's not—it's Charlene, a bubbly grandmother, who recently lost her husband, whose daughter and granddaughter live in Atlanta, and about a thousand other personal details about her life that she rattles off that I hear but don't really listen to. This is what Uber has done for humanity—even chatty grandmas can reinvent themselves.

As I stare out the window at all the passing familiar highway exit signs, I'm surprisingly not tired. I had taken a Benadryl and knocked out a solid six hours of sleep on the Heathrow–JFK leg of the trip, and I slept for nearly the entire ride back to Chicago. But my stomach is twisting as I get closer to North Grove and all of its suburban trappings. I wonder if Lauren and Samantha know I'm coming. I'm definitely going to run into someone because suburbia is not who you run into, it's who you try to avoid.

Charlene is rambling on about her six-year-old granddaughter with the genes of Einstein and apparently a gifted gymnast, and I toss back all the right responses, from "Don't you love that" to "God, I miss that" to "The best age ever, the best." We finally pull into my driveway and it's as if time froze and I had melted. The sprinklers are still on, just as I'd left them. Pablo is barking up a storm. I can hear him going apeshit from the other side of the driveway door. He knows it's me. I begin to tremble. *This is happening.*

The door flings open and Gabe stands there, leaning against the doorway jamb like the ghost from Christmas past, barefoot in his flannels and white T-shirt, his hair sticking up along the sides, and his arm in a sling, with Pablo at his side. I think of Holly the nurse and I don't feel sorry for him. Maybe a tiny bit.

"Girl, that man is a *maye—an.* Lucky you." Charlene lets out a long whistle, which sounds like a teakettle. The kind that pierces the ear and you want to scream *shut the fuck up already* as you race across the kitchen to turn it off.

"Yes, he is a man." That's about as much as I'm willing to give Charlene as I gather my things, thank her, wish her and her family well, and open the car door. Gabe rushes over and grabs the suitcase out of my hand. I let him do it.

"Thanks," I say, but refrain from telling him to *be careful of your arm and your ribs.*

"Wow." He stands back for a second. "You look great, Soph. Your hair. You look . . . so different."

"Thanks." I interpret "so different" to mean good.

Gabe, even with the stick-up hair, is still unfairly handsome. The kind of *maye-an* that every woman would tea-whistle at, even a grandma. Gabe is going to die with a full head of hair and a hard-on. As much as I hate him, he has not lost his sex appeal. Not even a little. The muscle memory flexes throughout my body, as I mentally chalk up his marital crimes against me.

As we enter our house, I reach down and embrace Pablo, who smells freshly shampooed. I stop walking, pausing at the edge of the laundry room, hesitating to cross over the threshold into my renovated kitchen. I fold my arms tightly and peer inside. All that vintage white on white with splashes of red and black that I was once so gaga about, and now means nothing. It's my kitchen but not my kitchen anymore. And it's huge. I forgot how big it is. I'd been living at the hotel and then in Lea and Jean-Paul's small apartment with barely any kitchen space. But this . . . I glance sideways at Gabe, who is intently watching me, still my husband but not my husband. It's all so familiar and so foreign—my life, but not my life.

"Ava is still sleeping," he says quietly, not wanting to interrupt my reentry thoughts, then carefully moves past me and heads into the kitchen, placing my suitcase next to the food pantry. "She told me to wake her up as soon as you came home. But I think it's best to let her sleep for a bit." He exhales deeply. "Come inside, Sophie."

He's trying. Nodding, I enter slowly and drop my purse onto the kitchen table and walk around.

"I made some coffee. It's a new bean—stronger than our usual. You know that barista with the nose ring, she recommended it." Gabe is talking in double time as he gets out the mugs. I see him but not really. I don't hear him either, the way I didn't really hear Charlene, like I'm in a thick fog or I've just woken up from a coma. I scour everything around me, trying to reconnect with what was once my life, my things. Nothing has changed physically. Even the same yellow sticky pad near the phone on the counter, which has "Things to Do, Bitch" embossed at the top, is scribbled with *Dr. Jerome at 11 a.m.*—as in my internist appointment over a month ago. *Before.*

"You okay?" Gabe asks gently, as he pours me a cup of coffee.

"I don't know. No, I guess. I feel off, shaky," I answer honestly as we both sit down at the kitchen table, not in our usual seats next to each other, but in opposite seats. We are tiptoeing, being so careful, so adult, right now. I suppose that's where anger lands after it leaves town: civility.

"Ava mentioned you are sculpting again. That's

really great." He is trying so hard to connect with me that it's almost painful.

"Yeah, I'm working with a very talented sculptor over there, helping her finish her installation." *On a major piece for which your daughter posed nude for her lover's lover. I bet she didn't tell you that part.* But I say none of this as I sip my coffee, which tastes weak and watery, now that I've gotten used to the full-bodied burnt-bean taste of French-roasted coffee. That conversation I'm saving for Ava, when we're alone.

"And your hands—you're okay?"

I glance down at my hands; hands that have been working overtime, day and night, on Eve without a hitch or even a twinge of pain. His eyes meet mine thoughtfully, and we are both thinking back to that awful moment years ago when I finally had to accept what four doctors had advised: *No more sculpting.* That night, after Dr. Number Four gave his verdict, I broke down completely in Gabe's arms. He held me, soothed me, saying repeatedly, "I wish I could carry this instead of you. I would rather me not being able to do surgery, than you not being able to sculpt." The ulti-mate sacrifice—*him for me.* The ultimate declaration of love—*I would take a bullet for you.* Were those words even true then? Did he feel that then? All I know is that

I believed him then. I look away from him, and out the kitchen window. *But not now.*

I sip the coffee, stare into the mug, the silence between us palpable and stretched. Finally, I look up at him. "How are you feeling? From the accident."

Our gazes lock again, so many words are left unsaid. Better that way. "Still hurts. Still healing, but improving, thanks. Still on painkillers, which I'm finally weaning off . . ." He stops there. I don't ask about the nurse and he knows better than to tell me.

His good hand cups tightly around his mug. "I'm sorry for all of it, Soph. And I really miss you."

Tears appear at the corners of his eyes, and mine remain dry. *How did we come to this?* I may have been able to forgive a drunken affair, a one-night stand. I may even have been able to work through a few Ashley Madisons with lots of couples therapy. Maybe. But the flirty nurse who he had once called me crazy and ridiculous for thinking that she was hitting on him—an affair back then that clearly continued until now? *And Lauren?* No way, I shake my head. No fucking way. That's where it ends. Lauren is family, my sister.

Instant replays of our friends continue to pop uninvited inside my head on a daily basis, as though challenging me to find the hidden clues—the *Where's*

Waldo within each scenario. I visualize Gabe and Lauren's shared looks, their inside jokes, most likely playing footsie under a table or thigh pressed against thigh—the sneaking in front of my face and behind my back, perhaps from the very beginning. I look at Gabe, sitting across from me, that electrocuted hair that used to make me smile in the mornings, that boyish yearning in his eyes that I used to love, and I have nothing left to give. *This broke us, Gabe. The others burned a hole through me, but you with Lauren shattered us.* I push back the rising anger inside me, and say, "Let's just keep things above board, nice for Ava this weekend. Okay?"

Not good enough. I can see it in Gabe's eyes. He's not done with this conversation that he clearly has been waiting for, prepping for. "I blew it, didn't I?"

I want to say something sarcastic like, *No, everyone blew you*, but I don't. I opt instead for the compromiser. "Perhaps we both blew this," I counter numbly. "Let's just keep things peaceful."

He stands dramatically. "No, don't do that. Don't protect me. You're not to blame at all." He points a finger. Gabe the hero gallops in. "It was all me. You were you. Good, loyal, beautiful. I royally fucked this up. I didn't know when enough was enough, until it wasn't." He picks up his coffee and downs it as though it were Gatorade or a vodka shot.

Until you were caught. That's usually the finish line for cheaters.

I can deal with Guilty Gabe, even Savior Gabe, but definitely not Victim Gabe. That's when I snap, when I pull the civility plug. No more tiptoeing. "It was Lauren all along, wasn't it?" My desensitized voice ejaculates into an accusatory hiss. "You really want to put this all on the table—then let's go."

His face turns red, he's caught off guard. He clearly prefers the civilized version of me. "It wasn't like that."

I shake my head. If I hear one more lie. "Oh, it was *so* like that. It went as far back as prom night, maybe even longer. You held back your feelings all these years, until you couldn't—both of you. How you must have laughed behind my back, thinking you pulled one over on me."

He sits down. "What are you talking about?"

"Don't make me feel like this is all in my head—like with that damn nurse." I slam my coffee cup against the table and it spills in a here-we-go-again moment. "You tell me, Gabe, what *am* I talking about?"

"Hi, Mom." Ava stands in the archway in a faded blue tank top and age-old gray sweats that read "Tyler's Bar Mitzvah 2009"—*how long has she been standing there?*

I jump up from the table and lunge toward her,

squeezing her in close. "God, I missed you. Look at you." She smells like Pantene. I hold her at arm's length—the wild, wavy mane, the flawless skin. I see her, but I also see Eve simultaneously—my sculpture and my daughter. The flare of the nostrils, the slight chin cleft, the doe eyes. *Nathalie's sculpture.*

"Love your hair," she says, winding a strand around her fingers. "Missed you too."

From the corner of my eye, I see Gabe watching us, left out—no usual three-way hug. *See, Gabe, this is the one three-way you lost out on.*

I point to Ava's chair at the kitchen table. "Go sit down." I snap into Mom mode, pouring her coffee and cutting her a piece of the banana chocolate loaf that Gabe must have just picked up yesterday from Whole Foods. I gently press my thumb into it. Still fresh. I open the refrigerator, which is surprisingly well stocked, and pull out a new container of strawberries while taking inventory: lots of fruits and veggies—all my favorites. He loaded up for our family reunion.

"So . . . ," Gabe says, as we all sit and face each other.

I ignore him and turn to Ava. "So, I slept pretty well on the plane, but not last night at the hotel. I'm sure the jet lag will kick my butt later. But let's hit Bed Bath & Beyond, Target, and the Container Store today—the usual suspects—while I'm still functioning," I say.

"Sounds great." Ava turns to her dad, then looks back at me. "We thought we'd all go to dinner tonight if you're up to it. That new sushi place. Mom, you will love it."

"Together?" I ask, knowing the answer.

She exchanges glances with her father again. "Yes, together. Is that okay?"

"Whatever your mom wants to do," Guilty Gabe pipes in.

Screw you. Don't go all Good Guy here. The anger from our unfinished conversation is still ballooning. "Sushi it is." I stand, knowing it's best to remove myself before my bubbling anger makes landfall. "I'm going to take a quick shower now, and we'll begin our day whenever you're ready, honey."

They both watch me with micromanaging eyes, as though I am Ava's photosynthesis experiment, her big fifth-grade science project. I remember how we all stood around the kitchen island watching that large jar filled with leaves in water for hours to see how oxygen is created. I know exactly what they are both thinking: *Is she going to go upstairs to the master bedroom or to the guest room?* It matters. Whichever choice I make tells the rest of the story. I see the dual anticipation in their faces. Ava's eyes are wide, Gabe's are wider.

My heart aches because there is no way in hell I'm

going up to the master bedroom. Choosing the unpopular Option B, I wheel my suitcase over to the guest room on the far side of the first floor. I hear their disappointed sighs in stereo behind me, and I feel even sadder. They clearly had a plan, an obvious collusion, and I've gone off script. The truth is, entering the guest room, which I have never slept in before, is one of the hardest things I have ever done. Choosing *me first* over their needs, disappointing my daughter and yes, even Gabe, takes us all by surprise.

Chapter Thirty

Dinner feels eerily like old times, and despite everything, I allow myself to enjoy it. The three of us together, eating sushi, ordering our favorite rolls and pieces, sharing and double-dipping, and for a moment I forget everything. I glance around the packed hip restaurant. "Love this place."

Ava is pleased. "I knew you would."

The restaurant, called Su-Chic, is very high-end for the burbs. It belongs in the city. It is decorated in art deco grays and brushed silver; vintage chandeliers shaped like lanterns hover over each table; abstract art lines the walls; and large three-foot-high glass vases filled with exotic Japanese plants are on each table. And the menus are one-page thin limestone blocks—no sushi pictures on sticky laminated plastic anywhere. Gabe and Ava are laughing, and if I don't let myself think and just feel this, feel *us*, there is something to it that seems so right. Ava in her entertainer role senses my participation. She is center stage, eagerly sharing her travel tales with Jake—no mention of Olivier, the cheating, me staying in the South of France, or our family brokenness. The dinner is the Old Us—Ava, first and last, Gabe and me her adoring audience. And then without warning, the curtain comes crashing down.

Over Gabe's shoulder, I see Samantha and Lauren walk into the restaurant. And then I realize that this family dinner was all a setup. The spell is broken. I glare at my deceptive child and husband.

"Really?"

Before they can respond, my ex-best friends make a beeline to our table. I look away, trying to pull myself together and pretend like I'm searching for something in my purse.

"Hi, Soph," Samantha says loudly, as Lauren eyes me closely but doesn't even look at Gabe. Everybody is beyond uncomfortable and I do nothing to help the situation. I can tell Samantha is dying to hug me and Lauren wants to make a comment about my hair but knows better.

I stand with crossed arms. "No way. Uh-uh. Not happening."

Ava pulls me back down by my shirtsleeve. "Please, Mom, just hear them out. They are your best friends. They want to talk to you. Just be you again for five minutes."

Me again? I stare at my daughter—*Eve in real life.* "You have no idea."

She glances at Gabe, but he is looking at me. I give him a cold glare. *Did you tell Ava you slept with Lauren?* I want to shout at him, and almost do. *Me again. Please.*

"Let's go, Dad. I will drive back with you."

Yes, we drove in separate cars to the restaurant. It was Ava's idea, and I thought she was being considerate of my feelings. Now I know why: they needed an escape vehicle for this so-called intervention. Gabe pays the bill, leaves exact cash, and follows Ava out the door. Bravo, I think. Well played.

I look at my former friends with unfiltered side eye. *I will give you both ten minutes and then I'm out of here.*

I tell the passing waitress to bring me another glass of pinot grigio. If I'm going to do this, it's going to be my way, and saturated. As Samantha and Lauren sit down, they are both visibly ill at ease, waiting for me to say something—anything—but I remain purposely silent. Samantha clears her throat. The opening monologue is about to begin. I can hardly wait.

Not so fast, I think, changing my mind. Samantha is not going to control this as usual, so I cut in, establish the format. "I'm really not interested in what either of you has to say. But for the sake of my daughter—say it quickly and then I'm leaving. Ten minutes." Samantha looks tired. There are dark circles under her eyes that were never there before. Lauren, on the other hand, looks great. She had a blow-out for the occasion—her red mane is voluminous around her shoulders. I can barely look at her.

"Okay, we get it. We fucked up," Samantha begins. "These past weeks have been hell without you. You know that. It's always been the three of us against the world."

Was the three of us, *was.*

"We want to do anything we can to fix this, Soph." She glances at Lauren, who is chewing at her lip, knowing her betrayal is far worse than Samantha's.

"I appreciate that you are here," I tell them, trying to be somewhat diplomatic. "But I can never go back to what was. This is not fixable. This changed me. I would never have come back to North Grove if it weren't for Ava—you both know that, right?"

They don't respond. Lauren's eyes are wide and unblinking and Samantha nods but barely. The ball still in my court, I continue, "The night of my birthday, Gabe's betrayal. So many women. But nothing—I repeat, *nothing*—hurt me more than you." I shoot Lauren a dirty look and refrain from pointing my finger in her face. "So many years you've had feelings for Gabe, from the beginning. I saw it at prom, damn it. I saw it when we were in Italy. And I can't stop thinking and rethinking that it was all happening in front of my face. You probably played footsie with him under my new kitchen table—while all of our kids were there. How could you? And you slept with him in Nashville when I was sick as a dog—how the hell could you do that to me?" My voice rises, people are looking, but I couldn't care less. My eyes are sizzling. I turn to Samantha accusingly. "And you *knew*. You were an accomplice to this. Shame on you both."

"It was once," Lauren whispers. Her voice sounds mousy and guilt-ridden. "Once. I was drunk and it happened. And I cannot forgive myself so I don't expect you to forgive me."

"If it were just once," I counter, "it would be one time too many. But it wasn't once—it was all the way through. At least admit it, Lauren. Admit it now."

A deafening silence looms for maybe five seconds, but feels like an eternity.

"Yes," she says and instant tears erupt, casting a shimmery mist over her green eyes, a color I realize that is very close to Luc's. Samantha's mouth drops open.

"Really? So surprised? Innocent? *Give me a break.*" This time I do point at Samantha. "We've both known that Lauren has always been jealous of us, even laughed about it." I sound mean, but I can't help it. The hurt inside is an open, festering wound. "How could you not tell me?"

Samantha doesn't answer that directly. Instead, she begins her prepared monologue. "Yes, everything you are saying is true. And if it were reverse, you would have told me, you would have told Lauren. We know that." She looks to Lauren for back-up support. "We messed up, Soph. I have nothing to say for myself—no defense, okay. All I know is that not having you in my life is far worse than even my mother's death."

Time stops. I knock the chopsticks off the table. *This.* This gets to me and she knows it. Lynda is the lone card Samantha possesses and she plays it. We all loved Lynda. I'm not inhuman. Breathe, I tell myself, just breathe.

Lauren's turn now. She knows she is going to have to work a whole lot harder. "You're right, Sophie. I am jealous. I am insecure. I've always felt that you and Samantha were closer than I am with either of you. And

I'm not going to blame my fucked-up childhood, but there's that." Her voice shakes. "And yes, I had a crush on Gabe all through high school, from the moment I saw him in the lunchroom freshman year. And when you started dating him, it killed me. *He chose you.* The night . . ." She glances at Samantha, who gives her a *keep going* look. "That night Gabe and I were together was not at all how you imagined it to be. I couldn't go through with it, couldn't continue. I realized . . . actually I had an epiphany, Sophie, in that awful moment of betraying you, that it wasn't Gabe I wanted—it was you."

Oh my god. I nearly knock over my wine.

But her watery, red-rimmed lying eyes are telling the truth. I know those eyes. I glance at Samantha for verification. She nods. "It's true," Lauren continues. "I'm planning on leaving Matt, only he doesn't know it yet. Just you two know, of course. After everything that happened with you, I realized it was high time for me to finally be true to who I am, whatever that means. I know it's not going to be easy on my kids. It's not what I choose to be, but I have to be comfortable at some point with who I really am. This was not the plan, right?" She looks at both of us and knows that this was not anything remotely near the plan. I'm speechless, realizing my mouth has dropped open and

I'm not blinking. "I'm not done here." Her voice seems to strengthen. "Forgive me for hurting you so deeply. But you need to know that it was you I was in love with, you who I was looking at during prom—*you.*" She sighs deeply, and then smiles slightly. "And Jenna from yoga is a close second."

We all laugh. Impossible not to. The marvels of our yogi Jenna's bendable body are beyond comprehension and the main subject of our numerous lunches after class.

But Lauren is still not done. "I take full responsibility for all the pain I caused you, Soph. Maybe somewhere inside of you, at some point in the future, you can understand and hopefully forgive me." The pent-up tears stream freely down her face now. "And your hair does look great, by the way."

We can't help it. We all laugh through the tears, because it is all so sad-funny, all too true-funny, all too Jo-Malone-for-three funny. *My best friend was in love with me.* Of course, I didn't see it. And how hard it must have been for her all these years to hide it. I cannot help but think of Lea—her radiant skin, that lithe body. But Lauren, as beautiful as she is, is my sister. This secret truth of hers I can work with. I can forgive this somehow. She was in love with me—*not Gabe.* She was looking at me at prom from across the gym—*not Gabe*. She wanted to play footsie with me under the table—*not Gabe*. She wanted to take from me what she could never have—*me*. None of it is right, none of it is okay, but in its twisted truth there is honesty and pain—more for her than for me.

There are no words for this. Samantha gently covers her hand over mine, Lauren over Samantha's. It's not simple. Our eyes lock. But it is forgivable.

"Okay," I say softly, and slowly cup my hand over theirs.

Chapter Thirty-One

Ava and Gabe are watching *Definitely, Maybe* when I walk in—one of our family favorites. Gabe presses pause and looks up at me.

"Thank you," I tell them both. I long to sit with them, share the popcorn, watch Ryan Reynolds, and play house.

"Come sit with us," says Ava, the mediator. Pablo chimes in with a wag of his tail.

"Can we talk first?" I sit on the long arm of the couch with just enough distance. Gabe turns off the TV. I have been driving around North Grove for the past half hour, rehearsing what I want to say to both of them.

They look at me as though I'm an impersonator. Neither is used to this new version of me and I get it. "I really appreciate that you did that for me," I tell them.

"This has all been so damn hard. I want to be with you both, I really do. But I can't pretend what happened didn't happen." I'm quiet for a few moments, and Pablo nestles up to me. "Ava, you are the love of our lives." I glance at Gabe, who nods. "The best part of us. I didn't ask for what happened between your dad and me, but it happened. And I can't go back."

"But maybe we can move forward," she says with a glint of hope in her eyes, and it kills me that I'm the one to add to her despair. "You guys have always been the best couple. Maybe you can work through the crap like Jake and I did."

If only there was a road map for working through the crap. I look at Gabe. "Please tell her the truth. Help me out here."

Gabe looks like he wants to throw up, but he muscles up, turns to Ava. "I didn't just cheat on your mom. And it wasn't once or even twice like I told you in Paris, which would have been bad enough. I had numerous affairs throughout our entire marriage. I betrayed this family repeatedly and I'm not proud of it."

Thank you, Gabe, for owning this, my eyes tell him. Ava tears up. This is all too much for anyone's child to handle. "I know, Dad. I heard all about stupid Ashley Madison from Caitlin. She told me that you were the number one cheater in North Grove. I know, maybe not everything, but I know." She chokes back the tears. "What am I supposed to do with all this?"

The level of humiliation and shame she must feel—and hearing the truth from Samantha's eldest, who is two years younger than Ava and who has always looked up to her. And yet Ava is still sitting here with Gabe anyway, watching *Definitely, Maybe*, still longing for us to reconcile somehow.

Ava clutches a throw pillow to her chest and turns to me. "It must have hurt you so much, Mom. I've done nothing but think about this and talk to Jake about it. In Dad's defense, when I was with Olivier, I never once thought of his wife. I mean never. It's easy to do, you know—to separate things, to compartmentalize—to just pretend other things around you don't exist. And it's wrong." She looks at her father. "Did you think of us when you were having all those affairs?"

My eyes pop. This could be a reality show, a Jerry Springer special, where Ava's fed her lines—and yet they are all hers. Our daughter is asking the Golden Question: *When you betrayed us, did you think of us, or did you pretend we didn't exist?*

Facing the two most important women in his life, Gabe is in the hot seat. He knows his fatherhood and husbandhood are riding on this. There is no more room for lies.

"Yes, I pretended." Perspiration lines his forehead. "While it was happening it was easy, but not the afterward. When I'd drive away from wherever I was, I never pretended. I felt it all—the guilt, the disgust, the shame, the disappointment."

"But it didn't stop you," Ava says, barely audible.

"No." He looks at me. His downturned mouth is childlike, remorseful. Part of me breaks for him, wanting to protect him from himself.

"So, what now?" Ava asks.

They both look to me, the only real adult in the room. I think of Lea and Jean-Paul—that first night we spent together when I was a novice sexual participant, and the one that followed, when I was calling the shots. I think of Luc's loyalty to his dying wife, despite Nathalie's betrayal. We are all just human, some of us a little more, some of us less. I love these two people with all their faults. I only wish I could deal with the crap and just move on. I wish I could curl up in that crook of Gabe's arm again the way we used to at the end of a long day and binge on Netflix. But I'm a rubber band pulled too far. Somewhere along the way I snapped. I can't go back, there are no steps to retrace. No pretend. *Even for Ava.*

I pull out the only response I can find from *The Good Mom Playbook*, the chapter called "It's Not Your Fault."

"No matter what happens between us, Ava, I will always love your dad. He was my first love, my first everything." I glance quickly at Gabe, thinking, *But now* not *my only*. "I won't lie to you, what happened—the numerous betrayals—have been beyond painful and I've been lost." I move from the arm of the couch and now sit next to them, closer to them. "The silver lining, if there is one, is that it forced me to really look at myself and ask what did I really want. The truth is, I wasn't very happy either. You know how you feel when you are not painting, Ava? You get edgy, irritable, parts of you feel like they're dying. Well, I stopped sculpting. First it was medical, and then it was fear." I look at Gabe. "I buried my passion years ago and I know that affected us. Now that I'm working again, everything seems to have changed. Who knows, maybe it took what happened between us to kick my ass in gear and find me again."

The truth is out. Mine and Gabe's, and now we have to address Ava's. I reach over and place my hand over hers. They feel cold and tiny inside mine. "There is something I wanted to talk to you about alone, but since we've started all this . . . like I said I am sculpting again, and I should probably tell you that I'm sculpting with Nathalie Senard."

Her eyes open wide. Gabe sees Ava's startled reaction. "Nathalie Senard—the famous artist?" he asks.

"Yes, her," I tell him. "She's dying of cancer and I was asked to help her finish her final installation in secret." I'm hoping I can skip the relevant detail that it was Olivier who connected us. I glance at Ava. *Your turn.*

"Are you working on Eve?" Her voice is barely there.

"That I am," I say, waiting.

"Who is Eve?" Gabe asks.

Ava's mouth drops. She knows I know.

Her cheeks blow out slowly. "What Mom is getting at is . . . well, during the semester, I posed nude for Nathalie Senard. Eve is me."

"Eve is you?" Gabe looks confused. "Where is this being shown?"

Ava's body tightens, she goes mute. There's no point in holding back, so I take over. "Eve is Nathalie's final sculpture. They're calling it the feminist answer to Michelangelo's David. I'd say there's a good chance it will be shown pretty much everywhere. I was concerned at first too, but now I have to say that I'm proud."

Ava's face breaks out with relief. It doesn't matter that we are a house of artists, and Gabe's a doctor. Our daughter posing nude is still our daughter naked in Gabe's eyes. "Everyone will see this." His mounting anger is more than apparent. "I'm not happy about this at all."

I wait for Ava's "it's not porn, Dad, it's art" retort. She's not one to hold back. Ever. She lets go of my hand and points at him. "At another time, Dad, you'd have a leg to stand on. Now, not so much."

Touché. But I interject reflexively. "Ava, he is still your father. Don't forget that."

"This is so fucking ridiculous." She jumps up off the couch, faces us with a steely glare, hands on her hips, and this time, points at me. "You ditched us, ran away from your problems. And Dad is the blue-ribbon cheater of North Grove, and you're still a united front? I posed because I wanted to. It's art, Dad, not porn. I'm an artist, and so is Mom—get over yourself."

And there you go. She crosses her arms, challenging either of us to say another word. Gabe and I look at each other. No matter what went down between us, we are hurting the one person we both love most in this world.

"A united front is something," I tell her gently. "It's a good thing, a start." I pat the couch cushion. "Come sit down, honey. Let's all just watch the movie together."

Sometimes saying nothing is the best option. Too many truths for one night. But at least there are no more lies. That *is* something. Ava reluctantly sits in between us. We watch the rest of *Definitely, Maybe* in silence, munching the popcorn, our hands meeting in the middle of the giant bowl, each of us lost in our own thoughts. We are still a family, only different now, stripped down and raw. Perhaps just a little more honest about our dysfunction. Maybe just maybe, now that the crap is out there, we will be better for it.

Chapter Thirty-Two

It's late after the movie ends, but none of us is tired. We decide to pack up Ava's jeep and the small U-Haul with the four stuffed duffel bags, the new futon and bedding, framed prints of her favorite paintings, the new microwave, the mini-fridge, and myriad kitchen appliances and bathroom supplies for her new apartment. University of Wisconsin–Madison is a two-and-a-half-hour drive from North Grove. Ava and I do the loading because of Gabe's arm and ribs. I made it clear to him that I'm taking her to school alone in the morning and setting her up. From there, I will be returning to France. He's not happy about it, but silently accepts it.

As we pack up the car, Gabe says nothing directly to me. He just belts out orders like "Put it over there," "Seriously? That's not going to fit," and "Stack it right, or it's going to break." He talks to Ava but looks past me. When everything is done, Gabe heads into his office and shuts the door and Ava goes upstairs into her bedroom. I wait for a bit, clean up the kitchen, go down to the basement and grab a large suitcase, and then make my way up to the master bedroom, which I've avoided.

Standing in the doorway of my bedroom feels even stranger than the kitchen. I enter slowly and pause in front of our tainted bed, staring at all the matchy-matchy decorative pillows, and know one thing for certain: I will never sleep there again.

My heart beating fast, I walk past my sculpture, enter my closet, and quickly rummage through my stuff. It feels as though I'm robbing someone else's closet as I toss shoes, shirts, skirts, jeans, and dresses into the luggage. I don't know exactly what I'm doing or even how long I will be staying. All I know is that I am going back to Saint-Paul, to the life—*the me*—I'm creating there.

Before I zipper up the suitcase, I snag the photo of me, Gabe, and Ava, taken on her first birthday, off my nightstand. It's my favorite. We all looked so happy then, so blissfully innocent. We *were* happy, were innocent. It was before the cheating began and the sculpting ended. I run my fingers along the chrome frame. This is how

I want to remember us—the memory I will always treasure.

I take one last lingering look at my bedroom, turn off the lights, and pass by Ava's room. Her light is still on. I leave my suitcase outside her door.

"Mom." She hears me.

I peek my head inside. "Hi. I will wake you up at around eight thirty. Sound good?"

"You're going back there, aren't you? No changing your mind?" She sounds so heartbroken.

Deep breath. I walk inside. Her room is dark; just her nightstand lamp is on. Her laptop is balanced on her stomach and her cell phone is right next to her; Pablo is curled up at the end of the bed. I sit next to her, remove the devices. "Yes, I'm going to finish the sculpture. And then . . ."

"And then what?" She sits up.

I shrug. "I don't know. No plan yet."

"That's not like you. Everything is always planned. You always seem to know what's next."

"Yeah, but that kind of went out the window." I smile sadly.

"Are you going to be okay?"

I reach out and hold her toasty hand, and she squeezes mine. "I hope so. How 'bout you? It was a hard night. Are you okay?"

"I think so. No, probably not." She pulls me toward her and I lie on the pillow next to her. "I'm worried about Dad, though. He's losing it."

"Yeah, I'm worried too." And it's the truth.

"He loves you, Mom, despite everything. I can see it." Still wistful. Still hoping. Still right.

Say something soothing so Ava can sleep. No, I correct myself, say something real so she can actually believe in it, hold on to it. "Love is messy," I say softly, borrowing from Lea. "I don't think I ever really understood that until now. But no matter what, even if life hurts like hell, sometimes you just have to pick yourself up and build again. That's what I'm going with."

She looks up at me, eyes large and round. "What if Jake cheats again? It happened once."

"Yes, but don't forget you were with Olivier at the same time," I remind her. Accountability is everything. Brokenness and betrayal are never a one-person show.

"I still think about him," she admits, leaning against me. "How did you get to Nathalie Senard anyway?"

More truth. There's no way out. "Remember you told me that Olivier was going to be teaching in the South of France? Well, I actually ran into him. I had taken a day trip to Cap-Ferrat and I bumped into him and his students at the Rothschild art museum. It took me by surprise, I admit. He told me about his friend

Nathalie, who he said needed help and thought I might be a good fit. He set it up, never mentioning to me that you had modeled for her. You can only imagine my shock when I took one good look at Eve." The truth is out there, bent a bit, filtered, but out. I stop at the edge of full disclosure.

Ava pulls the covers up to her chin. "It's crazy how it all connects, isn't it? How sick is Nathalie?"

"Very," I say, my head nestled against hers. "It's only a matter of time. I'm finishing Eve, working as fast as I can. She sits there all day and watches me, directs, and corrects me." I smile to myself, thinking of Eve's toes. I lean over and kiss the top of my daughter's head. "Last year in college—I still can't believe it."

"I feel so old and young at the same time," she says. "This summer, this whole year—it was so much."

And then she begins to cry. My baby finally lets it all out, and it's about damn time. She's been so strong, *too* strong. Ava cries for all the things in life that she can't fix. And all I can do is hold her, rub her head, and be present. It's the most powerless aspect of parenting. We can't take away our child's pain, we can't carry it for them. We can only just be there, a hand to hold, a shoulder to lean on, an ear to listen, and a hug to reassure. I feel Ava's pain more than my own. She flips over, and I rub her back until her tears dry up and the light soothing sound of her snore overtakes her sadness and carries her through the night.

By the time I climb into the guest room bed, I am mentally and physically exhausted and yet still wide awake. My mind is churning, rehashing the entire day that wasn't even a day—it was a life, an afterschool TV movie special. There's no way in hell I'm going to fall asleep now. I pop two melatonin and peruse an old *People* magazine from the bathroom that I'd already read a couple of months ago, when I hear my door open. I freeze.

"Soph."

"Yes," I say, my heart beginning to pound.

"I know you're leaving tomorrow." Gabe's voice cracks. "Can I just . . ." He points to the pillow next to mine. He wants to lie with me. I put down the magazine, uncertain what to do.

"Okay."

We don't speak at all as he climbs in.

"With everything that happened between us, somehow I just never envisioned goodbye. Is that crazy?" he whispers. His breath is hot and he's been drinking. Bourbon. "I think I must be the dumbest man alive. Book smart, life stupid. How did I let this happen? How did I not see the collateral damage of my actions? I mean, I pictured being caught, but not losing you—"

He doesn't finish. There is no transition. It all happens so fast that there is no time for me to even process what comes next or to put a stop to it. We rip each other's clothes off. And he's pretty skilled with one arm. It's our bodies in the room working it now, not our heads. It's our past clinging, touching, groping, not our present. We don't even see each other in the darkness, just feel each other, the excitement, the familiar, and, now, the strange. Suddenly, I'm not in the House of Lies, but I'm back at Gabe's old house where he grew up, and we are high school seniors sneaking off into his bedroom, tearing up his twin bed. His parents are sleeping. They thought we were in the basement watching TV, not fucking our brains out, just as we are now.

His hands caress my breasts roughly—much rougher than I ever remembered his touch. But after my Jean-Paul tutorials, I'm all in, up for anything.

"Jesus Christ, Sophie," Gabe pants. "I've missed you, this."

I say nothing back. I just close my eyes and absorb— his scent, his touch, his tongue moving everywhere on my body as though it's motorized. I feel the muscles of his well-worked-out abdomen and slowly inch my way down his long torso, teasing him with my lips, my tongue, and then taking him fully into my mouth. Gabe returns the favor, and we curve together, reclaiming familiar turf with a passion that has long been forgotten, catching glimpses of each other as lovers do in the grainy darkness. And then it goes from passionate to reckless. Him on top, me on top, me holding on to the shaky headboard—*we really need to fix that*—him hungrily exploring my body from behind. We are no longer a middle-aged beaten-down version of us, but fearless Cirque du Soleil performers free falling and twisting under and over each other.

"What the hell was that? Incredible. Man, I still love you," he whispers as he penetrates me. "You're still so goddamn beautiful."

"And sad," I say, spreading my legs wider.

"And mad," he adds, thrusting hard inside me.

"Yes, all of it—yes." His heart beats against mine, as he strokes my clitoris. This is not make-up sex or break-up sex—but the Final Fuck—and it's spectacular. And there, right then, we climax, together, a celebration of all that once was.

Gabe is silent, satiated, panting heavily next to me, and I cry just a little as I meld into the crook of his muscular arm, like a car pulling into its home garage for the very last time. The soapy underarm scent that I know so well, that was once so comforting, still is. But Gabe, once my hero, can no longer take the bullet for me—this time, he was the shooter. And there's no fixing that, no going back from that.

Seconds later, maybe less, he predictably falls asleep. How does he always do that? It could have been an earthquake, a fire, a robbery, a bomb going off, but once Gabe finishes, he's out for the count, undisturbed by the voices in his head, and I'm more awake than before.

Sitting up, I look at him beside me and use this sacred time to do all my goodbyes. I lean over, tenderly kiss his cheek, graze my finger along the light stubble lining his strong chin, kiss the tip of his nose and that scar lining his eyebrow. My lips brush his thick eyelashes and the slight cleft in his chin that mirrors Ava's. And at very last, I kiss his sleeping snoring mouth, those full lips that once belonged to me but now no longer do.

I lie there with my husband who claimed most of my life and once all of my heart. I watch his stomach rise and fall like a metronome. I even place my hand on top of his belly for a few sequences. My mind begins to quiet, and I realize that I am finally straddling the border of peaceful and okay. I reach up and remove a stray curl covering his left eye and know that I will always love this man despite his flaws, his marital transgressions, and weaknesses. But I also know that for the first time in way too long that I love me enough—enough not to stay.

VI.

The main thing is to be moved, to love,
to hope, to tremble, to live.

—AUGUSTE RODIN

Chapter Thirty-Three

I arrive in Nice midmorning on Tuesday, take a cab from the airport to the apartment in Saint-Paul. I'm wired from the travel, having slept on and off the entire flight. Now I just need to stay up until at least 9 p.m. to regulate, so I can start fresh and early with Nathalie tomorrow—one day later than promised, but I will make it up to her.

Walking around Lea and Jean-Paul's apartment, I realize how happy I am to be back in this cozy environment. I glance at the mismatched furniture and colorful shabby throw pillows. It's so vastly different from North Grove—so much less than everything I have there—but strangely in its own way, much richer. Real. Artsy. *Me.*

I unpack, lie on the bed for a few minutes, then pick

up my trusty guidebook off the nightstand and sift through it. I'm starving. I flip the pages and stop. La Colombe d'Or. That's it. I've been dying to go there for a good, long leisurely lunch. Now's the time.

I call the restaurant and make a reservation for 1 p.m., thrilled that I got in, knowing that people make reservations weeks, perhaps months, in advance. La Colombe d'Or is not just the most famous restaurant/hotel in all of Saint-Paul—it's known for possessing some of the most famous artwork in the world.

Apparently, the owners—the Roux family—had befriended many "starving" artists as far back as the 1930s and '40s. The restaurant became a cultural safe haven for struggling artists whose work could be exchanged for a meal or a night's stay. Paul Roux, the patriarch and a man ahead of his time, had the foresight to dole out meals to the likes of Picasso, Chagall, Matisse, Calder, and Miró. And the artists paid Roux back in kind—gifts of their artwork are displayed throughout the renowned restaurant and hotel. The guests, from Charlie Chaplin to Bono, are so legendary that the owners actually keep its visitor book filled with famous signatures of artists, actors, musicians, politicians, and VIPs in a vaulted safe.

I put away the travel guide, shower, and slip on a black maxidress and my favorite double-strand vintage antique silver necklace, which Ava bought me at one of my own art fairs a few years ago. It has an ornate oval locket, inside which she'd stuck a tiny picture of us, taken on her first day of kindergarten. Our heads are mushed together and we are both beaming. I smile at the memory, recalling the sheer joy in Ava's tiny face as she clutched her new Hello Kitty backpack, and the mixed emotion in mine. She was leaving the nest for the first time, and I had to let her separate and fly. And now . . . I think, fondling the precious locket, Ava is grown and flown and I'm just discovering my wings.

A half hour later, I park in the center of town, a few blocks from the restaurant, which is just footsteps from the village entrance. I then walk toward the densely framed ivy entrance of La Colombe d'Or, stopping briefly along the sidewalk to watch a group of old men playing a mean game of *boules*, a kind of horseshoes with balls.

As I cross the street, I stand back and observe the renowned façade of the restaurant for a few precious moments before entering. It is composed of old medieval stones and it's gorgeous, timeless. I gaze into the distance, down the road, at the high stone walls surrounding the village like a fortress from *Game of Thrones*. So much history in this little village. How I've loved walking through its labyrinth of narrow and picturesque cobblestoned streets filled with charming boutiques and art galleries, exploring the hidden gardens, the ornate ancient fountains—centerpieces—in the shady historic squares. It's such a far cry from North Grove, where all everyone talks about is the just opened Juice-ation, a neon monstrosity next to the car wash, that offers myriad anti-aging vitamin juices and smoothies, avocado toast, and acai bowls.

Inhaling the fresh air and letting its warmth fill my senses, I walk through the restaurant's small stoned archway, which opens up onto a sprawling terrace. Two steps in, and I'm greeted by a magnificent giant thumb sculpture by César Baldaccini.

"Oh my god, love this," I say to myself, stopping to observe the realistic-looking thumb sticking out of the ground, with its huge nail and defined ridges. What a strange, yet perfect introduction. The maître d', smiling at my reaction, leads me to a lovely small corner table shaded by ivy and a large overhanging tree. I look around the bustling terrace packed with faces from all over the world. The patio itself is the color of olive oil, rich with lush vines and vibrant flowers, which emit a spicy, intoxicating aroma. It smells like my yoga class *before* the workout—an infusion of essential oils. Practically every table is filled. My imagination begins to swirl. It's truly a gem—I can see why actors and artists flock here. So inspiring. My gaze freezes and my breath catches.

Luc.

His back to me, I spot him dining on the far side of the restaurant with a small group. His hands are moving animatedly, clearly in deep conversation. He's with a woman and two men—all well dressed, all around my age. *Friends? Artists? Art dealers?*

I tip the tall menu upward to hide myself while I take a better look. From my angle, he can't see me, but I can see him. The waiter, meanwhile, comes to the table and presents me with a magnificent basket of raw vegetables, artichokes, radishes, cucumbers, carrots, and celery, explaining that this is merely a pre-hors d'oeuvre, compliments of the restaurant. I tell him in my improving French mixed with English to choose something special for me—his favorite fish (only without a head) with baked Provençal tomatoes, beans, and eggplant.

I then peer over again at Luc and his friends. *Should I go over there—say hello?* Or just pretend I don't see him? Probably best to just leave it be. Is that rude? I munch on celery. *Why do I suddenly feel so nervous?*

The waiter returns with a goblet-sized glass of rosé—perfect. I pull out my leather journal, which I've learned is an excellent accompaniment while dining alone. Better than a phone, which makes you feel lonely, and disconnected. And better than a book, which looks like you are trying too hard *not* to look alone. A journal and a glass of wine, I've figured out, is empowering. *I'm writing. I'm drinking. I'm eating—I'm taking care of me.*

But instead of writing, I doodle aimlessly, and my mind wanders once more over to Luc's table. I can't concentrate. *That's it.* I put my pen down, take a long sip of wine, and decide to end this nervousness (Rule No. 4: Take control), so I can move on to other things and fully enjoy my lunch.

I stand, taking the wineglass with me as I walk over to Luc's table. I tap him lightly on the shoulder. "Luc—hi."

He turns, his eyes flash. "Sophie . . . what a surprise. When did you get back?"

"Today actually," I say, aware of the other guests at the table wondering who I am. "I am trying to avoid jet lag, so"—I gesture to my table across the terrace— "I've been wanting to come here and . . ."

He stares at me for an awkward moment, collects his thoughts, and turns to the others. "This is Sophie Bloom, from Chicago. A friend of Nathalie's . . ."

I nod, smile to everyone at his table, toss out a few *bonjour*s. "Sophie . . . these are friends in town from Paris, from the d'Orsay."

Ahh, I think, the Musée d'Orsay, where Eve will be unveiled in mid-October. Our eyes lock briefly, and it is clear to both of us that there will be no mention of my working with Nathalie as her ghost sculptor. I remember Olivier's words. *No one can know. No credit.* That was the deal. Luc probably received the same marching orders.

I smile warmly. "Well, lovely to meet you all, and enjoy Saint-Paul." I turn to Luc. "My very best to Nathalie." A few more pleasantries are exchanged, and I return to my table. I realize after a few minutes of sitting and staring at my journal, clutching the stem of my rosé, that I haven't let out a single breath.

I pay my bill and finish off a cappuccino and fresh berries. Just before I get up to leave, the waiter tells me, "Madame, you must go inside and see . . ."

I nod. "I plan on it. *Merci beaucoup.* This was truly *fantastique.*" I sprinkle as much French as I can into my closing sentence, and for a man who clearly takes his job and his French pride seriously, he grins with appreciation.

"*Pas mal?*" I add with a smile. *Not bad, ay? At least I'm trying.*

"*Pas mal,*" he replies with a wink.

I purposely walk around the opposite side of the

terrace, so as not to interrupt the lunch that Luc is still having with d'Orsay people. I stop briefly to admire the large colorful ceramic mural *Hands of a Dove* by Fernand Léger, perched on the wall between tables and shaded by fig trees.

Entering the hotel from the terrace, I walk past the concierge and the bathroom, and then stop in my tracks when I see the rustic dining room up ahead filled with white-clothed tables already prepped for the dinner crowd. It is chock-full of antique knickknacks and paintings. I peer in closely. Not just paintings, I realize, but masterworks. There's a Miró in one corner. A Picasso hanging over a table for two. That's a Braque over there. And in another crevice, hangs a Chagall. My heart races.

Looking around, I see no one around—not even a security guard. The lunch crowd is all outside. I'm sure there are hidden cameras. *Let them catch me.* I enter the vacant dining room to peruse the magnificent artwork up close. I practically have to stop myself from twirling around. Just me, hanging out with my idols. *Unbelievable.*

A good twenty minutes or so fly by, and I force myself to tear away, and check out other rooms. I walk through a windy corridor, and stop in my tracks. In the distance, out the large back window, I see the lovely pool filled with hotel guests, and spot a rotating Calder mobile near the shallow end of the pool, just as a little girl, oblivious to the famous sculpture, jumps in right next to it, with a giant splash. To the right of the Calder, as though dropped in haphazardly, sits a gigantic green apple sculpture by Hans Hedberg. *Am I dreaming?* It's as though I too have been dropped into the most marvelous home filled with hidden treasures. No guards that I can see, no thick bulletproof glass surrounding the artwork, no stuffy plaques naming the art and announcing its donor. Just pure simplicity. The art itself hanging out, as though it too is on vacation from all the pretense.

Reluctantly, I head back toward the lobby exit, and I see Luc in the distance, alone, his back toward me, staring at a drawing by Henri Matisse.

I clear my throat, not wanting to bother him, but there is no way around him, no other way to leave the restaurant. "We meet again," I say lightly as I approach.

He looks slightly startled. "I was just thinking about you," he says, pressing his lips tightly together. "I want to apologize. I wish I could have introduced you properly, and I know you were dining alone. I would have invited you to join us but the lunch was all business. They are representing the group of investors who commissioned Eve for the museum, and are underwriting the opening-night festivities. There were lots of details to discuss, and—"

"Please don't worry at all," I interject. "Really. I've had the loveliest time here. No need to apologize. How long are your guests in town?"

The corners of his eyes crinkle. He looks relieved. "They're leaving after lunch. They came out to the house last night to view Eve for the first time." He stops speaking. There's an awkward silence between us. "They were amazed, to say the least . . . but I also had to let them know how sick Nathalie is. It was a very emotional night, as you can imagine. Very hard for her. She didn't come out of our bedroom, didn't want them to see her this way. It was rough. I'm sorry, I . . ."

I hold up my hand, then place it against my chest. "I can't even begin to imagine. It must have been over-whelming for her. And she's so private that way."

"Yes, very. The art here . . ." He looks around, clearly wanting to change the subject. "I just love this place, especially the casual display of the artwork. It is as art should be—part of life, infused, not separate and standoffish."

"Exactly," I say, pointing behind me. "Did you see the Calder by the swimming pool? And that thumb at the entrance. Everything is so unexpected, yet so perfect."

His eyes, which seconds ago darkened, now glisten, the same golden green as the terrace. "Nathalie and I used to come here on special occasions, and whenever we have guests in town, we . . ." He draws in a deep breath, as though contemplating the "we" and all of its ramifications. "She's very sick, Sophie. She's taken a downturn since you left. I don't know . . . I just don't know." He averts his distraught gaze, and I see him wiping his eyes with his sleeve.

I can't help it. I touch Luc's arm, to comfort him. "It's going to be okay."

He shakes his head. "See that's the thing . . . it's not."

I gently remove my hand. He's right. It's not going to get any better. I wish I knew the thing to say. There are no words for a man who is grieving so much at once.

"And how was your visit home?" he asks, trying to reel in his emotion. "I know from our conversation the other day that it must have been tough for you."

In all his pain, he remembered.

"It was very tough at first. A lot to deal with . . . but then, surprisingly, there was closure." I think back to how much happened in those few days. *Lauren. Gabe. Ava.*

"I'm glad for you." He holds my gaze, as though he wants to say more and then changes his mind. "Well, I've got to go." He points over his shoulder. "I was actually headed to the WC. I'm sure they're wondering if I ran away."

I laugh. "See you back at the studio tomorrow. And again, my best to Nathalie. And Luc . . ." He turns to me. I notice a muscle in his jaw twitch slightly. "She's stronger than anyone I've ever known. I've seen her have really bad days and she always manages to turn it around."

Not this time. I can see it in his eyes. "*Au revoir,* Sophie."

Luc turns, and I watch his long stride move toward the restroom and then disappear. But something inexplicable is left behind, a thickening of the air around me, as though Luc is still here, still with me.

Chapter Thirty-Four

The early morning breeze lightly caresses my neck and cheeks as I pick up a café au lait and an almond croissant from the small bakery around the corner from Lea and Jean-Paul's apartment before driving out to the studio. I'm excited to get back to work.

When I arrive at the Senards', there's an Audi sports car parked in the driveway that I don't recognize. I wonder who's here. Entering the studio, I expect to see Nathalie waiting for me, smoking a joint and Claudia watching over her, making herself busy. But when I walk in, it's Olivier standing there instead, alone, surveying Eve. I'm startled, taken aback by his unexpected presence.

He looks up. "*Bonjour*, Sophie." As if it were normal. His eyes are baggy and his grayish face is drawn.

Something is wrong. He points to Eve. "Beyond what I even imagined she could be."

I look around, my heart pounds. "Why are you here? Where's Nathalie?"

"She's . . ." He shakes his head and his lips press tightly together.

Oh no. My whole body tightens with fear.

"Did she?"

"No, but soon. It's happening." Olivier lets out a hard breath and it's clearly an effort to speak. "Claudia called me last night, told me to come. Told me to wait here. I left Paris right away, drove all night."

She's dying. I think, panicking. *Luc.*

"You need to go," I say firmly. "You can't be here."

Olivier ignores my warning and circles Eve. "It's her best work. You have done a wonderful job. I knew you would."

"Listen to me, damn it." I raise my voice. "Her husband is in town. You can't be here."

"We're all friends," he says, standing his ground. "She asked me to come."

We're all friends. The lies. "Then trust me when I say, as her friend, leave now." I stop short of saying Luc knows the truth about you and Nathalie. I don't want to break Luc's trust or Nathalie's.

"It's the goddamn end, Sophie," he growls. "I was told to be here and I'm staying."

"Luc knows and Nathalie doesn't know he knows," I blurt out, betraying everybody's confidence. "This lie of yours, this lie of hers—he fucking knows. And I know, because I know you, that you're not just friends."

Olivier rakes his hand through his thick hair as though pulling it. His gaze is distant and sad. "I knew she was lying to me. She told me it was just a fling and it was over. But it wasn't for me nor for her. And now I'm about to lose her forever."

I feel my fists tightening. I've got to get him out of this damn studio now. "Do you understand that *you* are not about to lose her—*Luc is*. Don't do this. It's not about you for once. Give Luc the time he deserves with his wife. Leave now and I will tell her you came." I move toward him. If I have to drag Olivier out of here, I will. If I have to stab him with a chisel or knock him out with a hammer, I will.

He stands at the base of the statue and lightly strokes Eve's foot. "I've done so many bad things in my life. But Nathalie . . . I've always known it was her. She was the one. And now . . ."

The door opens and Claudia wheels Nathalie inside. She is propped up with pillows on all sides. She looks much worse than any time I have ever seen her look before. Luc was right—she has taken a downward turn. Her face is ashen and swollen, her chapped lips are nearly white. There is nothing left to her. Could that much have changed so quickly?

Claudia sees Olivier near the statue and looks fearful. She, too, knows he should not be here. She understands exactly how this is going to play out if Luc walks through those doors, and he will. I don't know where Luc is now, but he was in town yesterday. I can't bear this. I pick up my purse and grab my sweater. "I'm leaving."

"No." Nathalie clings to the sides of her wheelchair, her voice barely audible. "Stay. Don't go. Not today."

I stop moving, not sure what to do. My body feels feverish. She wants me here as a cover. This is so wrong on every front. "Please don't ask this of me. Claudia is here. She will stay."

"I need you." Her voice is so unbearably weak, but she is Nathalie Senard—she will demand and receive until her very last breath. "Eve is everything I dreamed her to be. Her hair . . ." She slowly reaches up, touches her own head, the patchy baldness beneath the violet paisley-patterned scarf. Her vanished blonde hair was once a lion's mane, thick and billowy, a golden river photographed in so many French magazines. Her barely lucid gaze does not veer from mine. She is asking me for one final moment with the man she loves. Who am I to judge? Her days are no longer numbered, they are at zero, I can see it—anybody could. But I feel Luc's looming presence like a tide in the distance you can see from shore, making its way toward you. I glance at Claudia for help. She shakes her head, her forehead furrows. Neither of us can stop the inevitable, neither of us can protect any of the players here.

"Work," Nathalie barks, half breath, half cough. "Please, finish her hair," she adds. The bark turns to a beg.

I put down my sweater, the purse, gather my tools, and slowly climb up the scaffold. From the corner of my eye, I see Olivier on his knees in front of Nathalie's wheelchair, his head against her lap. It's a version of him I've never seen before, nor could I have imagined. Her shaking hands stroke his head. Her turquoise eyes, the only part of her that is still vital, are now twinkling bright. She is a woman in love, even as she dies. And Olivier . . . even the fallen fall in love. I think of Ava, his rebound, his filler. I will never forgive him for that. But look at him now. A man who idealizes beauty for once doesn't care that it's gone. He is holding on to Nathalie's essence, his true love, one last time.

I put on my goggles and begin to work. Strand by

strand, using a sand cloth, I start to polish the long marble lines of nearly three feet of Eve's wild mane, scrubbing softly at first, then hard and angry, until the ivory marble starts to shine. But for the first time, I don't even notice. I glance down again. Olivier's arms are now wrapped around Nathalie's frail shoulders. His mouth is on hers, when Luc walks in.

I stop polishing, stop breathing, my hands go numb. Time halts like an electrical short as love, death, and betrayal all meet up in the same dark room.

There is no punching, no shouting. No explanations, no lies. Just an unbearable silence hovering before the storm. The sound of a broken vase crashing against the wall breaks the stillness. Luc looks up at me after he throws it, with a disbelieving accusatory *Et tu, Brute?* glare—and nothing, I mean nothing, has ever hurt me more. He thinks I'm in on it, part of the collusion: a duplicitous contributor to his ultimate humiliation and betrayal. The studio door flings open, then slams, and I hear the harsh sound of an engine revved up in the distance, the flooring of a car careening against the stony driveway.

Descending the ladder, I look at both Olivier and Nathalie, the guilty. Rodin's star-crossed lovers, doomed to an afterlife spent together in purgatory. My eyes meet Claudia's terrified gaze. *Go,* she begs me silently.

I throw down the goggles, my tools, my cloths, and race out the door after Luc. I feel the familiar betrayal pounding inside my bones, stomping me, choking me as it had the night of my birthday. Luc's pain is mine revisited. He's a good man, loving her despite it all, and now this, the greatest of all betrayals. In his face, and through his heart.

Panicking, I get into my car and race toward the village of Èze. I drive around until I finally spot Luc's parked car, near a guy who sells spices. At this point I don't care about getting a ticket. I park in a nearby no-parking zone, and jump out, glancing up at the cone-shaped rock housing the maze of shops, art galleries, perfumeries, restaurants, hotels, and at the very pinnacle, the exotic garden, known for its vibrant plants and flowers, sculptures of goddesses, waterfalls, and a panoramic view of the French Riviera. Luc had said it was his favorite spot in that article in the *Paris Match*. It's a long shot, my only shot. *There*. He has to be up there.

I move as though there is a motor beneath me, racing up the winding tiny cobblestone streets punctuated by vaulted passages, running amid the crush of pedestrians, neither seeing nor hearing them.

I'm out of breath when I finally arrive at the garden

entrance; my throat is parched and I'm dying of thirst. I stop in my tracks, and through the succulents and cacti, I heave a sigh of relief when I spot Luc standing in the distance. He is near the far edge of the overlook, alone near the rocks. *Don't jump*, I silently beg him, my heart beating fast. *But I understand if you want to.*

He hears my approaching footsteps against the grounds, but doesn't turn, doesn't move. I stand behind him and whisper. "Luc."

He turns slowly. His face is tear streaked, his eyes are blazing, pained. My heart breaks just looking at him.

"How could you do that to me—in my own home? Working as if it didn't matter. You knew . . ."

He is turning his anger on me, because there is no one else to blame. "I walked in this morning to work and he was there," I whisper. "I swear, I had nothing to do with it."

Luc shakes his head. He believes no one. Everyone is a liar. I get it. "And yet you didn't leave either," he counters. "You stayed, you sculpted, you allowed them to be together—you enabled. After everything I told you . . ."

I can't let him go down that road without a fight. "I told Olivier to leave immediately. I even told him you knew. I betrayed your trust just to get him out of the studio." My voice rises protectively. "Please believe me."

He stares blankly over my shoulder, then glares at me. "I believe no one."

I understand him. He needs someone to accuse—better than himself. Better than the dying woman whom he has loved his whole life but who betrayed him in the end—not just for the affair, but for choosing Olivier over him in her final days, perhaps moments. I wish I could take this harrowing pain away from Luc, but I can't. Just like I couldn't protect Ava. Or even Gabe from himself. Or me, from all the lies around me.

"I'm so sorry," I say, but he doesn't respond. He looks away. Behind him I see picture-taking tourists and young travelers taking selfies. Just listen to him, I tell myself. *Don't move, stay.*

He finally speaks. "I wanted the time she had left just to be with her, to be together. But the truth is, she chose Eve over me. I'm a painter—I understand her choice more than you know. But when I walked into the studio today I understood that Nathalie's choice wasn't just about Eve, it was him too. She chose him . . . over me." He shields his tormented face with his hand.

I want to hold him. Take care of him. Protect him. *Kiss him*, I admit, then scold myself. *He's not yours.* But something stronger, magnetic, propels me forward anyway. I lift my face upward, my lips move toward his. His eyes open wide and he pulls back. "How can you? Do you think I'm like them?" he shouts, and it's as if I've been slapped, shot. My whole body retracts.

"Nathalie is dying, you work with her." His green eyes are burning.

"You're right, and I'm very sorry. I just . . ." *Have I lost my mind?* I get up and walk away quickly, head held high clinging to whatever shreds of dignity I have left. Once I pass through the exit and out of his view, I run, rushing along the path with tears flowing down my face. Luc is mourning his dying disloyal wife—the woman he still loves—and I tried to kiss him?

Who's the cheater now?

Chapter Thirty-Five

I get the dreaded call from Claudia in the late afternoon. Nathalie, she cries into the phone, has passed. I can barely hear Claudia's words through her tears. The giant hole opening inside me seems to swallow me up.

I pour myself a glass of wine, and then smoke a joint to calm myself. There's a stash in Lea's nightstand, next to her condoms and an old picture of her with her mother taken at a swimming pool. I examine the photo closely. The white-framed Kodak print is crinkled from years of holding. That's when I really cry.

The phone rings again.

"Hello, hello?" I say, clearing my throat. I hear a man's muffled voice.

"Luc?"

But it's Jean-Paul calling from Capri.

"Are you okay? Is Lea okay?" I ask.

"Yes, yes." He laughs. "Everybody is more than okay—we're great. Sophie, we are pregnant."

"Oh my—wow—that's wonderful." A death and a birth simultaneously. Two calls, two souls exchanging places. I can barely breathe.

"I'm so happy for you both," I manage, fighting off tears.

"It's really crazy. We had been wondering why Lea was so sick this past week. We thought it was the flu and then this." I can practically see his handsome face smiling through the phone. "We've decided it's best to come home early. I gave my notice at the hotel. We are coming back at the end of this week, so . . ."

"Don't even say another word. I will figure it out." I inwardly begin to panic. *What am I going to do now? Where do I go? Eve is still not done. Nathalie is dead . . . and Luc.* "Give Lea my love. This is fantastic news."

I get off the phone and think of Jean-Paul with his chest-to-toe tats and Lea with all her New Age philosophies of life and relationships. It's hard to imagine them as parents, yet they are both so loving, so generous.

I sit at the table, downing more wine, and think about the timing. *Six hours.* Claudia had said Nathalie passed away six hours ago, which meant she died in the studio in Olivier's arms. *Not Luc's.* He never got to say goodbye. I don't think, I move. I get into my same clothes because they are at the edge of the bed. Tipsy and high, I call a cab to take me to Èze. Luc needs me, kiss or no kiss, whether he knows it or not.

When we pull up to the Senard home, I hurriedly hand a wad of euros to the driver and jump out. I clumsily type in the gate code and stumble across the pebble driveway toward the studio. The light is on, as I knew it would be. I can see someone moving through the window.

I fling open the door, and I don't find Luc—instead, I come face-to-face with an axe murderer. A crazed, shirtless man wielding an actual axe in his hand—*where did he get that?* And the studio looks like it has been hit by an earthquake. Luc has destroyed everything—random sculptures, the shelves, the tools, the vases—even the mini-refrigerator is bashed in. Everything is wrecked except for Eve. The best for last—Eve will be his final strike. I understand him. Everything inside Luc is broken, but I have to protect Eve from him no matter what. *For Nathalie.* He sees me. His face is blank and unrecognizable.

"Luc, stop, please. Enough!" I shout, as he moves toward the far corner of the studio and smashes through the lone standing shelf of tiny sculptures. Unfinished figurines. Nathalie's "rejection collection," she called them. But she could not bring herself to throw them out. One by one, Luc chops and destroys them.

I come up from behind him, this grief-stricken madman, and he stops in midswing. "Again? Leave me be. Get out of here!" he yells.

"No, I'm not leaving you!" I shout back, my head spinning, my thoughts and words not quite in sync.

"She died in his arms. *His* arms—do you hear me?" Luc's roar echoes throughout the hollow studio as though we are in a church or a cave.

"I hear you. Please, put that down." I'm wobbly but strong. "Give me that, damn it." I yank the axe out of his relenting hands and he stands there, limp and shattered. He sinks to the ground amid the debris, the marble, the glass, the clay, the plaster, so many pieces and fragments. I slip down next to him and gather him into my arms, and this time he doesn't pull away or shout at me or shame me. He melds into me.

"You've been drinking," he whispers.

"Yes," I say. "I could not bear what happened earlier between us, and then I heard about Nathalie. I'm so sorry. Look at me." He obeys, looking up. His eyes, the glimmery color of a forest just after it rains. *So beautiful, this man.* Give him something to hold on to. "Love is unfair and uneven. But she loved you deeply. You were her history, her youth, her passion. Things change sometimes when we're not looking. Sometimes it's one of us, sometimes it's both. But you did not live a lie. She loved you."

"She loved him."

"Perhaps, yes, at the end. But the beginning, the middle, the growing up together were all yours. *Only yours.* Hold on to that. Remember that."

I'm telling him these things as much for his benefit as my own. I'm mothering him as I should mother myself. We are the same, he and I, mirror images. Broken, left behind. I slowly pull away from him, feeling something so deep, a force so strong and inexplicably tender, but knowing that he was right earlier, that it's not right—and I'm not Olivier, I'm not Gabe: I'm still me. I will not get in the way of what belongs solely to Luc: his grief. *Be there for him. And for now, that is enough.*

I stand, wipe the dust off my jeans. My determined gaze boldly meets Eve, who has seen it all in this studio. She is now battle-ready and thankfully spared by Luc. I carefully walk across the room, never more coherent than I am now in my altered state. I grab a broom and begin to sweep up the debris. I sweep around Luc, hunched over, head buried in his hands. I brush away all the pieces, cleaning up the remnants of what was, hoping only to make way for what is.

Chapter Thirty-Six

Tonight is Eve's debut at the Musée d'Orsay in the heart of Paris, and I'm so excited that I can hardly contain myself. It took nearly seven weeks, working around the clock since Nathalie's funeral, to complete Eve and bring her to the level I know Nathalie would have wanted. This time instead of working on Eve from bottom to top, I began from top to bottom. I started with her hair—reminiscent of Nathalie's golden mane, and made my way down to her feet. No detail was spared as I toiled from early morning through the wee hours at the studio. My world was just me, Eve, and Claudia, whom I began to thoroughly enjoy and depend on. We would have coffee together in the morning, then break for lunch at the house. She would bring me a tray of dinner before she left for the evening. Luc had insisted she stay on, to be there with me, to give me whatever I needed while finishing Eve in time for the exhibition.

Luc did it for Nathalie. As betrayed and hurt as he was, he pulled himself together, separating his emotions from her art. Eve is Nathalie's crowning glory and no matter what, he would give her that honor. But Luc himself stayed away, living instead at their apartment in Paris, in the Sixth. I've seen him only once since the funeral, when he returned home to box up Nathalie's clothes and personal belongings, as well as all the memorable pieces defining their life together. I offered to help him and Claudia but he declined, which I understood. He needed those final moments in the house for himself to mourn and to perhaps begin the process of healing.

Claudia told me that Luc is planning to sell the house in Èze. I, on the other hand, decided to stay. I found a charming one-bedroom apartment to sublet in the village of Èze through December, and I've fallen madly in love with this medieval town and all of its eccentricities.

I flew from Nice to Paris two days ago to prepare for the exhibition. Eve was brought to Paris in an armored truck, escorted by two police cars driving alongside it for the entire ten-hour journey. Clearly, France takes her art seriously. But yesterday was lovely and all mine. I spent the entire day alone, walking along the Seine, and doing nothing but shop, eat, and drink coffee. No agenda, just being with me, and it was perfect. Today is all about the getting ready—the "car wash," as Samantha used to call it—hair, nails, brows, wax, and makeup.

I glance at the clock in the hotel room. Nearly two p.m. Time seems to be flying and standing still. In less than two hours, Ava will be here. She is arriving with Samantha and Lauren. They will rest a bit, and together, we will attend the cocktail reception tonight at the museum. Luc had told me to invite anyone I wanted to attend the exhibition.

I try on my new dress. It's tea length, black lace, form-fitting, off the shoulder, and elegant. I found it at a small upscale boutique along Rue Saint-Honoré. I gaze proudly in the mirror. I look good, ready—not just from the outside but from the inside. I feel the change, the lightness of being. I reach inside my suitcase to try on my jewelry with the dress. But instead of the jewelry case, I pull out my laptop. I look at it and smile to myself. *Why not?*

I sit on the bed and open it up to the "Me_The Sequel" file. My list—my recipe for healing.

I read through it slowly. Without knowing it, I accomplished everything I had set out to do, both the little things and the big: I changed my hairstyle, I eat what I want, I take long walks, I listen to music and no longer spend hours on TV binges, I got off all social networking sites, I got rid of everyone toxic in my life, I've taken control of those things that matter to me, I've stopped rushing, I've had incredibly passionate experiences, when I smile I now feel it, I am sculpting again, and more than anything, I have embraced and been surprised by life—*my life*.

I did it.

Glancing up, I catch my reflection again in the mirror: a woman all dressed up with somewhere to go. The wounded woman who came here to heal has done just that. I hug myself. I don't just like what I see . . . for the first time in so very long, I love how I feel.

Situated on the Left Bank of the Seine, the Musée d'Orsay is a grandiose turn-of-the-century structure, a historical landmark, which was once the Gare d'Orsay, a railway station that had been constructed for the 1900 World's Fair. The station was renovated in the 1980s to become one of the world's greatest art museums. And tonight, it belongs to us, I think, as Ava clings to my arm. We look up at the giant clock portal embedded in stone at the entrance of the museum. Without saying a word, we both know that Nathalie's exhibition is way bigger than we are. It's history in the making.

I glance at my daughter. Ava is stunning. She decided to wear a trendy white Calvin Klein one-shoulder jumpsuit, a perfect match to her gleaming marble doppelgänger awaiting us inside the museum. She knows that just as Eve is being launched, so will she as the young American model. All eyes will be on both of them. Ava is not only smart and savvy, but also, like all teens of this generation, she understands fully how to self-promote. I squeeze her tightly, protectively. My girls—Ava and Eve—will both be making their debut.

"I'm so proud of you, Mommy," she whispers as we enter the building.

Mommy, I think. Little girl and woman rolled into one. She leans her head on my shoulder just as a photographer snaps our picture. Samantha and Lauren are walking slightly behind us. An usher leads us all into the ballroom, dazzling with its impeccably preserved turn-of-the-century décor filled with paintings, murals, and opulent chandeliers. Ava grips my arm tightly and whispers, "Don't look, but there he is."

I follow her startled gaze and see Olivier holding court amid a circle of guests in the distance, drinking champagne, his arm wrapped loosely around a tall blonde clad in a glittery gold dress. I see only the back of her coiffed head but I know exactly who she is. *Sabine*.

"It will be okay," I reassure her, leading us in the

opposite direction. "We talked about this. He curated the show. Just stay classy. Say hello, smile, be polite, and move on. No more, no less. You got this, and I won't leave you."

Looking around, I search the room for Luc, but he is nowhere to be found. And then I spot Claudia in the distance. Out of her white uniform and in a strapless red dress with her dark hair piled high in a bun, she looks glamorous and ten years younger. That must be her husband, Maxim, next to her. She waves across the crowd and I wave back warmly. Still no Luc.

Eve stands strong and proud in the center of the ballroom, camouflaged by a massive canvas sheath custom-made to size. There will be an unveiling, dramatics. Perched next to Eve is an enlarged photo of Nathalie sculpting back in her glory days. Candles surround the image, illuminating her golden hair. I feel a chill course through me. Nathalie in her prime is a goddess, a genius whose work will be celebrated for years to come.

This is all for you, a tiny voice inside my head whispers to her photo.

"Mom, look who's here." Ava points across the room and I begin to laugh. I can't help it when I spot Lauren and Samantha mingling with none other than Dr. Vivienne Goldberg, the gynecologist.

Of course, she's here. She's a patron of the arts, friends with Sabine, and most likely an integral part of Parisian society. This evening is considered a major event in the art world—the great Nathalie Senard's final gift is being presented. There are photographers and journalists everywhere. But it is Lauren who catches my eye, flipping her glossy ginger hair back in the same coquettish way she used to when standing with a boy at her locker. She is a little too close to the doctor. Are they flirting? I wonder. Is that what's going on over there? I smile. *Good for her, good for both of them.*

Samantha signals she's coming my way. She leaves the two women to themselves and walks over to me. "Talk about being a third wheel," she says. "The new improved gay Lauren is in the house. It will take some getting used to, I admit, but she is happy. All that matters, right?"

"Yes." I loop my arm through hers. "Do you believe this, Sam? I feel like I'm dreaming."

"It's amazing." Her eyes shine. "I'm so damn proud of you. I know it's all about Nathalie tonight, but you, my friend, earn a gold star and smiley face."

Our joke since we were kids. We hug. Ava smiles. *Yes, we're back to us.*

"Only no one can know it, don't forget," I whisper as a reminder.

Samantha is having none of it. "You know it. I know it. Ava knows it. Your hands, your talent, made this happen. No one can take that away. Now after this, when you come home, your ass better be back in a studio. No excuses."

I gaze deeply into my best friend's eyes, and she pulls back slightly, raises a brow. I don't need to say another word. *She knows.* "The thing is, I'm not coming home. This is home now," I say anyway.

"Oh, you sure as hell are coming back home," she says adamantly. Samantha reminds me of Nathalie that way. Bossy, demanding, and all heart. You have to peel through the protective layers to find her vulnerabilities. An unexpected tear appears. "How am I going to do life without you?"

"I know, it's crazy," I say honestly, wiping away the lone tear with my index finger. "But we'll figure it out. We always do. Let's just enjoy tonight." My attention is immediately drawn to the entrance. "Come with me. I want to introduce you to that couple over there."

Jean-Paul and Lea, whose stomach is starting to pop, enter the ballroom. When they see me, they both smile broadly and walk in my direction.

When Ava turns around to grab an appetizer off a server's tray, Samantha whispers, "Tell me that's *the* Jean-Paul and Lea? Oh. My. God. You did that?"

"Guilty as charged."

"Holy shit, girlfriend." She lets out a low whistle. "I want every last detail. I'm so damn boring. All I've got is Eric."

"Eric is the best," I say.

"Yeah, he is. A pain in my ass but I'll keep him. But in my next life . . ."

Jean-Paul and Lea both kiss me, and I rub her tummy. "You look so beautiful," I tell her.

"If I weren't so damn sick, I would tend to agree."

I laugh. Lea is Lea to the end. I introduce them both to Ava and Samantha. Within seconds, predictably Samantha, the maven about everything, begins to give them pregnancy tips and parenting advice, and the two of them are ridiculously soaking up every word. And then over Samantha's shoulder I see Luc walk in. I gasp slightly. *Alone.*

"Be right back," I say.

Samantha, who has the sharpest eye in town and can read any situation, grabs me by my arm. "Now I understand why you're staying."

I smile tightly, and take a deep, nervous breath as I walk toward him. A crowd immediately clusters around Luc, and I stop where I am. Over shoulders, our eyes meet. He excuses himself and walks toward me.

He takes two glasses of wine off the nearest server's

tray and hands me one. He eyes me up and down and there is an unmistakable glint in his eye. "It's really nice to see you."

The way he is looking at me—*am I imagining it?* I beam anyway. The new black dress was worth every cent. "How have you been?" I ask. He looks good, back to himself in a navy sport coat, crisp white shirt, and jeans. The only person here in jeans. Casual elegance and perfect.

"How am I?" His wan smile belies his impeccable appearance. "I don't really answer that question anymore." He sees Olivier in the distance and his expression darkens. "He's here, of course."

"Yes, with Sabine." I lean in and reposition myself to block his view.

He laughs. "Still protecting me, are you?"

"Maybe so," I giggle. "What have you been doing?"

"Painting. Keeping busy. I try not to give myself too much downtime." His eyes bore into mine. "Any downtime, actually. You look . . ."

"Well, you at least have to finish that sentence," I say, my mouth curling upward.

"You look like . . . you." He quickly downs his glass of wine. "I will see you after the event. As you know, I am speaking tonight. Not my favorite thing to do." He looks at me intently, as if he wants to say something, but stops himself. I don't push him. Best right now to say less and wait for more.

The museum director makes a toast to the two hundred and fifty guests who have been invited to the gala, a fund-raiser for cancer research, which Luc had insisted on. He discusses the breadth of Nathalie's work over the past twenty years, her brilliance, her incomparable magic. And then *voilà*, he removes the covering and presents Eve.

There is a stunned silence at first, followed by thunderous applause. Everyone is awed by Eve's magnificence. Under the brilliance of the chandeliers and the glow of candles throughout the room, Eve stands even prouder—a radiant monument of womanhood towering above us all; a fighter, a feminist, a protector, a heroine. She doesn't just stand tall—she is a symbol of strength and fearlessness: a woman holding a spear in one hand and a serpent by the neck in the other. Don't mess with her—nude albeit defiant. She is breathtaking and shining. *And she is mine.*

The applause is earsplitting as Luc walks up to the podium. I hold my breath. Samantha squeezes my arm tightly. I lean into her. She looks at me. I place my hand on my heart. *She knows.*

It takes five full minutes for the applause to die

down and Luc looks overwhelmed. "Thank you all for coming tonight," he begins. "And a special thanks to the Arts Committee for making this memorable event happen." He names at least ten members and purposely leaves out Olivier. "There are so many things I could say but I thought it best to go personal. I want to tell you about Nathalie, the Nathalie I knew . . ."

He recounts her life as a young, ambitious artist, as a woman who'd lost her parents early on and had to survive. He describes her as a fighter, a workaholic, who yearned to be a mother more than anything but couldn't carry a baby to term. Her sculptures, he explains, had become her children. Nathalie never rested on her laurels. Art wasn't just her passion, it was her breath, down to the very last one. He pauses, choking up. "My friends . . . Eve is her opus, her greatest gift, the final piece that meant everything to her. She is the daughter Nathalie never had, the woman she wanted to be and to raise. And if anyone knew Nathalie—the word 'no' did not exist for her. Can any artist answer to the greatness of Michelangelo? No. But Nathalie was determined to do it. She fell in love with the David when we were art students traveling around Italy, and for the next two decades her dream was to one day create an equal, a contender. She began Eve over ten years ago. She stopped and started, sculpted and discarded. But once she discovered she had cancer, everything else she was working on took a backseat: Eve became her obsession. Nathalie was revitalized like I'd never seen her before. Even through the treatments and the worst of it, she was determined to create a woman who could take on a Goliath, if challenged." He glances up at the gilt-framed mural ceiling. "I know Nathalie is watching from above and this night means everything to her, and to me." He fights back the tears, but there is not a dry eye in the house. "But before I leave, there are two acknowledgments—actually three—to whom we owe this day."

Oh no, this was not the plan. This is Nathalie's day. I'm just the ghost. The heat rises to my face.

"Ava Bloom . . . a talented and beautiful young art student, an American, spent the semester here with us at the École des Beaux-Arts. She is the model. Nathalie chose her for her strength, her character, her willfulness. Ava, please raise your hand."

"Mom, what do I do?" she whispers nervously.

"Be proud, be you," I say, squeezing her tightly as she waves to the guests.

When the applause dies down and the cameras stop clicking, he continues. "And Claudia Martin took care of Nathalie around the clock when she got sick, and especially in the end as the cancer spread. Claudia made it her life's mission to make my wife comfortable. Every day that Nathalie remained alive is due to this incredible woman. Claudia, if you would . . ." He points in her direction. Blinking back tears, Claudia is visibly humbled by the roaring applause.

"And finally . . ."

I dig my fingernails into my palms.

"My friends, how is this for a twist of fate . . . Ava Bloom posed for Nathalie, and unbeknown to her, her own mother, a sculptor from Chicago and visiting as a tourist, was chosen to assist Nathalie in the end. She helped with all the finishing touches on Eve, to bring Nathalie's vision to life when her own hands could no longer work. It is my greatest honor to present to you the very talented artist Sophie Bloom." He gestures my way.

The applause is overwhelming and it seems to go on for hours. This time it is Ava who holds me tightly. I'm shaking as the flashbulbs go off and I spot Olivier clapping from across the room. I nod my gratitude. He deserves that. My euphoric gaze meets Luc's, and stays there. He is smiling.

What comes next is a whirlwind. Reporters asking questions, microphones shoved in my face and in Ava's. We cling to each other amid the frenzy. Part of me is sad, like there is an arm missing, without Gabe to see all this, to be here with us, to share this golden moment.

I whisper. "You will have to tell your dad about this, honey."

Ava looks at me with surprise. "You always think of him, don't you? Even after everything."

I nod. "And I always will. I can't help it. He's part of me. He would be so proud right now."

She squeezes my hand and I kiss her cheek lightly as a flash sparks in my face. We laugh. We're going to be okay.

Luc waits in the far corner of the room for all the media commotion to die down and then he approaches me. "I know your family and friends are in town. I want to show you something. Would that be okay? Can you meet them back at the hotel in say an hour or so?"

The *or so* part does cartwheels in my head. "Yes, I'd like that."

It's a gorgeous night, the kind of cool, breezy, lit-up Parisian night that you wish you could bottle. I feel ageless, weightless, as Luc and I stroll along the Seine, our arms grazing, my skin against his jacket, easily conversing and rehashing the night, omitting the obvious. I don't mention how he purposely left Olivier out of all the festivities and honors—never mind that he had organized it all. Luc doesn't tell me that he had given an ultimatum to the museum officials, that if they wanted Eve to be part of their permanent collection, Olivier Messier could attend the gala but nothing else. I don't tell Luc that I'd already heard it all from Claudia. I let all that go and instead wonder where he's taking me, what he wants to show me.

"We're almost there," he says. His pupils are dilated and a playful smile hints at the corners of his mouth.

"Where?" I ask, feeling a warm glow expanding throughout my body. "At least, give me a clue."

His eyes twinkle. "You'll see."

We turn right off Quai Voltaire to Rue Jacob, walk a few blocks and approach an ornate wrought-iron gate covered with climbing roses. We enter the gate, which opens to a lovely courtyard filled with artfully manicured potted plants and lavender, neatly trimmed hedges and shrubs, and white and yellow flowers filling large crackled vases. It's all so lovely. I inhale deeply, and the scent is divine. Luc leads me along the uneven cobblestoned walkway toward the apartment building thick with ivy growing up the façade. *His apartment?* My pulse races, my hands are clammy, and I feel butterflies swarming in my stomach.

"This way," he says, as we enter the dimly lit foyer

and he takes me to the closest door. Standing at the threshold, I realize that I am holding my breath as he unlocks it, flicks on the light, and ushers me inside. I can feel his eyes on me as I take in my surroundings. Paintings, canvases, brushes, oils, palettes, are scattered everywhere. The noxious piney smell of turpentine and the bittersweet scent of linseed oil fill the room. *Luc's sanctuary.*

"Your studio," I say softly.

"Yes. I've been working on something." His face becomes flush. He clears his throat, straightens his shoulders, gestures across the room. "For you."

Before I can respond, he takes me by my arm and leads me over to the large canvas on the far side of the studio. Its backside faces us, and he slowly turns it around. I look at the canvas, then at him. I feel the slight sting of tears gathering in the corners of my eyes. I move in closer.

It's the colors that draw me in at first—vivid shades of purple, lush lavenders, with splashes of blues and earth tones. Then it's the raw impulsivity of Luc's brushstroke, lending a rich, dynamic texture to the painting that engulfs me. It takes every bit of restraint not to touch it, to feel the raised composition beneath my fingertips.

I stand back and fully absorb the image. It is an abstract of a woman sculpting with a man standing behind her, his arms draped over her slim shoulders. His head is dipped, his mouth presses against her neck. The tousled dark hair with strands of gold. *It's me.* I turn, meet Luc's burning gaze. He doesn't look away. *And it's him.*

"It wasn't you alone thinking about us," he admits.

"I know," I say tenderly, my voice no longer a voice but a breath.

His jaw clenches slightly, and his eyes turn serious. "But I need to know something, Sophie. I *have* to know this . . . it matters."

"Anything," I whisper.

"Did you ever cheat on your husband?" A man who needs to know the truth. *This truth.*

I collect my disjointed thoughts, the images of past and present merging together. There are no lies in this room. "Once," I admit. "When we were dating. I was in college. I drank too much at a fraternity party and met someone. I told Gabe the truth, we broke up for a short while, and we dealt with it. Kind of." I gaze briefly at the paint-stained hardwood floor. "The truth is, we didn't actually deal with it at all. He hurt me right back to even the score. We never discussed it again." My gaze meets Luc's squarely and locks. "But never once did I hurt him like that again during our marriage. Never."

Forty-three times, I think. All that hurt, that betrayal. And yet, right now, it seems so very distant. Another woman's life and loss.

Luc presses his lips together, visibly relieved. "I believe you. There's something I want to tell you as well," he says slowly. "Before she passed, when you were in Chicago, Nathalie and I were sitting on the patio, and she told me that after she's gone she wanted me to find love again."

"And what did you say?"

"I said nothing . . . knowing what I knew about her and Olivier, I thought it was her guilt speaking. But it's what she said next that mattered. She told me that she wanted me to move on with my life—to remember her, remember us how we once were, that it would make her happy knowing I was happy. She said she wanted me to find a woman like you, Sophie. Good, honest, all heart . . . and loyal. She said that you reminded her of . . ." He stops speaking.

"Of you," I say softly, finishing his sentence.

I turn away from Luc, lean over, and inhale the intoxicating scent of the painting's still drying colors. He must have just finished it. I feel his hands lightly graze my shoulders, then wrap around me, enveloping me from behind, just as they do on canvas. Art imitating life, life imitating art.

"Yes, of me." His warm breath tickles my ear. "She was in love with Olivier and I won't lie. It hurt deeply. Her final moments were spent in the arms of another man. And that broke me. I remembered what you told me that night in the studio, and it was the only thing that got me through my deepest pain. You said I was Nathalie's history, her beginning, and her middle, and that no one can take that young love away. That was all mine." He gently lifts my chin toward him. "I've had time over the past several weeks to think, to grieve, to heal. Nathalie saw you and she saw me. *She knew.* She saw the possibility of us—before I was willing to recognize it and accept what I too had been feeling deep down."

His warm lips brush mine, and he pulls me in closer. Melding into his body, I feel the hardness of his chest, the quickening of his heartbeat. I inhale his woodsy scent, breathing him in fully. His long, lean fingers lace mine—*artist's hands* that match my own. I squeeze them tightly and he squeezes back: clasping not clinging, wanting not needing, knowing where we both have been and no longer afraid to embrace what comes next.

Shutting my eyes, I feel everything at once. Pieces, parts, fragments that somehow, fortuitously, have come together. I smile to myself, thinking of Nathalie and then Lea—their incredible strength. *Life is messy, love is messier. But pain is the messiest of all.* And yet in brokenness, there is rebuilding, a rising from a fall.

I graze my hand along Luc's clean-shaven face. Like a block of marble with infinite possibilities, perhaps we will create our own kind of love, a newness together. But no matter what happens, it is me who has changed, me who is no longer the shell but the pearl; me who is unbreakable.

Acknowledgments

Anyone who knows me KNOWS it's all about My Guy and My Girls—first, last, and in-between: David, Noa, Maya, Maya (Barski), and Izzi (my furry daughter and dialogue sounding board). You are the love, the light, the laughter, and, of course, the "dramatic" inspiration for all my work—the greatest chapter of all.

I can't thank enough my wonderful, large extended family for their unconditional daily support, showing up at all my book gigs, cheerleading, and distributing my books as gifts. A special shout-out to my very besties—my siblings and sibs-in-law (*muah*—love you guys). Much gratitude to my sis-in-law Bonnie Schoenberg—my first reader and "in-house" editor.

I'm so very appreciative of all the love and care you put into this manuscript.

To my Grandma Rachel, always—in spirit, watching over me from Heaven's Kitchen with that golden ladle. You are the voice in my head.

Huge thanks to my badass agent—the incomparable Stéphanie Abou and Massie & McQuilkin Literary for believing in this book. *Merci beaucoup* for everything, Gorgeous Mama. I'm so grateful that you're my gladiator. Sending deepest appreciation to the talented Randy Susan Meyers for making the *shidduch*.

I'm beyond grateful to my HarperCollins Dream Team: my tour-de-force editors Sara Nelson and Mary Gaule (#TeamCharles #TeamJosh), kickass publicist Katherine Beitner, and exceptional marketing guru Megan Looney. Thank you, Suzette Lam and Trent Duffy—my copy editors who shaped ordinary words into extraordinary. And to the art department's Joanne O'Neill and Robin Bilardello for this beautiful, expressive cover—it's perfect.

Special thanks to Ann-Marie Nieves of Get Red PR for her brilliant guidance and unparalleled strategic finesse. Steve Franzken for always making my website "changes" in the wee hours of the night (when I'm working the Insomnia Circuit), Marcy Padorr, my Chicago PR maven who has been by my side since the beginning, and to the ever-fabulous M. J. Rose for her spot-on advice.

My "Dalai Mamas"— I'm so blessed for all your love and support. I couldn't make it through life's journey without you: Lisa Eisen, Lisa Newman, Julie Kreamer, Rebecca Fishman, Randi Gideon, Dina Kaplan, Bonnie Rochman, Sharon Feldman, Amy Klein, Leslie Kaufman, Malina Saval, Melanie Killoren, Staci Chase, Lauren Geleerd, Julie Gorden, Susie Borovsky, Julie Samson, Cathie Levitt, and Marla Bark Dembitz.

Thank you #BocaBookBitches and Real-life Literary Heroines—Andrea Peskind Katz, Rochelle "YM" Weinstein, Lauren "The Good Book Fairy" Margolin, Jamie Brenner, Pam "PJ" Jenoff, Cristina Alger, Barbara Shapiro (my Beylah), Helen Hoang, Elyssa Friedland, Diane Haeger, Sande Boritz Berger, Abby Stern, Hank Phillippi Ryan, Weina Dai Randel, Kaira Rouda, Amy Blumenfeld, Mary Kubica, Patricia Sands, Jessica Morgan, Samantha Bailey, Amy Poeppel, Camille Noe Pagán, Leslie Zemeckis, Lynda Cohen Loigman, Alyson Richman, and Brenda Janowitz (the "List Whisperer").

Many thanks to the Jewish Book Council for its fabulous support, and to the myriad online book groups, book clubs, bookstagrammers, reviewers, bloggers, podcasters, bookstores, libraries, and publications. And most importantly, my readers. This is only a partial list. I could write a novel about all those who embraced me and my work along the way, including: Great Thoughts' Great Readers and the Fantastic Ninjas; my *Tall Poppy* sisters (Ann Garvin and the Pop-Stars), BLOOM; Binders; Barbara Bos (you rock) and *Women Writers, Women's Books*; Jen Cannon and In Literary Love; Kristy Barrett, Tonni Callan, and A Novel Bee; Charlie Fenton and THE Book Club; Bobbi Wiedel Dumas and Sharlene Martin Moore from The Romance of Reading for their friendship and Sharlene's gifted graphics; Readers Coffeehouse; Suzanne Weinstein Leopold; Jackie Pilossoph; Zibby Owens; Linda Levack Zagon; Robin Kall Homonoff; Jennifer Tropea O'Regan; Kate Rock; Elizabeth Silver; *Scary Mommy*; *Grown and Flown*; *Bliss, Beauty and Books*; *Writer Unboxed*; *BookTrib*; Richard Reeder (the man with the perfect name); The Book Stall, The Book Bin; Barbara's Bookstore; Shakespeare & Co.; the inspiring Jamie "Soul Cycle Book Goddess" Rosenblit; Leslie Hooton; Laura Coffey at *Today*; my hometown book club, the Happy Bookers; and my golden network of *GIRLilla Warfare* readers and staff writers.

Yaffa Siman Tov, my Israeli editor (Simanim Publishing House), *Toda Raba* for always believing in my writing.

A special hug to Ellen Katz for keeping me centered, breathing, and on my path (ILG).

Thank you, Guy Pederson, a gifted sculptor whom we met along our Napa adventure, for advising me on the ins and outs of sculpting, Michelangelo's habits, and who made it his personal mission to spread the word on *Fugitive Colors* (a girl never forgets her first).

My "beautifiers" (I couldn't do any of these gigs without you)—Elise "Leesi B." Brill and Diane Balke. And to photographer Tell Draper for showering me with light.

Marcy Glink (Great Events, Inc.) for her incredible warmth and creativity, and turning every special event I have into spectacular memories.

To "my" magazine editor—J. P. Anderson of *Michigan Avenue*. I've had lots of editors in this biz, but he is my fave.

My baristas—same corner, same place, same extra hot mocha—every day. This author couldn't function without her java, her wine, and a good bourbon (yes, it is 5 p.m. somewhere, if anyone's asking).

This book is not just my solo literary journey from prologue to epilogue, it's about those who enable me to live and breathe my passion on a daily basis. You know who you are and just how much you mean to me. Thank you for being my tribe. I'm so profoundly grateful. xoxo

About the Author

Lisa Barr is the author of the award-winning novel *Fugitive Colors*, a suspenseful tale of stolen art, love, lust, deception, and revenge on the eve of World War II. The novel won the Independent Publisher Book Awards (IPPY) gold medal for Best Literary Fiction 2014 and first prize at the Hollywood Film Festival (Opus Magnum Discovery Award). In addition, Lisa has served as an editor for *The Jerusalem Post*, managing editor of *Today's Chicago Woman* and *Moment* magazine, and an editor/reporter for the *Chicago Sun-Times*. Among the highlights of her career, Lisa covered the famous handshake between the late Israeli prime minister Yitzhak Rabin, the late PLO leader Yasser Arafat, and President Bill Clinton at the White House. Lisa is also the creator and editor of the popular parenting blog *GIRLilla Warfare* (www.girlillawarfare.com). She has been featured on *Good Morning America, Today, Fox & Friends,* and the Australia morning news show *Sunrise* for her work as an author, journalist, and blogger. She lives in the Chicago area with her husband and three daughters (aka Drama Central).